Betty Burton is the author of *Jude*, *Jaen*, *Women of No Account*, *Hard Loves*, *Easy Riches*, *Goodbye Piccadilly* and *Long, Hot Summer*, as well as the acclaimed collection of short stories *Women are Bloody Marvellous!* She has written for both television and radio, and won the Chichester Festival Theatre Award. Born in Romsey, Hampshire, she now lives in Southsea with her husband Russ.

By the same author

Women are Bloody Marvellous!
Jude
Jaen
Women of No Account
Hard Loves, Easy Riches
Goodbye Piccadilly
Long, Hot Summer

BETTY BURTON

The Consequences of War

This edition published by Diamond Books, 1999

Diamond Books is an Imprint of HarperCollins*Publishers*
77-85 Fulham Palace Road,
Hammersmith, London W6 8JB

First published in Great Britain by
GraftonBooks 1990

ISBN 0-261-67078-6

Printed in Great Britain by
Caledonian International Book Manufacturing Ltd, Glasgow

Set in Bembo

For my new grandson Ben Burton,
and
to the memory of my mother,
Lilian Archer,
whose work in the Second World War
gave me the idea for this book

Markham/Romsey

The Consequences of War is set in a fictitious small market town in Hampshire at the time of the Second World War. The town is called Markham.

However, in the descriptions of Markham there is so much of Romsey, where I was born and grew up, that it would be untrue to say that I was not thinking of Romsey when I wrote *The Consequences of War*.

I am sure that those of my family and friends who still live there will know that I chose to set this story in my home town because of my affection for the place.

The fiction is in the people of Markham and what happened to them. My Markham people were not drawn from Romsonians, but came to life in 1989 and live only within the pages of this book.

What is not fiction is the change that took place in the lives of many married women. The Blitz is real; so are the air-raids and the fire-bombings of Southampton and Portsmouth; the 'invasion' of Hampshire by Yanks at the time of D-Day; shortages, rationing and the kind of life led by people who lived in small, quiet towns in Southern England during the Second World War.

Betty Burton,
Southsea, Hampshire
January 1990

1989

Georgia Giacopazzi, treading carefully and slowly because of the very high heels she is wearing, comes down the wide sweep of thickly-carpeted stairs. And she wants to have a last look at the house about which she has from time to time over the last twenty-five years been curious.

The house is much as she had expected it to be – inherited money plus style (her contribution), order plus bits of bad taste such as the folly with its life-size plaster guru (his contribution). And to think it was he who told me that gin and orange was a common drink. 'A shop-girl's drink, Georgia.'

She had not imagined that they would have become such an old, old and ailing couple. Several times over the last forty-eight hours she had looked at them and thanked her own peasant ancestry from whom she had inherited robustness and a supple body, and maybe the English climate was kinder to the skin.

Georgia Giacopazzi has, since the Swinging Sixties and some gossip columnist interest, been known to the public simply as Giacopazzi. Giacopazzi's plumpish, ageless face has, for forty years or more, looked at her readers from the back cover of millions of copies of her novels, and smiled nicely.

Giacopazzi's novels are not nice – at least that is the impression one receives from jacket illustrations, for no matter what she writes her publishers see that on the jacket the illustrator spills blood, bares male torsos and drapes chilly (or aroused) women in wet satin. No, they are not nice, but she never intends niceness. Niceness is not a reason why she sells everywhere from Hudson Bay to Alice

Springs. Giacopazzi has the knack. She is a good storyteller of death and love, sex and mystery who keeps her readers page-turning to the end. She is a genre writer who appeals to people who know that the main ingredient of a book ought to be enjoyment for the reader. Giacopazzi has never won an award, never been seriously reviewed, never been invited on a TV panel of real writers, yet she is number three in any list of most-read authors. And her books have never been nice.

But she has now written another sort of book. It is the reason why she has left home and is visiting people, some of whom she has not seen for almost fifty years. The book is about them.

The house, whose stairs she now descends, was built in the Sixties in Johannesburg which, in that city, means that it is an old, mellow place. Designed to suit the nine months of summer, the place is spacious, airy, almost doorless, galleried and open-planned around a slightly Moorish courtyard. It is a rich house in a rich suburb full of Liberal Jews and of rich Rhodesians who ran away before it became Zimbabwe. Georgia Giacopazzi's conscience has sometimes been troubled by the size of her own income, but at least she has worked for it herself, worked long and hard for it over forty years. If she sold in thousands rather than millions, she would earn less than a teacher. These ex-Rhodesian ex-pat Brits have lived for forty years on the long, hard, hungry labour of others who finished up with nothing, not even their old age.

She can hardly wait to get away from them and their beautiful home.

Inside the house, sounds and light play tricks. The girl and her grandmother are not close by, but the girl's voice drifts clearly through fretted apertures and stone archways.

Georgia Giacopazzi coughs to signal her approach but she cannot compete with the girl's raised jaw-cracking English of a certain type of South African. The girl has always attended a school wherein the accent is fostered and enhanced – more English than the English, these Brits speak of England as 'Home' unto the third and fourth generation of settlers.

Georgia Giacopazzi smiles, not eavesdropping but listening professionally, for of course Georgia Giacopazzi is a novelist with an ear for convincing dialogue.

She slows her progress because she is curious to hear the rest of the conversation between the girl and her grandmother – after all, one of the reasons she has come all this way is not only to seek permission for some entries in her new novel, but to satisfy a long-lived curiosity about the grandmother.

The girl's voice comes clearly from the garden room. 'Well, Granny, *I* should be absolutely prepared to have hormone implants at seventy if it's the means of keeping old age at bay for twenty-five years.'

'Not twenty-five – ten, maybe – no way could she pass for forty-five. Those fair, plumpish Englishwomen of her type always manage to keep their wrinkles at bay; their problem is running to fat.' Her own body was spare.

'She's not plumpish, she's just not shrivelled up. You're seeing her as a contemporary, Granny darling. I see her from my viewpoint and I don't think she looks fifty even . . . I mean, just compare her to Ma . . .'

'Diplomatic of you, sweetheart, not to compare her to this old strip of biltong.'

'Oh Granny, you are just sweet.'

'Darling child, this country isn't kind to women's bodies.'

'Right on. So, when a thing like this HRT thingy is discovered, we should take advantage of it.'

'Never mind, darling, you are only just getting your hormones, it is forty years before you will have to think about replacing your lost ones.'

Georgia Giacopazzi clicks her high heels across the

terrazzo hallway and smiles as she approaches the girl and her grandmother. 'My packing's done, I'll be out of your hair in an hour.'

'It has been a pleasure.'

The politeness of her age and class armoured anything that might lie behind the formal cliché. For the two days of her visit, Georgia Giacopazzi had tried to find a chink through which she might glimpse in the old woman the girl who fifty years ago must have been passionate and unscrupulous. But nothing. She had revealed no more of her feelings about their common bond, if that is what it was, than Georgia Giacopazzi herself had done. Two women whose lives had been drastically changed by the fortunes of a war that had been over for forty years.

And when Georgia Giacopazzi had asked her if she was disturbed by anything in the draft of the new Giacopazzi book, she had said politely, 'I hardly think it matters, it is only fiction.'

1939

On the morning following Georgia Kennedy's husband's last day in Civvy Street, it suddenly came to her what freedom this coming war would bring.

For the last ten minutes, as her mind roamed lazily, she had kept glancing at Hugh's best working suit. Then the reality of its precisely-folded emptiness sank in.

I'm free again.

Hugh has gone!

Free of Hugh-centred routine.

Hugh, too eager to await the call-up, had resigned his Territorial Army commission, packed the khaki canvas bag and gone to Aldershot to join the regulars, all tickety-boo, polished, shiny and humming tumty-tumty-tum.

From the bed, she saw also his folded breeches and country-jacket of prickly lovat tweed and heard Hugh's grammar-school accent.

'The jackets and breeches must be dry-cleaned, Georgia, I won't be able to find the time; and put some naphtha in the pockets, it could be years . . .'

'But Hugh, you'll get leave.'

'Well yes, but you know . . . Don't make difficulties, Georgia.'

Looking now at his civvies – still not at the dry-cleaners as instructed and Hugh gone a whole twenty-four hours – Georgia imagined that the tweed was as much impregnated with Hugh's self-important voice as with the flour it gathered when he walked past the grain mills to his little white-dusted lab-office . . . used to walk.

She raised one arm above her head, allowing the shoulder-socket to lock so that the arm almost held itself aloft. Doing nothing except idle in bed and think about domestic freedom.

I'll be Georgia again.

Not Mrs Kennedy, not Hugh Kennedy's doubles partner, not the girl who married her boss, not Hugh Kennedy's wife . . . My Wife . . . The Wife . . . Housewife. She was free to be Georgia. She gazed up at Georgia's firm and slender arm, eight months since the 1938 Tennis Club tournaments, and still honey-brown.

Almost the last question he had asked yesterday, before he was caught up in the excitement, was about that very arm. 'Why on earth do you do that, Georgia?' Niggly. 'Is that supposed to be arm exercise? If so, then it's a waste of time, unless you use weights.' Niggly in spite of his elation at the prospect of Aldershot. She knew why: Hugh didn't like her to watch as he dressed. But unless he withdrew into the bathroom or the tiny spare bedroom, he had no option – either move would have been a statement of something. Of the state of their relationship perhaps.

Is he embarrassed in the open showers at the Sports Club, or the communal rugby tubs, or out on manoeuvres? Perhaps he isn't as well equipped as other men. How would I know? The last naked male I saw was Nick, and he was still only seventeen. The *only* naked male! Certainly from what she could observe of the lounging in bathers around the club pool, Hugh appeared to be no less well endowed.

Nick Crockford at seventeen was six foot tall and still growing, almost unembarrassed and nonchalantly proud of his body, diving and beckoning Georgia into the chilly clear green water of the lake that hot July after a day when they had been fruit-picking till their backs were broken. Sunburned dark brown except for where his body had been covered by shorts and singlet. Even then his hair had shown some streaks that, by the time he was twenty, would have spread until he was prematurely grey.

Yesterday had been a bit hectic, seeing Hugh off, then

typing up the letters he had left, and his various reports for the Sports Club. Today she could take more slowly; she thought again of her new state of freedom and life without Hugh.

Two years of marriage, of sharing four foot by six foot of springs and flock, of sharing boiled, blued, starched and ironed white cotton sheets, woollen blankets and padded art-silk eiderdown, two years of Hugh watching his next-of-kin raise her shaven-armpitted arms one at a time for a few minutes each morning – and always wondering but never commenting until the morning he left. Was that only yesterday!

'I like to stretch and look at my arms. They are the only parts of me that bear any resemblance to a ballet-dancer. It must be wonderful to be trained in ballet, don't you think, Hugh? As soon as I get up, they change shape and become a housewife's arms. They shovel coal, roll pastry and iron sheets. Nothing very wonderful about a housewife's arms. Eh? Is there, Hugh? Nothing exotic, not at all erotic.'

He had halted momentarily in pulling on his socks, those khaki fine-woollen socks that Gieves and Hawkes supplied not only to time-serving army officers but to Territorials, part-timers such as Hugh had been for years. He had reddened slightly, but had not looked up, had not wagged his head at her nonsense, had not smiled at her and said, as any man who wasn't Hugh would have said, 'You do say some daft things, Georgia.'

Yesterday, he had not heard much because of the clamour of his own thoughts of Aldershot, had been too deafened by the prospect of war and the prospect of permanent khaki to hear much at all except the zips and fasteners of his grip and hussif and toiletry roll, and the clink of the buckle of his Sam Browne belt.

And I do say some daft things. I do, because he never does.

If only he had just said, 'Georgia Kennedy, I shall never

make you out', and had come across to the bed and given her a playful kiss . . . or an intimate squeeze, suggestive caress . . . as he did in the fictions that went on in her head. If he had only said, 'I don't care if your arms are not exotic, but I know they are erotic, so move over and make room for me.' If only he had got back into bed and pressed down upon her wearing his uniform or . . . oh yes, wearing prickly thorn-proof lovat.

Desire sprang from the fantasy and made her wonder how she would feel if Hugh was away for long stretches of time. Hugh wasn't very good in bed, but at least he was there . . . used to be there.

Leaning on one elbow she drank the remaining half-inch of the lemon and honey she had brought with her last night – not their usual cocoa, but lemon and honey with – and for God's sake why not! – a large gurgle from the sherry bottle. It had not tasted very good last night, and was not improved with standing – but it had a faint flavour of decadence. Stale but exotic. Boozing in bed. A little bit of freedom from the male she had made promises to.

She ran her hands up her legs and felt her armpits. Perhaps . . . she smiled, remembering the time when she still lived at home . . . a customer, a White Russian woman refugee with lovely glossy black hair everywhere, used to come disturbingly sleeveless into the pub, always with a different good-looking man, and unwittingly be the focus of furtive attention from the regulars. Did Russian women not shave their armpits, or was she having her little bit of freedom now that she had escaped whatever it was she had? Perhaps I will let mine grow . . . but it would be reddish and insignificant compared to the Russian lady's.

Aloud, 'Get *up!*'

Her eye caught sight of a pile of papers Hugh had left for her to stow in a document folder he had provided – it had strings and looked as though it ought to contain something more legal or important than radio licences, car documents and the like. With these papers was his War Office marching orders envelope.

When it had arrived, he had turned the manila envelope over several times, smiling at it in a way that Georgia had once fondly imagined he smiled over her love letters to him. That was a fantasy, as she had soon learned: he had never set much store by letters.

'For Christ's sake, open it if you are going to, Hugh.'

'Keep your socks on, Old Girl, it's probably my Marching Orders.'

He was about to rip open the envelope with his thumb as always, when he stopped. 'Where's the paper-knife, Georgia?'

'I don't know, did we ever have one?'

Using his butter-knife he had carefully slit open the envelope. 'You want to get a box to keep them. Not many people realize it yet, but things like this will be like gold before many months are gone.' Having removed its contents, he smoothed the envelope and anchored it securely to the breakfast table by means of the knife.

'Hugh, it's only an ordinary envelope, I can't see how going to war will affect the production of envelopes – what do you think we shall do, press them into hard balls and throw them at the Germans?'

Normally, Hugh would have looked long-sufferingly at her facetious attempt at feigned ignorance. Being Silly. 'You're being silly now, Georgia.' That day he had smiled, smoothing back the longer side of his Brylcreemed hair with thumb and cupped hand. Some mornings she had counted him do that seventeen or eighteen times as he read his *Telegraph*.

'Put sticky labels on the list. Get a boxful. This Show's not going to be over by Christmas, I don't care what your captive oracle or anybody else says.'

'She's the librarian. And her brother is in the army and he is a sergeant. I should have thought he'd know a bit more about it than a playtime soldier.'

Sheer absolute bitchiness calling him that.

I have been bitchy. That time when she had referred to him as an office worker. Being in charge of the lab is so important to Hugh . . . used to be. Now he will not have to bring conversation around to the point where he can establish his status: he will have a peaked cap and insignia on his shoulders.

I once asked him to make love to me without taking off his lovely rough lovats. 'Hugh, why won't you ever let yourself go? Why is it that you'll never make love with your Tweeds on – and never with your pyjamas off?'

He looked at me as though I had made a lewd suggestion.

Jim-jams, he calls them. Jim-jams – man of his age!

The abbey clock struck seven. Outside the small forty-year-old single-bay terraced house, the spring morning had been going for hours. The earth had turned quite a few degrees since dawn so that now sunshine came directly into the room and turned the red and white Regency stripes to gold and tan.

Charlie Partridge, the postman, on the last leg of his morning round, loosens his tie and tips back his peaked cap. He's a good-looking young man in his solid way, resembling his mother. It is hot for the time of year, he has forecast a long hot summer – open-air type, he's always been quite good at knowing the weather.

He slows down and swings his empty sack round to the back. There are only a few letters left. Reading the envelopes he sees two for Kennedy further along the avenue and is reminded that Hugh Kennedy has joined up leaving Markham Town Cricket Club without a captain. Charlie Partridge plays but knows that he stands no chance of getting elected captain – born the wrong side of the tracks. And wonders, yet again, whether he should do the same and join up. He hasn't much time for Churchill, but Charlie has to agree with him in spite of him being a toe-rag. There will be a war and we'd better prepare for it. If I go it will be the RAF. He had not said a word to Marie, or to anyone for that matter.

1989

'Look, isn't that that novelist woman?' A woman, holding a large amount of hand luggage as she awaits the announcement of her flight, points.

'Which novelist?'

'The one who writes the dirty mysteries . . . you know *Lay of the Land*.'

'Yes, *Tricks of the Trade*, all those . . . there, look, coming down the corridor, the one in the white.'

'You're right, it's her. She looks just the same as her picture. I always thought it was touched up.'

'It's her face that's touched up I should think, plastic surgery. I expect her old chin is up behind her ears.'

'You've got to give it to her, though, she looks fantastic. Man, who would wear white silk to travel in?'

They gawp and press close to the window as the trail of passengers makes its way towards the fuel-suckling Boeing 747 gleaming in the clear, bright winter sunlight. Georgia Giacopazzi in her role of writer of blockbusters is used to being inspected and discussed by strangers.

'How old do you think she is really?'

'Nobody knows anything much about her. Not even where she lives. I read this big, in-depth profile about her in *Cosmo* and they said it was all true – about the mystery of her private life.'

'All invented by publicity agents.'

'She owns a London flat, a penthouse in Manhattan where she stays for a few days when she goes to New York to see her publisher, and a villa in The Algarve – isn't that in France or Spain or somewhere? – but she never, ever lives more than a few days in any of them. She has them just to keep people at bay. It said that she lives somewhere where nobody knows, not even her agent. She writes one of her blockbusters, goes on a big publicity tour, does TV and photo-calls all round the world, and then disappears again until she's written another one.'

'She gets three million dollars a book now.'

'How many rand is that?'

'God knows, but it buys a hell of a lot of face-lifts.'

' "An enigma" – that's what they called her in *Cosmo*.'

The enigma is now approaching the aircraft steps. All that one can tell from this distance is that she is of average height, has that whiter shade of white hair which indicates that it was once red, and walks upright with an air of assurance about her.

'You've got to admit, she looks pretty damned sexy still.'

The woman, the enigma, carrying an armful of fresh proteas, not huddling from the bitter winter wind of the high veld which ripples and billows her white silk coat, halts at the aircraft steps, turns towards the observation lounge window, raises her hand once then boards the London-bound aircraft.

1939

Spring

Georgia Kennedy got out of bed and, as she had fantasized doing many times but had never had the courage to actually do since she had been Mrs Hugh Kennedy, Manager's Wife, took off her Ceylonese pyjamas and walked naked down to the kitchen to make herself tea and toast, stopping to look at her face in the landing mirror.

A mane of reddish-gold hair that grew in masses of tendrils, straight high forehead, a firm chin and jaw-line which, she foresaw, would probably be plumply hidden in twenty years' time, and wide intelligent greenish eyes which would probably be surrounded by a mass of little lines in twenty years' time. Their embryos were already there. Leaning towards her reflection she raised her brows, pressed the star creases with her middle fingers.

What sort of a face is that Georgia Kennedy? Not beautiful, not lovely. Pretty. Good-looking. Handsome? You're a striking-looking young woman, Mrs Kennedy, and you look sweeter and kinder than you are. You've got the sort of face that used to make youths believe that Georgia Honeycombe was an easy lay. And now that you are Mrs Kennedy, it's a face that makes all of the Good Sports at the Club dances press their thighs closer to yours than they would dare to with the other men's wives.

What is it that gives men that impression of me? She searches her full lips, pink cheeks and golden hair and receives the answer that hers is the face of a young woman which makes men think of milkmaids in summer meadows. A country girl with a pretty face, and the Good Sports knew all about country girls and hay-cocks – easy lay, cock.

But they had all been wrong, she had not been anybody's

easy lay: when she had given herself to Hugh it was in well-deserved virginal white.

Given? Well, that's as good a description of it as any. He certainly hadn't taken her. Not Hugh. Hugh as a bridegroom was knocking the door of forty: if there had been wild oats, he had sown them years before. Wild oats no more rampant than those sown in the company of the entire touring team, and which were more concerned with policemen's helmets and thefts of public toilet signs than with women.

And 'well-earned' virginal white? Yes, because it had not been the nature of the pubescent Georgia Honeycombe to be chaste. She had strong lusts and vivid dreams in which she sometimes cried out. But she had parents who saw to it that she grew up to be a nice girl, a good girl; added to which she had been taught in a hassock and cassock school, in which God and his vicar kept an eye out for sins of girlish flesh.

Hugh got Georgia intact, and the honeymoon was almost over before he could bring himself to change that state. She preferred not to remember the honeymoon.

Hugh was better at firing off rifles.

They were not suited, but divorce in 1937 was not an option many couples considered, so they rubbed along and things got slightly better. Georgia was no longer intact, but she was disillusioned and unsatisfied. Married love was not what she had expected it to be. But, like divorce, in 1937 a more liberated sex-life was not an option open to a woman who had been to a hassock and cassock school. Not much of an option to many women who lived under the scrutiny of the community in a place like Markham then.

At the bottom of the stairs she halted at her unclear reflection in the glazed kitchen door to contemplate briefly the rest of Georgia Kennedy. Top heavy, well-defined waist, wide pelvis, rounded behind, long, solid legs – she would have made a good 'Gibson' Girl. Viewing herself objectively she knew that, had she been a mare, someone would no doubt have given her an approving slap on her flanks and said that she'd have no trouble when it came to producing. But Georgia did not want to produce. She smoothed the slight convex of her belly. She quite liked her own body but had never felt any desire to use it for the growing of tiny Hughs.

The letterbox, which had a flap like a man-trap, almost got Charlie Partridge's fingers this time. His attention was caught by a pink image behind the patterned glass which was intended to protect postmen from such unexpected visions.

A good bloody thing she an't my Missis.

Which, at least as far as Georgia Kennedy was concerned, wasn't true. It might have been quite a good thing for her to have had a husband more like Charlie Partridge and less like Captain Kennedy. But there, she had been only barely eighteen when Hugh had proposed, and girls of eighteen can't be expected to know that a dashing Territorial Army officer and captain of Markham Cricket Club isn't necessarily going to make a dashing husband. Certainly Hugh Kennedy had not.

1989

The straight-faced SAA steward asked, quite politely, 'Something to drink,' but delayed 'Madam?' just those few seconds too long after the question.

'Danke. Suurlemonene?'

'Certainly, Madam.' He smiled as he poured and handed her the fruit juice. 'Wull there be anything ulse I can bring for you?'

'*Danke. Ek is moeg, ek wil rus.*'

He offered her a blanket.

Although she was neither tired, nor wanted to rest, she accepted it. She had been travelling this route for years enough now to know that speaking a few words of their language to an Afrikaans steward could get a buzzer answered after the cabin lights were dimmed. With a British passport and a name like Giacopazzi, it was not a bad idea to ensure one's comfort – it was a long flight from Jo'burg to London.

Having finished the fruit juice, Georgia Giacopazzi settled back into her seat, grateful that the seat next to her was not taken by somebody who might have bought one of her paperbacks which were always on sale in airport and railway-station bookshops. Some people seemed to think that because they had laid out some cash, a small percentage of which eventually trickled down to the author, that gave them permission to ask personal questions. If they paid ten times the price of a book for a restaurant meal, they wouldn't dream of asking the chef, 'How old are you?' or 'I thought you'd be taller.'

It was partly her own fault, she had always agreed to a clause in her contracts that her books show a picture all glitz and glam. Image-making. Conning readers that I'm a nice lady – nice old lady. Her agent, Bruce, had said, 'Not *old*, Georgia. It's a charming picture,' and slid on to talking of the possibility of getting a mini-series for the new book. Georgia was still ambitious and normally egoist enough to want to see herself portrayed by some internationally-known star if the mini-series was made.

Who could play Hugh? Fascinated as always by looking down on clouds, her mind drifted. Ronald Pickup? He looked a lot like Hugh. If the Australians came up with their share for the series, then Hugh might for ever be transformed into Ronald Pickup. He would have liked that.

She had settled Charlie Partridge's part whilst she was writing the book – the American who played Columbo . . . something Falk . . . Peter! His face exactly Charlie's. And Dolly Partridge? Georgia knew who would be right to play Dolly. That bright woman . . . what was her name? . . . in the play and then the film . . . leave it and it will come.

The cloud was thinning and becoming islands in space. It had been quite weird how, when she started writing this book, she discovered that she had such an extraordinary total recall of those six years of the Second World War that she scarcely needed to do any research. She had done ten earlier books, but none of them was at all like *Running Away From the Smoothing Iron.* Why had she decided to write it at all? Merely to unload her memory, and free some of the cluttered old cells? Or was it to say the things she had never said to the people involved? Oddly, of all the questions she had been asked by interviewers, none of them had ever asked why.

'Mrs Giacopazzi, you have admitted that your new novel is totally autobiographical . . .'

'Yes, so far as a novel may be autobiography.'

'The events are factual?'

'As I recall them. But I say that it is still a novel – a fiction.'

'But for your characters you have used your husband,

your friends, neighbours, your . . . lovers – without, as one might say, halt or hindrance – using their real names.'

'Well, there seemed little point in trying to disguise them. In any case, it was all a long time ago.'

Respectfully, because Georgia Giacopazzi is becoming an old lady, 'May I ask why you did not write a conventional autobiography?'

'I think it is because it was the only way that I could know what those people I was so close to at that time actually thought and felt. A novelist is always inside the heads and hearts of her characters. An autobiographer is inside only her own, and merely an observer of anyone else.'

'I see.'

'It seemed important to me to try to understand the people with whom I spent the wartime years, the women especially. At the time, I was very young. Concerned only with myself. Those six years made up a very significant part of my life . . . not significant, that's not the word . . . *essential*, in the way of a distilled essence – condensed. Time during those years did seem to have the quality of denseness. So much could happen within the space of a few days . . . hours even. On VE Day, I was a very different woman from the young housewife I was at the start of the War. It was being with the women, you see. Had it not been for the war and being involved with the women . . . Good Lord, it doesn't bear thinking about.'

'How do you imagine they will feel, these people – finding themselves in a popular bestseller?'

Georgia Giacopazzi withdrew her gaze from the cabin window now that they had left behind the cloud landscape and there was only the endless blue of space to see.

Collins! Pauline Collins would be Dolly.

1939

Spring

Half an hour later and two long streets further on – the last leg of his early round before going to his own home where his wife Marie would have a mug of cocoa waiting ready to drink – Charlie Partridge went in by the back door of his parents' home in Jubilee Lane where his father, Sam, ready for work in his park-keeper's uniform, was as usual waiting with a ready-poured mug of well-sugared, dark-brown Co-op 99 tea at just the right temperature for Charlie to drink quickly. His mother, Dolly, on her way down the garden with a basket of washing and a bag of pegs dangling from her mouth, put her face up for a peck which she returned with a wink.

Charlie squeezed into the chair at the cramped coal-cupboard end of the table, nodded to his father. 'Dad.'

'Charlie.' The father, in his usual meal-time place beside the back door at the cramped larder end of the table, inclined his head in acknowledgement. 'How's Marie?'

'Right as rain.'

'Bonnie?'

Charlie nodded without giving chapter and verse of his daughter's health. His mother and Marie would chew that over when they went out shopping together this afternoon. Not that there was really anything to chew over, Bonnie was as bonny as she had always been for the entire five years since her birth. 'You all right then, Dad?'

'All right as I'll ever be.'

Which exchange of greeting they had been making ever since Charlie had got promoted from telegram boy to postal delivery service at the station end of Markham. On Charlie's round there were probably twice as many houses as on some of the other rounds, but people got few letters. At the railway end the houses progressed downhill – not in the literal sense, for this was the floor of the valley – from the streets of small shops and terraced cottages that spoked out from the hub of the centre of the country market town, the boss of which was the great Norman abbey. The best houses on Charlie's round were the rows of single-bays of Station Avenue where he had seen the hazy naked outline of Hugh Kennedy's wife.

Father and son sat with the back door open and watched Dolly as she looped up very white sheets and pillowcases.

Dolly Partridge, in her late forties, was still a very good-looking woman. Brown eyes and brown hair streaked with grey, and good teeth that had stood up well to the ravages of years of bad nutrition and lack of dental treatment. A handsome buxom woman with large breasts and heavy hips and veins that made her legs ache. Her only indulgence was powder, lipstick, and the best tight Eugene perm twice a year. Whether it be early morning when whitening the front step, or late at night putting out the milk-bottles for the Co-op, she had on a bit of make-up. She had married Sam when she was barely seventeen.

As a hero in the War to End All Wars of 1914, Samuel Partridge had been one of the first ex-servicemen to move into one of the six houses on Jubilee Lane reserved for such men. More aptly to *be* moved into, because one and a half of his own legs had not returned from France with him and artificial ones had not been ready. Sam, Dolly, their daughter Paula and two sons, Charlie and Harry.

Harry was the last child Dolly and Sam managed to make before all that kind of thing became difficult for them when Sam was blown up in that terrible French mud-hole. Sam could affirm that lightning did strike twice. The first shell split one leg and blew off most of the other, the second penetrated his groin with shrapnel. He still had nightmares in which he struggled to thrust a bayonet into a disembodied voice that called, 'Out! You can't play with two stumps and one ball.' When, in this dream, he wept with shame and frustration, a Red Cross official bent over him and said, 'Don't cry, corporal, it's not like castration, you'll still need to shave.'

Dolly talked him through the nights of his nightmares. But, being a young woman of normal appetites, she had had her own dreams that she could not speak of to anyone.

Between his park-keeping hours Sam sat in the kitchen or in the King William, spreading his Bolshie notions and running the Labour Party and a family Savings Club known as the Diddle'm. Dolly got fed up with politics, but she couldn't blame him, a lot of ordinary soldiers and their families had a rough deal – first from the nincompoop generals and then from a two-faced government. It's a wonder the men hadn't kept their guns and turned on them.

She came back in, wanting to get on with her chores, pushing round the two men filling the kitchen. 'Move yourself a bit, Charlie.'

'You know what I just seen?' Charlie asked. 'You know Hugh Kennedy, cricket captain?'

'A course I know him, works at the flour mill, lives in Station Avenue,' said Sam. 'Officer in the Territorials.'

'Got a blonde wife, years younger,' said Dolly. 'What about him?'

'Her . . . his missis . . .' Charlie leaned forward and lowered his voice '. . . just as I was putting the letters through, she was just going up the hallway . . . in the buff . . . without a stitch on.' His hands revealed that he was a man who liked bosoms.

Sam Partridge supped deeply, the star-creases at the corner of his eyes deepening as he withdrew his nose from the mug and heaved several quiet laughs. 'Hope you never got your fingers trapped in the excitement, our Charl.'

'You might laugh, I bloody nearly did. Theirs is one of those in the middle of the row that's had a frosted-glass door put in and one of them new-fangled rat-trap letter boxes right down where it breaks your back and every dog in the road can cock his leg on it.'

'You shouldn't put up with that, Charlie. See your Union about it.'

Missing the irony in his father's tone but hearing the word Union and knowing what would come next if he didn't go now, Charlie gathered up the few letters he still had to deliver. 'Ah. Well, I'd better get on.'

'It's what you got a Union for to protect you from that kind of thing. It's what you pay dues for.'

'Don't start, Sam,' Dolly said. 'Take no notice, Charlie, you go on and get your round finished.'

'You'd best tell the Union that that's what dues is for then, Dad: they thinks it's for building a bloody great office in Southampton.' Still not seeing his father's purse-lipped smile, 'So long, Dad.'

Dolly watched her son rebutton his tunic, run the crown of his uniform cap around his elbow and place it squarely on the fine head of hair which he had inherited from the Partridges.

'Charlie.'

Charlie swivelled his head to settle his hair inside the cap and patted the shoulder-strap of his delivery bag in place. 'I have to get on.' But he stayed until his father had had his say.

'You swore twice in the last five minutes. I never swore in my life and don't expect any of mine to neither, whether they're grown men or not – and specially in front of your mother. If you was still living under my roof, I should a had a bit more than this to say.'

'Ah, sorry, Mum. It just slips out.'

'No, it don't,' Dolly said, 'not if you don't let it.'

'All right, Mum.'

'Just watch it, lad.'

'I will.' Now he had got as far as the back gate.

'Oh, and Charlie,' his father called, 'your Diddle'm club's due.'

'I'll get Marie to give it to Mum.'

'Remind her, you'll be glad of it at Christmas.'

I'm twenty-five, Mum. I'm married, Dad. I've got a wife, and a child starting school in September. Stop bloody treating me like I was still a kid. Not aloud of course. Mum and Dad only ever had the best interests of the family at heart. Mum was right – she always was – they would be glad of the money at Christmas.

1939

Spring

On that same morning, at about the same time as Charlie Partridge was finishing off his round, Eve Hardy went down the drive so as to waylay Markham's longest serving postman, Mont Iremonger, before he rounded the bend in the drive where there was a view from the house. Eve Hardy was the same age as Georgia Kennedy but, unlike Georgia, who was a born and bred country girl, Eve was born in Markham and bred in the finest educational establishments that money could buy. Eve Hardy was the daughter of 'Hardy's Cakes Like Mother Bakes'.

'Morning, Miss Eve.'

'Hello, Mr Iremonger. Shall I take the post?' She put out her hand for the large bundle, but the postman held it back playfully but respectful.

'Shouldn't rightly do that, Miss. I'm supposed to deliver to the premises. But . . .' waggling the letters as though she was still seven . . . 'seeing there's so many ha'penny ones I reckon it's somebody's birthday . . .' Two-handed he presented them to her as he had done for nineteen years.

'Must be twenty, is it twenty-one?' He knew very well what it was, for as well as the unsealed ha'penny envelopes, there was a coloured postcard without an envelope from the Hardys' daily woman and another from their washer-woman. Both cards the same, a photo of a silver key and a girl with primroses and Happy Twenty-First. But Royal Mail employee Mont Iremonger had officially blind eyes to everything except names and addresses, particularly Longmile. This being a group of houses so grand as to suggest that they could scarcely be thought to be part of a market town at all. Even so, the Longmile address was Markham.

Eve took the cards and tried to be casual about riffling through them. 'Twenty-one today.'

'Congratulations, Miss.' Mont Iremonger knew what she was looking for, the letter with a Portsmouth postmark which he had placed at the bottom of the pile. A flush crept over her cheeks as she discovered it and slipped it into a side-pocket of her summer skirt. Charlie Partridge would have given her the letter and said, 'Well, here's your love-letter. You're still sweet on Dave Greenaway then? I'll bet your Dad would have something to say if he found out.' But then Charlie Partridge delivered mail to a very different part of Markham.

'Be back with another lot at midday, I dare say.'

'Pa's giving me a party, I'll save you a piece of cake for tomorrow.'

The Hardys' house being the last delivery, Mont Iremonger mounted his bike and headed back towards town. What would Young Eve's father say if he knew she was getting letters from the Greenaway boy? There wasn't much in Markham didn't eventually reach the eyes and ears of Councillor Hardy. He'd soon put a stop to it if he got to find out his precious daughter was writing to a sailor brought up in a Markham newsagents and tobacconists – and a Greenaway at that.

He'll never get to hear of it from me. Young Eve's been running to get the letters since she could walk, a proper little joy, like a godchild or a granddaughter. I wouldn't give her away to him in a hundred years. In any case I don't actually *know* that they're letters from the Greenaway boy . . . can't tell much from a cancellation stamp, can you? Only thing I know is that young Greenaway is in the Navy and he's in Portsmouth. No business of mine who's writing letters to who.

Twenty-one! He had reached the bottom of Longmile Hill before he was smitten with the realization that young Eve had stopped being a girl. Middle-age creeping up on you, Mont. Really though, in her pinky skirt and sandals, she didn't look that much different this morning than when she was about twelve. Young minx, though, going behind her father's back like that. But there, if you was a man like Councillor Hardy, you shouldn't be surprised if people went behind your back.

It was evening before other scales dropped from his eyes and revealed to him the truth about his own ageing. The thought of the lonely road that stretched to the cemetery clutched at his stomach and dried his throat. Next year this time, I shall be retired. He thought the sunset looked ominous and took himself off to The Orb and Sceptre for a pint of bitter.

1989

The lovely Tuscany golden terracotta rambling house, under the Tuscany morning sun, seemed empty now that the children had gone. A special visit to celebrate her seventy-first birthday. Celebrate? How Eve begrudged each year as her precious sands flowed through her fast-emptying hourglass. Each time they left, she wondered whether next time they came it would be for her funeral. Not that she felt ready to go, never had a day's illness in her life, but she was getting old.

Give me fifteen more years and I'll go quietly. Now that most of her life was gone, she wanted to stay alive more than she had ever wanted to. To see Josh growing up. One expected to feel strong emotions for one's children, but to feel such passion for grandchildren . . . and now a great-grandchild . . . that was something she had never expected.

'Grandma?' She would never forget Fergus's exulted voice down the telephone. 'Grandma, you've got a great-grandson. Eight pounds eight ounces, bald as a coot and noisy as all Hell – Joshua. Montague.' Fergus had an unsentimental feeling for family and history. In naming his first child he had remembered the old man who had been dead long before he was born.

'Thank you, Fergus.'

'No problem, Gran – any time.'

'Lucky little Joshua – having a Dad like you.'

'I'll bet you say that to all your grandsons.'

How the year had flown since then. She had never forgotten how endless her own firstborn's first year had been. How angst-ridden. Poor Melanie had had the worst of it. How had she ever managed to produce such a prize as

Fergus, who had had the masculine charm of Eve's own father but not a trace of the old devil's nature – thank God?

1939

Spring

At the end of her first day of freedom, Georgia Kennedy looked back upon it with slight regret at having frittered it away without having done anything very spectacular at all except to go into the Town Hall in response to an appeal for women voluntary workers, and to buy a half-bottle of Gilbeys. Gin, to her chagrin, she liked, even though, as Hugh had pointed out, gin was such a common drink compared to Scotch. Scotch and Soda . . . Whisky Mac . . . Scotch on the rocks, but gin and orange . . . Mother's Ruin.

'Gin, Georgia? That's a drink for a shop-girl on the razzle. If you must drink gin, at least learn to drink it with tonic.'

'But it has such a bitter taste, Hugh.'

'Try it. Scotch for me and a Gee and Tee for my good lady here.'

Presumably, because of its 'common' associations in Hugh's mind, they never had gin in the house, even at Christmas when he always got in a supply of port and lemon for the ladies.

It was early evening, and she sat in the garden drinking gin – and tonic, which she had learned to like – and wondering what she could do with all this freedom. The weather was exceptionally good, almost like July.

Hugh had been very put out when she had made her own suggestion.

'Georgia! Go out to work? For God's sake . . . officers' wives don't go out to work any more than managers' wives do.'

'I don't see why not.'

'Of course you damned well see why not, they just don't. . .'

As a kind of marzipan on the basic cake of her girlhood training in 'niceness', Georgia Kennedy had spent the last two years learning what women like herself 'just didn't'. Lately, she had begun to wonder why, instead of marrying a secretary with countrified origins, Hugh had not gone for one of the girls who were always so eager to partner him at tennis, or who at cricket pounced upon him with plates of sandwiches and cakes. They were his type – off-the-peg Officers' and Managers' wives. They knew unfailingly the etiquette of taking paid or charitable work, and the social position of a gin and orange, and what their set *just didn't*.

'Forget it! It's ridiculous! If you want something to do with your spare time, you take over my place on the Tennis Club Committee.'

'Oh Hugh! You know I can't stand them, and I didn't mean spare time . . . I meant . . .'

'If you can't stand the Committee, how do you think you'd fare with a room full of clerks?'

'I used to stand them all right before I married . . . and I didn't mean . . .'

'That was different. You worked in my office then.'

'It was just an office full of clerks and I . . .'

'And I was Manager.'

As in the past it had been with her mother, so her arguments with Hugh always ended with Georgia shutting up, silenced by their self-assurance and her lack of it.

She picked up the writing-pad and read over the four pages she had written to her parents, every line of which was what they wanted to hear.

Could I tell you, Dad, that I hadn't been married a week before I realized that I had made a mistake?

Could I explain to you, Ma, how hungry for *something* I always feel? That I'm not satisfied as I'm supposed to be with bed-linen Mondays, polishing Tuesdays, baking Wednesdays, cleaning Thursdays, shopping Fridays, Sports Club Saturdays and Cricketing Sundays, but starved of something filling and full of flavour?

I wish I could write and ask you things that really matter. I should ask you to tell me why you've always seemed ashamed of coming from country families, why you've kept the Honeycombes and the Gracelands at arm's length, why you are never satisfied and don't seem to be able to settle down. But their family wasn't like that, they never said the things that counted.

Georgia sealed down the letter, addressed it to *Mr and Mrs Honeycombe, Widdershins Guest House, Cults, Aberdeen*, and sat thinking of them, hoping that they felt rewarded now by their small guest house in Scotland, for all the years of budgeting to save minute amounts from the small profits of running the village pub.

Georgia poured herself a refill. Freedom from Ma, freedom from Dad, freedom from Hugh, freedom from their ideas of what is best for Georgia. It's my last chance to do . . . *something*.

1939

Summer

There was something in the air of Aldershot that worked on Major Hugh Kennedy like spiked wine. The bones of his vertebrae fused, his jaw squared off and protruded inches high above the strangling knot of his tie, and his heels went click, click, click, click to the strict beat of the dual metronomes of his swinging arms.

He faced the desk and saluted the King's Army in the person of his superior officer.

'At ease.' The old officer's voice was dark and gravelly from years of being raised so that damn-fool natives could understand his lingo. By rights, he should have been raising it at their damn-fool white counterparts in some piddling south-coast town like Lewes, or Hove or Southsea. But because of 'this little lot' about to start on the other side of the Channel, he was reprieved from expulsion from the only man's-life worth living.

Until the Hun was put down, and he with any luck had his own light put out with honour on the field of battle, the robes and runes and symbols of military life were still his. They were going to need every old war-horse they could muster before this little lot was over.

'Sit down, man.' He moved his cane a fraction closer to his gloves and smoothed the rim of his cap in which they were contained. Before he addressed his inferior officer, he ran his hands over his buttons, buckles and badges.

'Yes . . . Well, young . . . ah . . . Kennedy . . .'

'Sir!'

'Got these billy-doos from the War Office. Says here you've been in the Boys' Brigade then?'

'Sir?'

'Chaps here don't go a bundle on weekend soldiers, but never mind . . . right idea. Do with young blood. Get in now – and you'll get promotion goin' like a dose of liquorice powder.' He signed the papers with the dash of a cavalry officer with no time to waste on such damn piddling rubbish.

Young Kennedy waited three seconds to see whether there were any further formalities. There were not. He stood up and with two clicks was to attention.

'That's the ticket, Majah. Welcome to the Hogs. Best regiment in the world.'

Young Kennedy saluted.

The old war-horse returned the salute and felt to see if his epaulettes were still there whilst the young officer clicked his way across the shining floor and out into the sunshine.

The eyes of the two men had never made contact. Which was as it should be in the men's world.

1939

People had very ambivalent feelings about Connie Hardy. She had everything anyone could want – big house with acres of grounds, a car of her own, loads of clothes, holidays on ocean liners, people to do her work for her but . . . she was married to Freddy Hardy.

Councillor Hardy was a big fish in the Markham pond – so big that there was little room for anything else except small fry. In fact, Councillor Hardy was a pike with a successful mass production bakery business. Having consumed the local competition, he was ready to move into deeper waters.

He saw the approaching war as his chance to make a Million.

Aldershot camp was well within his delivery area, as were Bovey Tracey and Salisbury Plain: all encampments where many soldiers would eat huge quantities of bread.

Connie and Freddy Hardy had had only one child. Eve, whose twenty-first birthday it was today. The party was flawed in Connie's eyes, because she knew that, for all her planning, her husband would turn it into something unstylish and quite vulgar.

'No time, trouble, effort or money spared, Con. I'll supply the cash, and leave the rest to you.'

But he never could, never would, never did!

'Next to Eve's wedding, this will be Markham's event of the decade.'

He adjusted the white silk triangle in the breast-pocket of his dinner jacket. He was one of those men black tie dress was made for. He looked handsome, and knew that he looked handsome. Even more so now that his hair had thinned almost to baldness, giving him that remarkable combination of virility and maturity.

'How's that?'

Elegant Connie paused for a moment from rolling up her fine silk stockings and looked across at him. Neither of them looked their age.

'You look very handsome, Freddy.'

'Do I?'

'You always do, and you know it. As your mother says – Freddy could charm the birds from the trees.'

How else, Connie thought, did so many people tolerate him? Well, fear for one thing, I suppose. Fingers in everybody's pies. Wealth? Money buys a fair bit of tolerance. And charm. Power, money and charm – what else did a man need to take his place at the top of the pile?

He had good bones, sensuous mouth, deep-set eyes and straight nose, all of which, plus his well set-up body on which clothes hung perfectly, had the effect of making people believe that there was charm in his ruthlessness. There was not, of course – ruthlessness never has charm – but people will believe anything if it suits them or if they are flattered.

Connie Hardy knew every one of his faults and forgave him none of them, yet she was still attracted to him after nearly twenty-five years of marriage. The Councillor's enemies would say, 'She's such a lady and he's such a swine really – it makes you wonder what she ever saw in him.'

When he was at his worst, Connie Hardy often wondered the same thing. When at his best, she knew. In bed, they were very good together.

Twice she had decided to leave, only to find herself the next day in a state of satiety, as she always was when he turned on the charm – pleading and promising and stroking and combining romance with practised love-making. He was a double-dealer at heart. For twenty-five of her forty-five years she had been bound and gagged by him. Silver-chain bonds and silken gags, it is true, but she had never been free of him for a day. Her libido was strong, and had been fixed upon him from the day they met.

He picked up a complicated arrangement of black and tobacco-coloured georgette drapes and fly-away panels from the bed. 'Put it on and let's have a look.'

She abandoned her stockings and stepped into the georgette sack which immediately became a most elegant gown of the latest French chic.

He came and stood beside her, viewing their reflection with satisfaction. 'We two are OK, Connie. Still not a woman in the county to touch you for class, Connie. We'll show 'em tonight. Last fling before the lights go out.'

'We are not giving Eve her Coming of Age purposely to show them, Freddy.'

'Well no, Connie, but we shall just the same, shan't we?' He flashed his white teeth at her as he often flashed them at his secretary when getting her to work overtime for no extra pay, or at a bunch of old aldermen who were being difficult with their votes.

'Don't get into any arguments about council business.'

'So long as nobody gets into arguments with me.'

'That's just what I mean, Freddy. It is for you to see to it this evening – it is not *their* daughter's party, it's our daughter's.'

'I know.'

'Then don't go within twenty feet of Councillor Greenaway.'

Councillor Greenaway was the first and, so far, the only Labour man ever to be elected to the town council. He had set out to disrupt the cosy club that up till then had ruled the town and, although his one dissenting vote on matters such as how the rates were spent did not count for much, the pertinent – or impertinent, if the colour of your politics was blue – questions he asked in Council received a disproportionate amount of reportage, and created more discussion in the Tory Club lounge than was good for its Alderman and Councillor members.

Connie was ready now and sat smoking a cigarette and watching Freddy as he glossed back his hair and ran his fingertips over his Ronald Colman moustache. 'The man keeps a damn sweet-shop. If I don't want to argue with him, then I don't.'

'He's also one man who doesn't rely on you for his living, so it's no skin off his nose if you lose your temper at your daughter's party.'

'I could take him if I set my mind to it . . . buy up his lease or something. But he's all right. He's good for me, none of the kiss-my-backside attitude like the rest of them. If he wasn't a damn Red, I could quite get on with him – funny enough, we do get on in our own way.'

'Well, for tonight, you forget he's a damn Red.'

'All right, all right, you don't have to go on, I want it to be right for Evie just as much as you do . . . In fact . . . look,' he paused and felt in his jacket pocket. 'I went to Winchester today, for a special little present I had made, just from me to Eve.'

'Won't the car be enough?'

'That's our official present, look good in the *Clarion*, this is just from me – father to daughter.'

Connie Hardy opened the box and said an unambiguous 'Oh, yes' at its contents. A pair of ornate, sparkling dress-clips in the shape of letter Es, and in a kind of style that was most popular amongst girls who shopped for their jewellery at Woolworth's – in fact Woolworth's sold a very good copy of these very clips. It was the current fashion for girls to give one as a token of fidelity. They cost only sixpence, cheap enough for a girl to bestow her fidelity quite frequently.

Although he had the aforementioned health, money, power, etc., he unfortunately did not have any innate sense of style, and having found it very difficult to acquire, he had married it instead. Connie's own present to Eve was a slender art-nouveau statuette.

'Oh Freddy . . . they're . . . they're . . .' Oh my dear Lord! she thought, what can I say? '. . . they're *real* diamonds.'

'Of course they're real – wouldn't be much point if they weren't.'

In Pompey that same night, Able Seaman Greenaway and his two mates mingled with the shoppers in Lake Road. He had made up his mind that he would apply for transfer to where promotion was going to be fast. He was no fool: he knew that he had no serious chance of getting Freddy Hardy's consent.

'Let's all apply,' suggested David Greenaway. 'We should probably all go.'

'Och noo, Greeny, you'll not get me in a sardine can.'

'But think of the promotion, man,' David Greenaway said. 'We could be petty officers within a year.'

David Greenaway was of unremarkable height and breadth, made more noticeable when he was with the two Glaswegians with whom he had palled up on their first day – big, broad lads, one with flaming red hair, the other gypsy black with pock-marks of virility pitting his chin. With their little round caps and tight jerseys that showed off their physique, the young sailors swung along abreast through the market, turning the heads of Portsmouth girls done up and ready for a night out.

'Ye know, Greeny, these Pompey lassies are a bit of all right. I should'ne mind going to a hop.'

'Not for me, I'd rather just have a quiet pint. You two go, I'll see you back on board.'

'Come on, we'll find a dance-hall with a bar,' said the red-haired one.

'We'll toss ye for it,' suggested his pock-marked mate.

The Glaswegians lost, cheerfully.

'Come on, Greeny, cheer up. You look like a wet week in Dunoon.'

David Greenaway looked into his beer. 'It's my girl's twenty-first birthday.'

'Aw, and she'll be living it up without ye. Let's chip in and have a wee tot or two.'

The Scotch whisky loosened David Greenaway's normally tight tongue.

'She's the reason why I need to go on the subs.'

'You've no cause to bother your head about promotion, Greeny,' said the red-haired sailor. 'An educated chap like yoursel', with your old man owning a shop of his own, why, you'll be in a peaked cap soon enough.'

'Will she no have you as you are?' asked the other.

'It's not like that . . . though I *do* want to get some quick promotion. It's not Eve, it's her father, he's the big potato in our town. Rich . . . big house . . . owns a bread and cake factory. A borough alderman and a right swine with his employees. Fancies his chances with the women.'

Dave Greenaway's two mates understood: no decent working-class family would gladly welcome the daughter of the owner of a cake factory who had so many other points against him – alderman, skirt-chaser.

'And his darling daughter fancies ye?'

'More than fancies me. My God, she's lovely. I can never see her without thinking of big, ripe luscious strawberries with cream.' His gaze was away out of the sawdust and smoke of the bar. 'She's like that . . . pink and tender and sweet.'

The red-haired sailor nudged his mate. 'I can see ye've got it bad, Greeny.'

'I want to ask her to marry me.'

'Ye could run away to Gretna.'

'No, no . . . for a start my Mam wouldn't forgive me.'

Her beautiful, educated voice had not a trace of Hampshire breadth.

We could run away and be married over the anvil at Gretna Green, David.

His strawberry-flavoured girl would have run to the ends of the earth with him.

No, Eve, I don't want us married without our two families there when we come down the aisle of St Mary's, I want the Greenaways and the Hardys smiling at one another.

That's like waiting for the Montagues and Capulets to smile at one another.

It was, perhaps, an awareness of their universal, ageless situation that gave Eve and David such romantic notions about one another. They were very much in love with forbidden love – had been since they first met.

If we wanted to go behind their backs, Eve, we could simply get a Special Licence. Although Dave Greenaway thought himself and Eve to be beyond hidebound influences and convention, a Special Licence still held for him connotations of illicit sexual connection and hasty marriage. *I want my Mam to respect you.*

'Is she having a shindig for her birthday?'

'Oh yes, a great do with a marquee and a band, it'll be in all the local newspapers.'

'Well then, she'll no doot be dancing, so what about it? I'd not say there was much wrong wi' a dance for Greeny too.'

So, with his troubles shared and two decent Scotches inside him, Able Seaman Greenaway was persuaded to go dancing, and had not at all a bad time with a plump, blonde-haired girl who had sweet breath and whose breasts were like satin cushions inside her satin blouse and who wore his hat through the streets when she let him walk her home. But, of course, she wasn't Eve.

1989

The sound of Hildy's solid shoes on the stone terrace aroused the old lady.

'Don't bother with lunch, Hildy, I'll have what's left of that gazpacho from last night.'

'Cold soup do you not good. Old ladies should eat well.'

'Which old lady?'

'You old lady.'

'And you are a bloody sight too familiar with your elders and betters.'

'Somebody must be familiar with you or you never eat at all, I think. And I promise Mister Fergus.'

'I eat perfectly well when Mister Fergus is in Brussels. One day *Mister* Fergus will know what it's like. In no time at all, it will be Josh's turn to descend on *Mister* Fergus and tell him what to eat and what not to eat and how much.' She closed the book she had been reading and smoothed its cover.

Hildegard picked it up and riffled through the pages. 'He cares for you.' She was the younger of the two women, but was older looking – mistress and housekeeper. She went to sit on the low stone wall of the terrace.

'You'll get piles, sit on this.'

They had lived in one another's pockets for much of their lives, each telling the other what to do. Each dreading that they would be left alone, yet each wanting to protect the other from being the one who is left. That the housekeeper was well provided for in the mistress's will did not signify, they had been together for too long for the money to matter once one of them was dead.

'That Josh. Did you ever see such a baby, milady? Walking so soon!'

'Like his father. Fergus walked at a year, and stop calling me by that stupid name.'

'You called me Brünnhilde. You are wrong, the one who walked early was Melanie. You remember, we were still in Markham. My memory does not play tricks.'

'And mine does? I remember clearly, Fergus on the beach in Spain, suddenly walking off on his own.'

'Spain was Melanie, and she was one and a half years. Fergus was such a good crawler – he had no need to walk. Do you not remember, it was at Melanie's birthday party that she walked. The old man said that she was like a little wind-up doll?'

It was their pleasure to wrangle on about some small point like this. The gradually expanding family was at the centre of their lives, and the reason that they lived in a house with so many spare rooms. Such a wrangle was a way of saying, let's have a little session remembering when the children were young.

'You are probably right, Hildy. One gets so confused. Grandsons, great-grandsons . . .'

'I shall make tuna omelette? The fish will be good for you.'

'Gazpacho. My brain is perfectly all right, I do not need fish.'

The housekeeper nodded – she would serve both.

Eve opened her book again. 'And if the phone rings, don't answer it, I must get this book read.'

'Do you think that she has grown old well?' Hildy pointed to the photo on the book-jacket.

'I think I would recognize her, even though it's fifty years. Would you?'

'She looks just like any old woman to me. Perhaps I never saw her.'

'She has worn pretty well, she's my age.'

'But milady has not had her face repaired. You have good honest wrinkles.'

'Is that so? Well, thank you for that.'

'And you mean to go trappising all the way to England because this woman puts you in a book?'

'Traipsing. I am not the only one – all the women are in it. We were like a family in many ways. And I want to see who's left. And I want to see her, this old Georgia Giacopazzi without wrinkles who used to be my friend.'

'And the old Madam? She is in the book?'

'Yes, yes. Connie will be in it. Fergus said she was quite an eye-opener.'

'I will get the omelette and leave you to read your book.'

'Gazpacho – or you can take a month's notice.'

She started the chapter over again to refresh her memory. When Josh was in the house, everything else went from her mind. What a joy, to live long enough to see your grandson with a child of his own.

Did Georgia Kennedy have children? Perhaps the book will tell.

She had read the personal details of the author as they appeared on the book-jacket. There was nothing about any family.

Poor Georgia if, after all, she ended up with no one. If that is so, then perhaps she really does not have many lines and wrinkles, for they are the scars that children leave.

1939

Eve Hardy's twenty-first birthday celebration went perfectly. There was an abundance of everything, including guests with county names and accents. There was even a Sir – an unimportant one, but most of the locals couldn't tell one from the other, believing all rank had some sort of blue blood connection, and any kind of Sir added a touch of the exotic in much the same way as the pink bitters in the toasting champagne had.

Eve was a credit to her father – or was it her mother? Eve had inherited the Hardys' looks, which were immutable. Her inclination was to be gentle so that, as her care and training had been left to Connie and a sleep-in local woman known as Nanny Bryce, Eve had retained her gentle nature. Had she been a boy, and thus Freddy's to mould, there might not have been so much gentleness left by the time of coming of age.

Central to the evening were the speech, the cake and the revelation of her parents' presents. These proceedings were to take place on the lawns behind the house, with Freddy, Connie and Eve on the raised terrace where everyone would have a view of them.

Connie was aware that most of the people there had come to tuck in, drink up and see what opulent thing Freddy Hardy would do to keep Markham gossiping for a month, so she had pruned his speech. The *Clarion* reporter had already noted the servants dressed like flunkeys in pantomime, the iced puddings called bombes, the whole salmon which were decorated like cakes, and hoped that it wouldn't all be spoiled by a long-winded speech. Probably not, Freddy Hardy wasn't often long-winded.

After thanking the guests for making this such a grand occasion, and then thanking Eve for the twenty-one years of joy she had brought him and her mother, Freddy proposed a toast and presented his pretty daughter with the diamond Es.

Eve immediately clipped them to her neckline and kissed him.

'Thank you, Pa. Thank you, Mother,' and to the guests, 'Thank you all for making this such a nice party.'

Connie noticed a look of disappointment flit across the reporter's face – he had expected something more spectacular than diamond clips. Connie smiled to herself. He wouldn't be disappointed.

'The little bit of diamond nonsense is just a token of love from a fond father. Our – mine and Connie's – present to our daughter is a token of our wish for her to have some fun and some freedom whilst she is still young enough to enjoy it.' He nodded to someone at the back of the crowd who must have passed on the signal.

Suddenly there came a roar from round the bend of the drive which was out of sight of the guests. They all turned at the same moment to see the night cut by twin searchlights, then a white MG tourer, bound round with ribbon tied in an enormous bow and with a huge key fixed to the radiator grille, was driven up the drive, across the lawn, through the assembled guests and to a halt below the terrace. The jazz-band played a hot 'Happy Birthday to You'.

Eve Hardy blushed – as well she might. Never mind that Pa went a bit far when he did things, this was exactly the freedom she would have asked for had she been the kind of girl to ask for anything much. Eve Hardy was really a very nice girl, and she was head over heels in love with Dave Greenaway who came from the wrong end of town.

Connie Hardy blushed at an idea well, if vulgarly, brought off. He was convinced that the car had been his idea. A single woman with money and four wheels could have more freedom than any woman would have dreamed possible twenty years ago. Connie was determined to do what she could to see to it that her daughter had some life before she suddenly found herself thrust into the small band of a wedding-ring.

Connie looked again at the *Clarion* reporter as he watched Eve take the white car with its satin and silver trimmings on a circuit of the grounds. The *Clarion* reporter had been a man of little faith: he should have known that Freddy Hardy would not let him down.

1989

The aircraft cabin lights were now dimmed. Although the drone of the engines was soporific, Georgia Giacopazzi was quite awake. She could easily have buzzed the steward and ordered a gin and tonic, but she preferred to let her mind wander over what was ahead.

Even though for years she had not needed much sleep, she was always able to relax, giving her time to think through a problem or anticipate a sticky situation. When she was asked how she managed to fit so much into twenty-four hours, her smart answer was, 'When you are all asleep, I'm working', and it was true.

Then she had started work on something very different from what was implied in her smart answer. She felt apprehensive. It had all seemed so simple when she had talked to her publisher about using real people and real events in the novel.

'No problem,' (the book had an American publisher – Fiskess, Frankel Books), 'we'll write and get them to agree to it.'

'And if they do object?'

Nathan Fiskess had patted down the air. 'That's for our legal people to sort out. But I don't believe we're talking litigation here.'

'I think perhaps I should ask them personally.'

'Write the book first,' Nat had advised.

'You mean let them see what I've written?'

'They'll love it. Georgia – they're wrinklies now.'

'Thanks, Nat, they're my contemporaries.'

'Giacopazzi is nobody's contemporary.' Nathan Fiskess spread his hands. 'We can stand a little litigation now and then. I promise you, Georgia, watch my lips and put a dollar on my words – write what you like and they'll love it. We worry – you write. The Giacopazzi circus rolls again.'

She smiled wryly now as she remembered his grin as he flicked an imaginary whip. That's what the Giacopazzi industry had become: a great twenty-four-hour-a-day, world-wide glitzy entertainment of books and videos and films. Nothing arty-farty about Nat Fiskess: he was in publishing for the bread. If anybody had created Giacopazzi from the English novelist, it was Nat.

So far, he had been right. There had been no problems in Johannesburg, where she had expected some. To write the book, she had bugged her memories of those who had been her closest friends during the war years, and had written a fiction around the facts of their lives. And now she was facing them in turn – those who were left. Had they remembered her kindly? A flash came to her of the emaciated, drip-fed figure in the luxurious room in Johannesburg. I wasn't unkind . . . nor unfair.

She turned her mind now to how to handle the reunion.

A reunion of wrinklies who had once been young and who had been arbitrarily thrown together in wartime Britain. Hardly thrown, she thought, remembering their sedate first meeting. All of us wearing hats except Mrs Farr. I can't remember ever seeing Mrs Farr wearing a hat: she always wore a scarf tied behind like an Italian peasant woman. I suppose it was small things like that which made her different. There was something about Mrs Farr that was rather romantic. Why didn't I remember that when I was writing about her? Mrs Farr had taken to Markham, but Markham had never really taken to her. Has it taken to her now? Probably not, unless in the last fifty years Markham has changed out of all recognition.

1939

Summer

It was only in retrospect that the strange, golden spring and summer of 1939 was thought of as golden and strange by some of the people of Markham.

Golden, because it was the driest summer ever recorded in England, and green all but disappeared from the landscape.

Strange, because in that bee-humming, woodbine-scented, blue-domed land, people were burrowing holes in the earth and roofing them over with iron sheets to make bomb-shelters. Strange, because swaying carts loaded with fast-grown, sweet sun-dried hay, passed wheel to wheel with lorries taking to store piles of stretchers, hundreds of flat-folded brown board coffins and great bolts of pretty flowery fabric bought up cheap for the making of shrouds.

Markham. It had been a settlement long before its first tiny Saxon church had been built, or the Normans came to change it, influencing the style of windows, turning it into a great abbey for future tourists. At the time of that golden and strange summer, Markham was an insignificant market town, its days of any real importance long gone. The town was about a mile square. Five roads led out of it, three of them steeply uphill.

As well as being an ancient cattle market, it was now a bakery and a brewery town. At times the air made people salivate with its illusory aroma of home-made oven-baked. At others it reeked of hops and yeast and malt and pungent effluent. A town of 6,000 inhabitants and 101 pubs. Until one got to the town boundaries, it was not necessary to walk for more than five minutes in any direction to obtain a drink of beer.

There was an old saying: 'He's that drunk, he must have been to Markham.' These days there wasn't much drunkenness: Markham men could hold their beer. Or perhaps it was, as visiting Northerners said, that Markham beer was gnats' pee put up in barrels.

Until the summer of 1939, Markham had only dipped its toe in the twentieth century.

True there was a cinema, a Co-op, a new Woolworth's, and the railway station, but people remained parochial and life was still lived at a rural pace. There were very few cars, and cattle and sheep were still driven through the streets on Market Day. Milk was brought by horse and cart direct from the cow in brass churns, still containing its farm-fresh bovine TB. Beasts were slaughtered behind butcher-shops from where the occasional bullock escaped its tether and ran terrifyingly amok through the lanes and back-streets.

If Markham had a character, it was smug and phlegmatic; if it had a style, it was a century out of date.

Most employment for men and single girls was provided by Hardy's Bakery and the local brewery. There were one or two small employers, such as Southern Cereals where Georgia and Hugh Kennedy had been employed, and a bit of horticulture and retail shop-work. Almost all other men's work was beyond the town boundaries – farms. Southampton Docks, and Southern Railway.

Unlike their sisters in the potteries and mill towns, few women went out to work after marriage. Not only was there little employment available, a working wife was frowned upon and a working mother viewed with disgust. Of course, there was the Oaklands Estate mansion where there was occasional skivvying to be had, but Markham people didn't like working for The Estate. Years ago, a poacher had been hanged for the death of a gamekeeper. Markhambrians had long and unforgiving memories.

From a vantage point on any of the surrounding hills, the eye was always drawn to the elegant thrusting spire of the abbey and the twin erections of the bakery and brewery chimneys.

Whether or not the children of the town were aware that their parents were preparing themselves for war, it is difficult to say, for they scuffed their way to school and raced their way home as they had always done. To them, every summer was strange and golden and, as always in July and August, they gathered each morning by certain special hedgerows bordering certain special meadows, or at the places where the River Bliss provided a little shallow bay. At the chosen place they laid out their bags of lemonade, broken biscuits and dripping bread, and prepared to hurl themselves into meadows, trees, hay, water.

Old bent men leaned on bridges and watched, and their weathered wives halted momentarily and listened, remembering their own calling, laughing, squabbling, leaping and splashing, tiddler-jar days. Nothing had changed in a hundred years. In the rented terraces and council houses, the busy generation looked at their kids returning home late in the evening, river-washed and sun-burned, and supposed that the Germans must never have had that sort of fun. What else could account for them being like they were?

If Markham had a voice, it would have said, 'Don't nobody come here telling us what to do, we done all right up to now.'

1939

Saturday, thought Marie Partridge, Saturday, when Charlie had only the one round of deliveries, always had a different feel about it. Kids were about. Girls feeding chickens, fetching the bread, minding babies, doing shopping for grandmothers. Boys running errands, helping on allotments, lugging home a shilling's worth of coal in old prams. All of them scuttling about to get jobs done and be away to the river-banks or to the twopenny rush at the Picture House.

Women did the weekend shopping on Saturday mornings.

The choice of the weekend joint was the most important purchase. It provided a roast on Sunday, cottage-pie on Monday, stew from the bits on Tuesday, and if any stew remained with a few lentils and pearl barley, a good broth for the kids on Wednesday. Marie and her mother-in-law always went together, leaving Bonnie to go to the allotment with Charlie and be spoilt by him for an hour or two.

This morning there was an atmosphere you could cut with a knife between her in-laws.

'You all right then, Dad?' Ignoring what was obvious to anyone who knew him – that Sam Partridge's nose had been put out of joint.

'No, Marie, but there I dare say you knew all along what she was up to.'

Although she did not know what Dolly was up to, Marie flushed, 'I don't know what you're on about,' knowing that she looked guilty.

'Oh no? Well she'd better tell you then.' He flicked his head in his wife's direction.

'Who's she, the cat's mother?' said Dolly, rubbing her lips aggressively with a nub of lipstick.

Marie and Dolly exchanged sharp glances, and Marie knew it was best to keep neutral. Her father-in-law's tone was scathing. 'She wants to go out to work. A decent woman . . . at *her* age, too.'

'I'm still in my forties, Sam Partridge, not a hundred.'

'And just what do you think it makes me look like? Oh, I know . . . it makes me look like an old soldier who can't even keep his own wife.'

'Take no notice, Marie,' Dolly said, blotting her lips and setting the lipstick with powder.

'What about *your* Mum, Marie?' Sam said, determined to draw her in. 'I ask you, what would your dad say if it was her, eh?'

Marie knew well enough that her father would as soon lock Mum in as allow her to go out to work, but Marie kept out of it.

'And Charlie'd soon put his foot down. Make him look small in front of everybody . . . put his foot down all right.'

Sam already knew that Charlie *had* put his foot down, ages ago when Marie had been offered a chance to go back to hairdressing on Saturdays. Charlie had been incensed – 'If the day ever comes when I can't provide for my own wife and child, we'll be in bad straits. Till then you can forget about any Saturday job.' Marie hadn't broached the matter again, but had never let up the pressure when it came to making him shell out for decent things for their home.

'Don't try and drag Marie into it,' Dolly said. 'I've got the job and that's that!'

Marie was surprised into saying, 'You've got a job, Dolly?'

'Without asking me. Without saying nothing to nobody,' Sam said.

'*Yes*, Sam Partridge, making up my own mind and

without saying nothing to nobody. And don't drag Marie into it.'

'Marie's already in. How do you think she's going to feel married into a family where women goes out skivvying? Her family's like ourn, kept ourselves above that sort of caper.'

'God alive, Sam, anybody'd think I was going down the Docks and stand on the corner of Bugle Street to hear you talk. And I keep telling you, this is a proper job – it's not skivvying.'

Sam drew breath to answer back, but Dolly raised her voice and continued, 'People can do and think what they like, and I'll tell you this for nothing, if there's a war, there won't be many weeks pass before half the women in this road will be sorry they hadn't heard about this job, just you mark my words. It's a good, decent job and nothing to be ashamed of.'

'Oh you think so? Well, I'll tell *you* this for nothing. If there's half the women getting the idea of working, there a be half the husbands that a be giving them the rough side of their hand.'

'Oh, I don't doubt that for a minute, there's plenty of men trying to keep going on Hardy's wages that'd rather see their wives go all week on a Foster and Clark soup cube than see them get a few hours' work.'

'*You* an't never gone on soup cubes, Dolly.'

'I never said *me*.'

Dolly, now ready for Saturday shopping, wearing the beige straw summer hat she had worn for years, turned to face Sam and Marie.

'I'm sorry if anybody's feels hurt because of it, but I made up my mind and I mean to do it. It's a decent, respectable job working in the kitchens of the new Town Restaurant the Government is starting. It isn't any different from when I worked in hospital kitchens years ago, except that I shall get training under the cook.'

Sam, fiercely buttoning up his park-keeper's uniform, said angrily, 'A course it's different, woman – you're married! And a woman's place is in the home.'

'And I suppose that's wrote into your bloody Labour Party manifesto, too.'

Dolly, keeping her dignity, unwilling to be ruffled, picked up her leatherette bag and nodded to Marie that she was ready. 'When it comes to it, Sam Partridge, your lot and the Tories is hand in glove with one another about women. Half the world's made up of women and none of you ever been able to work that out yet, have you?'

Sam's fingers seemed to freeze to his metal buttons and for once he had no cliché to refute her accusation.

Dolly was exciting. Marie had never seen her mother-in-law so worked up: the thrill of it made her behind tighten and her eyes widen. 'Married women will have to work in this war, same as in the last one,' Dolly went on. 'You can see that can't you, Marie, and it will be first come, first served with the good jobs, and up to now the Partridges have been too proud to push themselves forward for anything like that.'

The two women left the house. Half-way across the yard, Dolly called back over her shoulder, 'And if Marie wants a job, there's one going.'

1989

The Boeing 747 was within half an hour of its first touch-down. Georgia Giacopazzi could see nothing in the cabin window except for her own reflection. An unruffled face whose outlines had been lightly padded and pouched by years. Lively hair controlled and drawn back in a simple chignon. Seen indistinctly like this, if she raised her head to stretch the loose skin beneath her chin, the well-preserved elderly woman looked much like the young Georgia Kennedy. As she had done when writing *Eye of the Storm*, she had for the past half-hour been thinking dispassionately about herself when young. Not only Georgia Kennedy, but Georgia Kennedy and the men who had meant something to her – none had been more difficult than Nick Crockford to put into the novel. Others had been easier, because once she began to write they gradually became characters in the novel, but not Nick Crockford.

In retrospect, events seldom seem to have been random: human beings are usually able to find a pattern, a design, and call it Fate . . . God's will – 'If I had only done so and so, I should never have . . .', 'If I had had 'flu that week instead of the next it would have been different . . .' or, 'If I had left the house five minutes later . . .' So it was with Georgia Giacopazzi. During the writing of the book, she had come to the conclusion that the events of the next fifty years of her life, about which she had thought so much over the last year, had had their beginnings at the meeting in the Town Hall.

1939

Early in June, a meeting, which had its beginnings, as did most meetings concerning Markham, within the walls of the Tory Club, was arranged for ten o'clock in the Council Chamber of the Town Hall.

Georgia set off in plenty of time with a feeling of elation because she was actually going to do something positive. The freedom from Hugh's domination, which a couple of months ago she had expected would change her days dramatically, had not come up to expectations. The first days of making spur-of-the-moment trips to Southampton or Salisbury or Winchester, simply to wander idly the streets and cathedral precincts, soon lost their appeal. Such trips were best shared, but since she had adopted Hugh's Sports Club-centred life, she had lost touch with her old friends; and she had never felt close to the 'girls' of the club.

But today . . . She had awoken early and completed the very small amount of housework and laundry engendered by a single, tidy woman within half an hour. She had bathed, and as she dressed she realized that she was singing quietly to herself, and feeling stimulated at the prospect of the meeting. The invitation to attend as representative of the Sports Club was to Hugh, but in reply to her letter about what to do he had phoned to say that in future she could deal with all that kind of thing. 'Just let the management committee know that I said it was OK, darling, they won't want to be bothered with all that fiddly sort of stuff. You'll do it wonderfully, you're good at those things.' He had been in a hurry to do much more important things with 'the men', so that she had no time before the line went dead to feel put down.

Never mind, it was not a fiddly thing, it was a gathering of all the representatives of organizations in Markham, from the fire service to the Girl Guides. It now seemed certain that war with Germany could not be avoided, and that Markham was lagging behind other towns in getting itself organized. In the interests of efficiency, Freddy Hardy, as leading burgher, decided that they should be brought together and put under his control.

So it was that on that warm morning an extraordinary meeting of the Markham Borough Councillors sat with invited representatives of 'interested and appropriate' bodies, with Georgia standing in for Markham's Sports Club Secretary and cricket captain. For half an hour before the appointed time, there flowed into the Town Hall an assortment of Hon. Presidents, Hon. Secretaries, of the Rotary club, the Tory and Liberal Clubs, Secretary of the Labour Party, which had no clubhouse, the Red Cross and St John's Ambulance.

God was represented by an Anglican vicar, a Catholic priest, some Evangelists and Free Church preachers, a Quaker Friend, a Salvation Army captain and three teaching nuns from the local convent school.

The Townswomen's Guild, Church Wives, Young Mothers and Co-op Women's Guild, Chairmen.

Scout Captain and Brown Owl, husband-and-wife team. Heads of all the Markham schools – C of E, Convent, Private, Council, as well as the Markham Sports Club, the Tennis, Swimming, Football and Cricket Clubs, and the Allotment Association.

No Markham Trade Union representatives had been invited – there were no Markham trade unionists.

Well, that is not strictly true. The Tolpuddle and Swing protests were as but yesterday to Markham, and the hand of Victorian-type employers was heavy on the work-force of Markham – heaviest at Hardy's Bakeries. There were a few postal workers and the NUR men who, although they lived in the town, worked outside at the Railway Works and so were free to be a Comrade.

And there was Councillor Vernon Greenaway.

Vern Greenaway was the owner of a large wholesale and retail newsagents and tobacconists in Markham, and had for years been an openly card-carrying member of USDAW. Vern Greenaway, because he owned a thriving business but was nevertheless one of Markham's Comrades, was incomprehensible to Freddy Hardy. Vern was shrewd and likeable and said quite openly, 'If this war comes, Hardy's will be unionized and he won't be able to stop them. It's our big chance, it will mean Comrades and Brothers will be everywhere.'

Freddy Hardy, as though possessing an inalienable right to take over any public event in Markham, had brought the members of his household along. Connie Hardy and daughter Eve sat at the top table, so did Nanny Bryce, awkwardly because she was really from the Station End of town and would have felt more at home sitting alongside somebody like Vern whom she had quietly voted for, even though she had been sent to the polling station in a blue-ribboned car.

Seated at what might appear to be the Opposition end with Vernon Greenaway were Sam Partridge, wearing his Labour Party badge; some pinkishly political people such as Rechabites and Free Church; Georgia Kennedy, who did not appreciate that she had aligned herself with Markham's rebels; and Nick Crockford. 'Nick!' Surprise and delight in her voice. She had not seen him since she married. His was the most familiar and friendly face in the Town Hall. The Crockfords had for years been close neighbours of the Honeycombes. Nick and Georgia had grown up together in Emberley village: Robert Crockford and his son on Roke Acre, a roomy cottage with land to suit its name, and Alice and Thomas Honeycombe and their daughter in the village pub.

He smiled and squeezed her shoulders familiarly. 'Well then, Georgia Honeycombe, what are you up to this morning?'

A moment of elation. To do with knowing that he still thought of her as Georgia Honeycombe. 'I might ask you the same thing. I shouldn't have thought this was at all your cup of tea.'

He raised his eyebrows, 'Ah well, we all get surprises at the strange brews our best friends get a taste for.'

Georgia Kennedy blushed.

'You shouldn't have married him, Georgia Honeycombe.'

'Nick! Do you mind just keeping your voice down.'

He grinned, and there came the same sudden transformation of his face that she had known since she was two years old and they had first played together in a pile of road grit. Solemn concentration, then the switch-on of his bright open smile.

'See, you know I'm right. You didn't say, "Don't be so ridiculous, Nick Crockford," only, "Keep your voice down." I can speak the truth so long as nobody overhears.' He stooped, resting his large and practical hand on her shoulder, and whispered in her ear, 'You shouldn't have married the old stuffed shirt, Georgia Honeycombe.'

She had not seen him since she married. Then he had been a youth not yet twenty, now he was a man. He had always looked like his father, and the resemblance now that he was grown was striking. Prematurely grey in his early twenties, outdoor skin, long straight nose, straight eyebrows beneath a lined forehead and straight-lidded eyes. There was in his face a fascinating combination of youth and age – almost white hair with a young man's face.

'How is Mr Crockford?'

'He seems better. He's writing a lot for the *Herald* and *Reynolds News* – I'll bet you don't see those papers in the Captain's house.'

'I'm glad. I've often wondered how he is.'

'You should go and see him. He's always liked you, you could sweet-talk him.'

Georgia felt guilty that she had let the months and years go by without once going back to Emberley to visit Robert Crockford.

'I keep intending to.'

'Go then.'

As a small child Mr Crockford had been no more strange to her than most adults. If he was strange, then it was because he chose to live as reclusive a life as was possible as a widowed father. He had come home from France in 1918 almost white-haired.

'I'm surprised that the Captain trusted you to come here on your own. I didn't have him down as a chap who delegates anything – especially to a slip of a girl.'

Goaded by the jibe, Georgia asked what she did not want to know. 'How's Nancy? And . . . it's a little boy, isn't it?'

'That's right – Pete, he's two. A real little bugger, actually.'

Even though Georgia had let Hugh sweep her off her feet when she was still only seventeen, it had been crushing to hear that Nick Crockford was living with Nancy Miles. At the time Georgia had expected that Nick's heart would have broken; instead of which he had been getting Nancy Miles pregnant.

The sound of the gavel brought the meeting to order.

Freddy Hardy, in his usual no-nonsense way, went straight into what he had to say. Georgia liked that. And the man himself. Attractive. Yet he was almost bald. Yes, attractive in the way that Nick was. The hair – or lack of it in the alderman's case – and a sensuous, handsome face. They both had the same straight mouth, thin top and full bottom lip. The same broad brows above observant eyes, the same serious expression that could snap into amusement. It occurred to her that they both enjoyed being who they were, and doing what they were doing.

As he spoke, one got the impression that he was addressing each person individually. Georgia caught his direct gaze several times.

Nick leaned towards her and whispered, 'He eats nice little housewives on toast.'

Georgia put on her mother's mouth and wrote the date on her notepad.

Freddy Hardy's voice, commanding and confident. 'You all know why you're here – if you don't, then read the notes that were sent you. There's going to be a war – make no mistake about it . . . What I plan to do is to head an organization of responsible bodies so that in an emergency there won't be any shilly-shallying about. I shall know whose responsibility any particular job will be.'

'Point of Order.'

Freddy Hardy's eyes glittered at his old adversary. 'Councillor Greenaway?'

Vern Greenaway, establishing something or other by remaining seated with his chair balanced on its two back legs in a manner unbecoming to the linenfold panelling of the Council Chamber, spoke. 'For a start, Fred Hardy, you needn't call me Councillor, this is not a Council meeting – it an't even an official meeting as far as I can tell – so let's dispense with any of that sort of argy-bargy.'

'Hear, hear!' called Sam Partridge.

The meeting tightened its collective buttocks in anticipation of a clash of horns of the well-known political adversaries.

'First off, Fred Hardy . . . everybody in this room knows everybody else – a lot of us went to school with each other. I say we make this meeting informal, because if we don't then we know who will have all the say, and we shan't hear from the people who matter because they'll be afraid to speak out of turn. And you needn't look like that, because I include myself alongside you when it comes to having a lot of gab.'

Laughter, and a slight shuffling of feet, murmurs that might mean agreement or dissension but certainly interest, certainly excitement as the many eyes turned to the Chair.

'What's the point of order . . . Mister Greenaway?'

Jokily, in the manner of kids asking, 'Who said you could have first go with the bat?'

'Well, for a start, who said you could be Chairman? This isn't Council Business.'

'Point taken.' Genially, 'I've no objections.' Confidently. 'I'll take nominations for Chairman . . . I take it you've no objection to that, Mister Greenaway?'

Open-handed, Vern Greenaway said, 'I trust you to do it with your usual efficiency.'

The Anglican Vicar proposed, 'As you are our senior alderman, Councillor Hardy, I propose that you keep the Chair.'

'Seconded.' From a few of the faithful.

'Any more nominations?'

'Yes!' Nick Crockford rose to his full six-foot-six by forty-four chest which nobody in the room could match. Georgia crossed her legs away from him in an unconscious denial of association.

His voice was deep and his vowels accentuated Hampshire. 'I propose Mr Greenaway and . . .' an emphatic pause, 'I propose a secret ballot – not a show of hands.'

There was a moment's rigid silence from the delegates.

'Very well . . . friend. We've always done these things in the old way . . . an open and above-board sort of way but . . . so be it. Any more nominations?'

There were not. Enough is enough, any more names in the ring would have doused the spark that was about to set light to the excitement that had been rising like petrol fumes since Vern Greenaway first interposed.

Eyebrows were raised, and 'Secret' hissed its way up and down the rows of representatives. What would happen to democracy if the great and good who held the reigns of power could not see how votes were cast?

What would happen was infiltration by uncomfortable people like Vern Greenaway who brought politics into local government when it had always been run very nicely without political controversy the Tory way.

However, Freddy Hardy was certain enough of his people to give them a charming smile and offer tea or coffee in the Mayor's Parlour whilst the ballot was arranged. Also it would give him time to find out about that great hulk.

In the Mayor's Parlour, there was a loud and excited buzz of conversation – even a few laughs and giggles. Nick continued to keep close to Georgia whilst they awaited the voting papers. Vern Greenaway, his clever eyes glinting at the unexpected turn of events, descended upon Nick and Georgia with a tray of tea and biscuits. He nodded at her and then at Nick. 'I know you, don't I? Isn't it your father who did that little book of poems against war?'

'My dad would prefer them to be called poems *for* peace instead of against war. There's a difference.'

'Ah, I can see there is. Good chap, Robert Crockford, pity he won't take part in local politics – we need him. You two know each other already, then.'

'Yes,' said Georgia, 'since we were children. We both came from Emberley village, born next door to one another.'

'Did you now? I never realized that you was an Emberley girl.'

'Georgia was Emberley Queen of the May in 1935 – before she became an officer's lady. That right, Georgia?'

Vern Greenaway sensed the air crackle between them.

'Nineteen thirty-six, actually,' and Georgia bent over her teacup.

Hello, hello, thought Councillor Greenaway, there's

something there or I'm a Dutchman. 'You keeping well, Mrs Kennedy? How's that man of yours? He's gone for a soldier then?'

She sensed rather than saw Nick's reaction.

'Yes, he's in the Regular Army now.'

'Well, well . . . a real officer's wife you are now then. How does it feel, being one of the toffs?'

Georgia laughed. 'Much the same as ever. Hugh was always the officer-type, even in the Terries.'

'Ah well, the Terries will have knocked some of the corners off him. Did you know my Davey's hoping to get himself transferred – he wants to be a sub-mariner.' He transferred his attention to Nick. 'And which of Markham's 101 clubs do you represent here? No, don't tell me,' he tapped Nick's broad chest, 'Swimming? Athletics?'

At that moment somebody dropped a biscuit tin, and it was not certain whether it was Nick's voice or the clatter that created the moment of silence in which Nick's voice was heard clearly and a little tetchily, 'Nothing so important – I'm a member of my Union, and I don't represent anybody but myself.'

Freddy Hardy heard, and looked across the room at the great hulk who didn't want a show of hands. TGWU? Where did he spring from? Partridge the park-keeper, harmless and a safety-valve for the local agitators. Greenaway, not so harmless, and now this one. The Markham Reds must be coming out of the woodwork, and would have to be watched. He looked across the room at the great hulk and guessed that there was a man who would break rather than bow the knee.

Connie Hardy looked across the room at the great hulk and undressed him behind her usual expression at public functions of ennui.

Eve Hardy looked across the room at the great hulk, and saw a tall, broad man who was very attractive but nowhere near as desirable as the neat sailor she longed for.

Georgia Kennedy looked at the great hulk and wished momentarily that her parents had never given her manners, or piano lessons, or a course in secretarial studies and a respectable neat and tidy life. *We had a lot of good times together.*

Georgia turned round to put her cup and saucer on a side-table, Freddy Hardy held back from doing the same with his own cup.

'Allow me.' He took the cup from her. He smiled. 'I shan't say, "Don't I know you?" because had I met you before this morning, I should certainly not have forgotten.' He took her hand which he held absent-mindedly whilst she introduced herself. He had the knack, when he wished to do so, of making people, specially women, feel that he was interested only in them. A warm, dry, firm hand that casually moved so that the ball of his thumb pressed the palm of her hand whilst his fingers moved over her knuckles. It was not a friendly action – too sensuous for that.

'What I came across to say was that we shall be having a kind of buffet-supper up at The Cedars next week. Why don't you come?'

'Yes, why don't I?' Georgia said. 'It seems ages since I had an evening out.'

Whilst most of Markham were intimidated by his wealth and power, Georgia was not. Without realizing that it had done so, the seventeen years of being daily with Nick Crockford had given her an insight into clever and sensuous men. She looked down at her hand, which he immediately released, turning his attention to Nick who said politely, 'Excuse me, I've got to find the Gents.'

When the meeting reassembled, and the result of the ballot was read out, Freddy Hardy put on a good show of a man who was relieved not to have to clutter up his important days with any more of Markham's problems, and when Vern took the Chair, the senior councillor, pleading a Board Meeting he had been neglecting for the sake of the town, left the room. Then the meeting got under way. The *Clarion* man, who had missed the fun of the first half, was now writing fast shorthand for his paper, and got himself elected Secretary.

Now that there seemed to be a sense of abandonment in the air, people allowed the old bastions to crumble and proposed one another for positions left, right, and centre with no regard to allegiance to Party or Faith. However, two walls appeared not to tumble easily, those of Class and Gender.

Somehow, even in spite of the earlier bit of applied democracy, people seemed reluctant to abandon entirely the safe caves they had always known. And the women knew their place.

Clerical positions went mostly to the class who lived in Mont Iremonger's delivery area, and the physical or tedious work finished up with the station-enders of Charlie Partridge.

Jobs that needed command, attendance at meetings or signatures on forms went to men, whilst domestic work, such as cooking, comforting, succouring and organizing foster-parents for evacuees, went to the women.

The morning wore on. People sat with bits of paper on which were details of their new posts and 'Responsibilities in Emergency or Time of War'.

Vern announced that there was a government scheme for nationwide public restaurants. Large premises in the town centre were needed.

'I should like to volunteer the Old Mission Hall.' The Anglicans got in first, foreseeing that money would have to be spent on buildings commandeered by the government.

A sub-committee was arranged.

A lady, tweedish even though it was warm, said, 'I should like to propose Mrs Hardy to chair the meeting.'

Vern Greenaway looked at Connie, who said graciously,

'Actually, I think I shall be occupied with Red Cross work, but of course I'll do what I can.'

Again Nick Crockford rose. 'If the lady doesn't think she wants to do it, then I nominate the representative of the Cricket Club.'

A little snicker ran round the room.

'Cricket Club? Ah, you mean Mrs Kennedy, who's here representing her husband – Markham's best cricket captain in years.'

'We have two nominations.'

'No . . . really,' said Connie Hardy, 'I should prefer to withdraw. I had planned to volunteer my services to the Red Cross . . .'

And so, with the *Clarion* reporter already assembling his headline, Markham's preparations for Emergencies in Time of War were got under way.

The crowd spilled out into the Market Square and stood around Palmerston's statue comparing their various wartime roles. Georgia had determined that she would not give Nick an inch, so she shook hands coolly and politely.

'I have to go. Nice seeing you, Nick. I promise that I'll go and see your dad.'

He held her hand just as the alderman had done, Nick's way of showing her that he had not missed the incident. His hand was larger, harder and rougher, the bones of his long fingers familiar. She knew every line and muscle of this hand, had seen it change from a podgy implement for patting mud into the grit pile, to almost an extension of herself when he massaged her wrists aching from hours of picking in Emberley Estate's commercial orchards.

When she looked down, he did not draw away as Freddy Hardy had done, but overlaid with his left hand too, 'Ah, it's good to see you, Georgia Honeycombe. You've become even more beautiful – and don't take it as a compliment, people get the faces they're born with.'

'That's nothing I don't know already, Nick Crockford. Now, give me back my hand, I've got shopping to do.'

He put on a face of mock tragedy. 'And when you've been in the Co-op with your little shopping basket, you'll go home and pop on your little pinny and stand at your modern sink peeling potatoes and think to yourself, If I wasn't the Major's wife, I could have gone off with that Nick Crockford and tickled trout in the Bliss.'

'Wrong,' she said. 'I'm off to buy some graph paper and some coloured pencils – I've got quite a lot of work to do before my Committee convenes. It was nice to see you again, Nick.'

1939

Getting under way as well, on a small island not far off the South Coast, was a new and extremely secret establishment known as Project XJ-R6, set up by the Ministry of War.

XJ-R6 – known in its own circles as Arsix – was a Special Corps of vetted military and naval personnel, created to organize, protect and support a team of 'boffins' who would soon inhabit the warren of underground rooms that were having the final licks of paint applied. It was hush-hush, *really* secret – not like the radar place on the Downs, which was so secret that everyone in Hampshire knew about it, nor as secret as the proposed fast little motor-torpedo boats on the drawing boards of secret offices whose doors were open to card-carriers of all persuasions.

As everyone involved knew, Arsix was *the* most secret establishment of any so far created. As well it needed to be considering what the boffins intended creating there. Had people living on the mainland a mile away known about the proposed experiments to be carried out there, then southern Hampshire might have moved itself to the safety of Yorkshire. And had Yorkshire known, they would have sent it back again – in a hurry. The cultures were but one of the proposed experiments. Arsix was to be a compost-heap of minds from whose richness new ideas of the means to create death and destruction would spring.

The names of personnel who were to be involved in the Special Corps attached to Arsix had been run through a long, close check-list of necessary characteristics and traits. These ranged from their loyalty rating and dedication through their financial and domestic arrangements to their marital status and physique. When the statisticians came up with their list in alphabetical order, amongst the 'Ks' was Kennedy, H. of the Princess Royal's own Hampshires. There was nothing listed to his detriment and in favour were his years holding a commission in the Terries, his approval of every aspect of the British establishment, both Church and State, his degree in chemistry and years of experience in laboratory management in the cereals business.

He was so elated at what had so far been revealed to him in the briefing room for trainees, that Georgia's news, which was that she was going to run some sort of committee in preparation for an outbreak of war, scarcely dented a single brain-cell.

However, he dashed her off a few lines explaining that his work would preclude him from leave for at least two months, and this being so he was delighted that she had found herself something to do and was it in the Townswomen's Guild? He could write nothing yet of the promotion that was bound to attach itself to the work he was undertaking. He rather liked the idea of one day turning up at the door glittering with new insignia.

He wrote nothing either of the female members of the Special Corps, who were surprisingly feminine with their uniform sleeves rolled up to the elbow, and hair that was kept rolled round their caps until they were off duty. It was as well not to start any stones rolling with a girl like Georgia: she could be a little strange at times, such as with the girls who liked to help out at cricket matches.

Meanwhile, Georgia felt that she was beginning to live; every day was exciting to her now that she was no longer a housewife. There was something about that long, hot summer that was both lackadaisical yet urgent – that war was inevitable and that the last moments must be used to the full. Couples who hadn't intended to married. Women who hadn't intended to became pregnant by men who had intended.

Georgia went to the buffet supper at The Cedars in one of Markham's only two taxis. She was surprised to find that it was quite a grand affair with the French windows of the house open and lights streaming from the house on to the terrace where there was music and a bar. She was surprised also to discover that Mrs Hardy and Eve were both away from home. She could not imagine Hugh, even in his bachelor days, having people to the house without a hostess present. The other half live differently.

It was quite late in the evening when Freddy Hardy came to ask her for a dance. 'Duty done, now I can concentrate on pleasure. May I?' He bowed in a delightfully old-fashioned way, then led her up to the terrace where couples were jiving to music from a radiogram in a walnut cabinet.

'Enjoying yourself?'

'Absolutely. It is very beautiful up here.'

Someone changed the record and a slow waltz was played.

'Oh,' Georgia said. 'I love to jive.'

'I'll change it back.'

'No, no, leave it.'

The way he held her reminded her of Hugh – the well-taught product of a formal dance school. He was good, and she had not realized until tonight how much she missed the dancing part of her life. In the deepening gloaming he held her close, not thrusting thighs at her as Hugh's friends did, but firmly and with much more of his body in contact with hers. I don't care, Georgia thought. Perhaps he is everything they say, but tonight I don't care. I long to just dance and be held by a man.

'Hungry?'

'A bit.'

His hand slid into the folds of her bodice. 'Practically starving.'

She didn't make a great thing of it, but removed his hand and pulled herself a couple of inches away from the warmth of his cheek and small, round belly. When the dance was over he brought her a drink with a lot of ice and they sat side by side on the stone collar of a formal pond.

'Gin and orange, my favourite,' she said.

'Pure guess-work though . . . don't see you as a G and T or Martini lady, nor Scotch or beer. You're more the G and O than anything.'

'More the shop-girl?'

'Meaning?'

'Oh, nothing really. But Hugh, my husband, says it's a common drink. Only shop-girls drink gin and orange.'

'He's one of the Sports Club lot, isn't he . . .? See, I've done my research. I never did get on with the Sports Club lot.'

'Some of them are a bit . . .' She felt it disloyal to continue.

'Whenever I've come across them they only seem to be bent on drinking themselves silly. Then they talk about beating hell out of the Irish . . . or the Jews . . . or the bloody miners and dockers and anybody else who comes from north of Leicester. I've got no time for a lot of Bolshie agitators like the miners or dockers, but I don't think that I'm *better* than they are. The trouble with the Club lot is that they *do*, and that the rest of us had better know it.'

Georgia thought such criticism was a bit rich coming from him.

'They're harmless, it's just that they like to cling on to the feeling of being Conquering Heroes. It's only the beer talking.'

'That's balls, if you'll excuse the language.'

When she didn't reply, he said, 'Sorry, I hope you don't love him too much.'

'He would never use bad language in front of me.'

'You're an unusual woman, Young Mrs Kennedy. You aren't phlegmatic, yet you appear to take things in your stride. I noticed you at the meeting . . . I wasn't surprised that white-haired Adonis was hanging round you.' 'Young Mrs Kennedy' said banteringly, in the way that Nick said 'Georgia Honeycombe' to her. 'Come on, I'll take you for a walk down to my little stream. You'll like it.' He took her hand and guided her through the garden, and the cigar and haircream scent of him caught her as she followed. His hands were surprisingly cold and hard. He said, 'Warm nights beside a stream take me back to my childhood, all that water-mint.'

'When I was a child we lived in The Cricketers at Emberley, and there warm nights smelt of beer, of ox-eye daisies and the Gents.'

'I like you, Young Mrs Kennedy.' He smoothed her spine.

'You should stop that right now, Councillor.'

The complications of the situation and her reaction to them intrigued her even as she acted them out. It was as though she could stand back and observe her behaviour.

She did not understand her ambivalence. She was aware of the gossip about him, that he couldn't keep his hands off women, yet she had walked away from the party with him and into this wild and unlit part of the grounds. She was wary of his every move, yet she felt almost hungry for the feel of him. Was it for him? She had felt the same way with Nick, longing for the feel of masculine hands on her bare skin and heavy moist breath in her ear, as there had been just now in the slow waltz.

'You are a clever and beautiful woman, Mrs Kennedy.'

'Thank you, and I'm also married and faithful.'

'Lucky man. Here's my stream, and a seat to sit and enjoy midsummer.'

His hand still clasping hers, they sat quietly. The stream swirling into tree roots and pouring over stones. *If Hugh had not gone away I wouldn't dream of behaving like this. I suppose this is what I meant by 'freedom'.*

'I really shouldn't be here,' she said quietly. 'If Hugh had not gone away, I wouldn't dream of behaving like this.'

'Like what? You are the soul of propriety.'

'As though I'm a free agent. I'm not, I'm a married woman.'

'But without a husband.'

'No. I have a husband.'

'Not in your bed where you need him.'

Hugh leaving. Hugh not being able to contain himself, expending himself like a boy dreaming. Hugh asleep in two minutes. Hugh unable to look directly at her next morning.

'I hope you don't listen to the gossips, I'm not what they make me out to be. I like women – I'll be honest, I prefer to be sitting here with you than jawing with a crowd of men. I thought you would appreciate my little stream. Don't you want to be here?'

'I don't know. It's peaceful and lovely and the mint smells wonderful. My senses tell me that I do. My common sense . . .'

'Well, ask yourself do you *like* being here?' He kissed her in a friendly kind of way but stayed holding her close and breathing close to her ear. 'Do you like being here?' His hand slipped inside the deep vee at the back of her dress.

'Yes, but . . .' She pulled his hand away. 'I'm a very proper person really.'

He kissed her ear lightly. 'I'm glad. Impropriety is boring.'

A small night-breeze moved the reeds and caused Georgia to shiver. He breathed once heavily as though capitulating, then released her.

'We should go back. Here, put my jacket round those bare shoulders.' He pressed one shoulder with his lips and Georgia stood up, knowing that if she did not do so now, then she might not do so at all until it was too late.

They walked slowly and quietly up the slope towards the house and the noise of the party. Before they reached the cultivated part of the garden which was hedged in clipped yew, Georgia slipped off the jacket and handed it to him.

'Thanks, but you'd better have it in case people get the wrong idea.'

'They get the wrong idea about me whatever I do. But you're right, they shouldn't have the wrong idea about you. I hope you won't find yourself judged by association with Freddy Hardy.'

'I don't really care. When Hugh left, I said to myself that there could be small freedoms to be gained for women in this war. And the one I've gained tonight is to be free to talk to a man without having to explain myself to anyone. It's been nice. Nobody ever showed me a stream on a hot night.'

'I have to go up to the house to see if the bar needs replenishing. I don't show many people my stream.' He laughed lightly. 'It'd never do if it got about that Freddy Hardy kept a bit of land so he could go there sometimes and smell the wild mint.'

Before they stepped through the yew hedge, he kissed her warmly, holding her close, as he might have had she been leaving for ever. She liked his soft, dry lips and the pressure of his convex belly against her own and kissed him back.

A flirtatious kiss. No harm done.

He said, 'Thank you for that, Young Mrs Kennedy.'

No one saw them step back through the yew hedge and rejoin the party. No talk, no speculation, no gossip. He turned as he went back up to the house. 'Mrs Kennedy. Did you know that you are absolutely stunning?'

At home, she unzipped her pretty party dress and slipped it from her shoulders. Standing before the long mirror, she considered herself. Stunning? Was that the line he was always shooting women? Why had he asked if she knew it? She could not be objective. In the mirror she saw only Georgia Honeycombe's hair, face and body. She slipped her hand beneath her breast as he had done, and again it tightened as it had on the terrace. It had not felt like Sports Club pawing.

What would you have done if he had tried to seduce you, Georgia Honeycombe? She closed her eyes. Didn't you go down to the stream to find out? What would his hand have felt like? Cold and hard and expert.

Opening her eyes, she watched herself move to the dance rhythm on the wireless. She smoothed nightcream over her skin and watched her fingers touch her own fair skin and allowed herself to enjoy the tender sensation. And for the first time since a young girl, she did not avoid her own eyes, nor did she turn away. There was nobody watching her. No headmistress, no vicar, no mother. She allowed herself to look at and touch her own body. No shame. No sin.

1939

The last couple of weeks of the school holidays in 1939 were as hot as anyone remembered. The children, who had lived in their bathers for a month or more, looked brown and wiry; endemic runny-noses had cleared up and their hair looked clean and sun-streaked.

Marie Partridge stood at her back gate and waved as one of the big girls took Bonnie off for the day. It was only half past nine, but Marie could see that the coloured washing was already dry. It was tempting to take it in and fold it down and get ahead of yourself, especially as she would probably feel guilty about Charlie getting back and finding it still hanging there. But greater temptation was to be going out on a Tuesday morning. Dragging herself away from the routine of the Tuesday coloureds, she dashed indoors where the kettle was already boiling for her stand-up wash-down in the bath.

In twenty minutes Marie was putting on her lipstick. She hesitated as to whether or not she should put a touch of Bourgeois behind her ears, but decided that perhaps it wasn't quite the thing if you were going to be involved in anything to do with food.

Before she left, she made a quick inspection of the house to see if there was anything out of place – she didn't want to provide Charlie with one single bit of extra ammunition. The plaster SS *Queen Mary* on the mantelshelf chinged the quarter hour: it was kept ten minutes fast, so she had loads of time. Time to get in the coloureds.

Once they were neatly folded and damped down ready for ironing, Marie felt lighthearted. She went out the back way and slipped the key under the lavatory mat. Her high heels clicked as she made her way from her house in Nightingale Road, along Gladstone Road towards Jubilee Lane.

Sam was in the garden picking runner beans. 'Marie! What you doing out on a Tuesday morning?'

Marie, taken aback at seeing him, feeling a guilty blush trying to rise, said very brightly, 'And what are *you* doing not at work? Those beans are looking good. Has Charlie seen them? He thinks nobody can grow runners like he can.'

Before he could answer, her mother-in-law came from the house. 'Come on then, Marie.' Marie hastened away.

Sam was halted in his tracks at seeing the two women wearing their afternoon shopping clothes in the middle of the morning, and with their faces made up and wearing ear-rings. 'Where you off to? You know it's my leg morning.'

'Well, there isn't nothing I can do about that, is there?' Then, low to Marie, 'Hurry up before he gets hisself worked up.'

Marie disappeared along the side of the house.

Dolly raised her voice. 'If we're not back by dinner time, I've left you some sandwiches in the larder.'

Close-shouldered, the two women hastened through the side-gate and away, leaving Sam with a feeling of mild outrage and a sense of being conspired against. There came one of the explosions of pain in his half-leg where the muscle had been blown away and left only bone. He thwacked the wooden replacement with his sturdy walking stick. 'I know you're not there, y' bugger.' The pain subsided like a beaten cur and lay quietly growling, waiting for the next time when it could pounce.

That he was the recognized head of the Partridge family was important to Sam. He might not have much left below the groin, but he was still head of his family. The family needed him. As he had said to his beer-mug cronies in the

King William, 'It's all right for women these days getting uppity and laying down the law about married women getting jobs, but when it comes to it, it's always a man who has to carry the can.'

This was the kind of unspecific statement with which the beer-mugs could readily agree. They nodded, 'A woman's place is in the home, Sam.'

'Right. Five halves of Boilermaker, Joe.'

'It's her natural place, Sam,' said Joe, drawing the beer.

'And one for yourself, Joe.'

The beer-mugs nodded as the Boilermakers flowed. 'And man is the bread-winner.'

'Men must work, and women . . . cheers.'

'Like in nature, Sam . . . the hen on the nest and the ewe with her lambs.'

The beer-mugs had pondered that one without perceiving that cocks and rams aren't much of providers. But still, it was the general feeling that counted.

'And no woman ever got her legs blown off like Sam there.'

Whenever Sam suspected that there was something going on in the family that he was not aware of, anxiety made knots in his stomach and gave him trouble with the bit of leg that had decomposed in France. He would admit it to no one, but he had felt bad ever since Dolly had gone behind his back and got her name down for this job at the kitchens at the Old Mission Hall.

And now where are they off to? Charlie didn't know about it, or he'd have said. On a Tuesday! There was too many things going on these days. Nobody tells me, oh no. No legs, so no brains. And then there was Vern Greenaway going about telling people that the Labour Party would have to stop functioning if there was a war.

Although he had denied saying anything specific, only that there probably wouldn't be enough members, Vern had looked pretty sheepish when Sam had tackled him about it. It all went towards giving Sam indigestion and shooting fires in his leg.

What was going on this morning? Another meeting? Dolly seemed to be here and there and everywhere since she had got herself this job. It wasn't even proper cooking, it was seeing if turnips would do instead of apples to make jam.

'Damn it, Dolly, the war won't stop us growing apples.'

'It's a question of shortages through distribution, Sam. So don't argue about something you know nothing about.'

Who'd ever think that somebody like Dolly would let a bit of authority go to her head.

If you didn't laugh you'd cry.

And now Marie was gadding off on a Tuesday morning.

Sam knew that if he lost his place, lost control of the family, it would go to pieces.

He took the beans into the house, and knotted his tie prior to going for his regular stump examination. There was always something when you were responsible for a family.

Harry, for a start, always wanting to be off somewhere, dancing, dancing, dancing. Never the same girl twice. All sorts of bits of things. There was lads like him that Sam had known when he was in the army: they'd pick up anything wearing skirts in the hope that they wasn't wearing drawers. Even Dolly couldn't make excuses for some of them he went out with, and now he was talking about selling his motor bike and going in for a car. A car!

'Can't you just see it – a council house with a car parked in front.'

The trouble with Harry was, he had come along five years after Charlie – not that that was Harry's fault – and seven after Paula, and they had treated him like a puppy; and I was out there having me legs blown off, not here to see what was going on. And he'd gone on being a blooming puppy.

'What you going to be like when you're forty, Harry?'

'Blue-eyed and fancy-free,' Harry said, not taking it a bit serious. Harry never seemed to take anything serious. A wonder he'd got his certificates. But he had. One thing you could say about the lad, he was blooming clever. Who else on the whole council estate has got a son working in the Town Hall?

Only you, Samuel Partridge, MM.

Charlie wasn't so bad, not bad at all really. Got a nice place, as nice furniture as you'd find if you like all that modern gloss and figured wood. The trouble with Charlie, you always had that worry at the back of your mind that he was *going* to do something. He never had yet, but there was always that feeling. Like Charlie betting on horses.

I know you do it, Charlie, because whenever there's a big race on you always got the racing paper in the front pocket of your bag.

And he's always late with his Diddle'm money.

You don't say nothing to him, Sam Partridge – Dolly always defended them – it's none of your business if he has a flutter or not. Our Charlie's master in his own house now. You'd have something to complain about if he went off boozing like some.

But there was always the worry that one day he might get a decent win and would start betting big money. Sam had seen it happen.

He took out his Rizlas and Black Beauty, rolling meanly as he'd learned in the trenches and set off to walk to the surgery.

Paula's all right, thank goodness for that. She's always been less worry than the boys . . . except that she was married to a docker, and dockers never knew where the next day's work would come from. What a system! Treating men like animals in a pound . . . 'You and you and you. No more! The rest of you can blow.'

What a way to run a country! It would have been better if Paula had married a local chap. A daughter ought to stop in her own town. Pity they hadn't got no kids. Paula never said about it, but you could tell how she felt about kids. She'd have made a blooming good teacher if she'd a been born the right side of the tracks.

There's still plenty of time, she's only thirty still. Thirty isn't old. It an't young. Still – she's healthy and plump as a corn-fed chicken.

1939

As she swept her front path, enjoying the lazy feel to the hot day that had started early with no children in the house and Dick bringing tea up and getting back in bed with her to drink it, Mrs Wiltshire saw her neighbour, Mrs Kennedy, checking her handbag for her keys before she slammed the front door shut. Grass widow. Grass officer's widow. She did look nice. Her hair looked . . . blonder. Certainly blonder. Well you couldn't say it didn't suit her with that pale blue dress and hat and the white ear-rings. She was a very pretty woman.

Mrs Wiltshire touched the front of her own hair, wondering whether she dare do a bit of bleach on the front. She would have loved to try it, but apart from the fact that Dick would be angry, Mrs Wiltshire did not know how bleaching was done. People talked about peroxide blondes, and you couldn't just put on that sort of stuff without knowing what you were doing. You heard about women whose hair turned green or fell out.

Dick liked blondes. He always got up and stood at the window with his hands in his pockets if he heard Mrs Kennedy's footsteps on the front path.

'She's a bit of all right is our Georgia,' he would say – not that he ever called her Georgia to her face. 'But you wouldn't get me off and leaving a wife like her alone in the house.'

'But you wouldn't mind leaving a wife like me then?'

'Ask a silly question,' Dick had said.

It had been quite like old times the last couple of weeks since Little-Lena and Roy went off for a bit of a holiday with Dick's mother. They had gone out to the pictures and a couple of times for a drink. Dick had been playful, like he used to be. Making a lot of noise going upstairs.

'Ssh, Dick. You can hear through these walls.'

'Never heard a sound from them.'

And you'd think you would. As Dick said, he might have been a bit of an old stuffed shirt, but she doesn't look like one who'd be quiet while she's about it.

'You're an expert then, Dick Wiltshire.'

'I reckon she could do with somebody a bit younger. The Chocolate Soldier must be forty if he's a day, and she can't be much over twenty.'

Mrs Kennedy came down the path, her white Cuban-heel strappy sandals clicking with that modern sound.

'How's Mr Kennedy getting on?'

'Oh he's fine. Loving every minute of it apparently. He's not much of a letter writer. But he's doing very well – been selected for something. I don't know what it is. Some new regiment I think.'

'Not staying in the Hampshire's?'

'To tell you the truth, I'm not sure. He said he wasn't at liberty to say anything about what he is doing.'

Mrs Wiltshire leaned her brush against the separating hedge. Georgia glanced at the abbey clock. Still plenty of time, she could always do her bit of shopping after the meeting.

'Fancy that. He'll be getting a bit of leave soon, then you'll get to know.'

'Well no, he says he won't be off camp for at least two months.'

'Two months! Well that's pretty steep, especially as he's only at Aldershot.'

'I don't even know if that's where he still is. All my letters have to go to some office in London for transferring.'

Mrs Wiltshire was impressed. 'Sounds very hush-hush if you ask me.'

'That's what I thought. Well, I must be going. I've got myself involved in this committee.'

'Well . . . lucky for some. Enjoy yourself.' Mrs Wiltshire smiled as she watched her walk towards the town. She liked Mrs Kennedy. Liked having a pretty, modern woman next door. It had done Mary Wiltshire no end of good herself. Mrs Kennedy said she did her eyelids with Vaseline and got that nice fine edge to her lips by using a little brush. Mary had tried it out and was really pleased. She had even bought a safety razor of her own once she learned that Mrs Kennedy had one.

Last night Dick had called her to the front window. Mrs Kennedy and the tall chap with the prematurely grey hair were standing outside next-door's front gate. 'Here, Mary, come and have a decko at this. Do you think our Georgia's being a naughty girl?'

'You don't want to go saying things like that, Dick. They aren't doing anything wrong or they wouldn't be standing out there like that. Anyway, you can't expect her to live like a nun.'

'And he don't look like no monk neither.'

What Dick and Mary Wiltshire had seen was indeed entirely innocent. A friendly game of tennis with Nick.

Georgia had been in the cottage next to the Mission Hall that was to be her office. The place had been dirty, so she had changed into a wrap-round apron and head-scarf. The physical work freed her mind to think about the pile of official instructions and forms she had received on the running of the office, but it had been side-tracked into thinking about Nick Crockford.

Last week, when she was leaving the tennis club, he had been outside.

'You look nice,' he said, and fell in beside her. 'Would you like to give me a game one evening? We used to have fun in the old days.'

'It's not the old days – what about Nancy?'

'Nancy never held a tennis bat in her life.'

'I didn't mean that.'

'I know you didn't.' A pause. 'As a matter of fact, she's gone. She's been gone since last spring. She cleared off with a ginger-haired relief signalman at Mottisfont.' Trying to make it sound comic showed that either his heart or his pride was hurt.

'I'm sorry about that, Nick. You didn't say, did you? I expect you miss the little boy.'

'Do you mind if we don't talk about it right now?'

Georgia fell silent.

'Well, Georgia, will you have a game of tennis one evening?'

'All right, book a court for a Thursday. I'm always free then.'

'Lead a busy life do you then? Did you enjoy your evening with the toffs?'

He was touchy about that. But it was none of his affair. 'As a matter of fact, yes. I could quite take to the high life.'

There had always been times when he had never quite known whether her tongue was in her cheek.

They had continued talking easily: at least, Georgia had talked at his prompting. He had walked with her as far as her gate, where they had stood talking for a few minutes.

'I'll see you then. Thursday evening.'

They had had their game.

'You've improved,' he conceded.

He was not very good, but could hit a ball very hard and kept her running about, laughing at her puffing. 'You smoke too much, Georgia Honeycombe.' She was the better player, and won. They laughed a lot, had a drink sitting in the garden of a pub and he had walked home with her. It had been really good to be with him again. Not like old times, those years when they were very young and had gone around together. Then, he was inclined to be very serious and solemn. Older now, he was still serious but not solemn. Man and woman now, each with experience of adult life.

Now, in her new office as she was hanging curtains, she heard footsteps in the passage and thought it might be Mrs Farr. Nick's head peered round the door.

She had not expected him. She pulled her apron across and her hand went to her scarf.

'What are you doing here, Nick?'

'I booked the court again. Will you come?'

A spark of irritation, he had booked the court. Men were all the same, expecting you to fall in with their arrangements. Even so, she had enjoyed herself last time. 'How did you know where to find me?'

'You mentioned it. I remembered. Here, let me do that.' He took the curtain spring she had been struggling with and fixed it.

Again the irritation. 'I could have managed.'

'I'm taller.'

'Now that Hugh's away, I have to stand on my own feet.' It sounded childish and unnecessary.

'Doesn't mean you can't accept help from somebody with longer arms.'

He was right, she had been about to give up on the spring. 'Sorry.'

'You're niggled because I didn't ask before booking the court. Come on, say you will. It'll do you good to bash a ball about.'

They had repeated the enjoyment of the previous Thursday, and again they had separated at Georgia's front gate, leaving her elated and a bit dissatisfied.

1939

It was the first meeting proper with certain other organizations of the 'Markham Committee for Nutrition and Emergency Local Food Provision', and Georgia was its convener and secretary. Her cool appearance belied her extreme nervousness and high excitement as she clicked her summer sandals along the pavement towards the Old Mission Hall premises.

Inevitably the bureaucratic and pompous title of the committee was soon humanized by the women who constituted themselves as The Restaurant Women. To the great and powerful, the preparation of food was domestic and thus female and low status work, which was assurance that there was no risk of any male wishing to serve as Chairman of their committee. Markham's great and powerful were content to leave the Restaurant Women to get on with it.

'Any guidance you may need, ladies, you have only to ask – this work will be most essential to the entire community.'

The men who said that didn't believe it of course. Essential work was that which could be seen in the streets: sandbagging, boarding-up, commandeering buildings, commandeering vehicles, ordering about lesser mortals and wearing badges and arm-bands and designating. Commandeering, ordering and designating was what would get the war moving.

The Restaurant Women, finding themselves in the unexpected situation of being in charge of themselves, soon discovered that they had no need of a Chairman at all. Georgia, the office worker, was adept at keeping the discussion close to what they had set out to discuss. Nobody needed any title except the one they brought with them – Mrs or Miss. There was nothing to commandeer, order or designate. By the time of the Tuesday morning meeting, anarchy seemed to be working quite well.

Georgia arrived at the Old Mission Hall at the same time as the contrasting Eve and Connie Hardy. Eve, small, plump and pretty, wearing a pink dirndl skirt and white blouse and flat sandals and floppy straw hat, looked a picture of English rosiness. It was really too warm for dark-blue serge, so Connie was a bit self-conscious in her new Red Cross officer's uniform, every seam of which Freddy's tailor had unpicked and re-sewn around Connie's svelte body. She looked a picture of elegance. Georgia wished that she had worn her own small discreet pearl ear-rings. Her nervousness at having to run this meeting was not calmed by Connie looking the picture of efficiency. But her mother's training and Georgia's own nature masked the anxiety.

'I say!' Georgia said. 'You do look absolutely splendid, Mrs Hardy.'

'Do you think so? That is nice of you. It is rather a hot day for this fabric, but I thought I must get used to wearing it. And it is best to try things out first among friends if it is possible.'

'You look marvellous. Only somebody as slim as you ever looks any good in men's-type clothes . . . all those pockets on the bosom.'

'I know, I can't think why they do it. Breasts look absolutely bulging if one puts so much as a flat handkerchief in these pockets.'

Georgia's natural friendliness had cut the ice.

'Mrs Kennedy, this is my daughter Eve. I hope that you don't mind that I have brought her along. You see, she is a very good driver, and I had heard that you need drivers.'

'Oh, absolutely.' Georgia and Eve shook fingers. 'We shall want as many drivers as we can get delivering food-containers to schools. I only wish I could drive.'

'I could teach you.' Eve Hardy's voice was unexpectedly low and very feminine, the sort of voice which Georgia thought of as having 'It' – like Marlene Dietrich. Quite at variance with the pink dirndl.

If Georgia felt less elegant and a bit overdressed compared to the mother, she felt quite 'the thing' compared to the daughter who dressed as though she was seventeen, but who must be quite the same age as herself.

'Could you really?'

'Of course, I should love to.'

'I don't think Hugh would mind if I got his car out.'

'Oh that's all right, we can use mine. It's a bit well . . . you know . . . but it's a nice little job to drive. You'd learn in no time.'

Suddenly Georgia's stomach warmed and relaxed. Eve Hardy seemed nice. The mother didn't seem half bad either – she had seemed genuinely pleased at Georgia's compliment, yet people must always be telling her how lovely she looked.

'Did you enjoy Freddy's evening? He said it was a working supper. Any excuse. My husband likes people in the house.'

For a moment Georgia felt gauche but quickly recovered. 'I can't say that it seemed much like work. I did talk to a few people about this place, which was why I was invited. It was a lovely way to be working. Your house and grounds are beautiful.'

'Thank you. Though I must say I was glad that I had an excuse – some of my husband's colleagues are frightful old farts.' The word that Georgia's mother would have made her wash from her mouth was not coarse coming from Connie Hardy's lips.

Her mother had always said, The Rich are different, they don't have to please anyone except themselves.

From outside, Georgia saw herself coolly talking to one of Markham's Rich, its first lady, whose husband had momentarily held her breast and kissed her – not passionately, but had kissed her. From outside, she saw a Georgia Kennedy she had never before seen.

They went inside the Mission Hall, where one or two women had already arrived. Immediately the rest of the women arrived, all at least fifteen minutes early.

The Restaurant Women were Mrs Kennedy, for her past experience of running an office, Mrs Partridge, who had good experience of working in the kitchens of a hospital before she was married, and for four years during the last war, and two athletic-looking women whom Georgia recognized as members of the tennis team. They were young and enthusiastic volunteers who had little experience of anything to do with cooking but were willing to do any kind of community work, as long as they would not be called upon to staunch blood. Georgia guessed that they wouldn't last long doing such unglamorous work. And Mrs Farr, a white-haired, youthful-looking woman who, after being a mystery when she settled in Markham years ago, was revealed, when she applied for the post of Head Cook, as having once been a cook with many years' experience at a famous public school.

Mrs Farr was a woman with an air of natural leadership and winning personality, and was therefore the person to whom they all deferred. Her references had been impeccable: if there was anything that Mrs Farr didn't know about producing puddings by the hundredweight, gravy by the gallon, and baked potatoes by the ton, then it was not worth knowing.

Mrs Partridge's daughter-in-law, Marie. Secretly, Dolly had wondered whether the others might think that she was getting Marie in by the back door, which of course she was, and good luck to her – if it wasn't Marie it would be somebody else. When Dolly saw that Mrs Nob of Nob Hill had brought her daughter, she no longer felt guilty about Marie.

There was an atmosphere of high old ladylike excitement in the back room of the Old Mission. Mrs Farr had come in good time and, having brought a large basket containing biscuits, cups and everything else necessary, had got the kettle on and had made a brew of good tea. In spite of the heat outside and the steam and lighted gas-oven inside, the room was chilly with that chill of all church halls where not much is spent on heating at the best of times: this one had been closed down for five years.

Georgia tapped her spoon on her saucer and the talk subsided. 'Shall we start before the men arrive, ladies?'

'Before we start looking at the place, I should say that Mrs Hardy – or should I say "Captain", Mrs Hardy . . .?'

'Oh Lord, no! The rank is embarrassing enough as it is. I really scarcely know how I came by it.'

We know how, thought Dolly. By knowing the right people. It was rumoured that Connie Hardy and Lady Mountbatten were like *that* – meaning in one another's pockets – though why a Lady should want to be in the pocket of a cake manufacturer's wife, nobody explained.

' . . . Mrs Hardy is here to inspect the building with a view to using one room for the Red Cross office and a store for their things – tea and condensed milk and cigarettes, I believe, for the troop-trains.'

They began their tour of the building. Georgia had taken a lot of trouble to anticipate that they would need lists to cover various types of work such as carpentry, plumbing and plastering, and had prepared a headed paper for each subject.

'I *say*,' said the tennis girl, 'that's terribly efficient, Georgia. Who did them for you?'

'I did them myself. They're just common sense really.'

'I *say*,' said the doubles partner, 'I am impressed. I thought your Hughie must have done them – he's always so good at that kind of thing at the Club.'

As they inspected the old building, each woman had a say

about what repairs were obvious, what changes were necessary, what installations, such as cookers, sinks, locked store-cupboards and cold-stores, would be needed. It went without saying that the hall itself, which had once been used for dances and socials, was to be the public restaurant, with a serving counter with heated plates at one end, next to the kitchens which could be installed at the back. There was a great feeling of conviviality . . . a lot of, 'That's a good idea' and, 'Oh yes' and 'I should never have thought of that.'

Georgia, with her forms and papers clipped to a board, thought, It's going so well. I wish Hugh could see me now. Then, no I don't, he would only be patronizing, or try to show me how to do it his way, and I should feel a fool and then I should act like a fool. For some reason, an image of Nick Crockford imposed itself upon her concentration.

The reason, though she did not know it, was that she wished that Nick Crockford could see her now. It was also that Georgia Kennedy's husband had been away for weeks, and it was not he who had been breathing close to her ear in her unfaithful dreams.

An inspection of the dank 'usual offices' brought her concentration back to her notes, and by eleven-thirty she had them completed. In their inspection, the team had – amongst other work – theoretically knocked down walls, built flush toilets, scraped surfaces and had them painted, widened doorways and had sheets of tin tiling affixed to the walls of the preparation and cooking areas.

They agreed that they must keep the stage so that there would be a chance for people to listen to a bit of piano music or singing sometimes, whilst they were eating.

'Or conjuring,' said the doubles partner. 'My Pa would love to, he's as good as a professional.'

'He is, I've seen him,' said Marie Partridge. 'At the Co-op concert. If there's a war, people will want things like that to keep their spirits up.' She flushed at having spoken at a meeting. Charlie would never believe her. Oh Lord,

Charlie. She turned off thoughts of Charlie. He would probably have seen her note and would know by now where she was. And would probably have gone down to the park to see his Dad. She glanced across at her mother-in-law, who was behaving as though she had served on committees all her life. Marie Partridge's spirits rose – they were in this together.

'It's no longer a question of *if* there's a war, my dear,' said Mrs Farr, and they all listened to the older woman, already recognized as wise and intelligent. 'There will be a war, and it will be soon. And it won't be over by Christmas, no matter what they tell you. And you are right, my dear, we shall need things to keep up our spirits, even more than in the last war. And you' (to Dolly) 'will remember all about what that was like, quite as well as I do.'

'I do. But I hope they write some better songs for this one. The others were mush. War isn't sentimental, it's degrading. I suppose it's because songwriters stop at home where it's safe – I never heard of a songwriter getting his leg blown off.'

The other ladies knew that Mrs Partridge was the park-keeper's wife and they lived on the council estate and even though they might not agree with her, were amazed at how well she could put things – at how 'deep' she was.

'Nobody's going to be safe this time,' said Connie Hardy, surprisingly.

Mrs Farr looked at Dolly Partridge, the only other woman here who really had any understanding of war, and was glad that such a very sensible sort of woman was going to work on the food scheme. I have always got on best with the working-classes, Mrs Farr thought. I shall offer her the job as cook's assistant: it will be better money than kitchen worker.

By twelve the first of the men arrived – fifteen minutes early, hoping to find some tea about – a man who said he was Clerk of the Works.

'This won't take long, and then you can get off,' he said, leaning familiarly on one elbow, having put himself at the centre of the gathering. He savoured Mrs Farr's freshly-brewed tea. 'We came yesterday and went through the place. But, well, we got to meet you official so that you can tell us what colour you want things. You're a proper official body now, an't you, ladies? Got to put this meeting in a proper report for the Town Hall.'

'Fancy that, ladies,' said Mrs Farr with a very odd look. 'A proper report for the Town Hall.'

The Clerk of the Works continued. 'I'll tell you this for nothing, the Borough Surveyor didn't think much of the place, nor did the Fire Officer, not worth spending the money on; but there, if you asks me it will all be over by Christmas anyway, so whatever happens it's going to be a waste. The Church people won't mind, though, give the old place a new lease of life all on rates and taxes.'

Connie Hardy's clear voice dropped into the women's stunned silence. 'Will you please explain exactly who came and went through the place yesterday?'

'Borough Surveyor, myself, Fire Chief, Inspector Knowles and Councillor Hardy, Ma'am.'

'So the five of *you* have already decided what is to be done?'

'Good as. You ladies will be able to be off by one o'clock. Just a matter of form.'

Georgia looked at the faces of the women, who were all looking at one another.

Connie Hardy held up a finger. 'May I speak with you and the other ladies, Mrs Kennedy.'

'Excuse us,' Georgia said. 'Help yourself to more tea and biscuits.' And led the way outside. They gathered in a close huddle, their backs to everything, facing only their unity and indignation.

Hello, thought the Clerk of the Works, they're up to something. But it wasn't his job to worry about that and the biscuits were delicious – not the boughten muck he got at home.

'Well!' Mrs Farr exploded first, and then the other established members of the committee exploded too.

Dolly Partridge said, 'It's not often I get het up, but I must say, I can't abide being treated like I was a child by somebody like Bert Bartram and – I'm sorry Mrs Hardy – by Councillors.'

'You don't have to apologize, Mrs Partridge,' Connie Hardy said. 'You have a right to be annoyed.'

Mrs Farr said, 'It is quite clear. Emergency committees (of which this is one) are set up by Government, not Councils. Council workmen will be employed, but Councillors have no authority to recommend what shall be done with this building. It is for *this* Committee to recommend.'

'Look,' Georgia said, 'I think we all feel the same: that we have put in a lot of thought and work into what wants doing in this place and if we let ourselves be walked over now, they will keep on doing it and we shall have only ourselves to blame. I must say, I feel pretty niggled about it.'

'Niggled!' said Mrs Farr, 'I feel angry. The kitchens and the entire preparation area at Melsbury School were planned by me, and when the new kitchens were to be installed at a new Navigation College, I was invited to vet them. And now I am expected to have my kitchens arranged by firemen and police constables.' With her smooth, unaged skin and pure white hair springing from her black peasant headscarf, she looked magnificent. Had there been people there who had known her in her younger days, they would have been reminded of when she had defied jeering crowds whilst she was chained to the House of Commons' railings.

'I'll tell you what riles me about it,' Dolly said. 'It's that five men, who probably never cooked a rasher of bacon in their lives, think that they can come in and tell us!'

Dolly Partridge, on one of her hobby horses, went on.

'They haven't got no idea what a kitchen ought to be. You ought to see the kitchens in the council houses. The gas-stove so you've got your back to the light, sink where water splashes the curtains, nowhere to put hot pans down safe – and it's all too blooming high.'

'Kitchens always are,' said Eve Hardy, speaking for the first time.

What she knows about kitchens you could write on a matchstick, thought Marie Partridge.

'I'll tell you what I think we should do.' All eyes swivelled in Connie's direction. 'Go across to the Town Hall now. There's a meeting of the Council Executive.' Knowing how it must look to them, and knowing better than anybody perhaps her own husband's reputation, she said earnestly. 'Look, I'll support you, and I can guarantee the Red Cross will support me if necessary. If you can try to ignore the fact that it's my husband who is Chief Executive, I assure you that I can. We are going to have to work together here. We ought to stick together.'

So, they went. And, united, they stood up to the Borough fathers, who were at first delighted to receive the charming ladies all in their summer dresses and hats, and Mrs Hardy in her delightful uniform.

Refusing their offer of sherry or rolls and coffee, Mrs Farr said, 'We intend to deal direct with the appropriate Government body, and so that there is no misunderstanding, we think it preferable that you give the Council's sub-contracted labour written notice that Mrs Kennedy is Administrator and that they must take instructions from her.'

Georgia Kennedy felt Freddy Hardy's eyes alight upon her and she knew that she must stand up to him.

'Thank you, Mrs Farr, I couldn't have put it better myself. You see, gentlemen, it is not that we want to be against any suggestions that you might have – I am sure we need the advice of the Fire Chief – but I have been appointed to organize and administer this restaurant and, in any case, I am sure that you will have more important affairs to deal with than the mass provision of meat and two veg.'

And it was done.

Later, Georgia and Mrs Farr met for the first of many 'Departmental Conferences' as they wryly referred to their informal talk about the administrative and practical running of the restaurant.

'I hadn't realized that you had been appointed,' Mrs Farr said. 'I must say that I am pleased. I had visions of having some retired bank manager telling me what to do. I certainly never in my wildest dreams expected that they would have the extreme good sense to appoint a woman as Administrator.'

It had not taken Georgia long to know that Mrs Farr was one of the straightest kind of people, somebody you could be honest with and know that she would never let you down.

'Well actually, I wouldn't give them credit for good sense too soon. Look.' She handed Mrs Farr a letter from the Ministry.

Mrs Farr read the closely-filled pages carefully, then looked up at the young woman who would be her boss and began to laugh quietly. 'Oh, I say, isn't that rich? *George* Kennedy.'

'It was Councillor Hardy as well as Councillor Greenaway who backed my application.'

'Well, for once they made a mistake worth making.'

'Do you think my appointment's legal?'

'*Fait accompli.*' The older woman's eyes sparkled with delight. 'Now you've started the job, it won't be easy for them to take it away from you.'

'What do you think I should do about my salary cheque?'

'Have you your own bank account?'

'No. I didn't know that a married woman could have a separate account.'

'Of course. Perhaps it might not be a bad idea if you open one: it would forestall any queries by the bureaucrats.'

'Goodness,' said Georgia, 'I feel quite conspiratorial.'

Mrs Farr momentarily squeezed Georgia's shoulder and smiled in a wry and serious way. 'Women do have to be, George.'

'I shall enjoy working with you, Mrs Farr.'

'And I you. What a wonderful experience, to have a woman in charge.'

'Goodness!' said Georgia Kennedy. 'Whatever will Hugh say?' at which Mrs Farr gave her a funny look. 'But I don't think that it would be a good idea to tell Hugh.'

'About George.'

'He would call it false pretences or something.'

'Least said soonest mended?'

Georgia covered her smile with her hand. 'It never occurred to me that one could enjoy a conspiracy.'

'My dear, if women are to get even the smallest freedom to work in the men's world, we sometimes have no choice but to conspire.'

Georgia warmed to this strong woman and seemed herself to grow stronger in her presence. 'You're right. Men conspire all the time, don't they, but they call it putting their heads together, or meeting over a drink.'

Georgia departed from her new colleague feeling stimulated and eager. She could do anything. Anything!

1989

'They want to take our picture, Dorothy.' Mrs Farr leaned towards her friend and sister inmate. Inmate was Mrs Farr's word: the matron (I wish you would call me Nancy, dear) liked her charges to think of themselves as Residents (It's what you are, dear, what we all are, Residents in Homelyside).

'Who, the *Clarion*?' Dolly Partridge's voice was pitched slightly higher and louder than was necessary, indicating deafness.

'No, the *Guardian*. And do an interview.'

'The *Manchester Guardian*?'

' "Monday Women". It's a feature . . .'

'I know what it is, I'm not senile – only deaf. What do they want pictures of us for?' Her body shook and wheezed slightly with amusement. 'Is the *Guardian* starting a page three?'

'No, it's a series on old wrecks.'

'You're fishing for compliments, Ursula. You know you don't look a day over a hundred.'

'You don't look bad yourself, Dorothy.'

'So I should, I'm younger than you.'

And neither did they look so bad for their century of hard wear, as they walked at the pace of Dolly's legs in the Homelyside garden.

Ursula Farr was thin and wiry from a lifetime of sensible eating and brisk daily walking, and she still swam. Her thick white hair she wore cut in the same Twenties bob she had worn it in since the Twenties. These days, her reading glasses lenses were thick, even so, she didn't miss much and her eyes were as intelligent as when Dolly Partridge had first met her in 1939.

Dorothy Partridge was plumper than her friend of fifty years' duration, deaf without her hearing-aid, and her legs didn't work at all well, but then Dolly had had four children, a poor diet for all her young years, and stood and knelt on more stone floors than she cared to remember. For a woman of her great age, with her sparse, fluffy hair and unself-conscious smile, she would make a good photograph for the papers. They both would.

After a few minutes' pause, Dolly asked, 'What did you tell them?'

'I said we'd do it. You don't mind, do you?'

'I thought you went off the *Guardian*. It makes my arms ache. Good cartoons.'

The postman, taking a short cut through the garden, saw the two old ladies helping one another slowly, and made a mental note to put them down in his Writer's Journal and do a characterization piece to read out at the group meeting. 'Shuffling, ancient, walking with two sticks, hearing-aid. Hair like dandelion clock. Companion wearing ethnic dress, shrivelled – ripe granadilla – contrasting hair like Jean Harlow.'

He winked at them as he passed. 'Morning, Girls.'

1939

Now August was well under way. The slow, comfortable pace of Markham appeared unaltered.

On Thursdays, carts rumbled through the narrow streets to the cattle-market. Horse-dung fell in the roads, and was quickly harvested in buckets by small boys who sold it for money to spend at the Picture House.

Dealers and farmers in breeches and gaiters crowded into town. In the stockyards they strutted carrying whippy sticks which appeared out of control, striking the backs of any and every animal. Having agreed a satisfactory deal, the weather-beaten men spat-and-slapped hands and went into pubs with all-day licences to tank up on enough pints to last them the week.

Downland-fattened sheep trotted and leaped into town, muddling their way from their peaceful fields to the riotous market pens, sometimes panicking wildly into front-gardens and up alleyways. Cattle moaned and pigs shrieked as soon as they sensed the slaughter-house behind the butcher's shop.

Market Day in Markham, with the exception of the use of some mechanized transport, had stayed unchanged over centuries.

But the self-satisfaction was beginning to crumble. In some back-gardens, little arches of corrugated iron which denoted an underground air-raid shelter appeared amongst the flowers. There were many fewer young men about. Although the school holidays had not ended, there was activity in classrooms. Piles of cardboard boxes containing gas-masks were being sorted. Buildings and rooms which had long been unused became offices from where ration-books, tokens, shrouds, coffins, vitamins and official information would be stored or issued.

As they had done twenty-five years ago, the people of Markham too scented the slaughter-house. National Socialism in Germany, which had at one time appeared no more threatening to civilization than the Scout Movement or British Communism, had grown terrifying and powerful. People like Sam and Vern Greenaway and Mrs Farr, who had yellow-jacketed Gollanczes in the living-room, and who had once been called Old Jonahs and prophets of doom for suggesting that Hitler meant trouble in Europe, were now asked when they thought the balloon would go up.

Not that Mrs Farr was asked often – for she was a separate, almost solitary woman. But rumour had it that she knew people who were now High-Ups. And she did know. Not only from men in the know who were old boys grown fat on her school spotted dicks but from letters direct from Germany where she had friends who were in danger.

On the last Thursday in August, Mrs Farr, having left her long, narrow house which faced the Abbey Walk, walked the hundred yards to what would be her new domain.

For some reason, which she suspected had to do with Mrs Hardy, the work had gone on apace. Those suspicions were only half correct: the other half was that Mrs Farr, in living so close to the Mission Hall, was better – or worse, depending – than a combined full-time Clerk of the Works, Foreman and designer.

When she arrived, Mrs Partridge was already at work scrubbing down behind the workmen.

'That shouldn't be your job, Mrs Partridge.'

Dolly Partridge did not stop creating spirals from the froth of soda and yellow-soap on the linoed floor as she smiled up at her new boss. 'Ah well, it wanted doing. Those chaps have got no idea, no idea at all. Wouldn't you think they'd done the distempering before the lino was laid?'

'If I had not been away yesterday, they would have. At least we shall know that this is perfectly hygienic when you have been at it.'

'You don't have to call me Mrs Partridge.'

'Thank you – it's Dorothy isn't it?'

'Everybody calls me Dolly – but I really hate Dolly.'

'Dorothy then? Mine's Ursula.'

'Yes, it'd be nice to be called by my proper name. Not much point having one, else . . . I dare say I won't call you by yours, it don't do.'

Dolly thought how blinking good it was going out to work, having somebody who appreciated that there was an art to scrubbing a floor. All the years that Dolly had spent on her knees at home, she had never once felt like humming, let alone singing in little snatches as she now did.

Mrs Farr and Dolly were, at the moment, the only two kitchen workers who were actually entered in Georgia's wages book.

'I had a letter from the Ministry this morning, Dorothy, which said in effect that we have got to have this place in working order by the end of the month. It's where they will bring evacuees to be fed.'

'Poor little souls. Can you imagine how they will feel, being carted off from their mothers and dumped down in a strange place?'

'Well, yes I can. The ruling-classes do it all the time. I have seen a great deal of it . . . too much, in fact. Even so, it has given me a good insight into how to make the best of it. Children like familiar food . . . children who are brought up by nannies go on liking nursery puddings and suet duffs.' She smiled.

Dolly said, 'There is something comforting about a spotted dick with a bit of custard.'

'I am sure that if you could see the menus at some Gentlemen's Clubs in London, you would find that the most popular puddings are exactly the same as in public schools. So what you and I shall do, Dorothy, is to make sure the children from the East End of London who like shop-fried fish and chips will not have to stand having nourishing country broth thrust upon them. Time enough when they've learned to breathe the air.'

Dolly nodded. 'That suits me, Mrs Farr. If there's one thing I know, it's how to make a good fritter and a good pancake.'

'Splendid. And very nourishing too.'

Mrs Farr might be a single lady with no children of her own, but she understood about people. In all her years, Dolly had never suspected that work could be anything but a necessity. She was beginning to think differently, which was why she sang as she scrubbed.

Mrs Farr, as she inspected the altered appearance of the premises, thought it was a damned shame that it had taken a war to bring a retired building and a retired woman back into life and use again.

'Young man, if you leave that protrusion of cement, it will collect dirt.'

The man touched his cap to the Old Battleaxe and got on with removing it, knowing that she would be back and he would have to do it in the end.

Mrs Farr wondered where the young man would be by Christmas.

1939

Saturday 2nd September

On the Friday when Britain made its British demand of Hitler that he withdraw from Poland, Dick Wiltshire, just as he was due to go to London and bring Little-Lena and Roy home, broke his leg and became immobilized.

His wife, whose reaction was to be irritable at anything that made waves on her calm domestic sea, said, 'We should never have let them stop on to the last minute, Dick. What if the war starts and they are in London? It's the first place the Germans will go to.'

Dick told her not to let it run away with her, that the Germans had got enough on their plates without starting on England. Even so, Mary Wiltshire was quite beside herself with worry, so much so that she swallowed her pride, took her courage in her hands and knocked on Mrs Kennedy's door.

'I feel really so awful coming like this, but I didn't know where to turn.'

'Of course I'll go and fetch them.'

'Dick will pay your expenses, of course.'

'That's not necessary. I shall be glad to do it. I don't know why you didn't tell me before.'

'The thing is, I can't really leave him all plastered up like that. The doctor says he mustn't move, he can't even go to the you-know without me there. I say they should have kept him in hospital, but there you are. People don't know what Dick's like. He's a Wiltshire all right: if he says he won't do a thing, then he won't.'

'It's all right, Mrs Wiltshire. I shall enjoy going. I know it quite well, it's not far from Putney. I did a week's filing-system training there once.'

'Oh that *is* a load off my mind. There's all this on the wireless about the train-loads of children ready to be evacuated from London, and I kept thinking, there's them being sent away for safety and there's Little-Lena and Roy there on holiday. Dick says Hitler's got his hands too full to think about bombing London by surprise, but I shan't feel they're safe till they're back. They won't like it: they run wild when they're with Dick's mother, there are a lot of children for them to play with – not like round here. Well, actually, it is a council flat she lives in, very nice, all mod. cons, but still a council flat . . . and that always means children. The people that live there call it "Sleepy Valley": you'll probably find Little-Lena and Roy running around like gypsies.' Having opened up Dick's origins, Mrs Wiltshire gave Georgia fair warning of what she was letting herself in for.

Next morning was Saturday. Georgia took the first train and was in London for nine o'clock.

Grandmother Wiltshire lived in a flat, one of a dozen or more blocks the like of which had no parallel in Markham. 'Sleepy Valley' had no traffic, except vans selling fruit and groceries, and hokey-pokey carts: consequently the entire area was used as a playground. As Georgia's Cuban heels clicked from the bus stop, she became aware of the noise of children. Scores of them playing, swinging, climbing. It seemed to Georgia that the tenants, this morning with doors open and radios playing, couldn't help but live in one another's pockets. No wonder Little-Lena and Roy would not want to go back to their quiet, tidy isolation in Station Avenue.

She found Dick Wiltshire's mother outside her flat on the third floor, standing with a group of women who did not, as would Markham neighbours in the presence of a private letter and family business, move discreetly away, but who read Dick's letter over Mrs Wiltshire's shoulder and called Georgia Dearie.

'Well, Dearie, I don't blame Gertie's son for taking the kids back.'

'I cou'nt never understand what they want to come and stay up The Smoke for when there's all open fields dahn South.'

'We was just waiting now to see the coaches go by. All going South to the country.'

A rush of brown, untidy, grubby children raced one another up the stairwell to be the first to tell breathlessly, 'They're coming, they're coming!' It took Georgia a while to realize that two of the dirty faces were those of Little-Lena and Roy, browner and more animated and assertive than she had ever seen them in Markham. Little-Lena had a great doorstep of bread and jam, Roy's face showed evidence of having already eaten his. Having brought the news, they all hurtled themselves back down the concrete stairs and raced to the end of the road and lined up as though to watch a carnival go by.

Then the coaches came.

Women in aprons and Dinky curlers came out of every flat and leaned over the balcony railings; then the men emerged in vests and braces and stood in doorways with folded arms. From the vantage-point on the third-floor top, Georgia got her first sight of the evacuation of some of the children of London. As she watched, it dawned upon her that, although war had not yet been declared, it had begun – not with gun-fire, but with separation, bewilderment and misery. And had started on the most vulnerable section of the population.

The council-flat children, with whom Little-Lena and Roy were standing, cheered and waved as coach after coach after coach went towards the Great West Road. Georgia Kennedy had never seen anything so awful and so moving as that endless parade of coaches and the cheering, happy, dirty, 'Sleepy Valley' children who, with the exception of Little-Lena and Roy, would within days themselves be hurtled away along the Great West Road or the Great North Road away from these rampant playgrounds surrounded by the open-doors which could no longer promise sanctuary or security. They would not understand who had betrayed them, or why.

She was as oblivious to her immediate surroundings as were the parents and grandparents amongst whom she now stood watching. Her throat was too stricken to swallow, tears welled and blurred her vision, brimmed and fell on to her smart, marina-blue crêpe dress, staining it irretrievably. The children began to return to the asphalt areas as soon as they were sure that the show was over.

Somebody further along the third-floor balcony blew their nose and broke the spell, and Georgia realized that it was not only herself, not only the women whose eye-sockets were wet; men too were surreptitiously cuffing their eyes.

A child shouted up, 'Dere was a 'undred firty-four.'

Whether she had counted correctly did not matter, Georgia thought, as she went into Gertie Wiltshire's flat to pack the children's things: even one coach-load of miserable, bewildered children leaving their homes because of war was too many.

At a Top-Secret location, known as Badger Island, just off the coast of Southern England, the afternoon of the Saturday when his wife was standing in a queue on Waterloo Station, Hugh Kennedy lay upon the narrow bed of a fellow officer, with his arms behind his head, waiting for the balloon to go up. Not a fellow Army officer, but a Naval type.

Hugh Kennedy was well and truly in the Army, and he loved it and thanked whatever god it was who had stirred up a war and then pointed at the ex-Terric. If one compared the insignias on the two uniform jackets hanging behind the door, the rank of the Naval officer was a touch higher than

Hugh's. But, with the formation of the hush-hush combined-force Arsix 'outfit', neither rank nor service seemed to matter too much amongst the officer class: such divisions appeared to have melded or been thrown overboard in the cause of making themselves into an effective outfit.

As he watched his fellow Arsix officer getting dressed, Hugh Kennedy thought that he had never been so satisfied with life. So absolutely . . . *satisfied* – there was no other word for it – in his entire life.

It had been a revelation to him.

There was something about being confined on this small island that seemed to break down barriers: not so far broken that the officers mixed entirely with the other ranks but, even here, there was a certain feeling of 'all in this together' – saluting had become little more than 'Hi there' with the fingers. Only the top brass and the boffins knew what Arsix was and what eventually would be going on here. Top brass kept well away and the boffins hadn't arrived yet.

For the present, it was life in God's Own Army for Hugh. Smiling and watching, and smoking a cigarette, he pondered upon the good fortune and the amazing sift-out of statistics that had brought him here. 'One thing I've never been, and that's a snob. No cricketer could ever be a snob. I've always been a good mixer. You have to be, all banged up together on a place like "Badger".'

He stretched luxuriously, pleased that he was in his prime. The Naval type smiled at the great sigh Hugh let out and went on dressing quietly. Where else, except on Badger Island, would one ever find an off-duty Army captain lying back on an August afternoon on the bed of a Naval officer whilst watching amazingly dark underarm hair disappear within the armhole of an immaculate white Naval shirt – and drinking whisky-soda.

'What used you to do on a Saturday afternoon? In the days before you became a lay-about Army Nabob?'

For a second, Hugh's conscience threatened to spoil the perfection of the day with thoughts of Georgia having to struggle with the lawn-mower whilst he was swanning around drinking whisky and wearing nothing but his tan. But the strange ambience of Badger Island – and the impression when he was over there of being beyond any life that was being lived, or had ever been lived; beyond where the sea broke on the South Coast, broke on the shores of England; that limbo, where there was as yet no war or XJ-R6 Establishment – salved any qualms of guilt that might otherwise have concerned Hugh.

'Play cricket . . . rugger.'

'You still play rugger?'

'I'm not *that* old.'

Hugh watched the Naval type rolling neat shirt sleeves to just above the elbow. 'If it hadn't been for being in the Terries, I think I should have liked the Navy.'

'What you mean is that you would have liked wearing the uniform. It is rather good.' Hugh envied the cut-glass, upper-class voice that spoke of breeding and money. As well as having achieved his ambition of becoming a time-serving Army officer, Hugh was in his seventh heaven living in such close and familiar proximity to this sort of class – actually rumpling its sheets, drinking its booze.

'I don't deny it. I'm very fond of white cotton shirts: always love going out for cricket or tennis in freshly pressed whites.'

'Puritanism and erotic suggestion of virginity. Powerful aphrodisiacs.'

He thought, with a little bit of regret, of the years he had wasted with Georgia, wasted because of his puritanical upbringing. The fault of having an inexperienced girl as a wife, an old man for a father, an old vicar, who would have been happier if little boys could have had their flies sewn up. The times he had brushed aside Georgia's tentative erotic suggestions because he had felt so embarrassed . . . so bloody *guilty*. God, how different it all seemed now that he had got away.

The Naval officer, now immaculately uniformed, came to Hugh and whipped the thin sheet away from his loins.

'Up, Kennedy. God, just look at the state of you! Have you no shame, lying there in full sail fifteen minutes before you are due on parade? Get yourself a cold shower.'

Looking at his state, Captain Kennedy grinned, and was not visited by his father – as he might have been had he not been on Badger Island where things were different. Where he had learned how the other half lived – and loved.

He reached out and put his hand up her skirt.

'Tut, tut, Wren Officer St John, you could find yourself on a charge of going on duty improperly dressed. As my mother would have said, What would people think if you were in an accident?'

'Do you know what my mother would have said? Be ready for anything – you never know your luck.' She picked up her bag and hat.

Hugh said, 'If you dare to put on that hat whilst you are still within my sight and range, I shall not be accountable for my actions.'

'Cold shower, Captain – and that's an order!'

He raised his whisky-glass to her. 'Any further orders, Ma'am.'

'Report for the night-watch here at oh-one hundred hours. And this time bring your own bottle.' At the door, the very lovely young Wren, whose complexion, lips and hair would outdo any Snow-White, pushed her hat over one eye and took up a stance like a tart, before she marched smartly to her office where for the entire period of her duty one might have felt convinced that the butter would not have had a chance of melting in her mouth. But then, the Hon. Angela's mouth was not her hottest part.

* * *

Marie Partridge never received letters which her husband did not know about.

This one, received this morning, stood behind the Queen Mary clock, as a source of friction. Marie had received from the MCN & ELF(P) an official offer, signed by G. Kennedy (Administrator), of a position as full-time kitchen worker. Ever since she opened it that morning, Charlie had been distant and sullen. That was not a surprise: they had already had one row in which the hot words which had been exchanged had not yet cooled.

He had said, 'Who's going to do the washing and cleaning then if you go traipsing off out every morning?'

Traipsing had annoyed Marie, so she had snapped back, 'Perhaps we could each do our own. And I'll tell you what, you'd have three times as much as me and Bonnie put together.'

And then it became ridiculous. 'And I'd have more towels than anybody else too, I suppose,' he had said.

'Not more, just dirtier, and you'd have to boil them.'

'Perhaps I'll stop doing the garden then.'

'You'd miss that before I should.'

At which point he had snatched up his sandwiches and gone off on his bike – presumably to the allotment. Now he was much later back than he usually was on a Saturday evening.

Marie was determined that she would not let Charlie browbeat her into turning down this job as he had browbeaten her about the Saturday hairdressing job, just to satisfy his stupid pride. Even so, she wished she hadn't got into that stupid row, especially on a day like today, when everybody was on tenter-hooks waiting to see what would happen. She had spent the day sewing black-out curtains for their house and Charlie's parents', and it had come home to her how silly they had been, when tomorrow the country could be at war.

I won't do anything to rile him. Charlie can often be

jollied into doing something, but he never liked to have the law laid down. He could lay the law down himself, but that was different. Anyway, if Chamberlain declares war tomorrow, then Charlie won't be able to say anything: women like me will be expected to pull their weight.

She heard his bike scrape through the back gate, and Bonnie running across her bedroom to call to him from the window. 'Come up and kiss me goodnight, Daddy.'

'All right, Bon, give us a chance to wash my hands.'

'And read me Worzel Gummidge.'

'We'll see.'

'You promised.'

When Marie heard him put the bags of vegetables down on the draining-board, she stopped treadling the sewing machine and went out into the kitchen.

'Oh, lovely little beetroots. They look as tender as mushrooms, Charlie.' Cheerfully. 'Shall I do a couple for your supper?'

'If you like.' Politely.

Neutral tone. Charlie could never be blamed for starting an argument: all you had to do was go along with his ideas and do things his way.

'Beets and a bit of ham and lettuce do you?'

'Oh yeah, that'd be fine – and a tomato.'

He washed his hands carefully, scrubbing and rinsing off every vestige of soil, and dried them on the roller-towel, whilst Marie put the beets on to cook.

'Won't be more than half an hour.'

'I'll go up and read Bonnie her story.'

As he passed her, she smelt beer on his breath, which meant that he had called into the four-ale bar of the King William where his Dad would always be on a Saturday evening. Of course, Sam would have had to be consulted about the letter.

As Marie consulted Dolly.

And hadn't Dolly said, Just stick to your ground with Charlie?

'Tell him you're going to do it and don't budge. Don't raise your voice or he'll only accuse you of going for him. Just don't let him put you down, Marie, and you know that I'll stick by you. He's got his union when it comes to demanding his rights; we haven't got nobody except ourselves, so we have to stick together.'

Marie let Charlie eat his supper and get his belly nice and full. The silence in the small kitchen was filled with the sound of the wireless. They sat, as they often did on summer evenings, with the back door propped open so that they could look into Charlie's beautifully-kept garden.

'It looks lovely, Charlie.'

'Needs syringing again: this hot weather and one or two drops of rain at night brings the greenfly on something awful. I'll have to do half the allotment again tomorrow, and the water-butt is getting low.'

'I'll do the back-garden if you like.' Suddenly, she felt sorry for him. Charlie was such a good man really. He was always cheerful. She and Bonnie had never wanted for a single thing. He never looked at another woman, nor ever would – that Marie was sure about. He was scathing about men who wasn't faithful, and women who went off the rails were worse than scum in his eyes. There wasn't a person in the whole of Markham who could utter a bad word about her husband. She had never loved anybody but Charlie Partridge.

If anybody had a good marriage, then they had. It was just that there were times when she was so *bored*, so fed up to the teeth with looking after everything. Not people, but things. Polishing the same bits of furniture, scrubbing the same lino, dusting the same picture-rail till she could scream or burst into tears at the monotony of it. It wasn't as if anybody would notice half the time if it wasn't done.

'All right then, thanks, it will save me.'

Marie hoped that he realized that she wasn't capitulating

over the job. She was determined now to accept. It was nothing to do with anything Dolly had said, it was that Marie had realized that if she was stopping home putting beeswax on wood as a sop to Charlie's manly pride, then it was time she stopped doing it.

'Your Dad was right, wasn't he, Charlie? He always said there wasn't going to be no "Peace in our Time".'

'A course he was right. That was a lot of bull. I don't know what they been mess-assin' about for. Sooner we're in, the sooner it will be over.'

She felt that he was avoiding looking at her. She could read Charlie Partridge like a book. Probably Sam had been putting him up to something.

'Do you think it will all be over by Christmas?'

'Can't see how it can be.'

'Charlie?' She put her hand over his. 'Let me take this job. Please. There's going to be a war and I want to do my bit like the rest. I won't let this place go downhill, you know that – I think too much of our home to let it go. But let me have the job, Charlie.'

She felt his knuckles tighten, but he did not pull away. He continued to look beyond the geraniums, lobelia and Little Dorrit in a hanging-basket by the back door, down the path bordered by roses to the hundred square feet of perfect grass surrounded by flowers and shaded by a pear tree.

The best garden in Oaklands Road, everybody knew that.

It wasn't only that Charlie Partridge had better working hours than most men and had time to garden, but that he loved every crumb of earth and every leaf and petal that grew there. He almost loved every greenfly for having the cheek to defy him. 'I'm sorry, you little buggers, but you should have gone and sucked somebody else's roses.'

He moved his hand from beneath hers, then, after a moment's hesitation whilst he tapped his fingertips on the table, he put his hand over hers and squeezed it.

'I'm sorry, Marie. I really am bloody sorry.' His voice was husky and she thought that he sounded as though he was close to tears.

'I wouldn't neglect the home, Charlie.'

He shook his head. 'I means sorry about the mess this country got itself in. It's a lot of our own fault. People should have listened to people like my Dad. I never really listened. You'd think that a chap whose father had his legs and bits blown off would have had such a lesson shoved under his nose that he'd have moved heaven and earth to see it didn't happen again.'

'Oh Charlie, people like us aren't to blame for wars. We can't do anything.'

'We all got a vote.'

'It wasn't much good giving women the vote if the men wasn't prepared to give us equality. People need self-respect, and if women have to get permission from their husbands to run their own lives, they won't ever get it.'

He started to say something, but she did not wait. 'It's like Bonnie. She thinks she's princess of Markham – because we tell her she is. She's clean and tidy, she gets good food and everybody in the family tells her she's clever and pretty and asks her what she's been doing at school and listens to her read. No wonder she thinks she's the princess.'

Marie was surprised at herself. She had often thought of herself speaking up like this though usually it was just a daydream after she had been to one of Sam's Party meetings.

'She's grown up like that, believing herself. If she was like one of Gladys Dotrice's little girls, you couldn't say, "You're a princess." They know they aren't, you know they aren't. They're too poor, too used to getting the dirty end of the stick, too often told they aren't anybody. Women got the vote, but men have gone on telling them that they aren't fit to have it. Not in so many words, but in things like telling them their place is in the home.' She paused for a few moments, but Charlie said nothing. 'Maybe it is, Charlie, maybe it isn't, but it is for us women to decide. Not men.'

'You're probably right, Marie. You usually are.' What else could he say when he was trying to find a way to tell her that, without consulting her, he had that day signed up in the RAF?

'Anyway, this time tomorrow, we shall probably be at war.' He nodded towards their view of the garden, at its best with the sun's rays catching it obliquely, gilding white flowers, subduing the reds. 'Take a good look at it, Marie, it won't be there much longer. It'll have to all go down to vegetables. The lawn will have to go.'

'No, Charlie, not your lawn.'

Sam Partridge came home from the King William much earlier than usual that evening. Dolly was sitting in the yard crocheting a pale pink bolero for Bonnie, to go with her new school dress, when she heard the controlled tread of his slow artificial feet. Inexplicably, on Saturdays, he came and went via the front door. Without needing to see, she now followed his familiar pattern of movements as he hung his coat on a hanger and hooked it behind the living-room door, took a glass from the sideboard, rummaged in the kitchen drawer for the opener, hissed open her bottle of Guinness and added a dash of Sandeman's port.

He came into the yard and handed her her Saturday night Guinness.

'Cheers.'

'Good health.'

On winter evenings, she would say cheers, and he would reply Good Health as they settled beside the range which would have its top open to reveal the red glow of a good fire. This evening he sat on the stump of what had once been a great plum tree when the Estate had been an orchard.

Dolly waited. He trailed resentment, a prickly humour that might have been brought on by anything: from somebody at the King William playing a dubious hand at cards, to ancient injustice towards his class.

Sometimes, his mood could be lightened by inconsequential gossip.

'Who was round at the William?'

'Only the usual. Charlie dropped in for ten minutes, says he's going to start making an air-raid shelter in the morning – in the cellar.'

'I wondered if he might.'

'He says his lawn will have to go down to vegetables.'

'That's criminal.'

'There'll be worse crimes than that before this lot's over.'

'That don't mean people like our Charlie should give up a thing like that lawn of his. There won't be nowhere for Bonnie to play.'

Sam poured himself a glass of the draught he had brought home from the King William, held it up to the light, then drank, savouring the pale brew.

Dolly said, 'Harry says he's going to make one for us.'

'One what?'

'Air-raid shelter.'

'Oh, is he! He never said anything to me.'

'I don't suppose he thought there was anything to say. I dare say he thought you'd be pleased.'

'I'm surprised he thinks he'll have the time. Where's he gone this evening?'

Dolly guessed the reason for his mood. Either somebody at the pub, whistling down the wind of their own problems, had made a blue joke that had hit home at Sam's impotence, or he had seen Harry with his new girlfriend.

Dolly thought, Anybody'd think it was my fault Harry got all his 'coutrements, and Sam haven't.

'I don't know, I think he's gone dancing in Southampton.'

'Is that right he's getting about with that new blonde bit of goods come to work at the Post Office? I don't need to ask – she's just the type. My God, the way she gets herself up – that much make-up plastered on her face, you could stick her to a wall. But there, Harry wasn't never very fussy, any bit of skirt that isn't nailed down and he's there lifting it. Only thing surprises me about him, is that he haven't got some girl up the stick.'

'You don't have to be coarse at home, Sam. He's your son. Don't you want him to build a shelter?'

'It don't matter much what I wants – if Harry says he's going to do it, and you agree with Harry, then we shall get a shelter.'

'Why are you always down on Harry, Sam?'

'Down on him? A course I'm not down on him. You say some blimmin stupid things sometimes, Dolly.'

'Well, don't be always criticizing him. He's done well for himself. What other lad off this estate got a scholarship and then a job in the Council offices – what more do you want?'

'I don't want anything more.'

'You do. He's always tried to please you. He's been trying all his life to get you to say, well, that's really good, Harry, I'm proud of you; and all you ever been able to say is that you know he's capable of being top.'

'That's a compliment, it's saying I think there isn't nobody better than him – if you had sense enough to see it. He's got so much in him, he could do anything he set his mind to.'

'Then why don't you tell him that sometimes. He might not need to prove hisself in other ways.'

'Harry knows what I think about him, you don't have to slobber over your kids to let them know things like that.'

'Nobody's asking you to slobber.'

Self-satisfaction at not having the last word, and having given vent to his irritable mood, the spark of animosity that had flared up between them went out, and they returned to their normal state of rubbing along together.

'I'll talk to him in the morning about where to start

digging. Two bloody legs and one bloody ball, Dolly – half a man, just when you could have done with a man and a half.'

'You haven't heard me complain, have you?'

Harry Partridge, having walked the new girl from the Post Office to the end of her lane where there were no streetlights, kissed her goodnight, long and open-mouthed, and remained holding her close. Having already investigated on the dance floor the fastening of her sleeveless top, he deftly slid his hand inside the opening.

'Mmm, your skin's like satin,' he said.

'I enjoyed the dance, Harry, I'd heard you were a good dancer.'

'I heard about you, too,' he said with a playful suggestiveness in his tone, and a friendliness in his casually moving hand.

His voice had a husky, silken quality, with little trace left of his working-class background. His looks matched his voice. He dressed well and was very good-looking, with fair hair, full, warm mouth and wholesome teeth. But it was not merely his voice and appearance that made him so attractive to women: he had, as had Freddy Hardy, a quality that was indefinable, charm plus sex appeal.

'Oh yes?' she said archly. 'And what's that you heard?'

'That you're a good sport.'

They were the young people of the Twenties generation. Nurtured on plenty of Hollywood, they learned to light cigarettes two at a time, drive with one arm round a woman, play hard-to-get whilst panting, and to flirt using double entendre. 'Is that so?' she said. 'Well, if it was a game of tennis you wanted, you should have brought your sports gear.' Her voice, too, had forsaken its roots, as had her accent its class, and her hair its dowdy colour. Like Harry Partridge, she was making herself.

He took off his jacket. 'We don't need anything special to

have a bit of a scratch single game.' He kissed her again, this time slickly achieving the lowering of her shoulder straps.

'You're a fast worker, aren't you, Harry?'

'Sorry. I'm not usually like this. It's just that I've never been out with a girl like you. You're a damned lot of fun, you know.'

'You are a liar, Harry,' she said genially. 'You've been out with every girl in Markham. But I liked going out with you.'

'That's what I'm saying. It's as though I've been searching. There isn't one to touch you. I've wanted to ask you ever since you first came to Markham.' He covered her mouth with his own, and so stopped any riposte that might hit a true note.

She pulled away from him. 'Hey, come up for air.'

'Deanna – you're wonderful! You aren't just a lovely face, and good fun, you've got all the rest.' His passion showed as he ran his hands over her body. He felt the signals of her response, and knew that she would be a good sport.

'I don't know what you've heard, but I'm not a push-over, you know. Everybody thinks that blondes are.'

'I know you're not, I know. I wouldn't want a girl who was.'

'Then stop that and be patient.'

'How can I stop? You don't want me to.'

She made a good gesture at protest, pulling up a shoulder strap. 'Not on the first date, Harry. Now kiss me goodnight properly and maybe we'll go out again.' She trilled a little laugh. 'Maybe fix up a game of tennis.'

'I thought girls comforted men on the eve of battle.'

'Eve of battle, my eye. The war hasn't even started yet. The only battle round here is the one I've been fighting the last ten minutes.'

He let his voice fall into deeper huskiness. 'I'm serious, Deanna. My folks don't know yet, but I enlisted in the army today.'

'The army? I should have thought Air Force blue would have suited you better.'

'I've joined the Paras.'

'Oh Harry, the red berets. But that means you'll be going away before we've even had a proper chance to get to know one another.'

'Then don't let's waste precious time. I love you, Deanna.'

Walking home whistling. Thinking.

She was a really good sport, one of the sort who told a man what to do. It was so enjoyable doing it with a woman who wasn't coy, who would guide your hands and say when it was right. I thought for a second I wasn't going to be quick enough. He remembered the tales of men who had found themselves with a wife and child for hanging on for just that second too long.

For two pins she would have gone all the way. His stomach clenched at the thought of being caught like that. I wonder what Dad will find wrong with the Paras? Thank God for putting girls like Deanna on the world. Idly thinking of the women he'd had and imagining those still to come, he became aroused. I shan't risk doing it like that again, it isn't worth it for one and six. For the two-mile walk home, Harry Partridge had mature thoughts on pleasuring women like Deanna and the making of a more satisfying love. And on his father's assured displeasure with something about the Parachute regiment.

1939

2nd September

The BBC news on the wireless was the final straw. The reality of what was happening flooded upon her. When Hugh had left, she had been lighthearted at the prospect of being herself again. Freedom, she had thought, a little bit of freedom.

When she had received her appointment from the Ministry, it was elation at getting such a post. And again she had felt excitement at the prospect of becoming somebody, no longer only a housewife. Hugh's weekend soldiering with the Territorials had been like his going out with any of the Sports Club teams – boys going off for the weekend. Suddenly it was all in earnest. Overnight Georgia Kennedy's world had changed.

At nine o'clock, with the sun just going down, she sat in her garden. Little-Lena and Roy, pale and wide-eyed after the stressful, arduous journey from London, had been reunited with their parents. As a treat for herself, Georgia had bought a hundred box of Du Maurier and a bottle of gin, both of which she was consuming settled in a big basket chair.

One of the bedroom windows next door was pushed up and Little-Lena's quiet little voice said, 'Mrs Kennedy?'

Georgia looked up. 'Lena?'

'I just wanted to say goodnight, Mrs Kennedy.'

Georgia waved at the girl, and was moved by her vulnerable appearance, her newly-washed combed-down hair, scrubbed look and clean, pressed pyjamas. She was such a good kid today, thought Georgia, I'd never really noticed her before. 'Ready for bed, Lena?'

'Yes. Roy's already asleep. I'm not tired.'

'Really? I should have thought you were worn out. Perhaps you're a bit overtired.'

'I'm glad I can't sleep. Dad said the same as you, that we had to come home from London because there will probably be a war in the morning.'

Georgia had never felt at ease with children, not knowing, until today, in what language to address them. From Little-Lena she had learned that children were no more difficult than an adult if you spoke normally. 'Your Dad was right to get you out of London. I should think Markham will be safe enough.'

'Dad's going to tell Grandma Gertie to come and live with us.'

'Won't that be nice for you – and her?'

Mary Wiltshire's voice was heard faintly from within the house.

'That's Mum, I'd better go in now. I'm not going to go to sleep though. I want to remember today. I expect tomorrow will feel different.'

'Goodnight then, Lena.' She had a sudden urge to kiss the clean, eager face of the girl and tell her that she had been a good kid today.

'Goodnight, Mrs Kennedy.' She pulled the window down to within a few inches of the sill, then added through the opening, 'Mrs Kennedy? Thank you. I'm glad it was you came to London.'

'Oh no, it's thank *you*, Lena, for being such a help and not complaining in all that crowd.' She blew the girl a kiss at which Lena put her own hand to her lips but shyly turned away without completing the action.

When she lit another cigarette, Georgia found that her hand was trembling and aching. It was as though she could still feel the clutch of Roy's fingers and the weight of their case and bags, with Lena struggling to help, as the three of them had made their way by every sort of crowded public transport across London and then home.

As she and the children had pushed their way, it had seemed as though she tuned in to the tension of other passengers: servicemen with full kit and new uniforms; people with clumps of labelled children; men shepherding their families on to trains; all of them, as she was herself, concentrating on their own immediate harassment. At Waterloo Station, she imagined that she could hear a kind of silent whine from all those outwardly controlled people who were fleeing in all directions. In the moments between talking to the children with calm assurance, she had clenched her teeth and gripped the case so tightly that her fingernails had left weals in her palms.

She was wondering whether to go indoors when the front doorbell rang. It took a second for it to register with Georgia that the long-legged caller in AFS uniform was Nick Crockford.

'Oh Nick! It's you.'

'Here.' He handed her a bunch of dahlias. 'I thought you'd like them. Grew them myself.'

'What lovely colours.' She took the flowers from him.

'You always liked them.'

'But not you. You only used to grow them for competition.'

He had brought her just such a bunch after her engagement was announced.

'I'm a primrose man. You know . . . full of hope.'

The memory of dahlias came back. When her engagement to Hugh was announced, Nick had picked every perfect bloom with which he had expected to win county prizes and had brought her the entire magnificent crop. She had pretended, and so had he, that it was just a bunch of flowers. It was not. And, knowing Nick, neither was this.

The lessons in politeness drummed into her by her mother – who had spent some years in service and knew the ways of polite society –came to the fore and covered her confusion. Don't keep callers standing at the door. Don't let the neighbours know your business. Politeness costs nothing. Always give visitors a name and a chair. She seemed to have little choice.

'Would you like to come in?'

He stepped into the hall, ducking his head to miss the porch-lantern.

The hall was an awkward place to be with an old flame. The sitting-room wasn't the place, neither was the living-room. 'I was just in the garden having a drink. Do you want one?'

'Why not?'

'I've only got gin and tonic, I'm afraid.'

'Just gin.'

She poured gin, he took it from her, went to the tap and added a dash of water.

'Do you want to bring it outside? There's another chair in the shed.'

'I'll be all right on the grass. It's warm. There'll be a storm in a few hours, though.' He removed his AFS jacket, then sat down beside her rolling his glass between his large hands. 'Nice place you've got. It's the first time I've ever been inside one of these houses, never realized they had such long gardens. It's nice out here.'

Georgia realized that it was indeed very nice out here, sitting beside a second flush of scented bourbon roses, their perfume hanging heavy on the still air, pink blooms glistening in the purple gloam and still humming with late bees using up the last bit of daylight.

'We don't use it that much: gardening's always been a bit of a chore to Hugh. I do a bit myself.'

'I shouldn't have thought there was enough here to keep anybody busy more than a couple of weekends a year.'

'Hugh never gets the time . . . cricket all summer . . .'

'Ah well, it would be, with a bit of tennis thrown in, and rugby in the winter, I suppose. Still the dedicated sportsman is he? I always thought he wore his whites as though he was going in for Hampshire. Not that he wasn't a good wicket-keeper – solid as a rock.'

She held out her hand for his empty glass, which he handed over without demur. She went into the kitchen and brought out a tray with gin, water and lemon slices. He was walking along the border looking closely at the rambling roses and clematis, hands in pockets as though in his own garden. Not that the Crockfords had ever had a garden as such but, like a lot of country families – like her own family too – they had a bit of land of their own. An acre or so on which there came and went, each in its season, every kind of edible plant and animal that would provide a meal or turn a sovereign at Markham market.

'Bit of greenfly. I should have thought he was in the right place to get everything he wants for the garden . . . sprays and that.'

She inspected a rose-bud. 'I'll get the syringe out tomorrow and give them a go over.'

At another level, Georgia was thinking that it was a peculiar conversation to be having with an old boyfriend who appears suddenly with a bunch of flowers. But then, it had always been like that with Nick, who could rouse himself from a silence and suddenly say, apropos of nothing, 'Did you know that there are these mushrooms in Mexico that can make people have visions. I should like to try that.' He had been a spontaneous and quirky boy – which was why she had always paired off with him rather than with the lads who thought they could make an impression by larking about and talking dirty. Nick was always different, interesting. Living with only his war-shocked father, he often went about only casually physically cared for, but always mentally groomed and well-fed.

Now they returned slowly to where the chair and tray on an empty flower barrel were awkwardly set out as for an amateur theatre production. He lowered himself on to the grass and lounged there as easily.

Georgia felt too formal sitting on a chair, so she too sat on the grass. Asked, 'How is your father these days?'

'Having a bit of a rough time . . . you know, the war. Brings it all back.'

'I saw he had a letter in *The Times*.'

He raised his brows in interest. 'The one supporting the Peace Women? It was a good letter – won't do any good though. One man against the tide. This country's got the fever, war looks too exciting and profitable.'

'Still thinking of going in for politics when you grow up?'

He snapped a look at her and, seeing that she was smiling, smiled too. 'That's the trouble, I grew up and found it wasn't worth the candle. How's Mr and Mrs Honeycombe getting on in Scotland?'

'Your guess is as good as mine. They say they like it, my Dad says they'll only come South again in their boxes. But of course you can't really tell from letters – they always were good at putting a face on things.'

'Right. Everybody thought they enjoyed keeping the pub, thought they were fixtures.'

'I know, but Ma hated it. She . . .'

He joined in, grinning '. . . thought it was common.'

Georgia laughed. 'You know my Ma, always afraid of behaving common.'

'The eighth deadly sin to Mrs Honeycombe – Behaving Common.'

He shook his head at her offer of a cigarette, but snapped the lighter and held the flame for hers, then inspected the lighter with interest. It had been his Christmas present to her years back. Before he returned it, he held it briefly in the cup of his hand, then ran his thumb over the ornate 'G.H.' he had paid sixpence extra to have engraved.

Her present to him had been a Parker Pen which he had used to draw hearts on each of their wrists. What with having started to smoke, and their exchange of expensive gifts, they had felt very grown up. They had exchanged their first open-mouthed kiss. Now, threatened with confusion at the memory, she inhaled deeply and blew a stream of smoke at the sky, glad that in the growing darkness he would not see the flush of her cheeks. Why has he come?

A memory of other times when they had been on the verge of falling in love, when they had lounged like this on grass, when they had sat like this with Nick suddenly going silent, withdrawing into his own thoughts as the rest of the gang of girls and youths were giggling and laughing.

A memory too of how she used to be aroused by him. He was the first one who had, when they were both hardly out of childhood: not by fumbling hands or awkward kissing, nor as later on with Hugh – Hugh went in for close-holding, back-bending, stylish tango-dancing and hard, dry kissing. Nick could arouse her with some simple but erotic touch. Perhaps as the gang walked home along the dark lanes. That first time was when they were all larking about by the summer river, he had lifted the long pigtail she wore and had run his tongue in the groove at the nape of her neck damp from swimming. And once, when they were resting from pea-picking he had . . . Even as she thought of it her thighs tightened . . . he had suddenly buried his face in her lap and then said some lines of a sonnet in his ordinary voice, as though quoting poetry was an ordinary thing.

She stole a quick glance at the profile of his hanging head with its beautiful thick curls worn longer than men had worn since the Prussian look took on. Nick Crockford's hair had always been something for her mother to latch on to when she could find no other fault with him – I know what I'd do if he was my lad . . . have that lot off straight away.

He had always been different. Difficult. Unpredictable.

He wasn't a suave and dashing sportsman like Hugh, nor did he have a safe, white-collar job like Hugh. Nick was a brown and weathered, large-fisted, broad-shouldered road-mender who, like his strange, intelligent, reclusive father was capable of doing whatever he chose in life. He had chosen to live as he preferred, doing physical work in the open air.

And so had Georgia chosen – to live a very different life from his.

They did not speak for a minute or two. Not an awkward silence, but an easy air of quiet between them.

If she had found him attractive then, she found him ten times more attractive as a grown man.

As Georgia listened to his breathing and watched his shoulder-blades rise and fall, desire, sparked off by the memories, spread up through her until she found her breathing shortened. Half-formed thoughts threw her into as much panic as they had when she was growing up. At a time when her Ma had said, 'Nick Crockford is no use to somebody like you, Georgia – tell her I'm right, Thomas.'

'Your mother is right, sweetheart, the Crockfords of this world don't never amount to much.'

'You've only got to look at his father to see that.'

Feigning a shiver, she rose to her feet. 'It gets really chilly once the sun goes down. Will you mind bringing in that chair, Nick?'

She tells herself that she shouldn't have drunk so much gin. But knows that she would feel the same without the gin. She knows it, but does not like to admit it. Throughout her marriage it has been Nick she thinks of when Hugh's body semaphores his desire, Nick she caresses, Nick's weight pressing down on her in the dark. Nick who wears Hugh's tweed jacket in the fantasy of making love in the afternoon. Nick who suddenly appears in her fantasies to make the kind of love Georgia desires and which she may not speak of to Hugh for he would be shocked at such excess in his lovely suburban housewife.

She knows why he has come, and suddenly feels afraid, and in danger of persuading herself, because they have both been abandoned by their partners, that it would be all right to sleep with him.

The same fear that she often felt before she met Hugh, when she and Nick used to go everywhere together. Fear of his seriousness, his way of making her face what she did not want to face – that she was like him, a peasant at heart, a country girl, the wild, wandering child that her parents had tried to smother with 'niceness', and piano lessons.

The Crockfords of this world never amount to much.

At the time, she had realized that if she did not get away from Emberley, she would find herself entangled in his life, find herself becoming like him, rejecting the things she was striving for: a car, a house in Markham, all sorts of dressy Sports Club dinners, pretty clothes, scent, and being somebody. She had not wanted to be a peasant, a country girl – had not wanted it then, or now.

'I think you'd better go, Nick. The neighbours don't miss much.'

'OK. The balloon goes up tomorrow, I'm being posted on Monday.'

'Nick! You mean in the forces? I thought you were a . . .'

'A Conchie?'

'Yes, you were always on about it.'

'I am. I'm going into the National Fire Service.'

'Oh.'

'Based at Southampton.'

'Southampton will be a dangerous place, won't it, with Fords and the docks? Mothers and children are already evacuating from there.'

'Not much point in having trained firemen in a safe place. At least I shan't be far away from here. I've got a room in Markham now, my landlady is going to keep it for me. Perhaps we could have a game of tennis when I get time off. Be like old times.'

Old and present times touched. Then she had found him

to be an absorbing youth – now she found him to be an exhilarating man. He began buttoning his uniform jacket.

'I wish . . .' She hesitated.

'Wish then.'

'I wish things had turned out differently.'

In the hallway he suddenly bent and kissed her gently, just missing her mouth. As the coarse serge cloth of his uniform brushed her bare arms, it was touch and go whether she returned the kiss.

But, instead of drawing Nick in, as she desired, she opened the front door and let him out, helped by her mother, Hugh and the thou shalt nots of her schooldays, for she was well aware that she could not kiss him frivolously – nor might it end there.

Whilst Europe was fast slipping towards war, Eve Hardy was driving out of Scotland where she had ostensibly been making a carefully manoeuvred visit to a girlfriend whose parents owned a hotel on the west coast.

Only Mont Iremonger, who had delivered letters with a Scottish stamp, might have guessed that she had other fish to fry in Scotland.

Late afternoon now, and she had been sitting and gazing at a signpost indicating that this village was Balmoral, after writing a view postcard to send home. At least, she thought, they can tell that I've been here. And then thought that they had no reason to believe otherwise. They trusted her. Guilt flushed over her. But it was their fault for being so snobbish, making her devious because she wanted to be with her boyfriend.

She had the car hood folded down. The day was so still and quiet that she could hear the sound of leaves as they fluttered their way through the twiggy trees and, although only just into September, she smelt autumn in the woodlands at the side of the road. An occasional car passed.

A game-bird gobbled, and then another. Oh come on, David, you're almost an hour late already.

She considered getting out to stretch her legs, but did not like to wander far from the car in case he should miss her. There was a telephone kiosk back up the road; perhaps she should ring his base. She longed to see him. But what if he has changed? What if I have? Perhaps he has found somebody else. Somebody he doesn't have to meet secretly. In a moment of panic, she could easily have turned on the engine and driven away. Instead, she opened up her wallet and looked at a small photo of him. Oh, he was so attractive, so smart and neat.

Kate, the girlfriend with whom she had been staying, had asked, 'How many serious men have you had, Eve?'

Eve had shown her the snapshot of David.

Kate had blown a smoky whistle. 'Go-to-bed eyes and a come-to-bed mouth. He's nice. Is he serious?'

'I met him when I was about sixteen. We were in the local carnival parade.'

Kate, still sounding like the girl she had been at their ladies college, shrilled, 'A carnival parade? Eve Hardy, I can't believe it.'

'Believe it. Everybody in Markham turns out for the carnival – the local hospital would close without that money.'

'All right, I believe you . . . so you were in the parade . . . ?'

'As the Gainsborough Lady – you know, the one who bows at the beginning of a Gainsborough film . . .'

Sophisticated. Amused. 'I said I believe you . . .'

'I was only sixteen, do you want to know about David or not? What happened was that the vehicle I was riding bust its radiator and I was stuck, and along came this beautiful young man on a big white horse – yes, a man on a white horse – there had been four horsemen of the Apocalypse, but David had got separated . . .'

'So he swept you up on to his steed and you rode together as Arthur and Guinevere.'

'You don't know how wonderfully romantic it was. It was like *The Sheik*. Kate Thompson! You have no sense of romance; you always did want to hear about dirty deeds.'

'You're a dark horse, Eve. An ice queen with a Latin temperament.'

Kate was nice, which made Eve feel very underhand at having used her as an excuse for this secret tryst with David.

Hearing the drone of a heavy motor, she started momentarily thinking it was the RN Stores lorry in which David was getting a lift, but it proved to be only a cattle lorry. They had arranged to meet here from where they could drive into Aberdeen. This entire holiday with Kate, with its half-truths and pretence, was centred around the climax in Aberdeen. Twenty-one and never slept with a man. It could be no other man but David: all her fantasies were focused upon him. For Eve Hardy, he was probably the most forbidden fruit in Markham – an ordinary seaman from the Station End of town. A local schoolboy, an uncultured accent and, according to her father, probably a Communist. He was, too, very good-looking, intelligent and most frankly masculine and sexual. It had been agonizing to have been sightseeing in Scotland, knowing that he was so near yet so far.

She had now been waiting an hour and forty-five minutes for him. She could never ring David direct, but he had a friend on the stores switchboard who passed messages. Again she was tempted to ring.

I will wait thirty more minutes. As soon as the time was up, she switched on the ignition and drove to the telephone kiosk.

It seemed ages as she waited for the burr-burring to be answered. The sun burned the glass of the box and heated the film of stale cigarette smoke upon it. The smell was sickening, so she leaned against the door to keep it open whilst she was passed from switchboard to various extensions, until at last she heard the cheerful voice of David's friend.

'Eve, lass, I've been hoping you'd ring before I go off duty. I'm that sorry. All leave's been cancelled. Davey's real upset, he wanted me to get a message to you, but you'd already left your hotel. Eh, lass, I'm sorry, Davey was so looking forward to seeing you. Are you still there?'

'Yes, I'm here.' Disappointment and the smell of the kiosk turned her stomach. 'Do you know where he's gone?'

'I can't tell you that, lass. I'm sorry, more than I dare do.'

'Can you get a message to him?'

'Aye, I can that.'

'Tell him to write to me care of Mrs Kennedy's office. He'll know where.'

Instead of going to Aberdeen to spend the night with her first lover, Eve Hardy turned her car south and drove right through the evening and the night.

Whilst she was driving south, Eve's father was supervising the storing of a cache of drums of petrol and oil in an old ruined cottage on the borders of his land.

'Freddy, don't you think that it is unpatriotic to hoard like that?'

'Unpatriotic my foot, Connie. I'm a long-sighted business man. Before this war's over, you'll be glad you're married to a man with foresight . . . friends in the right places.'

1989

Before the Boeing touched down at Palma, the young Afrikaner steward came to Georgia Giacopazzi holding her new paperback, *Flying High*, and asked her to sign it.

'Any message?'

'It's for my girl, Nel.'

It always was – always for my girl . . . for my wife . . . for my Mom.

'What is your name?'

'Piet.'

She wrote, conscious of the age spots on her hands, 'For Piet, *Eerste Offisie bediende* who flew Giacopazzi *ply na*. With love – Giacopazzi.'

'I have signed it for you. You must write the message for your girl.'

If it really was for his girl, then he could tell her that the message, 'First-class officer who flew Giacopazzi like an arrow, with love', was simply a personalized message. If not, then he would probably show the boys. The name Giacopazzi still meant something.

He read the message and looked pleased.

She said, 'My Afrikaans is not good, I'm afraid. Does it make sense?'

'I must tell my girl about your Afrikaans, or she might get the wrong idea.'

Georgia smiled up at him, 'turning on the Giacopazzi' as her agent put it. 'That would never do would it, Piet?'

In the waiting area at Palma, Mrs Giacopazzi, not wishing to strike up conversation with anyone and break her mood, drank iced bottled water and focused her attention upon a magazine.

Where had the Giacopazzi-ing sprung from? When I was young I was never conscious of turning on to anybody. Was I ever anybody but myself? Giacopazzi came after the first book. That had been a good, steady, readable tale. It had got enough reviews in places like Melbourne and Dublin for her publishers to find something to say on the jacket of her second. It was the second book, wasn't it, that had started the Giacopazzi legend?

Put the Blame on Eve.

Early Giacopazzi eroticism was to be found in *Blame*. Her publishers had hyped it up on the jacket with a pair of respectable though naked lovers, mouth to mouth at the remains of an apple. Undeservedly, *Blame*'s reputation for sexiness grew from a number of double meanings the author had not intended – at the time she had never heard of touching up, except in the restoration of paintwork context – and some Freudian images which she had. There were also a few typographical errors that were bizarre and funny. It was still read, but in the Eighties it was only a very mildly erotic book.

Mass-market readers began to expect Georgia Giacopazzi herself to be a femme fatale, seductress, sex symbol. And, to achieve her ambition to be rich, she had publicly become such. Even after she had turned fifty, the myths that surrounded her did not diminish. Nowadays, she had come to the conclusion that her age did not matter. Women loved her for the myth of agelessness that had grown up around her, and her assertion that it was good for women to express lust and desire, whilst men were aroused by her reputed extreme wealth and strings of young lovers: Giacopazzi at whatever age was a challenge – like Dietrich, Lenya, Collins.

The call to resume the flight to London roused her.

What in Hell's name will they make of me? 'They' being those women still alive, whose lives she had ransacked for *Eye of the Storm*; the women who had known her before she became Giacopazzi.

'Allow me.'

A too helpful arm encircled her waist to give her unnecessary and unwanted help up the steps of the aircraft.

'How sweet of you.'

'You're Georgia Giacopazzi, aren't you? My wife has read every one of your books.'

Until *Eye of the Storm* was in the bookshops, it was necessary to smile.

Momentarily, she was weary of the years of the hike, the hype and false front. For the first time since she had left, she longed for Markham, longed to turn the clock back to the eve of War, and leave it stopped at the time when she and Nick Crockford had sat on the grass in the garden of the old house in Station Avenue.

1939

3rd September

It is past midnight. The last day of peace in Britain is over.

Georgia Kennedy has left her bed where the pillow is wet with the tears that have released some of the stress of the eventful day. Resting her arms on the sill at the open window, she looks at Station Avenue where, until now, gaslights made yellow pools at night. Now, not a crack of light is permitted. The air is dry and hot, and the dark sky is lit very occasionally by the merest flicker of lightning, which is so far distant that the sound of thunder never does reach Markham.

As she has done for as long as she can remember, she tells herself a kind of story of what has happened during the day, keeps a kind of mental diary. She thinks of the coaches streaming out of London and wonders about the children who were in them, now in strange, frightening surroundings, sleeping in strangers' bedrooms where there are new night-time shadows in the cupboards. She tries to make order out of her experience – the drawn-faced parents on Waterloo Station evacuating their children privately. Middle-class voices, men in Anthony Eden hats, children in little clumps of grey and navy-blue serge. Why had those parents added stuffy school uniforms to their children's discomfiture? To create a good impression on the fostering parents? Would they give less care to children who travelled in cotton shorts or thin dresses? Mothers wearing straw plate hats, plenty of rouge and scarlet lipstick that had seemed to emphasize the false cheerfulness of their smiles. Children, labelled like game-hampers, being told lies.

'You will be quite all right, Deborah. Nanny Barnes will not forget to meet you.'

'I envy you, old chap. Lot of fun living in the country; you will simply love it – and Mama will visit. Chin up, we men don't cry, do we?'

'Just think how exciting it will be, Jack – Uncle Rollo says he will let you choose a pony if you're a real little man about this.'

Those children – hen-eyed with the knowledge of what happened to Hansel and Gretel, to the Babes in the Wood, and to the Princes in the Tower – were apprehensive of their parents' long smiles. Snow White's wicked stepmother had been as beautiful as their own smiling mother, hadn't she? Mrs Darling had left her children in the care of a dog; and the Water Babies . . . ?

Georgia feels, once again, Little-Lena and Roy clutching her hand tightly and that, seeing how the other children are being disposed of, they are now verging on the unthinkable – how do they know that Mrs Kennedy is not kidnapping them? Even so they cling to her because to be parted from that one familiar face amongst all those crowds would be worse. Waiting on the platform, Little-Lena asks Georgia, 'Mrs Kennedy? You know those mothers whose babies were killed by King Herod? Do you think that they ever had any other babies?'

A mine-field of a question. Georgia sees herself giving them coins to buy Nestlé's chocolate discs from the red machine on the platform. Now she wonders. Did they have other babies? And is Little-Lena reassured? And wonders too why she has taken so little notice of Little-Lena before yesterday.

Now that she has thought about the experience of London, she can allow herself to think of Nick.

Until tonight, Georgia Kennedy has shed few tears. From the window, she can see the pattern of a constellation and wishes that she knew which one it was. She knows that today was the end of her girlhood, end of that life which was given its expectations by her parents, by Hollywood movies, by Hugh's perfect tango and his Wolsey car, and by novels from Boots Library. Happy Ever After. The sunny housewife in her pretty green kitchen with its sprigged curtains, the golden-haired young wife of the cricket captain, the gins sipped in a summer garden surrounded by the scent of roses and philadelphus.

Until this evening, her cockleshell marriage to Hugh has kept afloat because the waters on which it sailed were calm. Nick's visit has whipped up white horses. Feeling the danger of being capsized, she longs to reach out to Nick and wonders now how she could have thought that marriage to Hugh and the sophistication of the Sports Club set was preferable to a haphazard life as Nick's woman.

Hugh had offered her his house, his status, his ability to tango and to come up with ace serves at tennis. Perhaps she should have looked up the true definition of sophistication before she discovered it from experience. Eighteen was no age for making life-long decisions about marriage.

Had she been only twenty, she would never for a moment have supposed that she was suited to the battle-loving Hugh Kennedy, after she had spent her youth knocking around with Nick Crockford, drifting in and out of romances with him. There were times during those youthful summers when she had felt that, had he said the word, she would have gone with him into the New Forest and lived rough and been a charcoal-burner or hurdle-maker and lived with him on birds' eggs and hedgehogs like the gypsies.

Now it's too late.

Before dawn, there came the first rattle of large raindrops followed soon by a steady downpour, cleaning and softening foliage, soaking into cracked and sun-baked fields, greening up tawny meadow-grass and sending up to open bedroom windows the scent of roses and wetted pavements. The chain of long, hot, dry weeks, when men's sinews have been dried and become tight thongs, and women have felt that their scalps were shrunken with the drought, was broken.

Georgia listens to the guttering rainwater, and wonders how she can bear to go on being married to Hugh, knowing now that she loves Nick and has never loved anyone else. But she will have to bear it, she is steeped in the thou shall nots and the solemnity of Christian marriage.

And you've only got to look at his father, Georgia.

1939

Sunday 3rd September

The abbey clock shows twelve-fifteen. Little-Lena Wiltshire walks slowly back from Greenaway's shop with the bag of sugar she has been sent for. Although she is only ten years old, she knows that, when she is an old lady like Grandma Gertie, she will be able to remember every detail of this day. It is Sunday morning and she has not slept since she awakened in Grandma Gertie's flat yesterday morning.

Mr Chamberlain, on the wireless, said that he had sent a note to the German Government and if they didn't answer it by eleven o'clock then 'a state of war would exist between us'. It was twelve o'clock and the Germans had not answered.

In her mind, Little-Lena saw Dad as he had been half an hour ago, his leg in plaster resting on a camping stool, and Mum leaning forward looking into the hole in the wireless where the sound came out, and Roy under the table fiddling with a magnet fishing-set Grandma Gertie had given him, sucking his thumb like a baby. She had herself sat rigidly aware of her father's words: 'Don't send her down to Greenaway's yet, Mary, she's old enough to understand what's going on. This is a bit of world history. It's the Prime Minister going to speak, Litt, so sit down and listen.'

The Prime Minister, he had sounded as he looked in photos, as though he had long teeth, like the School Doctor.

A State of War. Suddenly, with that phrase, Little-Lena makes sense of what has been going on all around her this summer. There had gathered in her head midge-cloud images. Of picnics, of summer-games, fishing and trekking, of half-heard conversations at home and half-understood talk on her Grandma Gertie's balcony, of seeing brick air-raid shelters being built on spare ground, and her mother saying, 'Oh, not Hitler *again*, Dick, not in front of the children, we don't want to hear any more about Germany'; of the one hundred and thirty-four coachloads of children, of the lost children at Waterloo Station and the terrible train-journey with Mrs Kennedy when they had had to stand in the corridor, Little-Lena thirsty from chocolate and bursting to go to the toilet until in the end she had had to tell Mrs Kennedy. And Mrs Kennedy being different from what she always had seemed.

What had been happening was A State of War.

Now that she knows, Little-Lena is no longer scared. The Prime Minister said, 'May God bless you all . . . it is evil things that we shall be fighting.' Her father had said, 'Not *you* won't be fighting, mate, you'll be tucked up nice and safe,' and her mother had said, 'Oh shut up, Dick, and listen.' Little-Lena, who had been going to the Church School for five years, knew it was important to get God on your side – and now he was.

Because of the war the school isn't going to open. Tomorrow, she will go with the others up to Princes Meadows. They will build a dam to float their raft. The over-tens will swim on the deep side of the footbridge bridge where there is water-weed and nine-holers that try to suck on to your legs. The girls will weave doll's-house mats out of the reeds; the boys will make bows and arrows and dare one another to take off their bathers and swim up to the girls. And they will make cigarettes from plantain-ribs and dried blackberry leaves, because a lighted cigarette is the only way to get a nine-holer off.

She skips and hopscotches the paving-stones. It does not seem like Sunday: the abbey bells have not rung, perhaps nobody went to Morning Service. She can see up as far as the railway ticket-office and back as far as Greenaway's shop, and there is not a single other person in sight.

The sun shines and sparkles the raindrops on Mr

Headley's roses. There is no school tomorrow. The conkers on the tree in the boys'-school playground are now quite big, but still green. To Little-Lena, it seems almost impossible to imagine that summer will end, that the conker-balls will eventually become spotted and split, that leaves will fall and the days will become dark and foggy.

Little-Lena goes along the back-way path so that she can lick her finger and dip it into the sugar bag. Perhaps she will see Mrs Kennedy and the wonderful man who had been in her garden.

1939

Christmas

As though some god played an even-handed game with the weather in Britain, the winter of 1939/40 was as long and bitter cold as the previous summer had been long and hot. Well before 24 December dawned, the myth that it would all be over by Christmas was exploded; though it must be said that, except for a silent Abbey bell-tower, a visitor to Markham might believe at first glance that It had never started and that nothing had changed in a hundred years.

But Georgia Kennedy, hurrying to open up her little office, noticed the changes. For a start, somebody had organized the evacuation of the statue of Lord Palmerston. On the wall of the bank there were large yellow letters, SWS, and an arrow indicating a water supply, and on the front of the Town Hall a finger-pointing notice – Breakfasts and Dinners, 8 A.M. – 3 P.M. – indicating Mrs Farr's domain and Georgia's own office. The Town Hall itself had a number of its windows blacked out and boarded up, and its entrance was flanked by piles of sand-bags, protecting the public toilets which doubled as emergency air-raid shelters.

But the rest remained unchanged and familiar in Markham Square that Christmas Eve. Three cakeshops, each with its speciality – yeast bakery, pâtisserie and iced fancies, Pinnock the glovemaker, W.H. Smith's, two chemists – Boots and a proper chemists, a greengrocer-cum-fishmonger, the Coach House, Post Office, three banks, Co-op, Woolworth's, Conservative Club and a shoeshop. A variety of architectural periods squashed together giving a charming, uneven roof-line and interesting façade. On Thursdays the Square still filled with the smells of passing cattle, sheep and farmers and, almost every other weekday, with the aromas from Freddy Hardy's factory bakehouse.

Georgia did not notice the town. It was still hardly daylight. She had Hugh's letter on her mind.

The office was cold and there was frost on the windows, so she kept on her coat, ankle-boots and fur Cossack hat until she got the little open fire going. Had it not been for its reprieve by the Emergency Committee, as Georgia's office, the condemned Georgian cottage would have fallen or been pulled down. Now, a few 'S' irons on wall-cracks, interior timber shoring and a bit of whitewash were beginning to bring the place back from decay, but there were still no utilities except gas, and the stairs and upper room were still unsafe.

Although she had been allocated only an 'issue' desk, two 'issue' chairs, two wooden stationery trays and a filing cabinet, Georgia was trained by her mother in the art of making things look nice. Short curtains with black-out lining, and a couple of matching cushions, two flowery pictures from the walls of her spare bedroom and, upon her desk, a variegated aspidistra in a pretty jardinière.

Leaving the place to warm up, she took her forms and clipboard and went to see Mrs Farr and her cook's helps.

At 7.30, most of the preparations for serving breakfasts were completed, and they were already well on with the midday meal. As she crossed the yard between her office and the kitchens, she heard the women's voices raised above the clatter of iron pans, kettles, shovelled coal and the odd line or two of a song, and she smelt frying bacon and roasting chicken. Whatever her spirits when she came to work, they were always boosted by the sounds that emanated from the kitchens when she went to consult with Mrs Farr first thing. She was, as usual, greeted by the Helps.

'Hello, Mrs Kennedy.'

'Morning, Miz Kennedy.'

'Hello, Miz Kennedy – you'm bright and early.'

'Likes your hat, must be nice and warm.'

'Too warm.' She took it off and several women had a try-on of it. The great coal-burning stove of an eight-plate hob and four ovens stood centrally in the room which was wonderfully hot and steamy after the cold morning air. Kept at simmering heat all night for the cooking of steak and kidney, or chuck or marrow-bone and lentil soup, the stove had been opened up by Mrs Farr at 6.30, and was now getting up a glow for bread and pastry-baking.

On racks above the stove there were trays of crisped-up streaky bacon, some of browned rissoles, others of thick slices of fried bread. The tea-urn steamed and lard sizzled bluely, waiting for the exact moment for eggs to be slipped in just before opening-up time. In the restaurant itself, crockery and cutlery were ready, milk was in cups, piles of bread cut, plates warmed and the serving containers heated. Except for the wafting smells, no one could have imagined from its unlit exterior what industry and life was contained inside the gloomy old Chapel Hall.

Nor could they have known the bits of joy that bounded in the hearts of the women who worked there. From seven o'clock till four, they scarcely stopped – skinning, peeling, washing, stirring, fetching and carrying and lugging and sweating. As they worked only six and a half hours, the jobs were considered to be part-time yet, to the women, these were jobs, proper jobs, in every sense – because they signed on and off in a Time Book, they had stamp cards, and at the end of every week they received a pay-packet.

Georgia hung her street-clothes in the lobby with the assortment of macs, woollies, scarves and knitted hats already hanging there. Mrs Farr was, as usual, in the cool pastry-lobby, mixing, kneading and rolling; working alongside Dolly Partridge who was cutting and filling.

'Hello, Mrs Farr, hello, Dorothy.'

Mrs Farr and Dolly greeted Georgia without spoiling the rhythm they had worked up.

In the two months since the Dinner Kitchens had been going, the women, under Mrs Farr, had established a working relationship and routine that was already as smooth and efficient as in any long-established business. It worked as well as it did because the women were determined that it should. They were aware that, although they were employees of the Ministry, the critical eyes of the Council and the Emergency Committee were upon them. Don't give them a chance to say, What can you expect from a woman, was the motto. Especially for Georgia who, as well as being only a woman, also had the fault of being a young and pretty one, and so by definition frivolous. She intended to be forgiven nothing because she was a redhead with a figure like Lana Turner.

Trixie, who had left Hardy's to come and work here, brought Georgia the mug of tea and bacon sandwich which she usually devoured whilst checking the stores. This morning being Christmas Eve, there was no urgent vegetable order to be made up, so Georgia perched on a stool and waited for Mrs Farr to tell her what supplies she would need after the holiday.

'Your man got his Christmas leave all right, Mrs Kennedy?' Dolly Partridge asked.

'Well, no, apparently they don't get any Christmas leave. But it looks as though he might get a day or two over New Year.'

Dolly Partridge saw the flush that coloured the young woman's cheeks, so turned her attention at once to crimping the edges of the great slab-trays of mince-pie. Somebody had said that she was knocking about with some chap, but Dolly couldn't abide gossip of that sort.

It was people's own affair, though it was a shame if a nice girl like Mrs Kennedy got herself in that kind of a mix-up . . . but there, when you're young and your man's gone away . . . Dolly knew what that felt like, and had more than once wondered what she herself might have done if the chance had presented itself. It never did to judge other people.

I just hope that Marie won't get herself into that kind of a mix-up . . . all Hell would let loose. But then, Marie never seemed to be all that interested – except in Charlie. But Charlie was in the Air Force now, and was on about being sent to Canada for training. Canada! The other side of the world. A postman talking about flying off to Canada as though it was only Andover or somewhere. There was some blimmin funny things going on.

Somebody said, 'I thought they all got Christmas leave. Makes you wonder what they can find soldiers to do at Christmas with nothing going on. You'd never think there was a war.'

'Our Charlie's coming home,' Dolly said.

'His first leave, isn't it?'

'Yes, Take him all today to get home. Kettering . . . or Catterick . . . one of those places – I always get them mixed up.'

'Just so long as he gets home. I expect Marie's excited, I must go through and see her before I go back to the office.'

Mrs Farr, deftly kneading and transforming rough crumbs of paste to smooth, pale yellow pastry, said, 'I told Marie that it would probably be all right with you if she went off straight after she shuts the till.' She glanced at Georgia for her approval. Marie, who worked the cash-till, did less hours than the other women and so was able to pick up Bonnie from school.

'It's all right with me. What about her little girl, Dorothy? The school closes at lunch-time.'

'Our Paula's going to fetch her.'

'I'll take over the cash-till and she can go straight after the dinner-time rush,' Georgia said.

Mrs Farr and Dolly glanced at one another without giving away their earlier speculation that Georgia might do that. Mrs Farr said, 'That's really nice of you, Georgia.'

'I've got no reason to rush off. Anyway, I've brought in a couple of bottles of sherry; I thought the Ladies would like to have a drink . . .'

'Why, that's lovely. I was just about to ask you what you thought – I made us a cake and Dorothy's done a lovely trifle.'

The three women, white-haired, pepper-and-salt, redhead, looked pleased with one another.

'Oh lovely!' said Georgia. 'The first Annual Christmas Party of the Dinner Kitchen Ladies.'

'Annual?' said Mrs Farr.

'Well, we could make it annual, whatever happens,' said Georgia, inwardly flushed with family feelings for this new and unexpectedly nice group she had become part of and who, if it had not been for the war, she would only have passed by in the street.

'Good Lord!' said Dolly gleefully. 'Fancy having parties at work.'

On Badger Island, Captain Hugh Kennedy was on duty. Wren Officer the Hon. Angela St John was on duty. They were on duty together. The fact that they were on duty and beautifully turned out in no way affected a bit of kissing and fondling – for they were on duty together and entirely isolated from the base camp. Each had been detailed by their separate divisions of XJ-R6 to survey a long hut recently erected by sappers, which would eventually become a hospital unit.

Although there was as yet no heating except the sun, it was quite warm there, the walls being extremely well-insulated and the windows sealed. Hugh, standing behind Angela as he unbuttoned her jacket, looked out across the brackish grassland and shingle to where the sea broke gently. Winter sun glistened on the wet shingle; competing bands of Black-headed and Great Black-backed gulls swept and glided gracefully; the dried remains of horned poppies and marsh grasses bent before the freezing wind.

'We could spend Christmas out here, Anny, and we could hunt for shark's teeth on Christmas afternoon.'

'Not the *entire* Christmas, my darling – one must have a few parties. But I absolutely *should* love to have a shark's tooth. What's Christmas without a party or two and getting nicely squiffy? You know I like parties and squiff.'

Hugh did know that, having often seen her capacity for alcoholic drinks – Gin and It before, Chablis with, and brandy after dinner. Equally intriguing to him was her capacity for enjoyment of sex, and quite Continental stuff. She was lovely, yet she could be both coarse and mysterious at the same time. It was like having Jean Harlow and Marlene Dietrich combined – except that film-stars were never seen with the slightest hint of body hair – nice women copied Hollywood stars. Anny wasn't nice in that way, she was *wonderful*.

Georgia had always had nicely clean-shaven armpits. And that was how he liked Georgia to be.

But not Anny. Not the long-legged ice queen whose loins were always afire: she was as blatant as an orchid with her urgent signals. Not bra-less, careless Anny who had, for some unaccountable reason, chosen him for a lover. He was absolutely besotted with her.

Several times recently, since the subject of Christmas leave became of interest to most of the Badger Island personnel, he had had to push Markham, Station Avenue and Georgia to the back of his mind. He did not want to leave, did not want to go home. He wanted somebody, somewhere in Whitehall, to decide that XJ-R6 was such a secret operation that he would not be allowed off Badger for the duration of the war. He wanted to be ordered to remain on duty – for ever if they liked, so long as exotic Anny playing wicked remained with him.

His caresses soon led to the release of the pins from her long black hair, and to the unfastening of her Naval buttons and his Army buckles. She retained her non-issue suspender belt, black issue stockings and flat-heeled WRNS shoes. She had a long, lean back which curved as elegantly as her throat. Her hips were narrow and her breasts were small and immature, apparently girlish and safe compared to Georgia's challenging roundness. She was complex and thrilling in her contrasts.

Hugh never ceased to marvel at how fragile she looked without the dark serge, the white poplin and the masculine tie. And he had never got over finding himself making love to a girl with an accent like hers. She had been presented at Court, went in the Royal Enclosure at Ascot and scoffed at both events – 'But darling, they are all grasshopping twerps. Really. And most of them such absolute shits when you get to know them. You are worth ten of them, my darling boy. You are all womanlover. Oh how I should love to do things in your cricket togs, all white and woolly.'

In the weeks that they had spent together, with few distractions either from duties or other desirable partners, she had taught him the art of holding back and the pleasure of fulfilling a woman. They had become finely tuned to one another. Hugh no longer gave the solo performance that left Georgia frustrated and both of them humiliated but, as he did now in the quarantine hut, clashed great climactic cymbals to Angela's vibrating, deep chords.

No wonder he was enchanted.

He had found a woman who was bold enough to challenge the old man in the dog-collar who had, late in life, somehow begotten a son and then attempted to castrate him with guilt. The don't touch, don't look, don't feel taboos of his youth were negated by Anny . . . Like this, Hughie? Now here and here . . . again . . . more. And he did not care where and how at only twenty-two she had learned so much about loving and being loved.

At last, in a great sigh of satisfaction he had said aloud what he had been saying to himself for weeks. 'God, Anny, how can I ever go back again?' They lay on the hard-wearing carpeting covered by his greatcoat.

'Pass the gaspers, Hughie darling.'

'You don't seem to realize . . . Georgia and I . . .'

'I know Hughie, you said. You can't come off with her and you can with me. It happens to vast armies of married people. It's called marrying the wrong man – or woman as the case may be. You will probably have to dump her, or both of you will have to come to some kind of sensible arrangement.'

'Anny! It's a small town, with ordinary people. We're not like the set you mix with. Nobody ever dumped anybody in Markham. Georgia's young.'

'Come off it, Hughie, she's my age, and she's not made of icing sugar.'

'She comes from a very proper family – so do I for that matter. We are what our parents and our schools made us. Georgia is quite a conventional person – she would never go about like this.' He kissed her armpit.

'Bullshit, darling, there's no such creature. When you get your leave, take her out to the woodshed or whatever you might have over there and try out some of your more imaginative Badger techniques . . . or take her out into sheep-country and try it on the Downs.'

But Hugh could not bear to think of Georgia doing the things Angela did, crying aloud as Angela did, telling him what to do next and what she was going to do, and afterwards watching him with smoke curling up past her face, arousing him before he was ready again and yet not being able to stop her, nor wanting to. To think of Georgia behaving like a whore was as painful to him as when, as a youth, he had come to terms with the fact of his own conception.

'You might find it quite a bit of sport, Hughie sweet. A spot of leave will do us both the world of good. A change of scene, change of bed, change of lover. And remove that expression – if you go all frightfully sullen, I shall pick up my knickers and be off. You know that I cannot bear a man who wants to possess me body and soul. I belong to me and I shall give whatever bits and pieces of me to whomsoever I fancy or need.'

Although she was very young, she knew how to quell him as well as to arouse him. It had been the core curriculum of her finishing school. Arouse and quell. At hunt balls, Henley, Cowes, Ascot and Commem balls. The art of upper-class seduction was not intended to bewitch an ex-Assistant Manager catapulted into a secret and glamorous military operation, but to throw a net over a prospective husband of the right sort, frequently a prospective husband who would prefer not to have to couple with a woman.

Anny St John knew that he loved her accent when it was perfect almost to the point of parody and that, whilst he wanted her exclusively, he could be aroused and excited at the idea of her having other lovers, so long as he was her chosen man of the moment. Again, on that Christmas Eve, she was doing both: keeping him on the knife-edge with promised satisfaction on one side and threat of deprivation on the other.

What Hugh did not know was what she had confided to a roomful of her Cheyne Walk girlfriends on a recent twenty-four-hour pass. 'I had no idea a man could be so phenomenally attractive. He's quite a bit older, oh, in sight of forty I should think, yet he's so unspoiled.'

'Not now you've got him, Anny.'

'I've not spoiled him, not one whit . . . quite the reverse, I have taken his raw clay and moulded it to my liking . . . well, of course, and to his also. I have only to . . .' She made a moue, raised her eyebrows and left it at that.

'Mean, Anny, mean. Tell.'

'What, and have Fiona tattle to her bandage winders? But, it *is* like having *the* most virile virgin every time – God, the bloody man is exciting – don't ask me why, he simply *is*.'

Her friends, of course, wanted to view this lover Anny had found for herself, this pistol of a Junior Army officer from some rural place in the Home Counties.

'You should join the Navy and find your own, my darlings – I know that there are plenty more clean-cut types, but I'm not letting you within a mile of my lovely unbuggered grammar-school Hughie.'

'They don't, you know . . . grammar-school types.'

'Right . . . mixed sex education.'

'How come your mixed-sex grammar-school Hughie is so virginal with all those girls available?'

'Oh, by not knowing what it was for, and putting everything into his village cricket team.'

'Everything? Anny!'

'Hospital wards are making you coarse, Fiona.'

Re-buttoned, re-buckled, hair combed and re-coiled, Hugh and Angela became uniformed colleagues again for the purpose of making written reports on the obvious – that this was a wooden hut with sealed windows and insulated walls within so many yards of the tide-line.

'Shall we come down here tomorrow, Anny?'

'Do you think I could find a shark's tooth?'

'A fossil one – of course, there are thousands.'

'All right, and we could have a swim – oh yes! A freezing swim before our Christmas Lunch . . . wonderful!'

'I haven't got my bathing trunks on camp, Anny,' Hugh said in all seriousness.

She scoffed at him by doing her trick of tipping her hat over one eye and looking him up and down clowning suggestiveness. 'Bathing drawers. Oh Hughie darling, I could eat you. You are so absolutely sweet.'

The Partridge sisters-in-law, Paula and Marie, greeted one another with the friendly reserve expected. 'Oh Paula, you shouldn't have.'

'Get on with you, Marie, if Robbo and me are going to be

here for Christmas, it's only fair for me to help out with the baking.'

Marie acknowledged this, and would have felt put out if Paula and Robbo hadn't expected to muck in, in the same way as when they went round to Sam and Dolly's on Christmas and Boxing Day and Marie's parents on New Year.

'I pulled the damper out an hour ago, so the water's nice and hot. You go and have a bath.'

'And Daddy's coming home tonight, isn't he?' Bonnie said.

'And we're going to make some mince pies, aren't we, Bonnie?'

Marie was about to say that Mrs Farr had given everybody a batch to bring home, when she realized that to stop the pie-making ritual of Christmas Eve afternoon would be to deprive Bonnie of one of the stepping-stones that must be trodden to get them through the Partridge family's traditions.

The bathroom was chilly and the water was boiling, so Marie lay and soaked in a roomful of white mist, drifting ahead through the next few days. As it was every year, all the Christmas baking had to be done this evening ready to take to Dolly's tomorrow. Paula had made a start. It wouldn't take long between the two of them.

I wonder what time Charlie will get home? The train that gets in about seven, I reckon. She hadn't thought that she would miss him so much – and in that way too, much more than she ever expected. Thank the Lord she had her little job. The girls were a load of laughs, the time went before you knew it. She was almost ashamed of some of the dreams she had been having lately. But you couldn't help what you dreamed: even so . . . she wouldn't have liked anybody to know. Worst part was, not recognizing the faces in the dreams. It would start off being Charlie and then kept changing to different men, and she didn't recognize any of them. Perhaps it would be even worse though if you did recognize them. Lord! Suppose it was somebody you met every day . . . out shopping . . . that would be awful!

And, as they always did every year, this evening, Charlie and Robbo would meet Sam and Harry and they would go down to the King William and carry home the crate of beer and the bottles of fancy drinks for the women.

If she had missed him in that way, what about Charlie? They say men need that kind of thing more than women do, but I don't know . . . At least Charlie wouldn't go with another woman. Never. Her Curse was due, it was a pity things couldn't have been organized a bit better . . . but you couldn't do anything about it. Just as long as I'm not early and we can have a couple of days. She never was, as a rule, but they said excitement could make you early – or late. It often happened to brides, so they said. The water was cooling but there was no room for any more hot, so she sank herself down to cover her shoulders.

As they always did, early tomorrow morning, Charlie would go up the allotment and pick the Brussels and get the parsnips and carrots and potatoes out of the clamp and take them down to Dolly's. Sam would prepare them whilst Charlie came home to change. Dolly did the cooking for dinner, Paula and Marie acted as her kitchen maids and made the trifle for tea; then they laid out plates of tinned-salmon, ham and tongue, celery and watercress. Since she had married into the family, Marie had always made the cake.

Before she became a Partridge, Marie had no rituals or traditions, and now she was as steeped in them as the rest. She liked them: it was, like Sam always said, building up something that would last. He said, 'My old Dad could look back down seventy years and see every Christmas Day he ever lived through.' Marie liked that. There was something safe in having traditions in a family. It was why she had let Bonnie help with the pastry on Christmas Eve before she hung up her stocking. Bonnie's children would do the same thing.

I hope he thinks I've been doing right with his old allotment since he went away . . . at least there had been some good frosts for the Brussel sprouts.

Then she wondered whether she had done right in buying the camiknickers. She had done it in a mood of loneliness and missing him and wanting to please him. Charlie could be funny about things like that sometimes, quite old-fashioned . . . could be quite funny about what was proper for a married woman. She tried to remember what he looked like in his Air Force blue. She heard the front door go and voices from the living-room. That must be Robbo; I shall have to get a move on. The water was now too cold to stay there any longer.

With a towel wrapped round her, Marie made up her face carefully, rolled her fair hair under and tied it back in a velvet bow.

Marie Partridge, anybody'd think you was going to a social instead of making sausage rolls. She smiled at her reflection as she blotted the bright-red bow of her mouth. Anybody'd think you wanted to get some man going.

She hooked her bra and tightened the shoulder-straps so that her breasts rose to Hollywood heights. This time of the month, she always filled her bra out. She could almost feel Charlie's eyes on her and felt shy to meet her own in reflection as she stepped into the powder-blue cami. It was almost like it used to be on weekends when they were first married, before Bonnie.

There's no getting away from what Mrs Partridge was up to: she had never worn art silk and lace in winter in her life, and she never had French legs like these, even on her honeymoon.

They reckon sailors' wives go funny when their men been at sea for months.

She stuck out her hip and half-closed her eyes at her

reflection, but knew that she could never bring herself to do that to Charlie in real life. Thought about it though. She only hoped that Charlie had remembered to go to the barber's, it would just spoil the whole Christmas if he hadn't. You couldn't borrow *them*, could you?

She smiled at the thought. 'Sorry to bother you, Mrs Miles, but we ran short of packets and the barber's is closed. Do you think you could lend us a few till after the holidays?'

'Of course, Mrs Partridge, don't know if they'm Charlie's size.'

She made her eyes crinkle with smiling and smudged her mascara.

I'll tell you one thing, Charlie Partridge, I'm not having any more babies. No. We've got Bonnie, and she's enough.

She clipped on her ear-rings.

And I want to keep my little job at the Dinner Kitchens. I couldn't bear it going back to being at home all day. I'm saving money. When Bonnie's older I shall get a proper job back in the salon. Then, one day, I shall get a salon of my own – The Salon Marie.

It would be all right, Charlie wouldn't forget to buy them.

Even as she said it, as she bent down to roll on her stockings, she realized that the story about anxious brides was true. Her Curse had come early.

Oh damn, damn, damn.

Tears gathered and she bit them back because Paula and Robbo would wonder what was the matter.

The blue camiknickers which were like something from a Hollywood film got thrust to the back of her underwear drawer.

I might as well have saved my money!

That first Christmas of the war was a strange one in Markham, spent in a blacked-out limbo, holding breath. Old men expecting a replay of trenches and ill-designed leviathans and mustard gas; old women not bearing to think about all the new widows and spinsters that there were waiting; young men wondering when the air would be filled with planes; mothers wondering why it was that they could make great ships like the Queen's, yet couldn't make a baby's gas-mask that would fit on a pram, and what did you do if you had twins or a toddler who wouldn't wear a gas-mask?

Markham children could not see that anything was much different from last year.

Evacuees could see that everything was different.

On the Council Estate, many people had their yearly taste of chicken. Many didn't, for there was still a lot of poverty. The Partridges did. For two days, the eight of them gathered in the living-room of 23 Jubilee Lane and, in the traditional style and order peculiar to their family alone, enjoyed, as usual, presents and food and drink all paid for from their thrift in Sam's Diddle'm Club. Except for Charlie having exchanged one uniform for another, and Harry in khaki, and the stiff tarred paper jammed into window-frames at black-out time, this Christmas would be little different from last.

Sam noticed that there was tension between Marie and Charlie and remembered how it often was when he had got home leave in the '14–'18 war. You got out of the swing of home life when you were in camp, and the women got uppity and used to doing things their way and didn't like to be told. Dolly had never stood up to him before he went in the army. Charlie was probably having the same sort of trouble. Well he'd have to put up with Marie being uppity and out of the home for the duration.

Dolly noticed that Robbo was quiet, and Paula was so cheerful that it made you wonder what was up between them. She wondered whether Robbo had decided to join up or Paula had missed a period – not things you could ask about. Just sit and watch and wait to be told.

Of course, as people always said, Christmas was the children's time. Bonnie, as usual, was spoilt by them all, but repaid it by enjoying every minute from the time she awoke in her Grandma's house, to the time she fell asleep from sheer exhaustion. Bonnie noticed that Uncle Harry drank rum which he always said he couldn't abear.

Charlie thought that Harry was knocking it back a bit. But then who wouldn't, training in the Paras? The very thought of jumping into space and not knowing whether the parachute would open made Charlie go cold.

Harry had only a forty-eight-hour pass. It was enough. Longer and Deanna might try to see him. He thought she had got the message that she had picked the wrong one if she thought she'd try pinning it on him. 'I don't take chances like that. If you're pregnant, it's not mine.' He hadn't heard from her since, so he guessed that he was in the clear, but he wanted to get back to camp away from it.

All down Longmile Hill, blacked out by heavy velour drapes, ten-foot-high Christmas trees filled the inner-halls and glittered with lights.

Connie and Fred Hardy had open house on Boxing Day for Army officers who had been billeted in a large, empty house two miles away. Connie saw that her daughter was not happy. But Connie, being Connie, could not find the right words to say anything to Eve. And Eve, being Eve, smiled at the officers and responded to her father's arranged good cheer.

Freddy Hardy used his Yuletide sociability like the entrepreneur he was, and got himself in very nicely with a high-ranking victualling officer.

There was no chink of light to be seen escaping from Mont Iremonger's house in Portsmouth Road: he had gone to Barton Stacey to spend a couple of days with his sister.

* * *

On Boxing Day, behind shutters that had been made to keep weather out rather than light within, in the comfortable sitting-room in Abbey Water, Ursula Farr sat reading a new Margery Allingham crime novel. An open fire burned on the low hearth. A white-maned, outdoors-looking man with sixty years' wear on his sunburned skin carried in a tray of coffee. Ursula looked up and they smiled affectionately at one another. Showing him the face of the book, she said, 'You should try writing a mystery, Niall. Make yourself a small fortune.'

'What would I do with a small fortune? What do I need? And there is nothing outside this room that I wish for.'

Ursula put down the book. 'Must you go back tomorrow?'

He nodded. 'The war hasn't stopped.'

'A thousand photographs and miles of film will still be made without you.'

'Ah, but most of them will miss the best bits.'

True, she thought. Whilst other photographers of his genius were accepting commissions to photograph winning racehorses, athletes and rural landscapes, Niall O'Neill had been in Spain, documenting in painful detail the massacre and distress.

'You'll never change, Niall . . . thank God. I only wish that you were here more often.'

Here and there in Station Avenue, small chinks of light shone out from front rooms that were only used on high-days and holidays and so were poorly blacked out. A dim light showed through from the back of Greenaway's shop where Vern was having a quiet five minutes on his own. Mulling over what Aunt Eadie had said. 'I suppose Freddy Hardy will be putting you up for the Freemasons then, our Vern, now our Davey's spooning with the Alderman's daughter.'

Vern had told her not to be so daft – they've never so much as been in one another's company.

'Oh? Well, you know best, our Vern.'

And now Vern, having a quiet smoke and five minutes on his own behind the shop, guessed that he did not know best. No smoke without fire. Subjects of gossip were always the last to hear.

From her bedroom window, Little-Lena watched the light fade. It was bitterly cold up there, but she didn't mind putting up with things sometimes, so that she could enjoy it more when things got better again. She didn't like having school spoiled by evacuees: they had scabies and nits and in her classroom girls had to sit three to a desk, the evacuated teachers were fierce and sarcastic – but things would go back to being nice as soon as the war was over.

She saw Mrs Kennedy's friend putting his bike behind her hedge.

'Hello, Nicholas,' Leonora whispered.

'Hello, Leonora, my darling,' Nicholas answered, kissing her on the mouth. 'How did you know where to find me?'

'I saw you from the window of my room, you were picking holly.'

'Ah Leonora, would that it had been mistletoe and you just happened to . . .'

Mrs Kennedy came out wearing her fur hat and ankle boots and a new red coat. Little-Lena rubbed a hole in the steamed-up window so that she could watch them going out together.

'I love your new coat, Leonora,' Nicholas said.

'You don't think it's too bright with my red hair?'

'Of course not, my darling, red hair looks best with red, especially with a black fur hat.'

Little-Lena ran the palms of her hands lightly down the bodice of her dress, lingering on the tips that felt like pocket buttons in the cold. Definitely. Hers were growing. The last time the school doctor had examined her, he had looked closely at her chest, screwing up his eyes and showing his long teeth. 'Has she started yet?'

Mother had blushed and shook her head and whispered, 'Good Lord no. She's only ten!'

'Well it won't be long. You should prepare her for it.'

Little-Lena had not understood what she was to be prepared for, but from her mother's embarrassment Little-Lena knew that it wasn't something she could ask Mother about – like asking why Roy had those little soft egg things. Those were still a mystery, even though Myrna said they were for holding the wee till it could find somewhere to go. Which didn't sound right, or why didn't girls have them?

She thought that what she had to be prepared for was for her chest to blow up so that she would have to wear a brassière.

'A Kestos, madam? Or a Maidenform?'

'A large Maidenform with lace.'

'What style would madam prefer?'

Once she was prepared, she wanted her chest to blow up as big as Mrs Kennedy's, and she would wear a brassière made of lace like the woman who lived next door to Grandma Gertie and who used to come out with her top undone and lean over the balcony. A man had put a paper flower down her front and the other women had laughed. Men liked women's chests.

Little-Lena had made up her mind ages ago that once she was prepared for It she was going to insist on being called by her proper name – Leonora.

Nicholas and Mrs Kennedy disappeared into the gloom. She didn't really like him going out with Mrs Kennedy because she couldn't see what was going on. But she supposed he had to go out with someone whilst he was waiting for Leonora. And she wanted Mrs Kennedy to be happy. She wondered whether it was allowed in England to share the same husband: they did in some places; Myra Turner had read her mum's library book about Salt Lake

City in America. Two husbands had shared Grandma Gertie, but that had been one at a time. There didn't seem to be any reason why it shouldn't be both together if Nicholas could afford it. She wondered why nobody had thought of doing it. It would be wonderful to be kissed goodnight by Nicholas and Mrs Kennedy.

Her hands were icy and her knees numb with cold. Now she would put on her new fluffy slippers and go back downstairs and sit in front of the fire and eat a slice of Christmas cake.

'Doesn't Markham look strange, Nick? Like some ghost-town in a cowboy picture.'

'I love you, Georgia Honeycombe.'

Having made it clear that her invitation meant nothing except that they would both be alone on Christmas Day, Georgia had cooked a Christmas dinner and now they were walking it off. They had reached Greenaway's when he suddenly drew her into the doorway of the shop and kissed her long and open-mouthed. 'And you love me, Georgia Honeycombe. You haven't ever stopped.'

For a moment, she allowed herself to be held close against his hard body, then she pulled away and resumed walking. 'Don't be silly, Nick, people will see us.'

'Let them! Anyway, you said it's a ghost-town.' He put his arm about her waist, but she pushed it down.

'Behave!'

'Just admit that you love me, Georgia Honeycombe, and I'll behave.'

As they passed the new air-raid warden and firemen's depot, they heard what sounded like a rowdy party going on. Hoping to take some of the heat out of their conversation, Georgia said, 'Let's hope Hitler doesn't choose tonight to bomb Markham.'

'Just in case he does, you'd better tell me you love me.'

'Oh Nick! I'm married. Hugh's been sent to some secret place – who knows what danger he's in.'

'But it's me who loves you, Georgia Honeycombe.'

It was dark now, and his voice seemed to echo along the deserted street. 'Nick! Stop acting the fool.'

From nowhere, as it seemed, a man was walking his dog in the dark, shining a small circle of torchlight along the edge of the pavement. 'Good evening. Happy Christmas.'

'Oh . . . yes . . . Happy Christmas to you too . . . thanks,' Georgia said. And the man disappeared into the darkness.

'There you are, Nick, see! You never know who's going to hear you these days, in the black-out.'

'But you know that nobody's going to see you.' Again, he stopped in a shop doorway and he kissed her until she couldn't help but respond.

'Oh Georgia, make a clean break. Tell your old man you made a mistake. People make mistakes.'

'I can't. Not while he's . . .'

'What? In the trenches at Aldershot?'

'Don't mock him, Nick. We're at war and Hugh's in the Army. Anything might happen to him.'

They reached the abbey where a service was going on. And Georgia's crumbling resolve was shored up by a choirboy singing 'Once in Royal David's City'. 'Shall we go in for a minute and have a look?'

They sat together at the back, looking at the nostalgia-evoking scene. He took her hands and sat chafing them between his own. The interior of the great abbey was a black cavern showing rounded arches where windows let in the lesser blackness of the night. The long aisle was a corridor of dark leading to where a few rows of firefly torches glowed on hymn books. In the choirstalls, one or two candles made cherubim of the faces of schoolboys.

Having spent a decade of her school life, metaphorically and literally, in the very shadow of the abbey, its architecture was so familiar to her that, even in the icy blackness, Georgia could visualize the detail – the stone columns, vaulted roof, Norman arches and Saxon windows, and she smelt the centuries of dust and incense that impregnated its entire fabric.

That unique odour brought back an image of herself in a short white dress, white shoes, white socks, white prayer book, kneeling in obeisance beneath the heavy, warm hands of Bishop Winchester. It brought back too the image of herself at eighteen in trailing white, with wreath and veil. Of her father giving her away to Hugh.

She had felt very emotional standing there with her father. Aware of her significant surroundings, the rood-screen illustrating the agony of bleeding and tortured saints, the stone busts of rich Markhambrians, the sentimental representation of the child who had fallen from the abbey walls to its death, the leper's window, the ancient font, tombs and plaques.

Hugh and all his friends had worn formal dress. There had been bells, organ and full choir. The Kennedys had not appeared much different from the Honeycombes except that they were more pushy and loud – though not as loud as the stags with whom Hugh had gone out the previous night.

Suddenly aware of her hand within Nick's, she withdrew it.

The singing stopped and strange, familiar echoes, caused by the rustle and shuffle of the small congregation, started up and flittered like bats around the galleries until they were sucked up into the roof. Nick took her hand again.

There was a clatter in the porch and the clang of the iron ring handle of the door. Hobnails sounded off the stone columns like ricocheting bullets as the intruder tried to creep along the aisle. Larger, noisier bats flew. Whispers from the fireflies and clattering from the choirstalls, the cultured voice of the vicar followed by the broad

Hampshire of the interloper. 'I'm sorry, Vicar, but you'll have to! You'm going to get us all blowed to Kingdom Come. Anyway the law's the law!'

The sound of retreating hobnail bullets accompanied the vicar as he mounted the pulpit steps, holding a candle.

'That was an air-raid warden. Our lights can be seen from the street. Until the cessation of hostilities, Evensong will have to be sung before black-out time.'

They slipped quietly out, Nick holding her arm tucked in his. At the porch door, he halted and they stood together as newly-married couples had stood there down the ages. 'I would give anything if I could put the clock back four years.'

'I'm married to Hugh, and nothing's going to change that.'

'Would you live with me, and none of this church nonsense?'

By the time he had walked her home, her eyes had dried and she was outwardly in control of herself.

'Nick, you seem to have no idea. I made Hugh a promise. Perhaps it was all right for you and Nancy, you never stood up in public and said you would stay together for always, but I did.'

He never liked her to mention Nancy.

'He took unfair advantage of you, Georgia.'

In his darkened shop, Vern Greenaway pondered sadly upon what he had seen when idly looking out.

Young Crockford was a good chap and a Comrade who had come right out at that meeting and said he belonged to a union. Vern's heart had warmed to him. As it had to the Kennedy girl who was making a damn good job of running the office at the Town Restaurant. Vern could never fancy her husband very much. A decent enough sportsman right enough, but he cracked his jaw and had a bit too much of the old school tie. Even so, the girl was married to him and young Crockford had already got a woman and a baby somewhere. Those two shouldn't be kissing in doorways.

Vern lit a cigarette and exhaled vigorously.

Who am I to talk? He'd regretted it since, even though he couldn't even remember the girl's name now. His biggest mistake had been to get it off his chest. It was still there between himself and Nora. Least said, soonest mended. He should never have told Nora.

A pity you couldn't protect the young against their own follies. He inhaled again, the glowing tip crackled and spat. They put some muck in fags these days.

He started to make his way back to join the warmth and laughter in the upstairs sitting-room. You couldn't beat having your family round you.

But bugger all . . . our Davey and Freddy Hardy's daughter!

1940

Again, the even-handed god saw to it that the bitterest winter in living memory was followed by a most beautiful spring.

Slowly, slowly, the war tightened its grip.

'We shall have to keep The Party going between the two of us, Sam, the best we can.'

'Keep the membership going anyway, Vern. We might have a social or two.'

'That's if there's anywhere not commandeered by the army. But the Women's Section could keep their afternoons going.'

'Hh . . . fat chance of finding a woman home in the afternoons these days. Is there any of them left who isn't off out doing something or other?'

'The Party needs to keep a bit of cash coming in somehow. We'll need it for the election, soon as This Lot's over.'

'Bit of good though, Vern. We got your seat on the Council guaranteed till the war's over.'

'Only trouble is, all the rest of them will keep theirs. I always hoped you'd get on one day, Sam. Never mind, drink up and put the books away, our day's going to come.'

And so, in the Tap Room of the King William, the Markham Labour Party was wound up for the duration. This reluctant action on the part of the old guard was an admission that this war was going to be a long one.

The winter snows melted, and the grass seemed to grow extraordinarily green; along the hedgerows of Hampshire every tree and shrub that was capable of flowering did so exuberantly. On the Council Estate the many fruit trees blossomed white and pink. Lord Palmerston's bronze eyes looked out from a funk-hole on his old estate, disdained horse-chestnut candles unfurling against clear blue skies, and glowered at early butterflies which had no business to be flittering about so early in the year.

Deanna from the Post Office disappeared and was soon forgotten.

Small, small changes. Tops of red pillar-boxes were painted green, stirrup-pumps and buckets of sand for putting out fire-bombs were allocated, a few more brick air-raid shelters appeared, fire-engines were painted grey and more and more and more ordinary workmen put on uniform for two shillings a day, from which pay those who were married must make an allowance to their families.

Gradually, gradually, the war gained momentum.

And the Prime Minister was losing the confidence of the people.

'Hitler has missed the bus,' he declared in a speech. But within days Germany invaded Norway and Denmark, and, within weeks, amidst muddle and chaos, the British forces were in retreat in France.

'That bugger's got to go, Sam.'

'Nye Bevan's the man.'

'Aye Sam, Nye'd soon get things hotted up. Ever heard him speak?'

'No, but he's the man to turn this country about.'

'But it's Churchill we shall get – you mark my words.'

The Markham stalwarts brooded into their pints at the prospect.

'Ah well, he can't be worse than the bugger we got now.'

'Don't you ever forget Sidney Street, Vern. People got short memories.'

'I haven't. I haven't forgotten that other old swine who used to stand in the Market Place – I haven't forgotten him.'

'Don't do to say these days.'

'True. Nora keeps telling me – you'll a get yourself

locked up, Vern Greenaway, talking like that against your own government. Drink up, Sam.'

'My turn.'

The old Bolshies of Markham were not dead but, like Sleeping Beauty, waiting for the prince of peace to come and awaken them to the new world they were sure would come.

1989

With the creak of Hildegard's shoes, her silent contest with the tiny sun-lizard over who would be the first to move was over: it scuttled from the terrace and disappeared.

'Hildy, you are like an invading army.'

'This letter came. See? It is the air tickets. I don't know why I must come. I shall be sick, as always.'

'Stuff and nonsense. You will love it. And you are never airsick.'

'Shall we visit Melanie?'

'Of course we shall visit Melanie.'

'Then I shall come. Here, drink your tea.'

Two elderly women – one arthritic, one breathless – who shared equally the family of the arthritic one – children, grandchildren, and now the delightful great-grandchild. One wealthy, one penniless except for the salary paid by the wealthy one, they had scarcely been out of sight of one another for almost fifty years.

'When we are in London, Hildy, remind me to bring back that little picture from my study.'

'The dragonfly?'

'"Demoiselle with Lilies and Irises", yes. It will be lovely in this light.'

'He was a very good man.'

'Yes, wasn't he?'

'We shall take him flowers, Milady.'

'We shall, Brünnhilde, if the gravestones haven't been whisked off or used to make paths.'

'Does Giacopazzi use him also for this story? Is he a good guy – he should be.'

'So far as I have read, she has done very well by him. She

has also done very well by me so far . . . I have been reading how I lost my virginity.'

'Never! You will not allow her to put that in the book?'

'Why not? It is charming, and she makes it much less mundane than I remember it. But it was in March, at the Savoy, and there were flowers and wine.' The sun-lizard eased itself out of the crevice, and she smiled at it for having claimed its place again in the wonderful golden light.

'But the family . . . Fergus, and Delia, how will they feel to see you written so in a Giacopazzi book?'

'Young people today *know* about such things. They know that a mother's maidenhead must have been lost. It will be good for them to know something of their ancestry. And why should they care about something that is a long-past history, and scarcely credible anyhow? I lost my virginity in 1940. Forty-nine years . . . so long ago.'

'I should not care to let the world read of my maidenhood.'

'Head. When you meet Georgia, you should tell her, and perhaps she will make it romantic and put it in a book.'

'There is nothing romantic in rape by filthy Nazis.'

'Oh Hildy. My dear, I had forgotten. I am sorry, sorry, sorry.'

'Pffft. As you say, it was so long ago.'

'Even so, it has done me good to read Georgia's version of my seduction. I look forward to meeting her again after all these years.'

'Meet Giacopazzi! Cheee!'

'Meeting Georgia Kennedy. We were such good friends . . . only you have been a better one.'

1940

March

'It was wonderful! You are wonderful, David. I love you so much.'

Leaning on one elbow, he studied her body, familiar in his imagination, caressed, glimpsed, but until now never seen by him. She wasn't that much younger than himself, yet she seemed such a girl compared to his own conception of himself; her naïvety, innocence almost . . . yet she had been so uninhibited with him. But wasn't that part of her innocence? Giving and getting full pleasure without self-consciousness, making her first love-making into a kind of precious deflowering.

'You don't need those things, David. I went to Harley Street and got myself fixed up.'

She was right: because of her sophisticated action, sex had been beautiful, a new experience for him. He had not been with very many girls, and none that had given any forethought about how to make it beautiful.

Looking down at her he thought, she is perfect. Not a blemish, not even a mole or freckle. He traced her body as though drawing her in outline.

'Burne-Jones would have loved you. He would have draped you in embroidered fabric, put a lily in one hand, a dish of pomegranates beside you, and painted you with your mouth just open, as it is now.'

She took the compliment gracefully, as she did everything.

'Even without your clothes you look expensive. You look as though you come from some great house called The Cedars, where you have a Nanny Bryce, and a gardener, and a daddy who owns a factory and gives you white MGs and diamonds.'

'I'm still just a bit of a tart who books a hotel room and brings back a sailor on leave.'

'Expensive tart. I've never been in an hotel like this. The Savoy. For Christ's sake, what would my Dad say to this?' Their room had flowers, drinks and a room-service tray.

It was the night of a victorious march-past in London to honour the men who had been involved in the scuttling of the *Graf Spee*. The country had been in dire need of it, to proclaim some good news for a change. David Greenaway, who had not yet been able to exchange his seaman's round hat for an officer's cap, and was still awaiting his new posting, had been at the Battle of the River Plate. Eve Hardy, without saying where she was going, had packed an overnight bag and gone by train to London to watch the march-past.

At another point along the route, Vern and Nora Greenaway too had watched. Vern had caught a glimpse of Freddy Hardy's girl in a First-Class compartment of the same London train on which he and Nora travelled, and had guessed rightly why Davey was not spending his twenty-four-hour pass at home.

If Eve Hardy was anything, she was a romantic. If she could do nothing else worth while, she could give herself to a returning hero. Not altogether selflessly, for her first venture into a true liaison was altogether quite as wonderful as she had expected that it would be.

'What are you smiling at?'

He outlined her features. 'Lovely, lovely tart.' In his grammar-school years, he had discovered the Pre-Raphaelites, D. H. Lawrence and Eve Hardy all within the same short time-span.

'Would you like to get married, Eve?'

She stared at the ceiling and considered, smiling. 'No, David, let's wait. Let's be lovers for a while. Secret lovers. Whenever you get leave, wherever you are, I will come to you.'

'I don't think you're serious about me.'

'You know that is stuff and nonsense. How much more serious can a woman be than to give a man her virginity?'

He laughed aloud. 'Eve Hardy, you could scarcely wait for it.'

Married or not, he wanted her very much. It was not so bad if their affair had been between a rich boy and a pretty girl from the local newsagent's. A man may take a girl up the social scale, but not the reverse. He could never imagine her living in Naval married-quarters, not even if he got promotion and it was in officers' accommodation.

She was right, they could wait. They had nothing to gain by marrying.

1941

Compared with other men serving in Britain, Georgia thought that Hugh came off a very poor second when it came to getting leave, but assumed, as he led her to, that this was because of the special nature of his work.

'There's a war on, we just have to lump it. Small team, darling; when one of the team is out of action, the whole shoot suffers.'

Although the war had been on for more than a year, and Hugh had been home very little, on the first afternoon of a four-days' leave at the very end of December, they had at once dropped back into their old ways, almost as though he hadn't been away. They had sat before the fire and talked. Georgia had enjoyed having something to tell him instead of always listening to him. And he actually listened.

'It sounds jolly impressive, Georgia. I never thought you'd stick it. And it's excellent pay. I must say working seems to suit you. You look terribly fit.'

'That's because I'm so happy, Hugh.'

In an answer to his question, she said, 'Darling, of course I miss you. I mean that I am happy about having such a super job. It is so satisfying. I can understand now why you were always so pleased with yourself. People who have jobs with titles are important. And I *like* it. I like being called an Administrator. I like being important, and I do the work very well, even though I say so myself.'

They walked around the garden which Hugh now seemed to view with some sentiment. 'And you haven't let the house go. Running a home is a job, and jolly important too. It's a great comfort to me when I'm out on The Project to think of you, and Markham, and the garden and the roses. I'm pleased that you have kept it up so well.'

'Well actually, I've taken on some help in the garden. I had to. I thought it best to get somebody who knew what they were doing.'

'You were lucky to find someone, especially if they are not overcharging, doing the job properly.' He had already approved of the way the roses had been pruned and the grass scarified. 'He did a nice job on the roses.'

'Actually, it's Nick Crockford. You remember Nick? He remembers you. He's in the Fire Service now, and does gardening in his spare time.' Omitting, of course, the fact that this was the only garden. She felt that she was rushing on too quick, but if she did not, then she would falter and the words would come stumbling out sounding like the lies she was in danger of telling. 'I'm glad you think he's made a good job. He always cleans things and tidies up before he goes.'

'Of course I remember him.'

Of course Hugh remembered Nick. Hugh Kennedy had stepped in front and removed Georgia Honeycombe from under the unsophisticated nose of the young Nick Crockford.

'Well, I met him at some meeting at the Town Hall. He's based in Southampton now, so that he can't spare much time, but he's a good gardener.' She did not trust herself not to go floundering on, so she turned her attention to taking in the shirts he had brought home for her to wash.

That night, they went to bed as they had always done, except that Hugh had worn only his pyjama bottoms. They made quiet love to Hugh's satisfaction. Georgia played her part adequately and added to her store of fantasies.

The following day was New Year's Eve. In spite of quite a few of the younger members having gone into the forces, the Sports Club had organized a party for those who were on leave. Georgia dressed in a tan-coloured dress which was a darker shade of her hair colour. Her hair she had had set in the new style, falling loose so that it hung over the right eye, and revealed her left ear with its white ear-ring as large as a penny. Her eyebrows were finely arched above shimmering Vaseline-traced lids and heavily mascara'd lashes, her full lips gleamed with scarlet lipstick, and her complexion had the fine peach-bloom of precious Max Factor powder.

'I say, Georgia, you really do look just the thing. Here, I bought you these, you should have had them at Christmas, but you know how it is, being on the Project.' His gesture suggested the difficulties of the hush-hush war on Badger Island.

As he said it, her cautious mind betrayed her with a glimpse of Nick when she had first worn her hair hanging down. He had stood in the hallway looking up at her as she came downstairs, pretending to hide his eyes. 'God help us, Georgia Honeycombe, there ought to be a law against you looking like that.'

They had been going dancing in Southampton, he had got some petrol and Georgia, now a proficient driver from Eve's tuition, had driven Hugh's car. He had been dressed in a dark grey suit, starched collar and exotic paisley tie. His curly hair had sprung forward on to his brow, and he had looked so rugged and handsome that she had wondered how she had ever come to believe that she preferred sleek and shining Hugh. And as usual she had behaved badly to Nick to atone for having such thoughts, but he ignored it until the lights and the music and the dancing drew her good temper back.

As Hugh made the excuse to Georgia, he too had a vision. A week ago, when there had been a Christmas Party in the Officers' Mess on Badger Island, he had seen Anny for the first time in a long evening skirt, velvet moving over her narrow hips and her unleashed breasts within swathed georgette. 'Anny, Anny, Anny! If you continue standing there looking so absolutely *edible*, I swear I shall not be able to stand upright in public.'

'Darling, you really are so so . . . ha! I shall not tell you again, or you will become quite swollen headed.' That had been the night she had dropped her off-hand and arch pose and had told him that she was head over heels in love with him. 'Absolutely ass over tipoff, darling.'

Hugh's hand trembled as he handed Georgia the little jeweller's box.

At the New Year's Eve party, Hugh was in his element. A few of his old team on leave, but the majority of the revellers were older men who fought their war through the young element. Hugh, the centre of interest, hinting at the secrecy of his job – something scientific. Elegant and smooth in his uniform. He had grown a Clark Gable moustache which really did suit him. They danced a great deal. There was little choice of drink these days, one took what one could get. They drank Irish whiskey mostly, and Hugh had kept drinking. Before the war, because he was usually in training for some event or other, he had seldom had more than one or two or a few beers.

Georgia preferred this almost lighthearted, urbane Hugh to the sports-captain type. That evening, there was something in the way he held her when they danced, more sexual, and when they danced Latin American, he half-closed his eyes, breathed heavily and hummed the music as he pressed her close, then flung her twirling away from him, unheedful of correct stance or steps. He had always been a very good dancer in the athletic way of some sportsmen, but that night as she watched him scooping and dipping the wives and fiancées of their friends, she felt that he had quite changed since he had been in the Army. He didn't keep smoothing his hair, but allowed the curving lock to fall on his brow. He loosened his tie – there was a kind of recklessness in him.

Watching him from the table they were sharing with a dozen noisy cricketers and tennis-players, she suddenly realized what was different. She recognized in him the same joy that she, even now without Nick present, had bubbling inside. *Joie de vivre.* Joy in life. Delight in being alive. Nothing she knew of him and his inhibitions suggested that it could be anything but enjoyment of Army life.

The New Year arrived at the Markham Sports Club to the usual cacophony at midnight, but this year there was no bursting into the streets, no snaking line of dancers, no Lord Palmerston to have a beer-mug put into his hand and a chamber-pot on his head. By one o'clock they were in the cold night air, with Hugh and his cronies exchanging maudlin farewells.

'God, Georgia, I put away some booze tonight.'

'You can sleep it off in the morning, darling.'

Georgia helped him stumble upstairs. 'Darling. Darling. Darling.' He held on to her like the drunken reveller he was. '*That* . . . is absolutely . . . the most beautiful word in the . . . Anny, I say, I think I've had quite a skinful . . . most beautiful word in the English . . .' He fumbled with the buttons of his uniform.

'Let me.' She had helped him undress and rolled him on to the bed where he had slid between the sheets which he had immediately flung back.

'No pyjamas, Georgia. That's the Army for you. No bloody jim-jams.' He had at once fallen into a heavy sleep.

Georgia had been wide awake and stayed a long while sitting before the embers of the living-room fire. Of all the things which she had anticipated might happen on that reunion with her husband, she had never for a moment thought of Hugh coming out of his shell. He was almost a different man, one or two of their friends had joked about it.

'I say, Rosie, look at old Hugh, he's going it a bit.'

'You can say that again, he was like an octopus with ten testicles when he grabbed me in the Conga.'

'Eight, Rosie, eight tentacles.'

'I know what I meant!' With New Year's Eve high laughter.

'Old Hugh's come out of his shell.'

'Looks a bit off his game to me. A bit off his game is he, Georgia?' Tennis-player guffaws.

Slowly it dawned upon Georgia that there was a woman somewhere. Although he had said that the hush-hush was a Combined Ops outfit, it hadn't occurred to her till now that it was a combined gender outfit too. Twice he had seemed to be calling her Annie.

When she at last climbed in beside him, he momentarily roused dozily from his sleep and said, 'Had too much, Anny . . . Irish.'

'Go back to sleep, Hugh.'

'Tired. Jus' hold me, sweetie.'

Sweetie!

Even though she was not entirely innocent, she had allowed Nick to kiss her on several occasions, she and Nick were not having an affair. But then, there was nothing to say that Hugh . . . but the pyjamas. And the way he had drawn her hand to hold him. Hugh had never been like that. His love-making always sprang from a kiss, an unspectacular arousal and an almost furtive connection, as though he ought to get it over before she knew what was happening.

She did not know what to think. Was her guilt about Nick colouring up some mild affair that was really only black and white? It could all be explained away. Annie could easily be a colleague, a name he used every day. Drinking and a carefree manner were not uncommon in wartime. And as for his bed manners . . . well he was home very little these days. Even so, Georgia was not blasé – who is when one has a glimmer of suspicion that one's spouse might be having an affair? Adultery is, after all, a major Thou Shalt Not.

On the final evening of his leave, when they were coming home from the Club and he was telling her something about some report, Georgia asked, trying for a small-talk voice, 'What sort of a chap is he, this Naval officer you work with. Is he a decent type?'

'St John's not a *him*, Georgia, she's a Wren Officer – one of the girls in blue, as they say.'

Georgia did not want to see the tell-tale indicators of his assumed casualness.

'I see, I see. When one hears "Naval Officer" one thinks "man". What's her first name?' She was sure that it would be Anne.

They had been walking linked, and she had felt the sinews of his arm contract. 'One tends not to get into first names on a project like XJ-R6. It's ah . . . Angela. Yes, it is . . . Angela St John.'

Angela! And he calls her Annie, or perhaps it was Angie. And he's lying through his teeth.

'Well, I expect women have a civilizing influence. I think all men together isn't good – you know, like with the rugby and the cricket teams when you tour on your own. You all descend to the level of schoolboys.'

The more she thought about it, the more convinced she became that the Wren meant something to him. She was very angry and confused, and jealous of the change in Hugh that this woman had brought about. She could not have borne to be thought to be like her mother, but Alice Honeycombe was a woman who could not bear clouds on the horizon or uncertainties in the present. 'Don't lie to me, Georgia. I can't abide it when things aren't out in the open. I don't care how bad a thing you've done – just tell me so that I know the worst.'

When he was packed and ready to go back, he looked down at her to say goodbye. Really quite handsome with his Clark Gable moustache and Brylcreemed hair, uniform immaculate, everything, as he said, tickety-boo.

'Be off now then, Georgia.'

Suddenly she felt that she could not let him go back without knowing. Not for rows or tears, but just to *know*.

'You've got plenty of time. Half an hour before it comes in.'

'Never like to rush – you know me, Old Girl.'

'Hugh, listen. There's something I wanted to say.'

'Fire ahead, Old Girl.' Absent-mindedly as he did a double check of the room for any possessions he had not collected.

She thought of Nick as she had throughout the weekend. Images of him hovered around. Going to pictures together, going dancing, keeping one another company. In spite of a few kisses, we are good friends. Nothing serious. We grew up together. How childish then to be jealous if Hugh went about a bit with a Wren. It was wartime, standards were different, people got lonely.

'Well, Old Girl, spit it out.'

'It's nothing.'

'Now then, what is it?' He caught her hand and spoke to her as though she were six years old.

'It's . . . well, I don't like being called Old Girl, women don't.'

He brushed back his glossy moustache with his knuckle. 'Ah, yes. Sorry, Georgia, mea very culpa. I'll be off . . . my dear.'

'"Darling", Hugh, we quite like to be called "Darling".'

'Can't change the habit of a lifetime overnight.'

'No, of course not.'

'Take care of yourself, Georgia.'

'And you.'

'I say Georgia . . . you did look absolutely splendid at the Club.' He found it so difficult to say. 'And you're doing splendidly at your war work – keep it up.'

'Thank you, Hugh.'

And he was gone, leaving Georgia still with a feeling that something major had happened, but she was not sure what.

1941

Midsummer Day

Glorious weather, the kind of day when Mont Iremonger loved to pack up and get out of Markham. As soon as he had finished his shift, he packed his watercolour kit, made a couple of doorsteps with new bread, beetroot and chutney, packed it all in the saddle-bag of his high-handled bike, and rode off through the town, over the stone bridge, and along the water-path until he came to the stile where Markham ended and the green Hampshire countryside began.

Mont's hobby and ambition were one. He loved to paint with watercolour, and many years ago he made a plan to paint the entire indigenous fauna and flora of Markham. It took him ten years to realize that he had set himself an impossible task. Hampshire was too exotic, too prolific. He would fill a book with pondside life, only to find that he had missed an entire species. It did not worry him that he had been over-ambitious, it was a comfort to know that he would never be at a loss to find a subject.

Today, he was not doing illustrations, but a composition that he could frame. He watched a male demoiselle glistening kingfisher blue. If I could only get that! Iridescent. Catch the light on its wings . . . its eyes.

Within minutes of settling down, he was lost in his search for the illusion, the magic. He never thought consciously about that search, he let his brush seek it out as his mind wandered.

He had heard a whisper that Freddy Hardy was being had up for using red petrol in his private car. What a fool. Everybody knew the police loved to get somebody for using business petrol for pleasure.

He helped his pencil discover the shape of the

composition. And he'd got a stash as it was. The mayor going in for black market. How can you have any respect for a man who goes in for that sort of thing?

Mont had often seen vans being offloaded with stuff. Once he had seen a soldier unloading some cans from an army vehicle. You could smell the petrol right across the garden. It was not only illegal to hoard fuel, it was downright dangerous. The man was plain greedy. There were a lot of people who were like that these days, couldn't rest unless they got more than their share.

Miss Eve had given up driving her little white car now. Driving a van for the school meals all week and a volunteer ambulance driver in her spare time. Mont missed her now that she was always out of the house before he got to The Cedars. Not Councillor Hardy's idea of a job for his daughter who had been to school in Switzerland. He would have probably liked her to have gone about dressed in a natty little uniform like her Ma.

You had to hand it to that lady – she was a knock-out in that uniform. People reckoned she wore her hat cocked over one eye like that because she was sometimes mistaken for Lady Mountbatten. Not a chance of that, as Mont had said when he heard it. 'Mistake Freddy Hardy's wife for Lady Louis? Why, Mrs Hardy haven't got hardly a line on her face.'

He touched cerulean, viridian and ultramarine and let his brush hover as lightly as the demoiselle itself.

People took the mickey behind her back. Lady Connie, they called her. The day might come when people would be glad of the Red Cross.

He had no tube of watercolour labelled 'Iridescent', yet somehow he achieved it.

It wasn't that people were vicious, but they got a bit resentful when people like her always got themselves into the top position in everything. It was as though they thought it was their right. Money talks! You couldn't argue with that.

There! It had taken him all afternoon, but he had got what he wanted. He had been thinking about it since the spring – a little painting for Miss Eve's birthday – but the demoiselles weren't about properly until now – and he had wanted to catch the water in just the right June afternoon light, with the yellow of the flags reflecting in the water, and the water-lilies opened to get the balance of their yellow stamens against the yellow irises. He imagined how it would look framed. A white mount – double, and a narrow white frame. No, plain pinewood! He imagined himself giving it to her. Nonchalantly. Oh, it's not much really, but I thought you might like it. I did it specially for you. I called it 'Demoiselle with Lilies and Irises', it's on the label on the back. Discreetly in the right-hand corner, *Montague I.*

He worked late that evening, making a perfect cut on the mounting cards, and sanding the edges of the beading, so that it was nine-thirty before he realized that the evening had almost gone.

He brushed sawdust from the folds of his shirtsleeves. Ah well, still time for a half.

The day had been hot, and the evening was hardly cooler than the day had been. A few men seated on a bench outside gave him the monosyllabic greeting of working men drinking and putting the world to rights.

'Mont.'

'Ev'n.'

'Hot.'

'Ah.'

'Aw bugger!'

'What's that?'

'Hark!'

'Aw Christ! Not a-bloody-gain!'

The weary note of the air-raid siren close by. Half a dozen

searchlights were suddenly unleashed across the sky and, even though no aircraft was visible, pom-pom guns outside the town opened up. From a distance, these deadly little guns sounded almost toy-like, but to be within a quarter of a mile of them was to have the vibration from the firing thrust deep into the ear-drums.

Mont jumped, but no more than the other drinkers.

'Christ Almighty! Didn't that put the wind up me!'

There was the sound of falling metal and tinkling glass.

'Shrapnel!'

As a body the drinkers scrambled back into the porch of the pub. The Landlady polished the same glass round and round. Every face was turned upwards and towards the direction from which they knew the bombers would come. The guns stopped firing, and the sudden silence seemed deep after the barrage. In the brief silence, searchlights swept the sky back and forth, back and forth agitatedly, catching nothing in their beams.

A few streets away, Little-Lena, still half-asleep, automatically stepped into the knickers that her mother, still in her day clothes but with the hem of her perm fastened in Dinkie curlers, held out for her. 'Come *on*, Lena, the siren went ages ago.' Roy whimpered at being woken up. Grandma Gertie clattered about the kitchen, following the routine she and Mary Wiltshire had worked out for air-raids: filling kettles, sink, bowls and buckets with water; filling a basket with some food in case it was a long raid.

'Quick now – whilst there's a lull.'

Roy whinged, 'I want Daddy. I'm frightened. I want Daddy.'

So did the trembling Mrs Wiltshire, but she said firmly but kindly, 'Daddy can't come. You know that. He's gone to fight the Germans.'

She hustled her children down the garden and into the little below-ground shelter that held six people comfortably, ten at a pinch, a crushed dozen in a life and death situation.

Gertie Wiltshire followed, but before she went into the shelter, she unlatched the garden gate so Mrs Kennedy could get in. As she did so, the sky was lit with a white light.

'Listen,' she said to Georgia, holding her head to one side. 'Can you hear them?'

'No. Can you?'

'Yes, they ain't coming from the usual direction. Listen.'

It was not true sound, but a disturbance of air that seemed to move something within the ear-drum, a sensation that went lum-lum-lum until eventually it became fully audible, when the sensation was transformed into the sound of fully-laden night-bombers homing in on their target.

'You coming down tonight, dearie?'

'If it's all right.'

'You know it is. Ain't it bright?'

'Must be the new searchlight battery.'

'Powerful.' She called out, 'Come and see, Mary.'

'No, Mum,' Mary Wiltshire called back from below ground. 'You should come down.'

'She gets nervy these days. It's understandable, I expect you do yourself with your man gone. How long's he been away?'

'Into the second year now.'

'And not much leave.'

'No, just the odd twenty-four-hour pass.'

'Dick's been gone six months, seems ages.'

Long minutes of near-silence. Georgia said, 'I think it's rather like at the pictures when a something is creeping up on the girl, and you can hardly breathe, waiting for it to pounce and the girl to shriek.'

'Blimey, look at that!'

One of the new wide beams caught and picked out an aircraft. High, but not as high as they came in daylight, was a long black bomber. A second beam arced its way with a flash to join the first. Then a third. Then another and another, until the many beams fused upon the bomber and accompanied it slowly across the sky. Then all Hell was let loose. As the great ack-ack guns that encircled Markham opened up, Georgia and Gertie Wiltshire dived into the shelter.

In Jubilee Lane, Dolly Partridge gritted her teeth at her obstinate husband. Sam, wearing a tin helmet, was standing by the blast wall of a shelter much like the one in which the Wiltshires and Georgia were seated.

'Come down, Sam. I've asked you a dozen times, we can hear shrapnel falling from here.'

'Don't nag. I'm all right. I can see what's what.'

Bonnie loved it when she was sleeping at Grandma's house and they had to take cover. It was cosy in the shelter. Tonight she had Auntie Paula as well. Bonnie cuddled up between them and sucked her thumb.

Dolly whispered to her, 'You tell Grandpa to come in. He'll take notice of you.'

'Come down, Granpa, I want somebody to read Long John Silver.'

As everybody said, Bonnie could twist him around her little finger. He came, wagging his head. 'Cheeping chicks and clucking hens.'

And crabby old capons. But Dolly did not say it aloud. Sharp. Too cutting – like Sam's own comments. Too many thoughts like this came these days – it was as though a spark had landed on her dry-store of resentment and, every day since she had been working at the Town Restaurant, a bellows was put to it. He was always sniping at her, picking holes.

Paula, when she was with her parents, felt immature, her feelings rushing back and forth between them as she sided first with one and then with the other. It was why she had been glad to marry Robbo and live in their little house near

Southampton Docks – just far enough away from Markham.

Mum's life had been nothing but work, work, work: she would be fifty before long and what had she done . . .? But then, it was worse for Dad, wasn't it – he had no legs. There couldn't really be anything worse than that . . . only, it wasn't Mum's fault yet he seemed to want to turn everything round to blame her . . . or Harry. When she was little, Paula sometimes sat with her legs under her, staring at her knees until the feeling went out of them, wondering what it must feel like to go to stand up and find that there was nothing there. Making herself believe it. Panicking, until in the end she would have to leap up to prove that it was only a game. The times she had frightened herself until she leapt up and somebody said, Oh Paula! watch what you're doing!

Later, it had seemed that she could watch her legs grow almost daily. Long and slender. Until the war, she almost always wore silk stockings and high heels when she went out. Her legs were her pride and her guilt. She often used to think that it was as though her father's legs had been a sacrifice so that her own could be perfect. When Robbo was courting her, he soon discovered what running his hands up and down the length of her legs could do to her. 'Cyd Charisse has got nothing on you, Paula.' Except that Paula was not much of a dancer. She wasn't much of anything except a docker's wife who couldn't get pregnant.

And now where was Robbo? Robbo was in the tank corps. Not in a tank, thank God. Paula's nightmares of burning men encased in an iron box would have been even more unbearable had Robbo been in the tank, a driver or something, instead of being one of the servicing team.

Paula slipped her arm round Bonnie and discovered her mother's arm already there. Bonnie, wallowing in the midst of warm female flesh and safety, listened to her Granpa's voice acting out the part of the pirate with a wooden leg, until she dropped off to sleep.

Bonnie was staying with her grandparents to give Charlie and Marie a bit of time to theirselves.

Charlie had four days before having to fly back to Canada, and at the Dinner Kitchens, Georgia had said that she would stand in and do the cash-till so that they could have as much time as possible together. Shortly before the air-raid warning sounded that June night, they were sitting where they had spent all day – in deck-chairs on the rectangle of grass that used to be Charlie's lawn. Charlie's threat to dig it up and plant it with winter greens had never been carried out. A bit of the lawn was reprieved, not velvet and weedless as in pre-war days, but still a pleasant bit of grass. 'You won't ever dig it up will you, Charlie?'

'Won't ever have the time.'

'I wish you could get posted in this country.'

'You get quicker promotion on this job.' He was already a corporal and expecting sergeant's stripes before long.

'I hope it's worth it.'

As darkness fell, Marie got up to collect things together.

'You don't want to do that, let's stop out a bit longer.'

'We can't stop out here. They'll be over tonight. They'll keep on bombing Portsmouth and Southampton now.'

'Southampton's not Markham.'

'Charlie – eight miles as the crow flies is nothing. Markham could get bombed any night by accident, or some nutty Jerry off-loading on us. It's happened enough in other places.'

'All right, but let's not go in till we can see the whites of their eyes. It's my last night, remember.'

'You don't have to remind me.'

'Well then . . .' He came and sat close to her and whispered in her ear.

'Charlie Partridge!' She darted glances at the walls on either side.

'No need to shout.'

At once whispering, she said, 'I'm not shouting. I don't know what's got into you. It makes me wonder what you've been getting up to in Canada.'

'Don't be daft. Come on, it will be nice. Nobody can see. It would be like when we were courting.'

'But that was out in the country.'

'And it was nice, wasn't it?'

It was . . . very nice. Like Markhambrian couples down the ages they had their special places for courting and love-making on warm summer nights. Places which, when passed by in the normal run of daily life even years later, drew the eye. Expecting to see what? To see meadow grass compressed into a nest? To hear a bit of happy laughter? Or breathlessness? A stifled ecstatic groan? A promise?

Places like the banks of Princes Meadows where they used to picnic as children, and the bandstand in the Park and the cricket pavilion, and . . . oh, there had been a fair few places where Marie had taken her chances. And with Charlie – respectable, respectful, careful Charlie – Marie could be sure that they were safe.

She softened. 'Yes, Charlie, it did use to be nice, didn't it?'

Relaxed, Marie sat back on her heels whilst he felt the movement of crêpe de Chine against her back. 'You've lost a bit of weight.'

What do you expect? I do two jobs as well as learning first-aid and going to emergency cookery classes. But not aloud, they had already spent too much time this leave with Charlie going on about her job, and about taking care of Bonnie properly, and trying to persuade her that she should either grow more on the allotment, or have another baby. Anything, she had thought, to keep me at home being Charlie Partridge's little wife.

'Don't lose any more. I don't like skinny women.'

It was as dark now as it would get on a normal

midsummer night. He's right, there's only our own house that overlooks the lawn, and Bonnie's away. He's going away tomorrow. It would be nice if his last night was nice.

Releasing herself from the kneeling position, she let Charlie's weight rest on her. The remembered feel from when they were courting, of stiff bents of grass prickling her body, that same smell of crushed grass, the feeling of space and being free and an excitement that never came in a bedroom.

'Charlie? Do you remember that time in the Dewpond Meadow? I said to you, Just think, Charlie, there could have been a girl and her young man lying here a hundred years ago and you said, Perhaps a thousand years.' Marie remembered it as the most romantic night of her life.

Until now. Charlie had been married to her for seven years, yet he still wanted to make love like this. It was romantic.

'No! Charlie, no!' An urgent, fierce whisper. She bent her knees in resistance, but he was heavy.

'Oh go on, Marie, why not?'

'You know why not. We had this all out. I will *not* have another baby.'

'Who's to say you would? Be a sport, just this once. I could be anywhere tomorrow.'

'You rotten devil! You damned rotten devil, that's blackmail. I know what it is, it's because you don't trust me.' She breathed heavily with effort and anger. 'I thought that when you were on to Sam about all the soldiers in the town. If I was going to be unfaithful to you, do you think getting me pregnant would stop me going with somebody else?'

'I never thought that.'

'Good as.'

He did not move the weight of his body, except to try to kiss her. 'Oh Marie, I didn't ever mean that. But Markham's swarming with soldiers, and you're a very pretty woman, and you can't trust men when they're . . .'

He was still aroused and holding her down.

'Oh yes . . . when they're away from home . . . wasn't that what you were going to say? You're one of the airmen swarming all over Canada; is this what happens out there?'

'Marie, don't be silly.' His voice was pleading. He pressed his face close to her ear.

She turned away from him.

'I love you. I'd be careful. It's just . . . you remember how good it used to be when you were expecting?'

She remembered. Which was why she struggled to get into a position where it wouldn't happen now.

'If you don't get off me this minute, I'll shout out so that the neighbours will know what's going on. I will, and I'll tell the whole family what happened.'

He hesitated. The siren wound up its warning note and the guns on the Oaklands Estate fired, pom-pom, pom-pom. Within minutes, the family from across the road, who had no air-raid shelter, were bundling down with Marie and Charlie, where they all began their long vigil.

Charlie to think about whether to be abject in his apologies, or to give her a tight-lipped farewell and show her he was still master in his own house.

Marie to decide to get on the bus tomorrow and do what she had been going to do for ages: go to Southampton and brazen it out with the prostitutes and low-class women she was sure would be at the Stopes Clinic. She would blush with shame and embarrassment, but never mind – it would be worth it. She would never trust Charlie again.

In another cellar – or basement, as it would prefer to be known at The Cedars – Connie Hardy blew upon the drying varnish on her nails, tacky stuff made up by the chemist and sold expensively under the counter. It took ages to dry.

The basement was vast and divided into rooms, holding the coke-boiler, utilities meters, a wash-house, dry-store, wine-cellar, games-room and indoor drying- and ironing-room. Since the blitz on the South began, these subterranean rooms contained bed-rolls and hospital cots, and on many nights Eve, Nanny Bryce and the help slept down here.

Now there was an ack-ack gun dug into the hillside not more than a couple of miles along the road: it was not easy to get to sleep once it started firing. Connie Hardy had lain awake for ages. The drone of hundreds of incoming German bombers seemed to drill down through the walls. The dry-store, being set apart by a passageway from the rest of the basement, was where she and Freddy sheltered at night.

The bulb in Connie's reading lamp had gone, and the ceiling-light was too dim to read by. It was *so* boring just sitting and sitting for hours. She had given herself a complete manicure and pedicure, brushed every speck from her uniform and even stitched the band back inside her cap. She had finished her G and T ages ago.

Where the hell was Freddy? As if she needed to ask. Sorry, Con, got talking in the mess with that Warrant Officer, and Jerry came over just as I was ready to leave. Couldn't chance it then, it was raining shrapnel.

Freddy Hardy was the world's most inveterate liar. An absolute damned shit because there was always sufficient truth in his stories to hold up to scrutiny. An absolute shit!

Connie knew where he was. Who he was with. What he was doing.

What he was doing was what he had been doing for years: wenching, whoring, seducing – how many words are there for it? –committing adultery, being unfaithful, womanizing. And what is he, as well as Company Chairman and Mayor? A lecher, libertine –probably a cuckolder. A shit! An absolute shit! A deceiver. Most of all he was that. He simply had to deceive anybody and everybody. If he was not involved in something just the right side of shady, then he wasn't happy. He seemed to need to take a crooked path, even when it was as easy to stay on the straight and narrow.

The guns opened up again, followed by a crump-crump as bombs fell quite close, then the whine of a crippled plane which sounded as though it would crash, but kept going in spite of a great barrage of anti-aircraft guns.

Connie's hands were trembling. She wanted company. More than anything, she wanted to obliterate the vision of Freddy in the arms of his latest. She was Eve's age. She wore khaki and was something to do with entertainments. Entertainments! Over the past months, since Freddy had become deeply involved with the girl and, separately, in some very shady deals, Connie had, almost objectively, watched their marriage coming apart at the joints. Connie wanted a drink and company.

Nanny Bryce, sheltering in the warm ironing-room, would be dead to the world. If only Eve were here. If only I had some idea of where Eve goes with her little weekend bag. Although they had always got on well together, they had never been close. Had never learned to be mother and daughter, any more than Connie and her own beautiful, remote mother had learned. Connie wouldn't have known where to start to enquire into Eve's personal affairs, which was quite funny when one thought of the very personal information she was expected to gather about other women in the course of her duties at various clinics.

Connie wondered whether Nanny Bryce knew who it was Eve went away to sleep with. But one could not ask.

Quite by accident, when searching for a lost ear-ring in Eve's room, Connie had come upon a box which had rolled under the bed. Connie was quite familiar with that type of round box. To the uninitiated, it might appear to be Max Factor face-powder, but at once Connie recognized the style as that of Marie Stopes from a private clinic. Thank God for small mercies, at least Eve knew what was what in that direction.

There seemed to be a lull in the air-raid, and Connie contemplated going upstairs to fetch the gin and some fresh tonic. Then she remembered that Freddy had a stock of it somewhere. Somewhere down here, he had been putting by a few boxes of things he said they might be glad of if it was a long war. She had little to do with it: it was he who unlocked the store to fetch a bottle or took stuff up to the kitchen when it was needed.

She had not been in the wine-cellar for ages. When she unlocked the door, she was astonished.

Perhaps it was not a miniature Fortnum's, but it was easily a well-stocked Home & Colonial Stores. She read the labels and stencilled boxes and crates. Golden Syrup, toilet rolls, tea, cocoa, light bulbs, condensed milk, tins of ham, Canadian salmon, fruit, chicken, American butter. All foods that had virtually disappeared from shops. Seeing it all together like that, the meanings of Racketeer and Spiv were brought home to her. Black Market of this kind was held in contempt by the people with whom she daily came into contact, for it was their men who ran the gauntlet of U-boats to bring it in.

Even so, she collected a bottle of the black market gin and poured a heavy measure. The familiar, comforting aroma, the sting at the back of the tongue, the awareness of its slide down the throat, the numb warmth in the stomach. Thus coated against anger and anguish, Connie Hardy began to think and allow herself to admit that things were coming to a head. For years there had been women . . . the loyal secretary then, but this was only suspicion, the typists staying behind to type up reports, and badminton partners to whom he gave lifts home. But since the outbreak of war, Connie was sure there had been numerous others who had succumbed to his charm and practised seduction. Shit or no, he was always so bloody good at it. And now there were ATS and WAAF girls around by the dozen.

The warm gin in her stomach turned to acid and she felt like retching. But why do I care? It all went long ago.

It was two o'clock in the morning. There was a lull in the air-raid, Connie sat on the terrace chain-smoking and looking out across the valley at the terrible red glow that stretched along the horizon. Had it been a couple of hours later, one might have thought, 'Red sky in the morning', but dawn was still making its way over Europe towards Dover in the east: it would not reach Hampshire yet. And that red sky was in the south, and not far away.

She still sipped her gin. Life with Freddy Hardy consisted of nothing but pettiness. A few drinks, official functions, the round of cocktail and dinner dates, dress fittings, trips to London, to the theatre and to Paris . . . all to boost his ego, to be seen in the right places amongst the right people – people who could do him a bit of good.

A useless, foolish life. I eat dinner and scarcely think where it has come from. I put on my uniform and tell mothers how much orange juice to give their babies, and give them advice I only know from Government publications. A basement full of luxuries whilst half the south coast is going up in flames. The only thing that she could think of was to run away from it all and . . . what? I can't even type.

The Landlord and Mont too had come up from the pub cellar to make tea and saw the shocking red glow in the south.

'That's the Docks.'

It was not necessary for these two elderly men to say more to one another. Each thought they knew what it must be like, although they could not in their worst nightmares have conjured up the reality of that night of fire-bombing.

Incendiary bombs had fallen like rain upon the warren of grotty shops, lodging-houses and pubs where there were prostitutes as young as ten, sailors of every age, and merchantmen of every race.

And where there were rows and rows and rows of terraced houses in which generations of dockers' families had lived. What had yesterday been bonded warehouses, grain-stores, coal-yards, timber-yards, rats, fleas, cockroaches, men, women and babies, had this morning become fuel to the vast conflagration that lighted up the midsummer night sky.

The two elderly men were stricken and silent.

Georgia Kennedy and Gertie Wiltshire took turns to stand guard whilst they each ran to the lavatory in the yard. The air seemed very still and warm. Quiet except for the occasional brief exchange between neighbours emerging after hours sheltering underground.

Grandma Gertie fished out a packet with two last cigarettes and offered one to Georgia, who hesitated because of their scarcity, though longing for one. 'Go on,' Gertie said. 'If they ain't got none in the shops tomorrow, then I'll give the blooming things up. My chest ain't never liked me smoking, anyhow.'

They smoked in silence, drawing deeply with relief. From where they stood, the surrounding garden walls and the houses in the next street prevented them from much of a view beyond the garden.

'Gone quiet.'

'They'll be back soon.'

She was right: soon the lum-lum-lum of returning aircraft could be heard over the south coast counties for the second time that night.

The two women stubbed out their cigarettes. Before returning to the shelter, Georgia glanced up at her own house. The little dormer-window of the attic glowing dull red. 'Oh God, look! Our attic's on fire.' She rushed indoors, followed by the slower woman. Even before war had been declared, Hugh had prepared for such an eventuality, so that there was always a bucket of water ready in the spare room and a bucket of sand on the landing. Her arms finding great strength in her panic, she grabbed both and rushed up the last few stairs.

The room was well blacked out with shutters and was dark. No sign of fire. Feeling her way across the room, she opened both the window and the shutters. From high up under the roof as she was, she saw across the roof-tops of Markham towards the south-east and could scarcely believe the brightness of the red glow in the sky.

Nick! That was where the docks lay, where Nick was on duty.

It was also the direction in which Badger Island lay, but it was only much later that it occurred to her that Hugh might be in danger.

The last wave of bombers had gone over half an hour ago. There had not been many of the crump-crump sounds of the high-explosive bombs that people were used to hearing in the nightly raids, yet there must have been thousands of bombers passing over Markham on that warm, June night.

All over Markham, people roused from the strange half-doze that passed for sleep during the nightly raids and rushed back indoors or came up from cellars. 'Never miss a chance to make tea or make water in an air-raid: you never know when you'll get the next one.'

At last the night was over. Dawn came at three o'clock.

In Markham's meaner streets, people exchanged cigarettes with their neighbours and stood talking in low, relieved tones. Their children – fresh from sleep and enjoying the novelty of being on the pavements at three o'clock in the morning – played hopscotch on yesterday's rinks.

On the hill, Connie Hardy flicked another cork-tip stub into the lily-pond and considered the plans she had made for herself.

Georgia, looking dark-eyed and pale, said, 'I'll make us some tea if you like.'

'We could have it in the garden – it's warm enough,' said Gertie Wiltshire.

'I must just pop indoors with Little-Lena first.'

'Let the kids have a bit of a run-around first – it'll do them good.'

Mary Wiltshire said, 'Roy can. You keep your eye on him for ten minutes.' She lowered her voice to a whisper. 'I'll have to take Little-Lena indoors. You should see the back of her nightie. She's started.'

Grandma Gertie raised her eyebrows.

'The school doctor said she wouldn't be long.' Mrs Wiltshire nodded in the direction of Little-Lena who stood on this warm morning with her mother's dressing-gown hastily thrown around her shoulders. Heaving a weary sigh, Mary Wiltshire continued, 'I'll have to go and tell her about it. I've been dreading this. After we've been up all night too. It never rains but what it pours.'

Gertie Wiltshire said, 'Tell her it happens to Shirley Temple and the Queen, and give her a day off school.'

Georgia, unable to avoid hearing what was said, thought, It's a pity you didn't tell the kid before.

Little-Lena intuited that she had not cut her leg – as she had told her mother because she didn't know what else to say – but that this was to do with the starting that she had been anticipating. She could tell by the way her mother had tied the dressing-gown round her and said, 'Stand there and don't move, I'm just coming.' Surreptitiously she felt her poached-eggs chest. Now she would get a brassière, and be called by her proper name from now on.

Leonora.

Leonora felt serene.

Mont Iremonger arrived home at half-past three in broad daylight. His next-door neighbours were watering their geraniums, keeping tabs on Mont as they did everyone in the street. 'We knocked to see if you was all right, but you wasn't there.'

'Went for a quick half at ten o'clock last night . . . longest quick half I've ever had.'

'And it was 21 June, did you realize that? – the longest day.'

'Aah . . . and the longest bloody night!'

1989

The plane was held up in Rome. She used the waiting time to read through some notes from a TV company. They had suggested doing some publicity shots of her in some of the locations she had used in the novel. They had particularly wanted to do something with the burning of the dockland areas of Portsmouth and Southampton. What on earth good to go there now; they were cities exactly similar to every other in England? It would need a film set and special effects to get anywhere close.

There was an announcement apologizing for a further delay. Georgia Giacopazzi felt irritated. This journey had been endless. Suddenly she was plunged into the need for some reality. She got some coins for the phone and dialled.

'It's me.

'Yes, of course I'm fine, have you ever known me to be anything else? It's just that I wanted to hear you.

'No, nothing that won't keep.

'Oh, it went off all right. He doesn't know anything, but she seemed quite pleased, didn't ask for anything to be taken out. I'm glad I went to see them.

'Of course I was curious. At our age one needs to compare oneself with one's peers from time to time. They look old. It's living all those years basking in the sun that does it.

'No, never! Two days was too long – Johannesburg is the pits! I can't wait to get back, it seems as though I've been away for ever. Did we get some good hay?

'Oh lovely. I thought about you. I was green with envy at the thought of it going on without me.

'Of course I rang to ask about the hay, why else would I ring from Rome?

'Yes, yes. Don't fuss.

'Yes, of course I am, how about you?

'Goodness, is that a promise?

'Bye. I'll be home in two days. Kiss Prince for me.'

She laughs. 'Well, pat him then. Bye. Love you too.'

1941

In the kitchens of the Town Restaurant, Mrs Farr stared down at the great slab of dark red meat laid out on the cutting board and could have wept for the slaughter.

She hoped that Niall would be down at the weekend. She would have to tell him about the piece of whale that had been delivered to the Dinner Kitchens. *It was devastating, Niall, twenty pounds of flesh, I could hardly bear to touch it. Nonsensical isn't it? I can gut a rabbit in thirty seconds.* He would understand.

He would remember 1930. Over ten years ago, when they already both had fine streaks of grey in their hair, they had at last gone on their 'honeymoon'. Twenty years late, but such a honeymoon. Sailing the warm seas for weeks on end – Niall doing a bit of writing, Ursula photographing dolphins, throwing back the flying-fishes that flopped on to the deck and, best by far, standing together watching the whales.

How much the whales enjoyed life. Niall had said, 'Whales have the kind of society humans should try to achieve. Caring, responsible and yet wholly joyful. One feels that they must experience love and enjoy their sex.'

As the school followed the boat, she and Niall had spent hours and hours just watching the huge, graceful shapes – skimming in just below the surface, coming close to the vessel, opening blowholes, then sounding with a show of those elegantly-shaped flukes. Niall had put their own passion and that voyage with the whales into his next novel, *Love-song of The Whale*. 'Beautifully written and deeply moving – Niall O'Neill at his very best.' Not a single reviewer, not even the usual right-wing snipers, had had a bad word to say for Niall O'Neill that year and it was now being referred to as 'a modern classic English novel'.

Ursula Farr covered the distressing sight with an enamel tray. It was as though the Ministry had taken to distributing carcases of people. Worse perhaps. For all they knew the great dark, limp slab that she was supposed to make edible might well be a species superior to humans. Those pacific creatures. No National Socialist whales. No Fascisti.

'Don't tell me it's got you beat too.' Dolly Partridge's voice broke into her reverie.

'Oh Dorothy, I was miles away.'

'You might as well make up your mind to it, whatever you do there's going to be a lot of complaining. And you can't blame people, nobody likes whale meat. Sam won't touch it.'

'And I don't like having it in my kitchens. Have you ever seen a live whale, Dorothy? Swimming free, cavorting and blowing.'

'Me? See a whale. I haven't seen any sort of fish swimming in the sea. I haven't never been to the seaside as much as twice in my life.'

Of course she hasn't, Ursula Farr, insensitive fool – the families of legless heroes don't.

Dolly, who would never stand and chat without occupying her hands, began peeling onions which Mrs Farr chopped.

'That's a shame, Dorothy. The sea's wonderful. I say! Perhaps we might all go together sometime. Would the girls like that?'

'I'm sure they would – just ourselves.'

'We could have a charabanc outing like they do at the brewery. Oh I wish I could show you whales. Everyone should see at least one school of whales in their lifetime. They're not fish you know. They're warm-blooded. Some experts say that the whole family stands guard when a female gives birth and that they look after one another's young.'

'Well fancy that.'

'And they mourn a death. Couples make love face to face like we do, and mothers breast-feed their young.'

Before she came to work with Ursula Farr, Dolly would have been covered in confusion at such open talk. She used to think that she would never get used to some of the things Mrs Farr came out with. Yet she looked so prim and ladylike. And she was really. Nothing coarse about Mrs Farr, never said anything blue, just the opposite really, she talked about all that kind of thing just the same as if it was ordinary. Which it was really. It was only that, if you had never been used to talking about the personal side of your life . . .

After a year in her company, Dolly was beginning to learn to be unembarrassed – but only with Mrs Farr. Ursula. Her friend. And, Dolly being the sort to keep herself to herself, the only real friend she could say she'd ever had.

Keeping her head bent over the onions, Dolly inched a little nearer to friendship by making her one and only revelation of that nature. 'But *we* don't you see – Sam can't . . . not proper . . . not since his legs.' Briskly, she took the dish from Mrs Farr and hurried on. 'Look, let me cut that up and run it through the mincer a couple of times. That's a start at least. I know – burgers! Like you see in America, at the pictures. We'll make them so full of herbs and spices and onion, coat them in spicy breadcrumbs and fry them in beef dripping, that they'll never know *what* sort of meat it is.'

Mrs Farr was not blind to the importance, to Dorothy, of such revelations as she had just made. Sometimes, Ursula Farr wondered whether Niall was right about pushing Dorothy.

'You could open up the most godawful can of worms, Ursula.'

'If I can open up her mind, I'll take a chance with the worms.'

'You're not the only one involved.'

'Dorothy Partridge is a level-headed, intelligent woman who has been put down all her life. It's all right for people like ourselves, we have chosen to be what we are.'

'And what are we? An old hack photographic journalist still dragging himself round the world when he should be dandling grandchildren; and a society dame who went political and kicked over the traces to join the workers.'

'As I said – we have chosen to be what we are.'

Dorothy did have potential. It was truly criminal not to give whatever help one could.

Niall had asked, 'And what are you going to make her into?'

'I shall not make her *into* anything. I simply give her as much responsibility as she wants and can cope with. Honestly Niall, she's extraordinarily inventive with the meanest ingredients. It comes of years of stretching hap'orth to look like penn'orth and knowing the value of good vegetables and cheap pulses. It's obvious that the entire family has been brought up practically vegetarian from necessity – yet I doubt if she's ever heard of Vegetarianism. Once she's learned how to handle staff, she could easily take over from me. We should all be better for somebody like Dorothy Partridge running the Ministry of Food.'

'You're probably right, Ursula, but you don't need to give me another lecture on feminism – I did help Ellen Wilkinson win her seat.'

'Then you should make one of your propaganda films about women like Dorothy.'

'*Information* films.'

'As you like.'

Now, the two older women worked as usual in companionable silence, broken occasionally by a comment, or by one of the young women – the 'Girls' – wanting instructions. Eventually Ursula Farr said, 'I'm sorry, Dorothy – what you said about you and Sam – all your years together spoilt like that.'

Dolly nodded. 'Thanks. It's a relief to have told someone. It has tended to make him a bit more aggravated than he might have been . . . to me and Harry especially. To compensate like . . . to prove to the world he's still a man. Trouble is, I never had nobody to ask about it before.' She washed basins vigorously, determined to say what had been in her head since she came to know Ursula so well.

Mrs Farr looked at the other woman quizzically.

'I just wondered if I was normal . . . you know . . . still wanting to . . . you know . . . with a man. I'm over fifty, you know, and a grandmother. I mean . . .' It appeared that she would not make it to the end of her sentence. '. . . well, do you?' The gushing water splashed into the basin and soaked her but she seemed oblivious to it. 'It's awful me asking like this, but . . . is that side of things still the same for you and your man?' She allowed her hands to float calmly in the full basin.

Ursula Farr paused to think before answering. 'Not the same . . . rather better I think. More quality than quantity, if you get my meaning.'

'I thought it might be. Women in my sort of class don't talk open about that – we can't really, we don't know the right words.'

Ten o'clock struck. Breakfasts over and the tables cleared and ready for re-opening, the time when all the girls and women had their mid-morning break. Eve Hardy came into the preparation room with her trays and tins. 'Sorry, Mrs Farr, yesterday's fish pie wasn't too popular with the Mixed Infants – they like fish-patties. Mmm, I say, what smells so good?'

Dolly thought how really lovely the girl was getting these days, but what a messed-up life they was having in that family if the gossip was true.

Mrs Farr said, 'I'm thinking of calling them "Dollyburgers" in honour of their inventor.'

Dolly busied herself getting the mid-morning break

ready. Georgia came in, and the girls from the restaurant, then Connie Hardy who, Dolly noticed, looked thinner than ever, and two WVS women – young housewives – joined them. Mrs Farr handed out slices of bread and jellied meat dripping, one of the wonderful perks for the Town Restaurant workers in these days of shortages and rationing. As usual they said, 'I really shouldn't, Dolly,' then biting into the savoury slices, closed their eyes and said, 'Mmm, beef. Wizard!'

They usually divided into women's and girls' groups, but this morning Eve went to stand with her mother, looking concerned and speaking in a low voice. Dolly noticed the mother pat the daughter's arm and smile reassuringly.

They're right, it looks like there's trouble in that quarter, thought Dolly, as she poured drinking chocolate from the enamel jug. Although they were always very nice to her and brought her into the conversation, except for Mrs Farr they were all either much younger or, like Mrs Hardy, of the class of woman that she would never have come into contact with in the normal course of events. Consequently, she either stood and listened to their smart, easy talk, or busied herself in a job like biscuit-making.

'How is your other son these days, Mrs Partridge? Have you heard from him?' Georgia Kennedy asked.

'Harry?'

'The one in the Paras. I saw you seeing him off.'

'That's Harry. I haven't heard for a fortnight. I think he was going to a training camp somewhere.'

'I used to see him at the Council offices,' said Georgia, 'but I never knew he was your son. Oh, is he a looker!'

'Oh, tell more, tell more,' said one of the girls, putting them all in a giggling mood.

'You know him, Trix,' said one of the kitchen girls. 'Harry Partridge – we used to go to the junior school together. You remember him, don't you, Cynth?'

'*That* Harry.'

'Yes, the one we used to call "Blondie". Pammy used to go out with him once, didn't you, Pammy?'

'When I was young,' said Pammy. 'All the girls was after Blondie Partridge.'

'Is he really your son, Dolly?'

'Of course he is,' said Pammy. 'He's Marie's brother-in-law.'

Cynth said, 'I had a real pash on Harry Partridge at one time. He had all that thick blond hair . . . used to wear it long on top and it used to flop down over one eye.'

'And lovely dark blue eyes . . . and a dimple in his chin – not one of those horrible deep ones, but one that just came when he smiled. I haven't seen him for ages. Is he still just as good-looking?'

Dolly's eyes sparkled at these pretty girls putting her beautiful Harry at the centre of the conversation. 'Well, I'm prejudiced I suppose, but I can't think offhand of a young man in Markham who could beat him if there was a competition for it.'

'Is he married yet?' Cynth asked.

'Our Harry get married? Somebody'll have to catch him first.'

'Oo, what a terrible waste. I'll bet he looks smashing in his uniform.'

Mrs Farr and Connie Hardy found themselves in close proximity whilst the young element was getting itself het up over yet another handsome and eligible bachelor. The women smiled at one another, perhaps with regret in the acknowledgement that they would never again be in a group so alight at a name and a male image. Remembering fleetingly how, long ago, somebody had dropped Niall's name . . . 'You must know him, he's the journalist Niall O'Neill', or jokingly, 'Fancy you not knowing Freddy Hardy, Con. Oh, he's definitely your type. Not only good-looking, he's loaded and he's really got It.'

Connie said quietly, 'Even Evie's secret romance is forgotten for the minute.'

Mrs Farr, who had noticed that Eve, like the rest of the young element, leaned slightly and eagerly towards whoever was talking at the moment, alive in the atmosphere of sex, gave Connie a questioning and interested look. 'Secret romance? Eve?'

Connie shrugged. 'It's not much good asking me. She has a man somewhere, but behaves as though it is the direst secret. I thought perhaps you might know something.'

Mrs Farr shook her head.

As the girls went back to the kitchens, Marie came in with her till-roll and breakfast takings.

'We were talking about your brother-in-law, Marie,' said Georgia. 'The girls vote him the handsomest man in Markham.'

Marie flicked a look at Dorothy – they never said anything about the family without first checking with one another. 'Harry,' Dorothy said, with a soft look in her eye. Marie knew that Harry was the favourite. It could be hurtful when it was Charlie who was the responsible one, who went with Sam to the Limb Centre and dug the garden over so his father could plant it, when Harry was just as capable. Everybody had always treated Harry as special. Looks isn't everything.

'Harry? I can't really think of him as a man. He is, of course – it's just with Charlie being older, more responsible.'

Georgia sensed Marie's slight pique, so poured her a mug of cocoa.

Marie always felt slightly ill at ease with the posher element. Not that Mrs Kennedy was on the same level as the Hardys. When she was Georgia Honeycombe she had gone to the same Church school as Marie, but afterwards she had been sent to Secretarial College, and then married a manager who was captain of Markham Town cricket team.

Those sort of things separated people. Like Charlie working for the Post Office and Harry working in the Council Offices had put them apart from boys they had gone to school with who had only got labouring jobs.

Because of cashing-up, Marie always came in later for her morning break, so that she was usually left with the WVS and Mrs Hardy and Mrs Kennedy. She would have felt easier if Trix and Pammy and the others were there. Not that anybody treated her any different from themselves, and Marie often wanted to kick herself afterwards for being so tongue-tied. I never used to be like that when I worked in the hairdressers; I could talk to anybody when we were alone in the cubicle.

Once, when she had mentioned it, Sam had said, 'You're worth ten of any of them. That sort is all froth. Not one of them knows how to make a decent meal, I'll be bound.'

'We're not talking about decent meals, you daft thing,' Dolly had said. 'I know what Marie's talking about. Manners and that kind of thing – saying the right thing and not saying the wrong one.'

'I know their sort. Have you ever really listened to what they say?'

'Yes, Dad, I have,' Marie had said. 'And I know what you're going to say – that they don't ever actually *say* anything.'

'Right.'

'Yes, but what I mean is that me and Mum would feel a lot more at ease if I could just answer in the same way. I'm not looking for any great discussion with them – just to know how to be as silly as they are sometimes – so that you fit in.'

Sam had raised his eyes disgustedly. 'I don't want you two coming home here talking like some Ladies' Circle. Soon as it gets like that you can pack it up.'

'Take no notice, Marie. He'd like us to spend our days up to our elbows in soda-water.'

This morning, though, a letter from Charlie saying how much he missed her had made Marie feel very good about Charlie.

'What's he like then, your Charlie?' Georgia asked.

Marie showed a photo of Charlie with his three new stripes.

'I know him,' Georgia said.

'I should think you do,' said Marie. 'He delivered your mail for enough years.'

'Our postman's a real sweetie, isn't he, Ma?' Eve said.

Connie nodded, and went on with the quiet conversation she was having with Mrs Farr.

'Monty Iremonger?' Marie said.

'I know the one you mean,' Georgia said. 'Always looks a glum-faced old devil.'

'He's not like that at all,' Eve protested in her precise crystalline accents. 'Really. It's just his expression. He's really a nice old grandpa sort of man.' To tell them of the picture he had painted for her which she had found so moving would have been, somehow, to betray him. She had not told them at home where it had come from, not that anyone except Nanny Bryce would be likely to ask – they lived very separate lives in that house.

Marie said, 'If it hadn't been for the war, Monty would have been retired.'

'Oh,' said Eve with absolute sincerity, 'that would be awful. I should really miss Mr Iremonger. When I was little, I used to be afraid of Santa Claus, then I began to pretend that, instead of it being that great man in black boots who was going to come into the nursery in the middle of the night, that it would be Mr Iremonger.' She laughed. 'Well, actually, I used to make up a story that he would marry Nanny Bryce and come to live in the nursery too.'

Marie again felt alienated – envious, almost, of girls whose childhood revolved around nurseries, and of girls like Georgia Kennedy who could join in so easily that you would think she had a nanny. Marie Partridge would never achieve that kind of sophistication in a thousand years. How had Georgia Kennedy done it?

Georgia flipped the trigger of her novel case, up popped cigarettes, which she offered to Eve and the WVS women. 'Go on, I've got a box of fifty.' Eve took one automatically and tapped the end to firm the tobacco.

'I don't,' said Marie at the offer.

'Haven't you ever?' one of the WVS women asked.

'Charlie never liked girls who smoked.'

'Doesn't Charlie smoke either?' Georgia asked.

'Oh yes. He's been smoking since he was fourteen, so he says.'

'Well, what's wrong with you having a gasper then?'

'Well, you know . . .' Well? What *is* wrong with me having one?

'Go on,' insisted Georgia. 'A fag will do you the world of good.'

And Marie saw that it would.

Saw their nonchalantly hanging wrists, as they dangled the cigarette, flicking and tapping it from time to time; saw their red pouting mouth as they touched the cork tips to their lips, the mysterious wreath of smoke curling and making them half-close their eyes from time to time, and the hand held at the height of the cheek as they exhaled.

And she saw something else. It didn't matter what half-baked thing you came out with if you were tapping ash from your cigarette, it was the cigarette that counted, not what you said. And their manicured and varnished finger-nails. And the way they always perched and twisted their legs, showing off their knees, or leaned on things with their backs arched and their bums stuck out.

'OK. I'll try one, if you don't mind.'

She lit one and inhaled gently.

'You do smoke – I'll bet you've been having gaspers for years when Charlie wasn't looking,' Georgia said.

'No, honestly.' Marie suddenly felt enormously pleased with herself. The smoke twirled through her buzzing head like a glass of sherry.

'I'll tell you one thing, Eve,' Georgia Kennedy said in her easy manner as she flipped her lighter to her own cigarette, 'if I was to have a postman coming into my bedroom, then I'd have Marie's Charlie – he's got such super hair.'

'Has he really?' Eve asked politely.

Marie nodded. 'It's very thick and curly.'

'All over everywhere?' one of the WVS women asked, giggling.

The rest of the young and classy laughed lightly.

Then Marie realized the double meaning. She couldn't look in Dolly's direction, but saw from the edge of her vision that Dolly was disappearing into the kitchen. She felt gauche. Froth, as Sam said. But Marie wanted to be frothy, frivolous. She wanted to have the same air of hardness and . . . knowingness that their class of woman had – and it came. 'Ah ah, now that would be telling,' said Marie, tapping her forefinger on the cigarette.

The other four shrilled at nothing in the constrained way of many respectable housewives of the Home Counties during the Forties War.

Women on long leashes coming out of their little homes, out of their respectable shells, women talking in groups with other women, drawing one another out, spasms of shared titillation about their own men or many men, moments of madness, opening up as they had never done since marriage had domesticated them.

Learning to talk with other women. Rolling up one another's hair, helping one another to brush on bleach. Grooming, comforting, envying, commiserating. Reclaiming a few of the small freedoms that their great-grandmothers used to have working with other women in the milking parlours, the threshing sheds and gleaning fields. Small freedoms which had been lost to townswomen in the south of England where there were no cotton mills or stocking factories or bath-houses or public laundries and where it was not done for married women to go out to work. Out of the home on a long leash.

'Come along, you young things,' Connie Hardy's voice. 'I think it's time we cleared out of Mrs Farr's work-place.'

'And you girls take your cigarette smoke with you – it's out of bounds in my kitchen.'

'Sorry, Mrs Farr darling,' Georgia called. 'Promise not to do it again.'

As the months of the war ground on, the changes taking place in Britain were profound. People were subject to dozens of new laws and controls. Children accepted barbed-wire, tank traps and gun emplacements as part of the environment. Older children began to take for granted that cakeshops displayed empty dishes and sweetshops faded dummies.

They accepted that the seaside had become a dangerous place but longed for it; they accepted the absence of, yet longed for, coach trips, Sunday School outings, banana custard, oranges at Christmas and Saturday cakes with cherries and icing. Except for a few days a month, they went without pear-drops, chocolate nuts and liquorice boot-laces and forgot that there had once been a time of long pencils in school.

In the Chapel Kitchens, a ritual morning gathering for cocoa continued even though the constituents of the group changed. Trix went into the ATS and Pammy into the explosives factory that had opened a few miles outside Markham.

1989

'Do you know, Hildy, I would not live through those middle years of the war again for anything.'

'I also. It is sad, but you read it so well, I like to hear what happened to all these people even though I know the truth. You remember the old Madam, how straight up she used to sit in that chair of hers?'

'The truth of Connie was that she was too fragile a creature for an old bugger like my father.'

'You don't swear like that when Joshua is here, or I shall tell you sharp.'

'What else? An old shit, as Connie called him? And he was. I believe I must always have known about his affairs, but it is not the kind of thing a girl wants to believe about her father. I once caught a glimpse of him in Winchester, helping a girl into his car . . . it was the way he did it, his hand accidentally-on-purpose on her backside . . . but I did not want to know.'

The old companion nodded.

'Can you imagine how Connie must have felt? Sharing his body with who knows how many women, sharing the same shower where he washed them off . . . and always having to keep up appearances. But I believe that there was a time when she really loved him in spite of all that.'

'How did Giacopazzi know?'

'Some of it surmise, but she has a finger on the truth. A lot of it from gossip: locals always know what's going on. Some of it from me: Georgia and I exchanged a lot of confidences, as girls do. But the thing one has to admire is that she observed us . . . knew us all so well. I suppose she must have been keeping some kind of journal. It is all so right.' She lapsed into silence, then went on, 'It was when I taught her to drive that we first became quite friendly, then again after Connie left, but closer. It is apparently the bits about Connie that she wants me to approve.'

'And?'

'The facts might not be exact, but it is probably nearer to the truth than any autobiography Connie might have written. Shall I go on reading, or shall we call it a day?'

'Read some more. I have never learned to read English well. I should like to know it all before we leave for London. When we get there . . . cheee! We shall have no time to read books.'

1941

Whenever Nick got time off, he came to Markham. And whenever she protested that really she shouldn't keep going out with him like this, he persuaded her.

'Admit it, Georgia Honeycombe, we always have a good time when we're together.'

'But we shouldn't be together.'

'It's innocent enough. Bugger it, Georgia, it has to be – you don't let anything decadent happen.'

Long ago, when the two of them were about fourteen and had truanted for a week, her mother had foretold: 'That Nick Crockford takes after his father, he's got an air of degeneracy about him – if you don't watch out, Georgia, he'll get you into something more than just naughtiness.'

The trouble was, it was that air her mother called degeneracy which aroused Georgia. Admitting it to herself, when they were together, she was more careful to keep control, both of herself and the situation. Kept to the straight and narrow by feeling guilty.

If the nuns oppressed little Catholic girls with threats of Hell and damnation, then Anglican teachers did as good a job on theirs by the use of conscience and guilt – and the Anglicans do not even provide the relief of the confessional and penance.

But Georgia was first and foremost a woman in full bloom, and only second a product of the C of E school. It was not easy for her during the time when Nick came to Markham and Hugh did not.

Sometimes he called to take her to the pictures or to a dance in Southampton or Portsmouth, but not in Markham. And she did enjoy his company greatly. They spoke the same language, were never awkward or tongue-tied, could argue fiercely without malice and laugh at small shared jokes. She liked his rambling conversation, ranging from the countryside, about which he would talk with great knowledge, to politics, about which he would talk with great passion, to books and history. She liked his attention to her, listening to her opinions, laughing at her jokes, behaving as though she mattered.

She liked him, because he was her sort. They knew one another to their depths, so that when she talked to him seriously about how bad she felt about deceiving Hugh, Nick said, 'All right, I understand. I won't try anything till you ask me.' And he meant it. 'You will ask me. You'll drop into my hands like a ripe medlar.' And he was convinced that she would. She never mentioned her suspicion – almost certainty – that Hugh was interested in the Wren officer, Angela, knowing that Nick would have no compunction about using this as a lever to prise her loose from Hugh.

On that July afternoon, as she entered a final total in a final column, there was a quiet knock at the back door of her office. Suddenly there was Nick's tall, broad body filling the tiny room.

'Nick! What are you doing here?'

'It's all right, nobody saw me sneak in – I was careful.'

'Fool, I didn't mean . . .'

He sat down upon the only other chair, elbows on knees in the relaxed position that was typical of him. She sensed that he had something on his mind or he would not have come to her office, but all he said was, 'I've got Sunday off, I thought we could take our bikes out in the country.'

'Lovely. I'll meet you along the road.'

'Right.'

'You didn't come just to tell me that.'

'No, you're right. I wasn't going to say anything till we'd had our day out. It's well . . . I've been transferred to a Liverpool brigade.'

Suddenly she was engulfed in confused emotions. She knew what it was like in Liverpool. As with all the great cities in Britain, Liverpool had been a prime target for the Luftwaffe: people went underground every night, and when they came up next morning there were pretty good odds that their home had been reduced to a hole in the ground. Liverpool was perhaps no more dangerous than Southampton, but it was at the other end of the country.

'You're a free agent, Nick.'

'They need firemen there.'

'If you want to go I can't stop you.'

'It's not a question of *want*.'

'And it's nothing to do with me anyway, is it?'

'What's up, Georgia? You're sounding like a niggly wife!'

'How would you know *what* a wife sounded like? You haven't seen yours in months.'

His cheeks became suffused, but his voice remained calm. 'You know that I haven't got a wife! Anyway, I thought you'd prefer it if I didn't see her.'

She knew that he had stopped going to see Pete, saying that it was confusing to him now that Nancy was set up with another man. But there were times when she knew that he longed to see his little boy. She concentrated on making pencil lines between wormholes on her desk top.

'It's none of my business.'

'Isn't it, Georgia, isn't it?'

She was silent.

'I said I would leave things until you wanted to change them. You know what I want.'

'I know.'

'Well?'

'How can I change them? I'm married to Hugh.'

'So what do we do? Shall I just go to Liverpool and that's that?'

Scraping the chair back, she stood up and turned away from him. 'I don't know, Nick. I don't *know!*'

At last he had got her to admit that their situation was not static, that they were not just good friends and dancing partners – company for one another, each with their partners gone.

He rose and came round to her side of the desk. She breathed in the familiar warm scent that was unique to him – harsh red soap, Erasmic shaving soap, and Nick's own wholesome sweat, skin and hair. The male scent that had enveloped her many times when they had sat close in the pictures, danced, and when he had sometimes suddenly, urgently gathered her to him and kissed her as though it was his last moment upon earth.

'I said I won't press you again to go to bed with me, Georgia, and I won't; but I never promised that I wouldn't tell you that I want to.' He held her face and ruffled her hair with his fingers. 'That I desire you, need you.' When he drew her to him, she did not pull back. 'I didn't say that I wouldn't kiss you. I didn't say that I wouldn't tell you that I love you.' He kissed her, lightly but fully on the mouth. 'I love you, Georgia Honeycombe.'

She still had her arms about him when there was a quiet tap on the door. It opened immediately and Eve Hardy's head appeared. She was at once flustered. 'Oh! I'm awfully sorry, Georgia. I just wondered if you had . . . Never mind. I'm sorry.'

Nick, unperturbed, released Georgia and said, 'It's all right, I was just going.'

'No, no. I'm sorry, but I was going to put the van away and I only came to ask if you would like a lift home, Georgia.'

In a moment, Nick had gone.

Eve said, 'How awful of me. I'm frightfully sorry, Georgia. I keep saying I'm sorry, don't I? That's because I'm embarrassed.'

Georgia smiled to cover her own embarrassment. 'It's not your fault. I shouldn't be entertaining men in my office, should I?' Suddenly there was a lump in her throat and so many tears gathered that she could not blink them away. 'I'm sorry,' she said. Then gave a laugh. 'How many times are we going to say sorry to each other?'

Eve came to Georgia and put arms about her. 'Would you like to talk about it? I'm a very good listener.'

Georgia was surprised at the mature tone of Eve Hardy's voice, which was usually cheerful and too girlish for her age.

'Yes,' said Georgia. 'Yes, I should like to.'

It was necessary for Eve to allow her shy look to roam a little before she let it meet Georgia's eyes. 'Maybe you'll be able to do the same for me some time.'

In Eve Hardy's eyes, Georgia saw there was the same anguish and hurt as in her own.

That was the first of many nights that Eve was to spend in the beautifully done-up spare-room which Georgia had decorated and refurbished herself.

On the Sunday morning, Georgia and Nick met on the road outside the town. It was warm, with breeze enough to make cycling seem the most pleasant pastime in the world. At lunch-time, they sat outside The Cricketers, which had sometimes been their resting place on other occasions like this.

He carried the shandies from the pub to the meadow where she was sitting beside the stream. They sat quietly, eating cheese biscuits and drinking. He studied her. The overhead July sun made her hair glow like marigolds and illuminated her lithe body in its striped dress. He traced one of the stripes from her shoulder to her waist. Her proportions were so much the reverse of those of Nancy, who had small neat breasts and broad hips.

How did I ever come to let her get away from me? he thought. Because I was young, and he had a posh accent and manager's job and his own house. Because Georgia was young and dazzled by his attention and I thought I wasn't good enough.

It was only looking at it from the distance of time and maturity that he could see how little it had taken for two country kids like himself and Georgia to be taken in. Hugh Kennedy was nothing, nobody. Captain of Markham cricket team and loud-mouth of the tennis court. Looking at it from here, Nick Crockford knew – I shall make ten of Hugh Kennedy.

He had recently received a letter from Nancy saying that she was going to get married, and asking him whether he minded if they adopted Pete. For a week he had prevaricated: not that he minded the marriage, but he did not want Peter to have the red-haired signalman's name. He knew that he was not being fair. To all intents and purposes, the other man was Peter's father now. He would have all the bother of bringing him up. Again he put it from his mind and turned again to thinking about Hugh Kennedy.

The trouble was, he had not known at the time that he was worth ten of Hugh Kennedy. Instead he had, unconsciously, made his life as different as he could from Hugh's by giving up his college place and going on the Council road gang, joining the AFS when Hugh joined the Territorial Army, going about with Nancy Miles because she was faintly sluttish, was good fun, wasn't afraid of enjoying sex, and didn't mind that there was no marriage ceremony. He hadn't bargained for the complication of Pete, yet had found a lot of joy in watching him develop over the months.

'I really love this place, Nick. Look, look, ducklings.' Neither of them had mentioned the scene of last Friday.

The heat of midday blended the pungent waterside herbiage, the dank rivery smell and the new-mown grass that lay in swathes about them. They sat on the bank and fed crumbs to the ducks, then lay back under the blue, cloudless sky slowly, unaware that this was all part of allowing themselves to sink deeper and deeper in love. At that time, in that meadow, the world was, for a moment, Eden.

The past was over as far as he was concerned. He had told her that he loved her – now it was up to her.

'Look, Nick! Up there. Look!' Georgia pointed immediately above their heads.

He squinted into the bright summer sky. 'I see it! Christ, there are dozens – I didn't hear any air-raid warning.'

So high that they would have been invisible had it not been for the sun gleaming off their surfaces, a shoal of whitebait in formation, the bombers moved slowly across the sky.

'Dorniers!'

'Junkers.'

'They could be. Listen.'

Behind them, the bombers trailed the lum-lum beat of precision engineering and drone of propellers.

'Dorniers.'

Suddenly, silently, all around the bombers appeared white puffs. Like balls of pulled cotton-wool, the shells of distant big guns burst; seconds later, each explosion, as it reached the meadow by the pub, sounded like the soft pop of a baked potato bursting its skin.

'My God, Georgia, if you didn't know, you'd say that was really beautiful, the way the silver shines against the blue, and the white puffs – there's something very artistic about it. Do you know what I mean?'

'It's like it is happening somewhere else. They seem so remote . . . you can't imagine that there are men there.'

The guns stopped firing, and the shoal, presumably temporarily out of range, swam steadily on.

Suddenly there was chaos amongst the shoal of bombers as it was attacked on all sides by fighter planes. Suddenly the silver fish in the blue sky stopped being beautiful. Suddenly the battle stopped being remote.

Vapour trails began to criss-cross the sky as Spitfires

climbed and dived in attack. The sound of machine-gunning sounded like nothing except what it was – aggressive and bloody. Georgia and Nick found themselves standing. Georgia gripped Nick's hand. A black streamer tinged with red and white appeared and ran down towards earth. 'They've got one!' 'Two!' Then a chrysanthemum of fire appeared and was smeared across the sky. Then the whine of the first hit and the explosion of the second reached the meadow by the pub. Within seconds the whine became a scream, followed by a ball of fire at ground level a mile or so distant. Then a series of other explosions as the bombs unloaded from the stricken German planes plunged into the woods and farmlands of rural England. Within seconds ripening fields of corn were afire.

It was not until someone said, 'The sods! That field was nearly ready for harvesting', that Nick and Georgia realized that other people had come out of the pub and that they too were standing along the edge of the stream to get a view of the air-battle. A stick of bombs, probably from a crippled plane lightening its load in an attempt to escape the Spitfires, landed in a field quite close by and something substantial began to burn.

One of the dinner-time drinkers, a man in working corduroys, shouted, 'That's the farmhouse! Come on, I got the tractor.' Men and youths leaped into the trailer.

Nick picked up his jacket. 'I'll come.'

'Nick . . .'

'I'll see what I can do over there. Wait here if you like.'

'I'm coming too.' The tractor roared, Nick leaped on the trailer and held out a hand to pull her on.

They were at the farm within a few minutes, already some land-girls and labourers were dipping pails in the stream and rushing to where the corner of a barn and an outside rick were burning. Somebody shouted excitedly.

'An engine come down on it. It was a burning engine from one of the Jerry planes, and it come down over there.'

Nick ran to the group of people who were dipping milking-pails and buckets into a large cattle trough and rushing back and forth. 'Form a chain, pass them hand to hand.'

Soon there were enough helpers to form two chains from the trough to the barn, but the trough was fast emptying so he shouted orders to re-form from the pump, telling the helpers to take turn and turn about at the exhausting pumping. Soon there was a rhythm to the passing of buckets, leaving Nick free to go to the head of the chain and direct the water where it would be most effective. The barn was old and dry and well creosoted.

Suddenly there was a roar as something inside the barn fired, blowing outwards at the fire-fighters. He felt the fierce heat and heard a frightening rush of air. 'Your hair, your hair,' he shouted to Georgia, and dashed water at her. 'Here, can I have this?' A land-girl, with her felt hat rammed down over her eyes, nodded as Nick ripped off her green neckerchief and plunged it in water. 'Tie this round your head,' he told Georgia. 'See if you can find something to cover your arms and tell the others.' To the tractor driver he shouted, 'What's in there?'

'Not much except a few drums of tractor fuel and that.'

'What else?'

'A dozen or so gallons of petrol.'

'Christ all bloody mighty! Get everybody back.'

'Let him burn hisself out,' said the farmer.

'And take your house and dairy with it? Whereabouts is the fuel?'

The owner pointed out where the store lay hidden: the fire was still well away.

'I'm going in, if somebody will back up the trailer.'

'Nick, no!'

It was as though Georgia had not spoken, and in a minute one of the men had mounted the tractor, backed the trailer through the end door and, in a few minutes more, was driving out again with the drums Nick had loaded.

'Now start pumping again.'

Like the others, Georgia pulled over her head a potato sack with slits hastily made in it and joined in pumping and passing buckets, bowls and milk-pails.

It was not an easy fire to quench, for scattered everywhere was bone-dry straw and hay. 'Get shovels and spades to beat out the sparks,' Nick shouted. 'Find some rakes and get that bloody lot away from here.' Automatically people obeyed him. It was a struggle. As soon as the flames seemed to be under control, something in the barn would pop or explode and feed the flames. Soon the flames had licked away one entire corner of the barn. Nick appeared to have an almost personal antagonism towards the flames: he attacked as though they were an enemy, not hearing the others shouting at one another, or their swearing and cursing as somebody slipped in the mud or stood on a charred timber – there was only the roar of burning.

He went closer and closer in towards the fire, hurling the water high so that it could cascade more effectively down the clapboard walls. Slowly, slowly the fire retreated. Then it was out, but Nick would not let the coming buckets stop until there was not a wisp of smoke. 'I think he's out,' said the tractor-driver, and there was a united sigh.

'It's out all right,' said Nick.

The shouting and noise faded and there was a peculiar silence, almost as though no one dared to breathe for fear of fanning a spark.

The farmer, black-faced and blistered, came forward and shook Nick's hand. 'I never gave it a thought, lad . . . you know, the tractor fuel and that.'

'You aren't the only silly bugger hoarding petrol,' Nick said, almost genially.

The farm-wife said to Nick. 'You done well, lad. I reckon you done that before today.'

'Not with buckets I haven't.'

'Well, you got in some pretty good practice today.'

The pub landlady and some other women came up to the farm with jugs of beer. The land-girls and the men had dropped exhausted and shaken to sit on anything handy.

'Here, gel,' the landlady gave Georgia a tankard. 'Give this to that man of yourn.'

'I can do with that.' As Nick put the tankard to his mouth he hissed through his teeth from unexpected pain. 'Aah . . . my lips!' He raised his fingers gingerly to feel; his hands too were covered with blisters and raw areas where others had burst. 'Am I a sight?'

He too was black-faced and blistered from the searing heat. His shirt, and a flowery scarf bound around his head, were spotted with brown burn-rings, not much of his eyebrows or lashes remained, and that part of his hair which had been left exposed was singed.

'Your face is burnt. And your hair.'

'It's not much.'

Someone brought out a bucket of salt and water for washing blistered skin.

Nick looked around him. The rickyard was a pungent, black mess, the farm labourers in singed and dirty shirts, soaked working trousers with yorks tied beneath the knees. The land-girls in khaki dungarees, soaked to brown with sweat and water, the farm-wife in old, drab, field clothes. Georgia, her summer dress grubby from the potato-sack and strappy sandals ruined, her face smeared with ash. For a moment, he wondered how these strangers saw her. It suddenly seemed an unreasonably important fact that she was a country girl. To anyone else, she probably looked as though she had never hiked a country lane or milked a goat in her life – he had a foolish urge to announce to them that she was not a town girl and that he loved her.

'How does that feel?' Georgia asked. The initial relief of

having dipped his hands and soaked his face in saline solution was wearing off.

He flexed his rag-bound fingers and winced. 'I'll survive.' He grinned at her and felt the soda-solution on his face crack and flake off.

As they walked away from the farmyard, the woman ran up to him and patted Nick's arm. 'Good luck, lad. Come and see us one day in your fireman's uniform.' To Georgia she said, 'He tells us he's off to Liverpool. If you asks me, we ought to thank God there's men like him.'

Georgia nodded, a faint polite smile. 'We do.'

1942

July

Quite late one evening, Ursula Farr, answering her door bell, was surprised to discover Connie Hardy in the porch.

'I'm sorry . . . it is so late, but I have no one else . . .' Her usual coolness was disturbed, her emotions were close to the surface.

'It's not late for me,' Ursula said, and without fuss took her through to a large old-fashioned conservatory and poured them both generous gins.

Connie struggled to retain what remained of her composure. 'This is delightful. It catches the evening sun. Such an atmosphere – oh, you have a datura – the perfume.'

'I brought the plant home myself from my travels. But you did not call to admire my datura.'

'I'm sorry. Yes. It is hopeless. I have to go away.'

'Are things so bad for you?'

'You don't sound surprised.'

'I find fewer and fewer things surprising – alas. It is perhaps a sign of age . . . of the state of society. But it is surprising that you use such a word as hopeless.'

'It is how I feel. I must go away. I'm already on my way to drinking myself into an early grave.' She downed the contents of her glass, but refused any more.

'It is your marriage, I suppose.'

Connie gave a soft snort. 'Isn't it always that which drives women to drink?'

'A good marriage is worth everything. But a bad one? It is certainly not worth being driven to drink for.'

'And Eve. It seems to me the worst thing that a mother can do is to abandon her child.'

'Eve is what, twenty-three, twenty-four? And why does

it mean that you must abandon her? Because one relationship fails, it doesn't mean that every other one involving you fails with it.'

'But the house . . . oh, everything!'

For a moment, Ursula thought that Connie would break down. She would have comforted her as she herself would have felt comforted, by close contact and arms, but Connie tensed at Ursula's gentle touch. A woman who had never learned how to deal with the contact of other women.

'A house is nothing. Bricks and mortar only.'

'But who will run it, if I go? I won't leave Eve to do it.'

'If the part you play in your house is as its custodian, then that isn't a big enough part for any woman, a mere keeper of furniture and fittings. Is that what you are there?'

'Yes. Except for trying to be *something* to Eve. I wish that I could have made a better job of it all – but you see . . . I had no idea . . . no idea at all. Perhaps Freddy would not have needed other women if I had been better at everything.' She forced a cigarette into her holder and held it to the flame, drawing it into the tip; as she inhaled deeply her hand trembled.

Ursula felt both close to and distant from Connie Hardy, sensing that the younger woman might, at any moment, withdraw; so she merely nodded non-committally but said nothing.

Connie continued. 'Freddy and I have always been poles apart. There was always that one thing . . . that was . . . was good between us. You understand? I hope that I don't embarrass you.'

'You don't. Sex has never embarrassed me.'

'I see now that our entire marriage was held together by brief moments of physical attraction. Then, about a year ago – it was during one of the night raids – as they say . . . the scales fell from my eyes and I was able to see us as we are. In the middle of the night, I was sheltering in the bowels of my house and searching for gin, whilst he was charming an ENSA girl. Eve . . . well, she was God knew where.'

'If your marriage has failed, then it has failed you both . . . if you will only stop taking all the blame upon yourself . . .'

Connie stubbed out her cigarette and refilled her holder, using the action, Ursula suspected, to cover her emotions.

Eventually, she said quietly, 'That's right! I'm not entirely to blame. I have never been unfaithful.'

Soon after that she had left.

Having made the move to talk to Ursula that night, Connie Hardy was able to tell Eve something of how she felt. It was typical of Connie that she asked her daughter to meet her in the impersonal surroundings of a large, once-fashionable hotel out of town. They sat in its still-splendid restaurant talking quietly, as their training dictated, in controlled and unemotional tones.

'It is now or never, darling. I have to go. I couldn't bear the thought of the Markham gossips watching me slide downhill as people watched your grandmother. They probably say that I am a parasite and a social butterfly, and I may be; but I have my pride.'

'Ma, don't say such things, don't put yourself down.'

'I am down, Eve, but I do not intend to stay there.'

'Have you told my father?'

'No. I want to discuss it with you first.'

Eve looked at her mother. Why do we behave like this? If she were Dolly Partridge and I Dolly's daughter, or Marie, we should be weeping or showing our anguish. Do I feel anything for her that I would not feel if any other woman sat there telling me that she was leaving her husband? Does she feel for me? Is this only a step away from the kindly way she dismisses servants – the informal interview in Madam's sitting-room?

She remembered Trix, who used to work in the kitchens. 'My Mum's cleared off. I don't blame her. D'you know what? She left the wash-boiler full on and cut the flies out of my Dad's best trousers because he only wore them when he went off to see his floozie. He thought I was going to stop home and be skivvy. I told him (Christ! You could have heard us t'other end of town going hammer and tongs), I told him, Serves you right, you dirty old devil, don't think I'm going to wait on you, if you was mine, I'd a cut off more than your flies. That's when I cleared out and went to live with Pammy.'

And we sit on this expensive, neutral ground. If ever I have children, I shall touch them, hug them, shout and cry at them. There will be no holds barred when it comes to showing them I love them. Perhaps she doesn't love me. Never has. Nanny Bryce was my surrogate mother from the day I was born.

'What will happen. . . ? At home, I mean.'

'That is what I wanted to discuss first – though your father may have other ideas once I have gone.'

'He wouldn't . . .' Eve could not bring herself to articulate the thought.

'Bring in his woman? Probably not, because if he did then she might be led to believe there was a commitment on his part. No, I rather thought that he might see you as hostess and Nanny Bryce or someone younger as housekeeper. I wanted to give you fair warning. He can be very persuasive . . . pressing, even, if he thinks that you owe him some due.'

Eve fiddled with her napkin. 'I have been thinking about taking up nursing, or something more useful than driving the school meals van. Perhaps now I shall. I don't think that I could live there.' How to say it? 'Actually . . . I shouldn't like to live at home if . . . if you were not there. I should not think it was home.' She blushed.

Connie twisted a new cigarette into her holder. How to deal with Eve being so emotional? 'That's sweet of you, Evie, but you must be practical . . . I mean about affording . . . We have both been used to not having to think about that. I have a little money still from your Uncle Douglas's legacy.'

'And I have never touched what he left me. You know, Mother, if you think about it, it has been Pa's style of living that has made us expensive women. Georgia Kennedy never went skiing or sailing, she doesn't give cocktail parties – so she needs none of the clothes or equipment. If I lived more simply, I should not need his allowance.'

'I will not influence you. You are a grown woman, and must do whatever you decide to do. I am sorry that my actions will put you in the position of having to make any decision at all.'

'I think Georgia Kennedy would be glad of someone to live with her – she has hinted at it once or twice.'

'Are you sure that she meant another woman?'

'I'm sure.'

'I shall not leave for two weeks – you have time to consider. Don't do anything hastily.'

'Why in two weeks?'

'That is when I join my unit.'

'Mother! A unit? What unit? You have it all planned?'

'Yes. It is about the only thing I can do where age is of no importance. They are so short of aviators that they will take anybody who can fly anything.'

'Fly, Ma?'

Suddenly Connie looked eager, became animated. 'Collecting and delivering aircraft. I've had a full pilot's licence all my life. I've had a try-out at Eastleigh – they welcomed me with open arms. It is essential work.'

'Goodness!'

Had her mother said that she had joined a troupe of acrobats, Eve Hardy would not have been more surprised.

Connie blinked nervously and smiled with caution. 'I thought of a hundred different ways of breaking the news to you, but there seemed to be no easy way.'

Eve's hand crept across the table to take Connie's. 'Oh Ma, I'm so proud of you.'

1942

The outing that had been talked about came to fruition. The pre-war type of works' outing to the seaside was out of the question. Charabanc hire was restricted, and many seaside towns in the south were badly bombed, their beaches inaccessible because of mines and barbed-wire or travel restrictions. But once Georgia had suggested that they should all go for a day out in London, there was nowhere else they wanted to go.

Dolly was the only woman in the Dinner Kitchen who had a man to answer to for her movements.

'You must all be daft to go up there,' was Sam Partridge's opinion.

'It's what we need just now, to be a bit daft,' Dolly snapped. 'There's still a bit of life going on up there, not dead like this place. We shall have our lunch, go to a matinée and be back home by bedtime, which isn't any longer than you're gone when it's some Labour Party rally.'

'There hasn't been a rally since the war. But there, if Dolly Partridge has made up her mind to go traipsing off for a day, then Dolly Partridge will go. It's no good me saying anything these days. And what about Marie?'

'And what about Marie? Paula's going to look after Bonnie same as she always do.'

Paula now lived with Marie, an arrangement that worked very well for both of them. Marie saw to the house chores in the morning and got Bonnie off to school, and Paula, who had an early shift job at an engineering works, did the shopping and fetched Bonnie from school.

'Charlie's going to be upset.'

'And just why, may I ask? And in any case, who's going

to upset Charlie by opening their big mouths about it? There isn't anything wrong with Marie having a bit of fun. I suppose you think Charlie never goes out to a pub or to pictures.'

'It's different for him. And women on their own going round London isn't nothing like going for a pint. Any case, he's away from home.'

'And living in lodgings in the lap of luxury. And being a man I suppose entitles him to gad about, but Marie mustn't even have a day out with her workmates. To hear you talk, anybody'd think we was going to Brighton for a fortnight.'

'It's no use talking to you these days. You got an answer for everything.'

'No, I haven't, but I'm trying to find one.'

All of the women who worked in the old Chapel Hall buildings, the Restaurant staff, the WVS and Red Cross storekeepers, went by train to London. Even though they sometimes went shopping in the rubbled cities of Southampton and Portsmouth, they were shocked at the flattened area of London, but astonished to find that some of the boarded-up shops were selling luxuries that never seemed to reach them in Markham. Peering through the slits in some blanked-out shop windows they saw synthetic cream cakes or fancy coloured shoes, and one or two tobacco kiosks had a few real packs of cigarettes on display.

Astonishment. 'The tobacconist says that anybody can buy those fags – Players or Craven A, ten per customer.'

'Why don't we ever see stuff like that?'

Trading furtively on the pavements were men with suitcases full of branded lipsticks, or stockings, or ear-rings, talcum powder, mascara, clockwork toys or tins of salmon or ham with strange foreign labels. Compared to Markham, London was an Aladdin's cave of goods in short supply.

'Oh bliss, two packets of hairgrips,' said Georgia, having secured as well cigarettes, a cream spongecake, a Max

Factor lipstick and pair of silk stockings. 'If we went home without doing anything else, I should say I'd had a day to remember.'

Marie had found a velvet snood with flowers for Paula and some plimsolls, with white soles instead of the ugly wartime black or orange, for Bonnie.

Ursula bought three Chandler books with pre-war bindings and made the girls giggle at her delight. 'Look at the margins, oh, and the white paper, look, isn't that lovely? I can hardly bear reading the economy editions.' Hugging the Chandlers, she felt happy anticipating Niall's face when he saw the books and happy to see her girls who worked so hard and so well together giggling like schoolgirls. Over cups of Oxo which was all the coffee-shop proprietor could offer that morning, Ursula announced, 'I've got a surprise, ladies. A friend of mine has booked lunch for us. And tickets for the matinée should be waiting there for us to collect.'

'Where?' they wanted to know.

'Wait and see.'

'Lyons' Corner House, I bet. You can still get real sausages with meat at Lyons'.'

'Wait and see.'

Before lunch they went to look at Buckingham Palace, all dull and sandbagged, and at Westminster Abbey, mostly because they felt that that was part of going to London, travelling by underground, momentarily subdued at the sight of the provisions that had been made for Londoners to sleep there during the blitz.

They had expected to eat at a British restaurant such as the one in which they worked, and had only wished for Lyons' Corner House. But it was to the Café Royal that Ursula led them. There, Niall O'Neill had not only arranged things, but had settled the bill in advance.

'Oh my God,' said Pammy for them all. 'It's like stepping into heaven.'

There is no saying what any of the usual clientele thought

of the troupe of happy women with shopping bags who, having lost their initial awe of finding themselves amidst such splendour, chattered and laughed their way through a three-course meal and four bottles of wine between them.

'This is *chicken*,' hissed Pammy, 'all of it, real chicken, not even out of a tin.'

'See what it says on the menu?' Cynth said. 'Customers may be served only *three* courses.'

'And not on coupons either,' Dolly said. 'Sam's always on about how you don't need coupons if you can afford to live in posh hotels, but I never believed him. Fancy being able to live like this every day.'

They ate canned fruit salad with ice-cream – a pudding so exotic and rare in wartime that they had forgotten its taste – and cheese and biscuits.

'Look at all this cheese, it's a week's ration. I feel that guilty eating it all. I feel I ought to be taking it home,' said Marie.

'Don't let your guilt spoil your enjoyment. You've all earned it,' said Ursula.

They wondered how it was that places like this could get hold of proper coffee when whole families were lucky to get a bottle of Camp a month, but savoured every last dreg and sugar lump, urging one another to 'go on, have it whilst you've got the chance.'

Ursula, Eve and Georgia were the only ones who had ever been to a London theatre. The girls thought it wonderful and gorgeous; Ursula, keeping her thoughts to herself, saw it grim and gaunt and seedy compared to pre-war. But then the music started up and the curtains swung back on the opening of *The Dancing Years* and for a couple of hours there was light and respite from the grim times.

With the money left in the kitty, they voted to go to a tea dance. A group of laughing, unescorted women, out for a bit of fun, was exactly what the surplus of uniformed men hanging around the dance-hall needed. Even Dolly danced.

'I haven't done that for donkey's years.' She looked ten years younger and quite radiant when a sergeant in the REMEs twice asked her to dance. The third time she saw a khaki figure bending over her shoulder, she thought that it must be him.

'Harry! Oh look, Ursula, it's my Harry!' She leapt up and hugged him.

'Mum. What are you doing here? I was up on the balcony having a drink and I couldn't believe my eyes. My Ma, with a soldier, and swinging round the floor like a twenty-year-old.' Dolly hastily explained how they both came to meet in such an unlikely place. Marie came back to the table, kissed him and was quite proud to be seen doing it. But not as proud as Dolly. 'Everybody, this is Harry, my youngest son. Ursula has heard all about you . . . too much I expect. You know Pammy, don't you, and Cynth you went to school with.'

'And I know Mrs Kennedy.' He smiled directly into Georgia's eyes – as he had all the other women's. To Eve, 'I know who you are all right, Markham's own deb.'

Harry was charming to all of them. The arduous training programmes he had undergone had broadened and weathered him. He wore three stripes and had the dark red beret of the Paratroop regiment rolled up and buttoned down on his shoulder. Because of his good bone structure, his looks had not been spoiled by the cropped service style – he was an extremely handsome soldier. 'There can't be a town in the kingdom that can boast such a bunch of pretty women.' His eyes took in all the women, then flicked from Georgia to Eve and back to Georgia again. 'Save a dance for me, Mrs Kennedy – after my Ma's had one with me.'

As soon as they were on the dance floor, holding Georgia close, he said, 'Can I call and see you next time I'm on leave?'

'Well, you don't let the grass grow.'

'With a girl like you? It's far too chancy to waste time. I was watching you from up there. You've changed.'

'You don't know me.'

'I've seen you about since you were a kid. You're different from the rest . . . I'm a great woman watcher.'

Georgia pulled a face. 'Not only "watcher" from the girls' gossip.'

'Markham's premier industry, gossip. I'd love to take you out. Please, please. Only to go to the pictures if you like.' Urgently.

Georgia felt arousal and excitement growing. She suspected that he was, like Nick, that rare combination: an intelligent and physically attractive man who did not need to boost his self-esteem by behaving like a pouter pigeon. She could tell that he was weighing her up at the same time as his eyes looked uncompromisingly into hers.

'We have to grab every moment that's given to us these days. Please say you will. Come dancing with me. You're a wonderful dancer.'

And with the thrill of recklessness that was clearly signalled to him, she said, 'All right, why not?'

Later, after an interval when he danced with Marie, with his sensuality pouring over her, he whispered to Eve as they quickstepped, 'I wish I could tell you what is racing through my mind.'

Relaxed in the company of the women she worked with, and having enjoyed herself for the first time in months, Eve said archly, 'Very well, soldier, I grant your wish.'

'You might be shocked.'

'Shocked? When I work with them?' Affectionately she indicated the five kitchen girls grouped round some American soldiers, and added, 'And you know who my father is; I'm not easily shocked.'

Harry raised his eyebrows, surprised that the icy-looking maiden was so pert. Lord, he would have to play this one carefully. The redheaded princess who looked so hot for a man that he felt sure that he would have no problem there, and the blonde ice-maiden who he had always assumed was toffee-nosed and wouldn't be much fun and turned out to be a bundle of surprises. And both on his home patch.

'I'm pondering whether you're like your clever father as well as your beautiful mother?'

'You would need to know me better to answer that. I rather think that I'm like myself.'

'A man in your life?'

'Yes.'

'Are you going to tell me?'

'No.'

'Good.'

He twirled her away and she followed expertly. He gathered her back again and pressed her close in the exotic light flickering from the rotating mirrored ball.

'You're a flirt, miss.'

She laughed, showing her teeth. 'I granted you the wish to say what you were thinking, was that it?'

'No. I was thinking that I should like to go to bed with you. Are you shocked?' But he knew that she was not. Neither was she a virgin, she was too sure of herself for that. Perhaps she was a chip off the old block.

'I would guess that most of the men in this room might say the same,' she said. 'Men are always ready for bed, and I've been told that I have a bedable look about me.'

'Must have been a discerning man to describe an ice-maiden as bedable.'

As Georgia had, so did Eve respond with uncharacteristic flirtatiousness. Placing a warm palm on his cheek said, 'Feel. Warm-blooded.'

Moving his own warm hand round from the small of her back to her left breast. 'But not cold-hearted. I have a spot of leave coming up.'

'Have you now?'

'Can I meet you?'

'In Markham? Oh, the gossip, the gossip.'

'I have a short course to do on the station at Nether Wallop. Do you ever go to Salisbury?'

'I do go to Salisbury sometimes.'

'And what about the regular man in your life?'

For a moment her face straightened and he thought that he had made a wrong move, but he needed to make it clear that he was offering nothing more serious than a jolly roll in the hay.

'He has been gone a long time.' Direct as he, she made her position clear. 'I'll be waiting for him when he gets back. But I wasn't designed for a nunnery.'

Good God, thought Harry Partridge. What is happening to the girls of Markham, is the shortage of men so bad that ice-maidens are melting in their own heat?

There was something in what he said. The kitchen girls were playing enchantresses to Yankee soldiers as blatantly as Eve and Georgia flirted with Harry Partridge. There had been bravado in choosing London for their one day of luxury in the midst of daily meagre life in Markham. That, coupled with the romance of the *Dancing Years* show and being surrounded by so much rubble and charred timber, created a sense of being on the edge of danger which they found stimulating and which made them feel reckless.

As they were leaving, Georgia remembered her bags with the precious stockings and cake, and hurried back to retrieve them from the balcony table where she had left them.

The band was playing 'La Compasita', which was the music Hugh had played over and over when he was teaching her to dance, and momentarily she was drawn back to six years ago. She picked up her bags and for a moment idly gazed down on the scene below as her mind drifted back to the first months of her marriage, when life had been full of everything a girl expected of marriage, before ennui, before disillusionment, before she found herself wanting more from life and from men than Hugh could give her. A life where Georgia Kennedy amounted to something.

In the bedimmed, smoky light, the revolving mirrored ball sprinkled glitter on the couples moving in and out of the stylized love-making poses of the Tango.

Her eye was drawn to a couple skimming across the floor making a path through other dancers by the authority of their skill. Because of his stature and the way he danced, the man reminded Georgia very much of Hugh. The girl, dancing well but without the stiff and dedicated seriousness that Hugh used to demand, had long raven hair that she flicked like a true Latin as she and her partner turned. Arms stretched, they danced close. The ballroom was crammed with dancing couples, yet it was these two who held her attention.

The music reached a climax and the dance was over. The floor began to clear. Georgia's couple, before they walked off, kissed briefly but quite passionately, each holding the other fast about the neck, then pulling apart but holding one another's gaze as the lights went up. Georgia had a pang of envy that she had no man to be so totally absorbed in her. Talking close, intimate, smiling and oblivious to what was going on around them, arms about one another, they walked directly to a table below where Georgia stood.

Now she saw them clearly as, cupping his ears in her hands, the girl drew him until he was only a fraction away from her face, then briefly ran her tongue along his lips. It was as intimate a gesture as Georgia had ever seen in public. The woman was about her own age and wore WRNS officer uniform. The man was Hugh.

Downstairs, she found the group waiting for her whilst watching the dancing. Only Dolly, searching to get a last glimpse of Harry before she left, had seen what Georgia had seen; only Dolly had seen Georgia watching the dancers and the act of intimacy. Dolly recognized Hugh Kennedy.

'Come on, girls,' she said as Georgia appeared, 'quick march, or we shall miss our train.'

1942

By the time she was thirteen years of age, Little-Lena had trained almost everyone to call her Leonora. She had grown leggy and as full-bosomed as she had often dreamed of becoming. However, by the time her mother had taken her to the corset department and got her fitted out, the days of lace and shapely Maidenforms, Kestos and Gossards were long gone. They had been replaced by functional Utility brassières.

'Mrs Kennedy?' By now Georgia Kennedy was used to the girl's polite but eager preliminary. 'I hope you don't mind . . . but where do you get your pretty bras?'

'Utility. I trim them myself.'

Almost overnight, Leonora became an expert embroideress.

'I don't know what you want to waste your time doing that,' her mother grumbled, 'nobody's going to see it. You'd be better off doing a bit of make-do and mend.'

It was no use trying to explain, Mam didn't understand. Leonora didn't want embroidered bras and pants for anybody but herself. She hated the whole idea of making-do and mending. Mam's knickers were darned and her petticoats made from old nightdresses and she always hung them on the clothes-line as though she was proud of them.

To Leonora, her mother seemed obsessed by getting round shortages, she was always trying out recipes and writing tips on backs of envelopes.

There was a bit-bag in the hall cupboard into which the gleanings of any kind of 'turn out' went – serviettes to make handkerchiefs, lace from the edges of afternoon table-cloths for dress trimmings, odd pieces of cord, buttons, buckles and felted knitting to be unravelled laboriously stitch by stitch and remade with the same care. Behind the larder door was the essential bag-of-bags, the care of which was in Roy's hands; it was he who salvaged grease-proof butter and margarine wrappings for re-use to line cake-tins, who straightened and ironed brown paper and food bags which one seldom got direct from a grocer or baker. It was Roy too who was prodded into 'helping the war effort' by collecting kitchen waste from several neighbours for the national pig-swill collection, and old newspapers for recycling.

Mary Wiltshire's favourite admonition was, 'I don't want to hear you grumbling. If your Dad has given up his liberty, the least you can do is put a cheerful face on it and not grumble. You wouldn't hear him grumble.' But it wasn't true that Dad had given up his liberty: the Germans had taken it from him, and Leonora was pretty sure, knowing Dad, that he would do a lot of grumbling about that.

These days Mam seemed to get crosser and crosser. She had kept on and on falling out with Grandma Gertie until she had gone back to London. Mam told people, 'She *would* go back. But there, Dick's mother always found Markham a bit quiet. She's a born Cockney, misses London, and it does seem pretty safe these days.' Leonora knew why Grandma Gertie went back to live in Sleepy Valley, and wished that she might have gone with her.

There had been a big row just after they had heard about Dad. Leonora had felt sorry for both of them. She imagined that they must feel as bad as she did herself about Dad when they first got the news that he was in a prison camp; you wanted to lash out, take it out on somebody, but there wasn't anybody you could blame. Leonora had taken it out on Roy, who went stupid and babyish, and Mam and Grandma had taken it out on each other. Roy had been really awful, always picking fights, bunking off school and wetting the bed.

Whilst it was all going on, Leonora spent as much time as she could at Mrs Kennedy's. Mrs Kennedy was always ready to talk to Leonora. Even that had been wrong too. 'I don't know what the attraction is next door. I suppose your own home isn't good enough for you these days? Georgia Kennedy spoils you.' But to Mrs Kennedy's face she was all honey, getting Mrs Kennedy to show her how to bleach the front of her hair and how to make a fat page-boy bob.

Overnight, it seemed, everything in Markham began to change.

All through the Battle of Britain, the inhabitants of Markham had lived in the eye of the storm, surrounded by violence and destruction. Thousands of bomb-heavy German aircraft flew overhead with an arsenal of high-explosives and incendiary bombs for neighbouring cities. For two years, Markhambrian families huddled in their shelters at night, and in daytime children's lessons were constantly disrupted by rushing to air-raid shelters or to the abbey, or by running to and from home.

But, throughout those long months, only one house was destroyed. Yet how could they relax? For at the back of the mind there was the nagging knowledge that Markham was only minutes flying-time from plum targets, anti-aircraft guns, Naval bases, docklands, aircraft factories, marshalling yards and Spitfire runways. And only seconds from the bomb-doors of any bomb-laden German aircraft caught in the searchlights above them.

Eventually the Battle of Britain was over. Whilst many terribly injured towns and cities lay licking their wounds, Markham, its fabric unharmed, had grown downtrodden and sick and weary. Much of the young blood of the town had left, many would not come back. Paula's brother-in-law was dead, so were two of Pammy's brothers. The men in Trix's family had always been merchantmen: now her Dad, an uncle and two cousins had gone down. The husband of one of the WVS women had been taken from his rear-gunner seat on which had remained parts of his vital organs.

Three years of war, two of which had been punctuated at frequent intervals by the shock of violent death and grief that never lessened with familiarity. Georgia never knew why they chose her – she had never considered herself as the type to exude sympathy – yet they always came to her office to pour out their misery. As they cried for their menfolk, she put her arms around them and wept for the women as they let out their grief and guilt. Awkwardly the first time, for Georgia had no woman upon whom to model herself. Alice Honeycombe, in priding herself on being a practical woman, had never known the value of offering a handgrip or an enfolding arm, preferring, 'Sit down and I'll make you a good sweet cup of tea. Best thing is to just get on with things.' Georgia's mother was not unsympathetic, it was that she did not know how. Georgia did it naturally.

It was a grim time, during which there were few treats or pleasures to lighten it. The dance-hall and swimming-club had been long ago closed. Pubs, often short of beer, opened short hours; shop windows were empty; and women queued endlessly, for bread, for cake, for fish, carrots, shampoo, elastic and an occasional cheap toy. The only place of entertainment was the Picture House which was always full to overflowing.

Then, after three years, came the change. Yanks descended on Markham.

Hugh had a twenty-four-hour pass.

At the end of the day before he was due home, Georgia went into the preparation room where she knew Mrs Farr and Dolly Partridge would be alone working out next week's menus.

Normally, Georgia enjoyed being in the kitchens late in the day, but on this day she scarcely noticed its quiescence and orderliness. The place was scrubbed and warm. Tins and jars in neat rows, knives and pans in graduated order and clean check tea-cloths spread on preparation surfaces. A place of safety, impregnated with smells of foods, soap and clean damp floors. Mrs Farr poured tea for Georgia.

'To me,' said Dolly Partridge, 'a twenty-four-hour pass sometimes seems worse than none at all. It takes you twenty-four hours to get used to each other again don't it? Then, before you know it, they're gone again.'

Georgia concentrated on initialling some forms. She had tried to sound casual about the phone call from Hugh saying that he would be home for twenty-four hours, but her throat tightened and thick tears welled beneath her eyelids.

'I haven't got those totals wrong, have I?' Dolly asked. 'I used to be good at figures at school, but I haven't . . . Oh my dear, what's the matter? Me and my big mouth. Is it embarkation leave? I never thought.' She looked anxiously at Mrs Farr who nodded encouragingly. Tentatively, Dolly put an arm about Georgia.

At the feel of the older woman's warm, soft body close to her face, Georgia broke down into quiet weeping. Dolly held her, rocking, saying, 'There, there. It's all right, it's all right, let it come out, it does you good to have a cry,' until Georgia's tears subsided and Mrs Farr offered her a tea-towel to dry her eyes.

Eventually, Georgia heaved a sigh. 'I'm sorry, I'm sorry. I feel so stupid. I don't often cry.'

'One should never apologize for crying,' Mrs Farr said.

'That's right,' said Dolly. 'All the time we've been working here, I can't say I've ever found you moping about anything.'

Georgia, now almost composed, tried to cover her embarrassment with a wry smile. 'Stiff upper lip and a lot of fast blinking – it's the way I was brought up.'

'It is the English way, not a good one,' Mrs Farr said. 'As a child I was brought up to behave like that, never show your anger or anguish. What happens is that when one needs to, we have never learned how to do any of it properly.'

Dolly said, 'It's took me all my life to find that out, and I might never have done if I hadn't come here and worked for Mrs Farr. She said that everybody had a right to their feelings, didn't you, Mrs Farr?'

'We aren't ashamed of happiness, why be ashamed of other emotions?'

'Is it embarkation leave?' Dolly asked.

'Yes.'

'Well, they don't all get sent into the fighting.'

'It isn't that. I don't think he is being sent anywhere dangerous.'

Dolly remembered what she had seen at the Lyceum: Mrs Kennedy watched her husband messing about with a pretty young WREN, not just casual like Harry was when there was a woman about, but full-blown stuff by the look of it.

'His whole unit is being transferred to some remote island. I've an idea it is somewhere off Tasmania.'

'Goodness, what on earth is our army doing in Tasmania?' Mrs Farr said.

'It's just this unit Hugh's in. I don't know what it is they do, but it's something to do with noise – sound waves – not Hugh, he's to do with personnel and accommodation. I'm not supposed to know, but Hugh can't stop himself, he's a bit like a child in some ways, has to show off . . . It's very advanced experimental work . . . I shouldn't be telling you, should I?'

Dolly said, 'With Charlie, Harry and Robbo in the Forces, my dear, I ain't likely to do no careless talking.'

'I don't really know anything anyway, and from what Hugh says, they don't always know themselves what they are up to, which is why they can't risk doing any more experiments close to a civilian population.'

'Noise you say?' asked Mrs Farr. 'You mean sound waves?'

'I think they break things with sound . . . like breaking glass with singing.'

'If only the human race were to put half as much ingenuity and resource into construction as it does into destruction,' Mrs Farr said.

'Well, at least he won't be in the war,' Dolly said. 'You don't want to upset yourself, why don't you just try to forget where he's going, and make the most of the twenty-four hours.'

Suddenly Georgia felt an overwhelming relief at finding herself in the company of these two wise and kindly women. She shuffled idly through the time sheets, then blurted out, 'I'm not upset because he's being posted . . . I believe he's having an affair and I don't know how to deal with it.'

'Oh,' said Dolly.

'A serious affair?' asked Mrs Farr.

'I don't know. But I believe it is, and if it is, then I want to have it out, I couldn't go on living with him not knowing . . . but how can I even broach the subject with only twenty-four hours, it's too big a thing. I mean . . . you can't just say, oh, before you go, are you sleeping with another woman?'

'Are you sure you're not just imagining it?' Dolly asked. 'It's easy enough when they're away such a lot . . . and you hear so many things.'

'I don't think so, it's only a couple of incidences, but I'm sure he's involved with someone. I just don't know how serious. I'm sorry, look at the time . . .' She began to initial the time sheets. 'I'm keeping you; you don't want to hear my troubles.'

'You don't have to keep apologizing,' Mrs Farr said.

'There's not a lot we can do for each other these days,' Dolly said, 'half an hour of time isn't much. There's only

Sam at home, it don't hurt him to wait for his supper sometimes.'

Mrs Farr brewed fresh tea.

'I don't know what to do,' Georgia said.

'What would you do if he had seven days instead of twenty-four hours?' Dolly asked.

'I had rather thought that I would just tell him I saw him with a woman and see what he said.' She paused, then, having made up her mind, plunged on. 'It was that afternoon at the Lyceum . . . I went back for my parcels . . . he was down below. He had phoned me the day before to say that all leave had been cancelled.'

'There might be an explanation,' Dolly offered but, remembering what she had seen, thought that his explanation was not likely to be a very honourable one.

'I had already suspected something.' Georgia gave a faint smile. 'I always thought stories about people giving themselves away by talking in their sleep were a bit thick. He didn't exactly do that, but he once had too much to drink, he thought that I was somebody else. And . . . well, he's different . . . changed. And he can't wait to get back to camp – he hums to himself just as he used to when he was going on tour with the cricket team.'

Ursula Farr, whose relationship with Niall had always been shared with another woman, always encumbered by a second presence, wondered, not for the first time, whether she would have felt aggrieved in Georgia's situation. But over the years that she and Niall had been together, she had always known whose name and whose bed he shared. In their case, it was always Ursula who was the intruder into a marriage.

'What if there is somebody else?' Mrs Farr asked.

Without hesitation, Georgia answered, 'I should ask for a separation.' At last, she had said aloud the word that had been struggling to find its way to awareness. 'I think . . . yes . . . I should want to divorce him.'

'Even supposing you are right, that's a big step to take.'

'I know, that's why I got so worked up. You can't decide something like that in a day, can you? If I say anything, it's going to be all up and over and we shall break up, but how can I do that if he's off to the other side of the world, and maybe he won't come back . . . If they are moving his unit because it's dangerous to the civilian population . . . it's got to be dangerous for the unit, hasn't it?'

'Couldn't you just ride the twenty-four hours?' Dolly asked. 'Get through it and leave the sorting out till he gets home again?'

'If . . .' The two older women watched Georgia struggling to say something that Dolly guessed was probably against all the rules of her upbringing – the not letting the neighbours know your business. 'If . . . I didn't have to sleep with him . . . you know . . . I mean have intercourse . . . I could manage it, but all the while that there's this suspicion hanging over me . . . well, I couldn't bear him to touch me. But if I refuse . . . then I'll have to tell him why.' She studied her thumbnail scratching the table edge. 'He . . . sort of . . . well, sees it as part of a marriage duty. It has never been very enjoyable for either of us. Oh, I don't know what to do . . . it's all such a mess.'

'For a start, it's not really your mess, is it my dear? Keep that in mind whatever you do,' Mrs Farr said quietly.

Georgia paused as the implication of that sank in. 'No, it isn't, is it? But I do have to sort it out.'

A short silence fell between them, broken by Dolly, who said, 'I tell you what I think – you should have the Curse.'

'But it's not my time.' Momentarily she withdrew her gaze. 'He wouldn't know that, though, would he? I mean, I could just leave my Dr White's in the bathroom as I always have done – to let him know. Dolly, you're a blessing.'

'You haven't solved the problem, Georgia,' Mrs Farr said, 'only shelved it. If you'll take my advice, these things are better cleared up than allowing them to drag on for years. And I'm not talking out of my hat.'

Georgia found herself observing Hugh closely. He certainly appeared not to have a troubled conscience and, although she continued to see that there was something changed in him, she wondered whether it was the style of his brother officers brushing off on him. The new Hugh was the officer of the tobacco advertisements – Erinmore, smoked by men who knew what they wanted – and what they wanted was women who admired them.

He was full of his recent appearance before a selection board.

'Brass Hats, Georgia. Ten Brass Hats. You never saw anything like it. Who'd ever have thought some Whitehall Johnny would have put a list of requirements through the mincer and out would pop Hugh Kennedy? If just a single one of them hadn't jelled, then it would have been no-go. If I'd had an Irish mother, or had gone to a soccer school, or hadn't got a pass in physics . . . I'd have been out! As it is . . . well, there's no knowing where this posting could take me.'

He had accepted the phantom Curse without comment. Georgia concluded that he was pleased that he didn't have to perform. Saving it for her – the WREN with the long legs.

Dog in the manger Georgia, she thought.

In observing him, she saw what a curious situation she was in, finding herself married to a man who turned out to be a complete stranger. Was he always like this but I was too young to notice? Did he have a string of girls before he married me? Why did he want to get married? Was it because the rest of the team had got wives, and Hugh Kennedy wanted one too – younger, prettier, fuller breasted and with a lot of shockingly noticeable hair? There had been no doubt about the stir he had caused when he had taken Georgia to a Clubhouse dinner and announced that she would be Mrs Hugh Kennedy – the Cricket Captain's wife.

The leave sped quickly by. Then, shortly before he was to return to Badger Island, in the midst of packing, whilst strapping his cricket bat to his grip, he sat down and began filling a pipe. 'Come and sit down, Georgia,' he said, thoughtfully tamping down the tobacco. 'We may not see one another for quite some time, and I have something serious to say to you.'

She sat down and waited for his lecture about bank credit, paying the rates, not worrying about him.

'I have thought of every possible way of saying this to soften the blow, but there isn't any way. Straight facts, more honest.'

He clicked his lighter and drew on his pipe and got it going.

'And the fact is, my dear, that I want a legal separation. I have met someone I love and who loves me. She's a society girl. Rich, actually, and she's got a bun in the oven. I'm sorry. She doesn't mind about getting married, so it's all right for things to stop as they are. You can still be the wife and keep this place on until we come to some arrangement. Anny has money. And of course you would still have my marriage allowance. That way there's no scandal. I'm sorry, Georgia, but we do love each other. It is happening everywhere – people falling in love with people they wouldn't normally meet – the consequences of war, I'm afraid.'

Two years ago, Georgia would never, in any fantasy, have imagined that scene. He must have rehearsed the speech and worked out the best time and way of delivering it.

Georgia had always supposed that marriages ended with flaming rows, exchanged recriminations in loud voices with tears, which was what she had imagined when she had confided in Mrs Farr and Dolly. For many moments they sat in a silence that was broken only by his crackling tobacco. Then she got up and moved towards the door where her outdoor coat hung: she put it on, tied a scarf about her neck and picked up her keys.

'I'm going out, Hugh. Just be gone when I get home.'

Judging by his expression, he too must have anticipated something other than this composed exit.

'You are a thorough-going shit, Hugh.'

'Georgia!'

But she was gone.

By the time XJ-R6, minus ex-Wren St John, reached their destination, marriage separation papers were being drawn up by Georgia's solicitor.

Also by the time XJ-R6 arrived, one of Angela St John's Cheyne Walk friends had wangled her a flight to Tasmania. There, money being no object, she set up 'a darling little nest on the coast' to which Hughie might come with ease from XJ-R6.

Hugh Kennedy never did work out why it was, when he told Anny what had happened and Anny said, 'Oh Hughie, you were a bit of a shit blurting it out like that,' that he had been so shocked at Georgia's use of the same sort of language. Perhaps it was that in Georgia's mouth the description held some truth.

1942

'Did you know there's Yankee soldiers in the town?' Dolly asked.

'I did,' said Ursula. 'I saw half a dozen wandering round. What lovely uniforms.'

'Sam met some in the park, apparently there'll be thousands when they all arrive. I expect that's exaggerated, but there's a big camp on the Andover Road. Sam asked these lads to tea. Lord knows what I'm going to do, I never met Americans before.'

'Give them what you'd give your own boys, anything to fill them up.'

'I didn't really mean that.' Dolly, unused to articulating her concerns was hesitant. 'Well . . . people like us aren't really like you when it comes to strangers. Ordinary working people just aren't used to having strangers in their houses. Our house has only got the living-room and kitchen.'

'Young lads away from home won't mind, they'll be glad enough to be away from camp and with a family. Ordinary American homes aren't much different from English ones – plenty of them aren't as good.'

Having seen America at the pictures, that was hard to believe.

The young soldiers came. Dolly could scarcely wait to tell Ursula on the day following their visit.

'Did you like them?'

'Oh yes, they were lovely. No different from anybody else once you got used to the way they spoke. Bonnie didn't care, she wanted them to keep saying things. They didn't mind, and kept making her laugh.'

Ursula Farr worked on, encouraging Dolly by gestures and smiles, knowing her well enough not to ask too many questions if she wanted to get the whole story. Niall could have made such a wonderful documentary film of the first meeting between the Partridges and the first Americans.

'I tried to give a good impression. I used darned-near the whole of the family's high days and holidays hoard of sugar and dried fruit and made cake and pies.'

'I've got a bit you can have.'

'Oh, I didn't mind. It'd be a lie though if I didn't admit that I felt a bit peeved when I saw my only tin of peaches disappearing as though they weren't a treat, and the sandwiches with my only put-by tin of red salmon. I never expected them to eat so much. Poor little Bonnie, I had to rescue her a few slices for later. But I kept thinking to myself about Charlie always getting invited into people's homes in Canada – it's the least we can do.'

In spite of the quick despatch of the salmon sandwiches, Dolly had felt pleased with her first try-out of having strangers to tea. The only time Bonnie had ever seen such a spread was at Christmas. 'Because it's there, doesn't mean you can take it all,' Marie warned beforehand. 'Don't go mad: choose cake or fruit, but not both.'

The four soldiers seemed to have about them an air of explosive vitality that was meat-fed and sugared. At first there was a polite awkwardness when Sam was effusive in his welcome and Dolly, Marie and Paula showed excessive politeness.

The young men had been made freshly aware by their sergeant of their delicate situation as a visiting army '. . . not invading, not conquering . . . but a *visiting* army.

'The British have been at war for some time: it didn't start for them at Pearl Harbor. You might not like it, but some of them think we should have come in before we did. These people are short of things like sugar, so their food might be kinda unappetizing, but you eat the goddam lot and enjoy it.

'An' you wanna take a good look at the section on Language. Bum's a butt, and a rubber's an eraser – they call rubbers johnnies – and don't nobody ask me why. And carry the goddam things. Don't talk about 'm, don't even think of need'n them, keep off the women. I'll have the goddam balls off any sonofabitch touches local ass.'

The soldiers had enough to think about in their capacity as ambassadors to worry about the correct terms for a rubber. They worked at not being unmannerly by refusing the food, consequently they accepted generously of everything and, to their surprise, found it not half bad and not so different from what their own mothers might have made. They kept saying how real good it all was and refilled their plates.

'I don't reckon that camp feeds them properly,' Dolly said later.

Strangers from abroad, coming like that, made it one of the most important occasions in the Partridge family's history, and in the neighbourhood generally. Many of their neighbours went by, glancing or craning to see if it was true that there were Yankee soldiers at Number 24. Marie, Paula and Dolly had dressed themselves up, and as they both had a bit of money to spend on themselves these days, had had hair-dos – Paula's brown riot of curls showing through the mesh of a red snood and Marie's silken fairness tied in a large velvet bow.

Neither of them had seen their husbands for a long time, for both Charlie and Robbo were now in Africa – Charlie in the north, and Robbo in the east. The Americans, ambassadors for their country and especially for their own states, tried to keep lechery from their eyes, but Paula, whose legs went right up and didn't stop till they reached her neat little ass, moved like a chorus girl, and Marie was as curvaceous as a movie queen – it was not easy for the young men when they discovered that an old English park-keeper had such unexpected women in his family.

Sam, who seldom talked about his war, soon found himself with an audience who were keen to hear about it. They called him Sir.

Dolly, enjoying having sweet-smelling young men round her table again, wondered at the craziness that sent Charlie and Robbo to Africa and Harry to train in God-knew-what secret place, and replaced them with boys taken from their own mothers in faraway places with names like Talahassie or Mobile.

Over the food, the formality began to ease. Fascinated at Sam doing his one-handed roll-up after tea, the ice was finally broken by a square young man called Studely but known as Studs.

'Say man,' said Studs. 'Ah never seen that one-hand roll done outside a movie. Could you teach me? Say, Ah hope Ah'm not out of turn, Sir, but would you care to smoke a Camel?'

Bonnie giggled, and kept giggling until first Marie and then Paula was set off.

Sam hung the dartboard on the yard wall, and in two teams they played until the sun went down, when the Yanks left, having thanked Dolly profusely with renewed praises for her baking, left Sam with an entire carton of Camels, Bonnie with a box of wide-eyed candy-bars, and Miz Paula and Miz Ma-ree an invitation from their Commanding Officer to a camp dance.

1989

Georgia Giacopazzi thought that the last leg of the long flight was always worse than the rest. A man seated across the gangway, wearing expensive aftershave and gold jewellery, tried to chat her up. He was an American and he set her off remembering the first time she had met one in real life. Nineteen forty-two, just after Hugh had gone off with Floozie.

Mrs Giacopazzi guessed that her seat partner dined out on any name he collected. He didn't come on to her. He was in his late forties, the wrong age to find well-known women anything other than interesting items. She could recognize those men who were stimulated by gossip column legends. Giacopazzi's serious chatters-up were either under thirty, or over fifty and not given to scent and talcum. The men of forty or fifty were too insecure, too busy spreading their thinning hair and shoring up a fading macho image to think sexually of women older than themselves.

She did her PR duty with this one, then she allowed her eyes to close so that he would think she slept. At some convention, he could say ha-ha that he had slept with the Giacopazzi woman, and that her chin sagged and she had wrinkles that didn't show in publicity shots . . . and Christ, how the woman snored.

She drifted back into her favourite project. If the mini-series was going to be made of *Eye of the Storm*, then it was crucial that they got Nick right. She knew who she would *like*. Ever since she had seen him in the Butch Cassidy film and then when she had met him for real a couple of years back. Of course they weren't likely to get him, but he had had exactly that same unaffected sexuality as Nick. Of course he was more handsome than Nick, but the kind of production they were likely to want to make of *Eye* was sure to be internationally glitzy. It was more important to get *Eye of the Storm* right than any of the earlier films. If Ukay-Ozzi Pictures made the series, they would never put the Nick character in an unglamorous AFS uniform.

That period when Hugh went overseas and Nick was in Liverpool was the longest part of the war. Nick wrote regularly, on each neat page she had been able to hear his voice. His voice angry at the living conditions of Liverpool people, his intelligent voice coming through in his forecast of a changed post-war Britain, and his voice tender with love and passion for Georgia Kennedy.

Nearly fifty years ago now, yet she still remembered how much she had longed for him, so that every love-song on the wireless about separated couples seemed directed at herself and Nick.

'The very thought of you, and I forget to do,
The little or-din-ary things that ev'ryone ought to do . . .
I see your face in ev'ry flower, your eyes in stars above,
It's just the thought of you, the very thought of you, my Love.'

The man with the gold jewellery glanced sideways at the old woman humming quietly to herself.

Nick had received two bravery awards for going into explosive or dangerous situations. When it had come to writing the scene in the book about how he had tackled the burning farm, she had seemed to have total recall, and she had awakened many times since with the smell of burning straw in her nostrils.

I wish Mary Wiltshire was still alive, I should have liked to know what she thought when she saw me and Nick going about together.

Once, before Hugh had come home on the awful embarkation leave, Nick had come back to Markham with seven days off. They had gone out together every day. A goodnight kiss, and that had been all. Ages before, he had said that in time she would fall to him like a ripe medlar. Before Hugh's leave, it had seemed that that time might be near, but she had been faithful to her vows to Hugh.

Lord, how naïve I was. She still had the letter Hugh had written to her after he got back on the XJ-R6 station, could remember the words, they were stuck in her memory. 'I did not imagine that you'd be so upset. I had heard the gossip that you had been seen playing tennis with Crockford. When you said that he was doing the garden, I felt a lot easier in my conscience. I thought you were having a fling with your old flame and we could call it Love-All.'

Oh . . . too long ago . . . too long a-go.

Yet, the knowledge that she had not been able to see him for what he was when she married him still rankled. For she considered herself something of a judge of character who was seldom wrong in her first impression of people and who saw through her fictional characters as soon as they hit the page.

At least it had rankled until a few days ago when she had seen them. What nothings they were. Rich, idle, boring, selfish nothings. She pictured it now: Hugh lying there served by houseboys in white uniforms and red sashes wearing gloves to serve at table; maids in caps and aprons; gardeners in khaki work-clothes and leather kneecaps, keeping the swimming-pool immaculate and the lawns bright green . . . Old Hugh, his white Clark Gable singed yellow from thousands of cigarettes. Old Hugh with dewlaps sitting staring or lying abed half paralysed and pathetically ga-ga. And Floozie . . . walnut-skinned and juiceless, her sexy legs shrivelled to sticks. With children who talked of nothing but the state of the rand against the dollar, and the unreliability and ingratitude of servants . . . only the girl of all of them had been worth expending any effort on – at least she was whilst she was going through a liberal, protesting phase. Let's hope it's more than a phase.

God what awful, useless lives, living off the tobacco crops which other people grew for them. They had never planted or harvested anything – except the money.

Georgia Giacopazzi thought of the fields and meadows surrounding her own home. Good growing land in a fertile valley. On acres where the earth had once been impoverished, they had brought it back into good heart themselves. She smiled faintly, and clutched her thighs at the imagined feel of the great old-fashioned tractor seat vibrating as she drew the chains across a rutted field; then the live smell as their boots crushed clods when they inspected the new grass and clover; then the years of growing crops. Although she loved to be in the throes of writing, she worked quickly because she could hardly wait to get out to do something in the fields or milking-parlour.

But . . . in the beginning it had been the novels that paid for it all. And then the meadows and fields and animals began to pay for themselves.

Her mind again drifted back to Hugh as it had occasionally over the years. It is a recurring theme in many of her novels, the puzzle of a man approaching middle age who marries a young girl and who, once they are married, tires of her and leaves her unfulfilled and takes an equally young mistress. She felt in her briefcase for a pencil and her notes for *Goodnight, Broadway Baby!* – the novel she had talked over with her editor before leaving for Jo'burg.

Reading it again, it sounded crass. Perhaps I'm dried up . . . written out now that I've done *Eye*, now that I've seen Hugh. Perhaps it's all done with. Well, that would be a relief. Wouldn't it? Forty years of being addicted to fictitious lives, fictitious people, and never feeling free for long enough to enjoy her other life. Would it be a relief not to feel compelled to keep saying something?

The aftershave man perked up. 'Another bestseller coming on?'

Georgia Giacopazzi smiled at him and winked conspiratorially.

'Do you take your characters from life?'

'Very often.'

From now on he would be sure to read the new Giacopazzi paperback – hoping to find himself in it, recognizing himself not as the foolish, perfumed, middle-aged character with his hair parted too low, but as the absolute and utter shit that the young heroine fell for. Her male readers usually quite liked the Hugh character – or Chris, or whoever was the current utter cad who dropped his wife and went off with a rich society bird.

1942

It was not until the evening of the day after the changed Hugh had gone, and Georgia was walking homewards in Dolly Partridge's company, that she had anyone she could tell about what had happened.

'I tell you, Dolly, I was . . . I was absolutely speechless.' Her voice was tight with emotion. 'I mean, I had been keeping my end up ever since he came home, down at the Club. I cooked us a couple of nice meals, took him breakfast in bed, mended his socks. I thought he was enjoying being back at his own fireside and that he would have a nice memory of home. He said, She's a society girl. The way he said it . . . it was as though that was a perfectly reasonable explanation for leaving your wife.'

Dolly felt sorry for the young woman. She must have felt humiliated enough that time when she had watched him at the Lyceum doing that mucking about with the girlfriend. Her pride might not have been quite so wounded if she'd been able to tackle him about it; got on her high horse and had a row, chucked him out even. But for him to be so brass-faced.

'Sounds to me as though you could be well rid of him.'

'It doesn't alter the fact that I've been ditched by my husband.'

'You don't want to go about saying things like that, it will only make you feel worse. In fact, if you don't mind me saying so, you won't go about saying anything at all. You know what Markham's like for a bit of gossip like this.'

If she had been a girl from off the Council Estate, or was one of Paula's friends, Dolly would have said for her to come round for a cup of tea; but they only had the one room, and Sam would be there.

'Look,' she said, 'do you feel like a trip out to Southampton this evening? *Gone with the Wind* is on. You're welcome to come. I mean . . . You know . . . if you wanted to get out this evening.'

'Oh Dolly, could I? Could I really? I'd love to see it.'

As Dolly said to Paula, 'She seemed that pleased, you'd have thought she never went anywhere.'

'Well, if what you say is true and she hasn't got any friends except the lot that hangs out round the tennis court, it isn't surprising she'd enjoy going to the pictures with somebody nice like you.'

Dolly blushed, she wasn't used to that sort of compliment, even from her own daughter. Especially from her own daughter, but then Paula had changed a lot in the last year or two, had got a lot more open. She was getting about a bit these days. But there, she's a grown woman – none of my affair.

It was the week following that Georgia answered her office telephone to a speaker whose voice she couldn't quite place.

The voice was masculine, the tone amused. 'Oh dear, oh dear, I'm devastated. After that afternoon at the Lyceum, I thought that you'd never forget.'

'Goodness! It's Harry, isn't it? Harry Partridge. Of course I recognize you.'

He had a lovely warm laugh. 'Listen, Georgia, could you get a message to my Mum? I've got an unexpected bit of leave. Do you think that you could tell her I'll be home tomorrow?'

'Of course, at once. She will be excited. She thinks the sun shines out of you.'

'I know. And what about you, don't I make the sun shine for you?' That laugh again.

Flirting down the telephone seemed safe. 'Sergeant Partridge, I'm a respectable married woman.'

'I know that, but I rather thought that you were more my

kind of woman. Will you come out with me? No strings. Just good friends.'

'I'll think about it.'

'Now. My three minutes is almost up. Please? Can you get off on Friday afternoon? Have you got any slacks?'

She laughed, 'No, I can't get off, and what have slacks to do with anything?'

'Have you? What colour – let me guess, red.'

'Of course not.'

'Red slacks would suit your neat bottom.'

'You'll get cut off before your three minutes is up if the operator hears you.'

'Right, in jumper, slacks and scarf then, at twelve o'clock, Saturday. And tell Mum I wouldn't mind a pond pudding if she can manage it.'

'Pond pudding? You'll be lucky – don't you know there's a war on?'

'Mum will do it – she loves me.'

The operator cut in. 'Your three minutes is up, caller.' Harry rang off making kissing sounds.

He turned up on the August afternoon wearing a leather airman's jacket, and goggles pushed up on his blond hair. He looked extremely dashing and handsome.

'Come on. Tie up your pretty hair. I've borrowed my mate's Vincent. Isn't she a beauty?'

Georgia, laughing, clasped a hand over her mouth at the thought of it. 'A motor bike! I've never been on one. I should be afraid of tipping off.'

'It's easy. You just sit on, hold on to me and let yourself go with the bike.'

Ever since Hugh had gone, she had been in a state of mind which alternated between wishing never to set eyes on him again, at the same time as wanting him to walk in through the door so that she could scream and throw things at him. Wishing too that she hadn't been such a fool, but had made love with Nick who was worth a thousand of Hugh. Heaven knew, she had longed to. Recently she had seemed to think of little else but a love scene with Nick – lust scene.

Just at that moment, a date with a good-looking, amusing man like Harry Partridge was exactly what Georgia needed to cheer her up. Oddly enough, it was because of his reputation as a lady-killer that she felt he was just the antidote for Hugh. Not that she would ever be seduced by his type, but because he knew how to make women feel good, feel special.

'All right then,' she said. 'Where are we going?'

'Where do you want to go?'

'Anywhere out of Markham.'

'The sea?'

'Can we really? It's ages . . . absolutely wizard!'

The ride was exhilarating: he drove fast and skilfully. She held on round his waist and, as soon as they had roared up the hill out of Markham and out along the Bournemouth road, she got the hang of letting her body go with the movement of the machine. From time to time he shouted something back over his shoulder, but she could not hear what it was. Speeding, they went through the New Forest, past villages, past clusters of tents where soldiers whistled, over the heather-packed moorland. Suddenly she saw the bright line of the sea.

'Look, look!' she shouted in his ear as she hugged him excitedly. In response, he pressed her arms to him with his elbows, his muscular leather-clad back, firm buttocks between her thighs, and the vibrating and roaring bike elating and reviving her. The only sensation she was aware of was the roaring bike. Markham, Hugh, Wrens with buns, work, her own lusts, and the longing for Nick – all of it was sucked into the slipstream of the roaring motor bike, and lost.

Bournemouth looked as seedy and neglected as a less prosperous resort, but Georgia was delighted to see it again after so long. 'We came here on holiday once,' she shouted at him, and he nodded, pressing her with his elbows again. Many of the beaches along the coast were inaccessible, so he drove on beyond Bournemouth. Then, a few miles out into the country, he turned down a long narrow track, ignoring a notice which said, MINISTRY OF DEFENCE – DANGER – STRICTLY NO ADMITTANCE, and on over dunes and hummocks to a wonderful little isolated cove that looked as though it was more likely part of Dorset or Devon than Hampshire.

After the roaring of the bike and air, Georgia at first heard nothing, then the silence became filled with breaking waves and calling sea-birds.

'There!' Harry ripped back the fastenings of his jacket, flung off his goggles and twirled Georgia around by her waist. He was such an easy man to be with that she felt that she had known him for years.

'Ah, just breathe that, Missis Kennedy – a bit of fresh air left over from before the war.'

'The whole place seems pre-war. How did you find it? I thought that all this part of the coast was inaccessible.'

'Out of bounds – but not inaccessible if you know where to come.'

'It's not got mines, has it?'

'No, it's just a bit of MOD land that they purloined and then probably forgot they had.'

Leaving the bike against a white-sanded, tussocky bank, they went down to the water's edge, where Georgia took off her shoes and stood in the clear waves as they flipped on to the pale sand. 'Oh, it's marvellously warm. I wish I had brought my swimsuit – I never thought we'd have the chance to swim.'

'Come on, don't be shy. I promise you nobody will come down here.' And he began to undress.

'Harry!' She looked around her. 'We can't!'

'Come on, little Church School girl. God won't strike you

down for swimming as naked as He intended that we should. In any case, it's the only way to really enjoy it.' He sat down on the dry sand and unlaced his boots. 'You must have swum in your skin-suit at Princes Meadows – there's more than a few girls have seen all I've got. Don't tell me the Markham boys haven't seen yours.'

'I didn't swim at Princes Meadows. I was a country girl, remember?'

Quickly, and without embarrassment, he had stripped down to broad sun-brown shoulders and pale buttocks, and was swimming away from the shore.

'Don't watch then,' she called after him. He waved acknowledgement and kept swimming. Nothing would have made her walk naked into the sea, so she retained the lacy bra that Leonora admired, and her cotton briefs. When Alice Honeycombe had taught her daughter, always look as good beneath as on top, she had had in mind accidents and hospitals, certainly not being enticed into the waves by a naked Paratrooper.

'It's wonderful! Marvellous!' she shouted when she had swum to where he was treading water.

'Isn't it just? I had forgotten.'

They splashed and played as they each had done fifteen and more years ago: he in the River Test at Princes Meadow and she in a cool, dark-green pond where there were natterjacks and dabchicks in the reeds. 'Look, nobody comes here. It was a naturist beach before the war, then the Ministry took it over. We came here once, but it's useless as training ground. You could swim here every day and nobody would know.' He sounded so certain that she felt convinced that she was not the first girl he had brought here to swim. 'You should take it all off and feel how good it is. Here, let me, and I'll take them back up the beach – you'll have to let them dry, anyhow.' Deftly, he unhooked her bra, removed it and held it between his teeth, whilst she wriggled out of her briefs.

He was right, the sensation of freedom was good, it was as though her shyness was in the lacy and provocative covering, in which she had felt more undressed before him than now.

She watched him wade through the shallows and up to the motor cycle, where he attached the two garments so that they blew like pennants. She watched him as he strode over the white sand. He was, as were most men for that matter, a smaller man than Nick; pale-skinned beneath the tan, and sturdy. Although Nick's hair was now totally white the hair on his chest had not gone through the same premature change but remained dark, whereas Harry's blond fairness was the same all over him. The muscles of his shoulders, arms and legs were very well developed, which she assumed was from his training as a Paratrooper.

She watched him all the way down to the water. The first grown man she had ever seen totally naked. Where was the immorality in a super body like that? Where was there any sin in their being together like this? She felt free. Clean. Wholesome. Harry Partridge had taught her more about wholesomeness in five minutes than her mother and the hassock and cassock school had done in years.

She turned to float on her back and, relaxed by the blue sky and the warmth of the afternoon sun, with her hair moving like foxy seaweed, Georgia floated parallel to the shore, allowing the waves to move her gently back and forth. She did not turn when she heard him swimming over-arm towards her.

He plunged into a rippling wave and came up beside her, salt water darkening his fair hair, glistening on his lashes. 'Didn't I tell you?'

'Mm. It's *the* most voluptuous sensation. I could stay like this for ever.'

Holding her easily with one arm, he paddled them both gently along with the other. Like this, exchanging desultory remarks, they drifted back and forth along the shoreline for a long time.

'Your mother was awfully pleased when I told her you were coming home.'

'I knew she would be; and she made me the pond pudding.'

'She's nice, your mother.'

'The best. She says the same about you, you know.' He dropped into what had once been his normal broad tongue. 'You know what, our Harry – that there Mrs Kennedy is a real nice girl. And she's clever, do's that job as good as a man.'

'Did she? Did she really? That's a real compliment coming from Dolly. One can never tell what she thinks, she keeps herself to herself.' Has she told him about Hugh? Probably not, Dolly's not the sort to gossip.

'That's because she doesn't feel . . . oh well, I don't know . . . it's this class thing, I don't think she would ever get used to working side by side with "Them".'

'Don't let's talk about work.'

'Fair enough. Shall we go and dry off? Perhaps we might find a tea-house or a café open along the front somewhere.'

He spread out the thick leather coat and they lay side by side, resting on their elbows facing the sea, allowing the soft breeze and hot sun to dry them. How naturally she had done it, slipping off the shackles of her nurture, freeing her nature, so that when he began to brush the dry sand from her back, she did not pull back but allowed herself to relax into the sensation of his fingers and the rough feel of salt and sand, and her damp hair and the sun burning her skin. She felt lighthearted and joyful.

'Have you always been faithful to your husband?'

'Why do you ask?'

'I don't know, only that I think that you are the type who would be.'

'There is a type then?'

'Yes.'

She turned so that she could see his expression: it was

enigmatic. His hair was so fair and short that she could see his scalp shining through it. He will be one of those men who are bald at forty and even better looking than now . . . he'll be like Maurice Chevalier and Eve's father – he'll always have women round him. 'You don't look at all like your brother.'

He laughed. 'No . . . our Harry an't nothing like our Charlie. Anybody who knows us would tell you that. Charlie's the good son, Harry's the bad lot.'

'I meant looks. Dolly is extremely proud of her sons, and she obviously adores you. I'm sure you aren't good and bad sons – that's sibling rivalry rearing its ugly head. It's been doing that since Cain and Abel.'

Now it was his turn to look her full in the face. 'You're full of surprises.'

'Oh?'

'Come *on*. Para sergeants don't often get to take out a girl who drops phrases like "sibling rivalry" into the conversation.'

'Perhaps you don't give them the chance to.'

He grinned, displacing a miniature avalanche of sand from his cheek. 'Let me plait your hair.' She lowered her head, resting her chin on the backs of her hands, conscious of her breasts and knees cool against the moist sand, her back hot in the sun, the sound and smell of the little rushing waves.

She closed her eyes and drifted into the red world behind her eyelids, idle with pleasure and a contentment she had not felt for years. She could not have said why she could lie under the cloudless summer sky naked with this naked womanizer whose knee and shin was in contact with her hip, and feel so at ease. He sat breathing quietly as he finger-combed and divided her hair. From a long way off she could hear the occasional lowing of cattle and the call of gulls. Eden before the Fall she thought.

'I haven't plaited a girl's hair for years. I always loved doing it.'

'Nobody's done mine since . . .' Remembering when that had been, she trailed off. Since summer 1935, under the willow, beside the Test when Nick and I and some of the others went swimming after pea-picking all day. 'Whose hair did you plait, or shouldn't I ask?'

'Paula's – my sister.'

'I know Paula – a little.'

'I've always adored her . . . still do.'

'No sibling rivalry?'

'Paula's nobody's rival.'

'Not even the good son's?'

'Is psychology your bedtime reading?'

'Only digests, The Idiot's Guide to Freud – nothing too hard.'

'I can't tell whether you're serious or taking the mickey.'

'I'm not taking the mickey. I find psychology fascinating, and now that I'm on my own and there's nobody to answer to, I can read what I like when I like.'

'Do you have to answer to your husband when he's there?'

'Can you read what and when you like when you're in barracks and there are other people around?'

'Touché. You're a bit of a dark horse though. I'll bet you *are* faithful to him.'

He noticed the shadow that crossed her gaze when she answered, 'Yes.'

'I guessed you might be. You're an unusual woman these days.'

'Oh no, I don't think you're right. I don't think there's a woman among those I work with who isn't faithful. Perhaps you don't look.'

He laughed. 'You're right, I can't say I search very hard.'

'Then why date me?'

'Because you intrigue me. Even in all that crowd at the Lyceum, my eye was drawn to you, even before I noticed my Mum. I thought you looked familiar, but it wasn't that;

I loved your whole air of a woman thoroughly enjoying herself. I suppose I was surprised. I mean, I'd seen you when you were a schoolgirl, then occasionally here and there – then suddenly there was this woman with her head thrown back, laughing and jitterbugging with absolute abandon. There, a nice fat pigtail. It suits you, but it's too restricting for all that beautiful hair.'

He smoothed dry sand from her, turning her over, moving from her arms and shoulders, to breasts, to belly where he let his hand rest, warm and heavy.

'I realized then that I'd misjudged you, imagining you as Miss Frosty Knickers when you came to the Council Offices.'

'I was enjoying myself that afternoon. They're a wizard crowd to work with. Now tell me about the crowd you work with.'

'Soldiers. Just soldiers like any others.'

'I don't believe that. The Paras are a crack regiment. People are reverential when they mention The Paras: you are the *crème de la crème*.'

He raised himself on one elbow, she opened her eyes, he smiled down.

'What are you smiling at?'

'The way you use a phrase like that – as though to the manner born.'

'You think it's too posh for an innkeeper's daughter? You talk posh yourself.'

'Not in front of my Dad; posh talk is pansy, affected.' He picked up a handful of the fine, warm sand and trickled it on her body, making spiral patterns. 'I realized something about him only recently . . . my Dad is not simply a man – he is a Working-Class Man. He's not a socialist so much as a Labour Man. A Working-Class Labour Man with capital letters. Sure of himself. Did you know he got his balls blasted in the war?'

She blushed at the word and the unexpectedness of the question.

He went on, 'Now there's some psychology for you – a man who loses his virility and expects his sons to compensate by proving that they are better than the next man in everything. Except that when it comes to the sons growing up and getting "full use of their 'coutrements", as my Mum says, he can't stand it. He's eaten up with anger and bitterness. And he's every right to be – but not with us, not with his family. There are times when I feel so sorry for him that I'd like to put my arms round his shoulders and say, Cry, Dad. For God's sake have a bloody good cry. But he's so prickly you can't get near.' He kneaded her belly, moving his hand absent-mindedly. She detected the same love-tinged bitterness in his tone that would come into her own voice when talking to Nick about her mother.

'Yet you like him.'

'I don't know about *like*, but I love the old bugger. Nothing I've ever done has been good enough for him: at grammar school if I got best marks in all subjects, scored the winning goal, got made Prefect, he could never bring himself to say he was pleased. I've never been able to please him, to get him to say just once, that's bloody good, son.'

'Is that why you've become Markham's Don Juan, to get back at him?'

He slapped her playfully. 'A surfeit of Freud. Tell me about your parents.'

'Boring story. Came from farming families originally,' she said, 'met when they were in domestic service. They longed to be "naice" people, who knew which knife was which. Ma longed for gentility. Ma's family were small brewers, so she knew the trade; Pa got the licence for the Ruddleman, near Ower, about the time I was born. Then later they took over the pub at Emberley.'

'What about their little Georgia, is she a naice lady?'

'It's really strange: when I'm with Hugh's friends, I always want to make it clear to them that I'm absolutely *not* nice, not one of their sort.'

'And when you are with the hoi polloi?'

'I don't feel that I belong there.'

'I recognize the feeling. But you see if I'm not right . . . after the war there's going to be this other category of people.' His tone had changed and for a moment she could have imagined that she was with Nick in one of his earnest moods. 'Not a class in the present sense of the word, but people like us who don't wear our origins like hair shirts or coats of arms. My social class was hammered and riveted on to me like leather armour. But I'm gradually popping off the rivets. People like ourselves will make the first class-less class.'

They were silent for a while, occasionally the smell of civilization wafted across them in the form of oil and petrol from the motor bike.

'You're gorgeous, Missis Kennedy.'

'I think you must have the knack – I actually feel gorgeous lying here. Is that vain?'

'You've a right to a bit of vanity with a face and body like this.' He continued trickling sand and brushing it away. Georgia guessed it wasn't as absent-minded as it appeared, for whenever she opened her eyes he was looking at her; but she enjoyed the sensation. It was as though her body, starved of human contact, fed upon the sensual touch of his hands and the appreciative looks. Hugh was never playful nor attentive, seldom asked her serious questions, never really looked at her as though she was an interesting person. Hugh had never valued her. Only Nick, till now, had done that.

'You used to come to school on the Country Bus,' he said. 'Your hair was always shining and plaited; you always looked pink and scrubbed.'

She laughed. 'I was. My mother saw to that. She wasn't going to let me grow up to be a country innkeeper's daughter.'

'And you didn't, you learned all the tricks that got you

out, like I shall. In peace-time I wear a white collar to work, I speak proper and use the correct knife and know enough to use my fingers to break into a bread-roll; I've eaten guinea-fowl and I know what game chips are. I'm probably the only fellow brought up on the Markham Council Estate who does.'

His absent-minded hand wandered and caressed, she put her hand over it to stop its progress to her loins. She could so easily have let him go on.

He continued, 'You got away from your family.'

'Well, they went away from me actually. They went to Scotland. They looked after an old couple for little money in return for the house when the old people died. They wanted me to go, too, but I hated the thought of Scotland.'

There was a little swish of waves as the tide turned. 'It is so beautiful here,' Georgia said. 'I shall remember this afternoon next winter when the coal has run out and I'm burning briquettes and sawdust and my fingers are freezing.'

'You are such a beautiful woman that I'm surprised that you haven't had fifty lovers.'

'It isn't only the Catholics who tied the fear of God round little girls' knicker-legs, you know.'

'I know. My sister suffers from it.'

'Paula?'

'I think she would have got pregnant ages ago if she hadn't thought that the Trinity were watching her in bed.' He laughed, but Georgia guessed that he knew his sister well enough.

She said, 'It's not easy to forget the Vicar's eyes ferreting out our sins. Perhaps he really does believe that daughters of the poor are lustful and immoral.'

His smile crinkled his temples as he bent over and kissed her soft and full on the mouth. 'Probably hasn't read any psychology.'

'On the other hand, perhaps he was right.' Encircling his neck, she kissed him back.

His face, close to hers, was hot from sunburn, his lips were salt and grainy. He was a lighthearted, romantic man who knew the meaning of enjoyment. He had made her laugh and relax and had stripped her of some bits of lace and inhibitions. Lying close to him, feeling the movement of his hand, seeing his handsome, wholesome face, smelling the sea on his skin, hearing his soft rhythmic breath, she felt overwhelming affection for him. Not so much erotic, but of course it was that too, but carefree. She *liked* Harry Partridge.

At that moment in that isolated cove, where the only Thou Shall Not was the Ministry of Defence warning, she wanted nothing in the world except that they make love.

Harry Partridge, since his days with Deanna from the Post Office, had learned a great deal about women and sex and waiting. He did what Hugh never had – he waited for her so that she too achieved sustained and intense pleasure, so that it equalled and paralleled his own.

The intensity of her response exploded upon Georgia and was amazing to Harry. He assumed that such a perfect encounter was because of her experience, rather than the reverse.

Afterwards, when Harry said, 'Your man's bloody lucky,' she smiled enigmatically. Hugh Kennedy never knew what he had lost.

They smoked cigarettes, swam once more, dressed and went looking for a tea-house.

Night had fallen when he dropped her at her front door.

'Thank you, Harry, it was absolute pleasure. A trip to the seaside will never be the same again.'

'We must do it again some time.'

'Yes.' But she guessed that they probably would not – perhaps hoped that they would not, for to do so would diminish that day.

Later, leaning against her back porch watching the night sky and making her last measure of gin and her last cigarette last, she searched around in her conscience for the guilt that she had expected would have engulfed her by now. The story of a Woman Taken in Adultery was not read to girls until their last year at school, when they were impressionable enough for it to be tattooed upon their minds. In Markham the crowd still reached for its stones, but Georgia felt free of it all.

1942

'What a mess. What a shame . . . a bloody shame.' Mont Iremonger, living at the eye of the storm of war, could not bear what was happening to his town and in particular to the houses on his round. 'Everything decent has gone, the roses have gone to suckers, the lawns will take years to get back from what the goats and geese have done, even the railings and the gates. If it's true and all that iron we thought was going to the war effort is being dumped at sea, then the Government ought to be . . .' Mont Iremonger couldn't think of anything bad enough for such a cynical action. 'The Cedars used to have the finest gates round here for miles.'

As Mont trudged up the drive with the Hardys' mail, he thought back to those happy days a few years back, when The Cedars was still recognizably the property of Markham's most renowned burgher: shiny windows, well-painted and clean woodwork, and gleaming brass fittings. From April to September the lawns always showed lines and never a weed in the gravel drive or between the York stone of the terrace. He recalled the time when he had carried Miss Eve her first love letter which she did not want her parents to see. And the day following her twenty-first birthday, when she had waited for him seated in that pretty little car, 'Come and sit in and eat your birthday cake, Mr Iremonger.' He still had the little flower-spray that had ornamented the cake. There was another day – when Miss Eve was off holidaying in Scotland. He didn't think anybody else knew, but Mont had supposed she had gone to meet Vern Greenaway's lad without telling her people – that day when he had met Mrs Hardy. She was as pretty as a picture outside her front door, gathering roses in a basket.

He had thought she looked like one of them American Southern Belles. He had asked, 'Miss Eve enjoying her holiday, ma'am?'

'I am sure that she must be, but you would imagine that she was in Australia instead of Scotland, and that the telephone wasn't invented.'

'Ah well,' Mont remembered saying, 'we don't think when we're twenty, ma'am, do we?'

'I'm afraid we don't; we don't give two thoughts for anything else whilst we are enjoying ourselves.'

'Got to enjoy ourselves when we're young. Especially now, as things are.'

'True. Who knows when there will be holidays again?'

'And that's a fact, ma'am.'

Now, more than three years on, as the December cold stiffened the leather of his boots, he remembered every detail of that exchange. Poland was in trouble and Mrs Hardy had been wearing a pair of heavy, silky trousers with wide legs so that they looked like a skirt till she moved, and a blouse to match printed over with pale roses, just like the ones she had been picking. Looking back, it was as though that morning there had been a kind of summit to which he had been steadily climbing since the end of the Great War: once he had reached that summit there had been nothing else, not even a pleasant route by which to descend. All you could do was to remember how it used to be.

The only letters he now held were addressed to Councillor Hardy. Mont was not supposed to do so, but unofficially he sorted and extracted any letters addressed to Mrs Hardy and, as she had asked him to do, he readdressed them to an address that was unknown to anybody in Markham except himself and Eve. It was against the law, but the least that he could do.

He reached the bend in the drive where in years gone by Miss Eve had often come to meet him to collect the post whilst taking her little dog for a run, and there she was, coming towards him.

'Well I'm blowed, Miss, quite a time since I saw you. I was just thinking about you as a matter of fact. Hello, old feller.' He rubbed the little dog's ears. 'You're getting like me, a bit old and stiff, an't you, old chap? He must be getting on a bit now, Miss.'

'Yes, he's ten.'

'I remember when you first had him, he was called Jap then, wasn't he?'

'He was, but I changed it to Yap because people might think I liked the Japanese. Fancy you remembering that, I had quite forgotten.' She picked up the dog, smoothed back its ears and smiled indulgently at it, then set it down again. 'With a face like that, Jap still suits him. I'll walk with you,' she said. 'Where's your bike?'

'Have to leave it at the bottom these days. Not enough puff to get me up the hill.'

'Is there anything for me?'

Mont shook his head and handed her the bundle of mail. 'Afraid not, Miss. Was you expecting something? The post's all to pot these days. They say there's that much armaments and troop movements during the night these days, that Royal Mail has to come second.'

'Not really. I don't get much post these days.' He knew that Vern's son had been posted 'Missing' after his ship had been torpedoed. When Mont had heard this from Vern, he had immediately wondered how Miss Eve would get to hear of it. There was nobody in Markham to tell her, so he had decided to break the news to her himself.

It had been one of his worst moments, plucking up courage, trying to sound casual, yet serious. 'Have you heard about Councillor Greenaway's son, Miss Eve?'

Mont had seen that she already suspected bad news. She had almost whispered. 'He isn't dead, is he?'

'No, Miss, but they have been told he's missing.'

'Missing.'

'He's not "Missing believed dead", so that's hopeful.'

At that time she had just picked up Yap and walked off into the spinney beside the drive, and Mont had let her go. Later, he had condemned himself for being the stickler for formality that he had always been. Never again: there's times when you have got to put yourself forward for people you think is worth it – and it's hard luck if you get snubbed for it. You just had to make sure that you didn't overstep the mark. She didn't have nobody now. Her father was a womanizer and nothing but a glorified spiv, her mother had run away, and now she didn't get young Greenaway's letters for comfort.

They walked in silence for a minute. When they reached the gate she did not leave him but kept walking steadily beside him, tucking Yap into her coat when he began to get breathless in the chill wind. 'Is my mother's mail all right . . . I mean, do you mind? You won't get into trouble or anything of the kind? She told me that you were sending it on. She thought it extraordinarily kind of you. You might not believe it, but if you knew my mother, you would take it as a kind of compliment that she took you into her confidence.'

'Believe you me, Miss, I do know that. It was a pleasure to be able to do something.'

'She is very grateful, things are quite difficult.'

'She sent me a Christmas card, and some tobacco. Fancy her doing that, I never expected it. I've kept the card.'

Again a short silence.

'Don't mind me asking, Miss, but is she all right? She never said much on her card.'

No, thought Eve, that's not Connie's style.

'She is absolutely fine. And happy, and feeling very useful.' Eve Hardy laughed, and for a moment Mont saw again the pre-war face of the young woman in the girlish frocks and sandals. 'I went to see her just before Christmas, you would hardly recognize her . . . well, you would, because in many ways my mother will never change. But she wears trousers and heavy jumpers and shoes. She has had her hair off, and her fingernails – you can't fly planes with manicured nails. I thought that she looked years younger than me. People thought that we were sisters.'

Mont remembered the baggy silk trousers with printed roses. He still had the vision, the reality was gone for ever.

To Hell with propriety. 'And what about you now, Miss? Are you all right?'

'Yes, I've been staying with one of the girls I work with. She's on her own, we were company for one another over Christmas.'

'That was nice.'

'You knew about me and David Greenaway. That was why you told me about him being missing, wasn't it?'

Mont nodded. 'Only guesswork, Miss. Because he stuck stamps on upside down, all the Greenaways do. They're Republicans – don't ask me why they do that with the stamps.'

'If my father hadn't always been so much at daggers-drawn against Mr Greenaway, then David and I wouldn't have had to be so hole-in-the-corner.'

'That's politics for you, Miss.'

'I don't think so, Mr Iremonger. I think it is my father cannot bear the thought that there is a businessman in Markham who is not in his pocket.'

Mont did not offer a comment. 'Well, here's my old bike, darned near as decrepit as its owner.' He carefully wrapped his trouser-legs round his ankles, 'Like gold these are,' as he put on his cycle clips.

'Mr Iremonger?' Eve put a restraining hand on Mont's handlebars. 'I came down to meet you on purpose to ask you something.'

Mont waited, quite anxious at the frown folds that had appeared on her brow.

'I wondered if . . . when you are on your rounds . . . you might know of somebody who would take Yap for me.'

'Take him?'

'Look after him. I mean really care for him, be with him all the time; perhaps some lady who is at home all day and would like his company. It's either that or I shall have to think of having him put down – I can't bear to think of that. He's been all right till Nanny Bryce left.'

'You can't have little Yap put down. He's got a year or two to go yet. Lord above, he isn't no more stiff and breathless than me, and I an't going to let nobody put me down.'

'I know. But I just don't know what to do. I've asked quite a few people, but they've either got dogs or cats – and Yap is so quarrelsome with other animals, it wouldn't be fair. I just can't find a suitable home: if they haven't got pets already, then they are either out all day or they are not the kind of people I would want to hand Yap over to. I thought you might be able to think of somebody. Father is hardly ever at home, he's bought a place in the country. I simply have to do something more useful than delivering school dinners. I want to train as a nurse, I've wanted to ever since I heard about David, I've hung on thinking that Yap wouldn't last another winter, but he really is quite healthy.'

'He can come and live with me. No, no . . . he'll be all right. I won't leave him alone for a minute. You'll be all right, won't you, old chap?' He picked up the little dog and scratched into its silky hair. 'You always liked me, didn't you, eh? We'll be all right together. You won't be too fast for me, and I shan't be too fast for you. There look, Miss,' he took off his scarf, wrapped it round Yap and placed him on an empty mail-bag in the deep basket on the front of the Royal Mail bike, 'that's how we'll solve the time when I'm out at work. You'll just love it, won't you, my ole dear, getting some air in your lungs without crunching your arthritis too much? I've got just the little soft blanket for you at home – you'll be snug as a bug up front of my bike. I could take him now if you like, Miss.'

'Would you really? Oh, it would be a relief. I'll bring his basket later.'

'You come and visit him any time you like.' The dog put its paws on the handlebars and looked ahead, as though it was a regular thing to take rides in a bicycle basket. 'Don't you worry, Miss Eve, we shall get on like a house afire.'

'This family is never going to get out of your debt, Mr Iremonger.'

'Don't you say that, Miss, this has perked me up no end.'

Which was how Mont Iremonger's life took a strange turn that he could never have foreseen.

That same day, Eve went to tell Georgia that she would have to find another driver for the van.

Freddy Hardy – whilst feeding on their firmness, and drawing pleasure from the Texan sun-tanned tip-tilted breasts and rounded arms of a new mistress more youthful even than his daughter – lamented to her the fact that no matter how many diamond clips, expensive scents, cars and finishing schools a man might shower upon a daughter, there was no guarantee that she would stand by her father in his time of trouble.

The Texas-born WAC, newly drafted from the USA to the cold and lonely wilds of England, was comforted to find such a nice Poppa who seemed to have plenty of everything she liked most, and promised to be his own faithful little girl.

A couple of weeks before Eve was due to leave to take up her new career, they were all together having their usual morning break when the office phone rang. When Georgia returned from taking the call, she had lost her natural pinkness, so that the small freckles beneath her eyes looked oddly painted on.

'You all right, love?' Min, one of the cleaners, asked.

'That was the police. It's my parents . . . they're dead.'

Everybody stood staring at her as though an omen had fulfilled its prophecy.

'Dead? Both of them?' said Dolly.

'You was only just saying you was going to Scotland to see them,' said Min.

Georgia frowned. 'And my Dad, he's dead too. The policeman said they were both dead . . . killed.'

'Sit down, Georgia,' Eve ordered.

Ursula said, 'Dorothy will get you some brandy from the Red Cross locker.'

'Was they bombed then?' Kathy asked.

As Georgia drank Dolly's brandy, two red spots flared on her cheeks. 'No,' she looked puzzled. 'He said a tank went out of control and drove through the hedge and . . .'

She came-to hearing loud clanging and crashing, which gradually quietened and became the familiar sounds of the kitchen. She choked on the ammoniac salts that Ursula was waving under her nose, and then focused on Eve and Dolly who were holding her.

'I've never done that before. How stupid.'

'Shock,' said Dolly. 'You should be at home.'

Which was where Eve drove her and stayed until the completion of all the complicated arrangements to have their bodies transported and buried, as they had wished, in the village whence they had come.

1989

During the writing of *Eye of the Storm*, Georgia Giacopazzi had been able to recall the six years of war and women friends vividly but with objectivity. It was only now, with the proof copies out, that she could allow herself to become involved with the people who, in the writing, had been fictional characters. A long air journey was the perfect place to let the memory drift.

When interviewers and features editors wanted to know about the early years.

'When did you first know that you wanted to be a writer, Mrs Giacopazzi?'

'I have never wanted to be anything else. I guess I've always done it.'

'Making little books like the Brontë children?'

'Nothing so marvellous as theirs, of course.'

The truth, Mrs Giacopazzi?

The truth is that until the day of their funeral it had never occurred to me to want to write or that I could. Before that day, I had supposed that modern writers were men like Robert Crockford, educated but poverty stricken, or like Somerset Maugham, who travelled to exotic places and knew all the right people, or Jane Austen, who was special. I had supposed that modern women novelists must have been educated at Girton or at least to have been born into those circles where uncles and fathers had contacts in the publishing world. And a room of one's own and an income of two hundred a year as Virginia Woolf said was necessary.

The truth is that it never occurred to me until the day when I first met my own people. I scarcely knew of their existence.

And you wanted to write about them?

To put them down on paper, yes. To make some sort of record of their existence. It was a short step from there to writing fiction.

And getting published.

Yes, but it wasn't too difficult just after the war.

1942

Georgia was surprised at the number of people who attended the funeral. She had invited those Honeycombes and Gracelands with whom her parents exchanged Christmas cards, people whom she knew only by their handwriting. Relations of Georgia's father she could now, in their presence, pick out by the various shades of red in their hair or that solid white that carroty hair changes to in old age. Her mother's relations, sharp-eyed, frizzy-haired people who knew how many beans made five – one for the rook, one for the crow, one to rot and one to grow and t'other for I. Solemnly, and with faces set in moulds that those who do not know country people often take to be sullenness, they knelt tight-lidded and prayer-handed in the village church.

As one-time neighbours of the Honeycombes – and long ago from this village too – Nick's father had come countryman-fashion to pay last respects to neighbours, people of his own kind. Nick wangled a week off and had got Hugh's neglected car back on the road. On the drive from Markham, Robert Crockford had sat alone in the back of the car as politely remote as Georgia had remembered him from when the Crockfords and the Honeycombes were neighbours at Emberley, speaking only when spoken to in the well-articulated voice which Nick had inherited but had learned to roughen up at school.

Country-fashion, too, in order of precedence, the mourners walk from the church to the graveyard, behind the coffin carrying their wreaths that are made mostly of ivy, snowdrops and early wild daffodils.

'We none of us begrudged the money for a good wreath,'

an elderly woman had said whilst they all waited for the hearses to arrive, 'but it's wartime and all. We done what we could for Cousin Thomas. We should a liked lilies or chrysanths, but 'tis the wrong time to go like, if you wants much in the way of shop wreaths. I'm Hyacinth Jepp (Honeycombe that was), your Pa's first cousin.'

Now at the graveside, wearing an expensive grey suit loaned by Eve from her mother's abandoned wardrobe, black shoes, and a new black pill-box hat which emphasized the rampant colour of her hair, Georgia, escorted by an uncle she has never met, throws down two small handfuls of earth, its sandiness sticking between her fingers. The smell of earth is everywhere, it blends with the naphtha of funeral coats, and the green wreaths, and wet crushed grass. She notices that her parents' male cousins wear suits that must go back to the turn of the century; probably their wedding suits, yet these still fit their work-lean frames. The women all seem to be short and have wide hips and large bosoms. It crosses Georgia's mind that they probably all went to the same village school, where there was no segregation amongst them because their bus journey was a nuisance, where they were not scorned, not different as she and Nick and the other Country Children used to be.

Dry-eyed and distanced, Georgia looks at the scene objectively.

Even the emotive 'ashes to ashes' phrase does not stir her. Although the brass plates are engraved with the names Thomas Honeycombe, Alice Honeycombe, née Graceland, it is as though the coffins side by side contain strangers. Perhaps they do, for it seems to Georgia that she understands this uncle, John, of the Christmas cards more than she did her Pa.

As they walked slowly to the empty grave, he had said, 'You looks strung up, gel. You a feel better when you've had a good howl and got it off your chest. Nobody here won't take no notice. We all needs a cry at times like these.'

Pa would have said, 'You don't want to start crying in front of everybody and letting yourself down.' But Georgia's only grief was for the mean act of death itself, snatching away twenty years that were still due to Thomas and Alice. She would have felt the same about the sudden death of strangers.

The Honeycombes and Gracelands had combined resources to provide what was proper on such an occasion. After the ceremony of death, still in procession, they walked from the graveyard through the village where people stood respectfully at their gates and along a tar-macked, pot-holed lane with high hedges on either side. Georgia felt a strange kind of excitement as she listened to twenty or thirty broad Hampshire accents, and knew that Nick would be easy and happy in their company. They had not seen one another for many weeks, but on the journey their conversation was curtailed by the quiet Robert Crockford in the back seat.

'This here stream comes straight from the chalk,' John Honeycombe said. 'The fishing rights is tied to the land and nobody can't take them.'

'Really?' Georgia had never considered fishing rights, but she looked into the bright stream.

'Best trout in the whole of Hampshire now we seen off the pikes.'

'Is that one?'

'He is. He's a right ole devil, you'd never tickle him in a month of Sundays, nor he won't take nobody's bait. He been there so long now that I don't know as I'd fancy him neither poached nor baked.'

Over his shoulder, John Honeycombe said to his sister, 'What about that Hyacinth Jepp, she spotted the ole devil soon as she looked in, she's turned out sight more of a country girl than our Tom.'

The strangeness of Pa, who spent his weekends dressed in stiff white collar and waistcoats, being 'Our Tom' to these ruddy faces. And the sudden realization of the praise in being called Country Girl by Uncle John.

Hyacinth Jepp broke ranks and came to walk beside Georgia. 'Your husband couldn't get here, then.'

'No. He's somewhere off Tasmania.'

'Well, he's safe and warm at any rate. And they're friends of yours drove you here?'

'From the same village as us. Mr Crockford grew up somewhere round here.'

'And the other one would be the son, then?' asked John Honeycombe.

'Yes, he and I went to school together. He's in Liverpool now – fire service.'

'That's a nasty job, very nasty,' Mrs Jepp said. 'Well then, here we are. After you, Georgia.'

John Honeycombe held aside a wide gate that barred a cattle-yard obviously brushed and hosed for the occasion. From a little way off the grunt and squeal of pigs could be heard.

'I never realized that it was an animal farm . . . you know what I mean, I imagined that you grew corn and potatoes.'

'An't nothing much we don't grow,' said John Honeycombe. 'I should have thought our Tom would have told you.'

Georgia shook her head. 'I don't think that he liked farming very much.'

'No,' said John Honeycombe with a sharp edge, 'No. No, Tom never did.'

John Honeycombe led the way diagonally across the yard, along a rough path through a patch of long grass. An ancient tree trunk stood there, with only two branches, from which sprouted young twigs. Geese and a few hens grazed.

Good Lord, thought Georgia, it looks like a calendar, and thought of her Pa hating it and studying hard in the hope of getting away.

Following where she was looking, John Honeycombe said, 'She's a rare old apple. Hyacinth won't let her die without a fight. She budded some of the last young shoots year 'fore last and damme if most of they haven't took.'

The grass was surrounded by a border that had evidently grown herbaceous plants last year; there was a bottomless bucket from which straw protruded; clay forcing-jars and glass bells under which some green plants flourished; here and there clumps of snowdrops and windflowers bloomed.

The path ended at the porch of the cottage, a low thatched building with a steep roof from which dormers protruded like shaggy-browed eyes. Because the cottage was tucked into the slope of the rising downland, Georgia guessed they must look out over the valley. A farmhouse with some of its history evident in its structure: part old brick and knapped flint with leaded casement windows; part red brick with sash windows; uneven building and roof lines; a few bulges and iron ties; but a place that seemed as old and solid as the hill in whose shelter it had been built many generations ago.

Once over the threshold, the mourners dropped their formality in honour of the dead for the practicality of comforting the living. Hyacinth Jepp was obviously in charge here. 'Now my dear,' she said, 'while our John sees to the whisky, you come with me.' Putting into Georgia's hand a glass containing a large measure of brandy, and taking one herself, she ushered Georgia from the living-room into an enormous kitchen. 'Drink up, it'll drive the graveyard out of your feet. Now . . . I hope you don't think I was taking things over, but I knew you wouldn't have no chance of putting on anything, seeing you're in Markham and all.'

'It's wonderful . . . I never gave a thought to food.'

'Well no, I doubt you had many funerals.'

'None. I don't even know if there are special rations or anything.'

'Well there you are then, I'm glad I got on and done

something. I know our Tom was always a stickler for doing things right. Just so long as you don't think I'm butting in, I wouldn't want you to think you had that sort of kinfolk. Tom was still my brother, even though we haven't met for thirty years and more.' To a redheaded girl a few years younger than Georgia, 'Heather, get hold the other end. There!' Proudly Hyacinth and Heather flung back the sheet from the longest kitchen-table Georgia had ever seen: it was laden with food. Hyacinth and Heather were obviously well pleased with the laden table.

'Heather, you go and fetch that there young man what drove Georgia – he must be starving by now, great chap like that – and his father.'

'Mrs Jepp, the last time I saw a table laid like that was at a big centenary dinner in Southampton.'

'And I'll wager a penny to a dollar your dinner in Southampton wasn't home-cooked. Every bit of this was done by Honeycombe women, most of it grown by Honeycombe men. I an't Mrs Jepp to you, niece – but you don't have to call me Auntie if you don't want. Most folk call me Hyacinth.'

The table was a work of art of woven swags of greenery amongst which were placed best china dishes displaying glazed game pies decorated with complicated paste leaves, puffy fruit pies oozing juice through sugar frosting, decorated galantines, plain pressed meats, a brown-skinned baked ham, a leg of cold pork, beautiful shiny loaves, patterned golden butter and several substantial wedges of cheese – yellow, white, blue-veined.

'Ma and Pa would have been very proud.'

'Well, who knows, seeing as how Tom had a wish to be buried here; perhaps he come to realize that he was still one of us. The Honeycombes has always been one for family, no matter what. I said to our John many a time, you see if I an't right – our Tom will come back.' She wiped her eyes with the back of her hand. 'He was a pretty lad. A pity he had to come back like this.'

Suddenly Nick was beside her, and Georgia saw Hyacinth Jepp's sharp eyes flick from him to Georgia and back again.

Nick slapped his large hands together in appreciation of the table. 'Will you just look at that, Georgia.' Amongst these people, Nick had easily lapsed into the broad tongue he had used throughout his boyhood, but which had recently reverted to the more cultured one taught from the cradle by his father. 'An't that the most beautiful sight you ever saw? A work of art, 'tis a shame to break into it, Mrs Jepp.'

The praise satisfied Mrs Jepp and she beamed at him. 'We don't want none of that, lad. That was all made to end up in hungry bellies.'

'Here you are, Georgia.' She handed Georgia a large knife. 'Give that lad a slice of something. You take over now, 'tis your do.'

'But . . .'

'It's the proper thing. Brother Tom was head of this family, you have to do the honours. I'll give you a hand.'

Willing to take part in this extraordinary family burial rite, half-party, half-harvest festival, Georgia thrust a knife into the crust of a large game pie.

Hyacinth garnished the wedge with pickles and cress and handed the plate to Nick. 'There lad. I'll show you work of art. Now you must have a bite too, Georgia, before all the rest of them gets in here. And what about Mr Crockford?'

'Have you seen my Dad, Georgia? He's in there talking away nineteen to the dozen to one of your uncles.' He smiled, 'Well, for him it is nineteen to the dozen. I gather they knew one another when they were young.' To Mrs Jepp, 'He's a man who usually keeps himself to himself.' He savoured the pie and closed his eyes. 'Oh . . . wonderful, Mrs Jepp. My mother made game pies like this: I can just remember them, all succulent and herby. Taste, Georgia, just taste.' He held the slice for her to bite into as Hyacinth Jepp observed with satisfaction.

1989

Had she been flying in from a publicity trip organized by her publishers, a white Daimler would have been awaiting Giacopazzi at the London end; as it was, a discreet black BMW with a discreet brown driver awaited her. The driver took her hand-luggage and held open the door. 'Hello, ma'am, nice to see you again.'

'It's nice to be back, Salim.'

'Been somewhere nice this time, ma'am?'

'Jo'burg.'

'City of gold, they say.'

'They can keep it.'

The car slid away and headed towards London. Georgia Giacopazzi sank into the comfort of fine leather. 'I swear they keep moving Johannesburg further away from London. Or perhaps it's old age.'

He moved his fine Asian profile to the left. 'Not old age, ma'am. I have it on the best authority that they have in fact moved the entire continent further east.'

Only the best for Giacopazzi. A driver with a sense of humour, who handed her out, dealt with the hotel reception, took care of her bags, saw to it that she had everything she wanted, saluted without subservience and went. Alone for the first time since early yesterday, she kicked off her shoes and sank on to the bed. She longed to phone home but it was a bad time to do so. Her body ached with the fatigue of disguising the nag of arthritis and of keeping on her public face for so many hours, but her mind was afire. As when an idea for a novel was building up, she closed her eyes and allowed her thoughts to take whatever turn they wished.

The phone purred gently. Thinking that they must be phoning from home in spite of the hour, she answered at once.

'Room eleven hundred.'

'Mrs Giacopazzi? A call for you.'

'Georgia?'

Mrs Giacopazzi's heart leaped. 'Yes.'

'This is Eve.'

'I know . . .'

'Georgia? Oh, I thought we'd been cut off.'

'No, it's just the surprise . . . you sound exactly the same as ever.'

'I'm an old lady.'

'Who isn't?'

'Georgia, I don't know about you, but I hate telephones. One cannot see the other person's face. But I wanted to tell you that I think the book is very good.'

'You do?'

'Very good. But not at all the usual Giacopazzi story, except the hint of mystery . . .'

'My instincts are to make the reader wait.'

'I couldn't wait. I read the end – I wanted to know . . .'

'And?'

'I wish that you had told me.'

'It was all too bizarre, I simply couldn't.'

'I had no idea, Georgia.'

'Of course, how could you? I thought it best to do it short and sharp.'

There was a short silence while Georgia retained her composure. Eve's voice came through again. 'Are you still there, Georgia?'

'Of course. It's only that with a fifty-year gap, one doesn't really know what to say first. Could we meet? Where are you now?'

'Boston.'

'Mass?'

'Yes, visiting with Melanie – my daughter. But I shall be in London again in a couple of days.'

'I shall wait here for you.' Another short silence. 'Eve?'

'Hullo . . . yes, Georgia?'

'You said you thought the book was good . . . does that mean you don't mind that I've written it?'

'It's the truth, and you've been kind to us. Which is mostly why I have called you.'

'Until you get back to London then.'

'Yes, until then, Georgia.'

1943

Eve Hardy entered her nursing career in London. She was obliged to live in nurses' quarters, but had a room in Connie's small flat where she kept some of her things and to which she could flee to sleep like a log on her days off. When nothing had been heard of David for almost two years, she became convinced that he was not only missing, but was dead.

There were moments when she wanted desperately to go to talk to the Greenaways, but thought that they would not like to hear about their son's involvement with one of the Hardy family or, even if they did not mind, would probably not have much to say to her. She started entertaining young men in Connie's flat, cooking for them, sewing on buttons, and then wrapping them around with her arms and legs.

Connie would come home and be unsurprised to find a Canadian greatcoat on the hallstand, or a young man with frizzy hair and a black torso washing at the handbasin, or a supply of luxuries from the American PX or the whiff of Gauloise or Camels about.

Once, she had said, intending lightheartedness, 'God's buns, Eve! You're as dissolute as your father was.'

And Eve, stiff and tense, her eyes blazing, had gone white and said fiercely, 'Don't you ever, ever, say that I am like him. He's a cruel, self-centred and dishonest bastard.'

Connie was taken aback by the passion in the attack: she had never supposed that Freddy's behaviour had so affected Eve. When she had broken it to her daughter that she was leaving home, Eve had appeared quite sanguine: 'Oh Ma, I'm so sorry for you, because I know how you hate messiness,' although she never called her Ma or Mother from then on. Apart from her tendency to be secretive, it had seemed to Connie that Eve sailed through life untroubled and unperturbed, never hankering, but content with what she had. Nanny Bryce's little pet.

Whenever Connie thought of her daughter, she had a sketchy mental picture of a pink, plump eighteen-year-old in a dirndl skirt and a straw hat on pale curls, walking at the slow pace of her pekinese dog. Suddenly she was confronted by this stranger, a strong, blonde woman in grey and red uniform with her hair scooped into a large knot, wreathed in tobacco smoke, knowingness and confidence.

'I . . . My dear child . . . I meant nothing. Take no notice, I'm not with it half the time. My work, you know . . . but that's no excuse. I really am frightfully sorry about how you feel. I had no idea – none.'

'It doesn't matter now. Forget it, forget it, forget it.'

As far as Eve could tell, Connie herself seemed to be content with complete celibacy, for in the flat there was never any sign of men except for those Eve brought there. Connie seemed to be fulfilled, living only to receive her instructions to collect or deliver an aircraft.

Sometimes she was away for days, returning pale-faced, burning-eyed and exhilarated. When Eve saw her like this, she was reminded of some of the ever increasing number of outpatients she encountered who were brought in in a drugged stupor after a ship from the Far East had docked. But Connie did not take even gin these days – she did not need it. Nothing could surpass the sensations she achieved from her secret and dangerous missions which often took her to the other side of the English Channel.

Late in 1943, when she was nearing the end of the first part of her training, Eve was called into Matron's office and told that if she would like to volunteer, then she could have the rare opportunity of training as an auxiliary in the nursing of psychiatric patients. Several small hospitals were being opened in suitable locations away from large centres of population. These training hospitals were looking for girls of a certain intelligence and calm disposition.

'Only suitable candidates are being selected, Hardy, level-headedness and attitude being of prime importance. Psychotherapeutics!' She fired the word at Eve, who waited for her superior to continue. 'Have you heard of it?'

'Treatment of madness?'

'Of psychiatric illness, yes. It is a fairly new and special branch of medicine. Many have ill-informed knowledge of its value. I value it highly. There will be a great need for trained personnel when men are released from captivity. In the last war, many men were shot as traitors or cowards for presenting psychiatric symptoms. We have come far since then.'

'Yes, ma'am.'

'You are the right type. I have put your name forward as a volunteer for training. I'm sure that you will not let me down.'

'Yes, ma'am.'

'Good. There are three new training centres. I have volunteered you for one intending to specialize in the effects of long-term incarceration and the effects of extreme physical abuse.'

Eve pulled her brows together questioningly.

'Torture, and solitary confinement, Hardy. Our enemies are evil in the extreme. The personal rewards in terms of promotion will come swiftly to those willing to put a year's training into a month. The wards must be fully ready to receive patients within six months.'

'Ma'am?'

'Ask ahead.'

'Does that mean that they are expecting to be bringing back POWs in six months?'

'I have no idea, but you may draw as many conclusion as I.'

'May I ask where and when I begin training?'

'As soon as your transfer and travel documents arrive. As for where . . . the Oaklands Centre – I'm told that Lord Palmerston once owned it – located in a place called Markham.' She smiled a rare and lovely smile. 'I believe you know it.'

Oh Lord! She thinks she's done me a favour.

'Yes, ma'am.'

'Always nice to have a spell close to home.'

Connie said, 'Turning Oaklands into a nuthouse, Eve? I am sure that it must be quite unsuitable. Of course you will refuse the posting.'

'Of course I shall not refuse. Have you ever refused an order? And it's not a nuthouse. And for goodness sake, Connie, you aren't to mention what sort of nursing home it is because you aren't supposed to know.'

'Oh don't worry on that score. I know no one who is likely to be the slightest bit interested in an insane asylum in the wilds of Hampshire. Poor Oaklands, though. What a shame, they'll probably destroy all the lovely friezes and use the orangery for something dreadful.'

'Depressed patients aren't likely to destroy friezes.'

'But Oaklands! It does seem so . . . inappropriate.'

'Inappropriate! For God's sake, Connie. To what better use can an uninhabited country house be put? It's not as though they won't have a roof over their poor heads – they have at least three mansions, a sea-front house in Southsea and a London flat.'

'It is still their home, even though it has been visited by kings and princes.'

'And Nazis – Ribbentrop visited in thirty-six. No worse psychotic illness than Fascism. Oaklands is very appropriate, if you ask me.'

But Connie was not really seriously perturbed about the fate of Markham's great estate; she was preparing to travel to an isolated aerodrome from where she guessed she would be flying a small plane which she would land in a field the other side of the Channel. In any case, Markham was in her past. She had cleansed herself of Freddy and, as far as she was concerned, he could bang himself to death. But she had made up her mind that she would never divorce him.

'Once the war is over it won't matter, Connie. All the estates will come under common ownership.'

'Not you too, Eve? Everybody you meet these days is a damned Red. I can't stand them, they're all so damned *fair*.'

'Good. And I should have thought you'd had enough of the other sort to last you a lifetime.'

Connie shrugged. 'He is opportunist, not capitalist.'

'Is there a difference?'

'Eve! I suppose the next thing you will do is to join some union.'

'I already have.'

'Don't tell me, I don't want to hear. It's everywhere, like some damn disease. It is one thing I agreed with your father about; he would allow none of that in his factory. Can you imagine that great Welsh Bevan and his wife running this country? Too ridiculous for words. The country would never be the same again.'

'Well good for *it*!'

Connie, uncharacteristically ramming her change of clothes into a grip, altered her tone. 'Who cares anyway? Live for the day. Listen, darling, I'm off . . . shan't be back for a few days. Take care.' She brushed Eve's cheek with her lips. 'I dare say you sometimes wonder . . . well . . . I *did* want you, you know . . . you're the one thing that's been worth while.' She zipped the bag. 'And look, it's your affair, but these men . . . they aren't going to take the place of the man who has gone, you know. Nobody can. You really do have to put it behind you and start again.'

She kept flicking short, shy looks at Eve, then suddenly she took her daughter's hands and drew her to her slim, girlish embrace. 'Darling girl, I'm not much to go on, except as a lesson on not wasting the best part of your life hanging on to something in the past long after it is dead.' And then she was briskly gone.

Until then, nothing, even David Greenaway being posted Missing, had pierced Eve's placid armour quite so much as that unique moment of real contact with her mother.

1989

'Ladies?' Used to senility and deafness, the Wardress raised her voice so that it echoed round the glass span of the conservatory.

Hand over deaf-aid microphone, Mrs Partridge said, 'No need to shout, we aren't deaf.'

Good-hearted beneath it all, the Wardress smiled at her pair of celebrities. She propped open the double doors. 'It's like an oven in here. Hottest day for a hundred years; hottest summer since '76.'

'Going to get hotter,' said Dolly.

The Wardress fanned her neck with her collar. 'Ladies, The Press is here again. It's *The Independent* this time. Aren't you suddenly the famous ones?'

'I preferred it when I was notorious and they weren't all so damned patronizing,' Ursula said. 'Shall we go to them, Dorothy, or summon them to our rooms?'

'I've emptied the small sitting-room for you,' said the Wardress.

'Let's go there and make a grand entrance together, Ursula.'

They progressed at their own pace from the conservatory, where they had been tending their coffee and banana plants, towards the house.

'*The Independent,*' Mrs Partridge said. 'Isn't that the heavy black-looking one?'

As it turned out, the feature-writer was Charlotte, a slip of a girl in a silky suit and ear-rings like bunches of grapes and she was from Independent Radio. 'I understand from the matron that you have had other meeja people here recently.'

'That woman has a big mouth,' said Dolly. 'It'd be all the same if we didn't want you to know. She could take up broadcasting on her own account, without a microphone.'

Charlotte, having smiled her way through getting her equipment tuned to the pitch of her interviewees, explained that she had been given a half-hour slot and she wanted to do something on older women that would make Woman's Hour sit up. 'I'm hoping it will get me noticed – nobody does anything serious about the *really, really* aged as real people; and when I read the piece in the *Guardian* I thought *te-rrific!* Centenarians and friends of Giacopazzi. It will make a smashing piece.'

When Charlotte had got her piece about the really, really aged real ladies and gone, Dorothy made a pot of tea which Ursula carried to the conservatory, a building which they considered theirs and which few other residents cared for because it was about the only room in the home where there was no television set.

'What about *that* then, Ursula? Fancy my film coming to light – after all these years.'

'And she made the connection between the mention of Niall in the *Guardian* interview and the film in the archives. She's a clever girl, she'll make a good journalist.'

Like many who went through the years and years of shortages and economies, the two old ladies poured their tea carefully and drank it sugarless, not talking too much as they savoured flavour and caffeine.

'Shall you accept her offer to go and see it again, Dorothy?'

'I think I might, so long as you come too. Will you mind?'

'No, of course I should not mind. Why should I?'

'I wondered – when you said that you weren't sure that you wanted to see it again.'

'That's not because of you and Niall – you know that never bothered me greatly.' She laughed her almost silent laugh. 'I'm not likely to start after fifty years.'

'I would have stolen him from you if I could have.'

'I can't say that I should have blamed you for it: he knew how to make a woman feel exceptional.'

'He was the sweetest man, wasn't he?'

'Dorothy, let's be honest . . . he was a libertine.'

'That's a word you don't hear much these days.'

'He screwed around.'

'And you married him. After all those years, you got married. I never thought you would. Thought your feministy side would have put the mockers on marrying.'

Ursula smiled, deepening the deep vertical lines of her mouth. 'The flaw in many a good feminist, loving men . . . a man. I never much enjoyed women in that way.' Switching off for a minute or two, the old women lapsed into dozy contemplation. 'Trix did. Did you know that? It was Trixie, wasn't it, whose mother cut the flies out of her father's best trousers? Or was that Pammy? Remember Pammy from those days?'

'It was Trixie. If it hadn't been for the war, she would have ended up as knocked-about and unhappy as her Mum. If I remember right, it was her sergeant in the ATS that fell for her. Didn't they set up home together when they were demobbed?'

Ursula said, 'She had never heard the word lesbian until she joined the WAAF.'

'Well, you didn't in those days, did you – well, not in our sort of circles; but I'll bet your lot knew all about it. I knew that there were men like that, you used to see them in Southampton – especially round by the docks – old chaps with long hair and wearing lipstick. Lord, it's no wonder they got called queer the way they used to go about. I just always thought it was men like that.'

She drifted back to the sub-world where she saw the past in such detail, where, more and more often these days, she discovered interesting facts she had never had time to notice at the time. Dolly Partridge could sit for hours roaming about there. Eventually she said, 'There used to be a couple of ladies lived in Markham – before you came here – when I was a girl – they was getting on in years. One was tall and thin, walked like a stork, the other was tiny and very sweet-looking. They was real lavender and old lace. They had lived together donkey's years, since they were girls . . . never went out without hats. Had high boned collars. Never wore anything except cream and fawn, fashions that was about fifty years before . . . a lot of scenty powder the same colour. It's funny when you look back, I don't think nobody ever thought anything about them living together. They were Sunday-school teachers. Nobody thought twice about it. You see what I mean . . . nobody much knew about women then . . .'

'Or cared.'

'. . . Just as likely they was just friends but you know, once you find out a thing and that they got a name for it, you begin to think about things you never thought about before. It's like what you just said about young Trix. I can see now. She was very against her Dad . . . and her brothers . . . and men. She never blamed her Mum for going off and leaving them all. The war didn't have all bad consequences.'

'Here.' Ursula tipped a small shot of whisky into each of their cups. 'Drink before you start getting maudlin. You always do when you start thinking about the old days.'

'Why do you always make out you are so tough? It's why I never thought you'd get married.'

'Because I am tough . . . and your batteries must be running down, you're raising your voice. I married Niall because I couldn't have coped with being the Other Woman to you. One can only sustain being the Mistress if one despises the Wife.'

'You never said that before.'

'The film never saw the light of day before.'

'All the years we've been together and you never said you was jealous of Niall's little fling with me.'

'I never meant that I was jealous; what I meant is that I could never despise you. You are the best of all people. I guessed what would happen if you and Niall got together: you are the kind of woman men like. You look after their creature comforts.' She spoke quietly, watching her friend twiddling the volume of her hearing-aid. 'Oh Lord, Dorothy, why don't you carry a spare battery – I shall never repeat all that if I live to be a hundred.'

The plump old lady peered. 'What's so funny, Ursula? This thing's on the blink again.'

'I said, Georgia Giacopazzi . . .'

Dorothy Partridge winced, 'Ah, that's better.'

'Georgia Kennedy didn't know everything that was going on.'

'You're right there. If she *had* a known we should be getting ourselves interviewed by the *Sun*.'

'Or the *Sport*.'

Dorothy looked blank.

'It's a dirty paper . . . likes three-in-a-bed stories. You are behind the times, Dorothy.'

Turn of the Tide

1944

When Eve got her transfer to the Oaklands Centre, she had been working in London for eighteen months or so. In spite of the fact that she had wanted to get away from Markham, she missed the place more than she had expected whilst she was living in London. It was a time when the harsh sound of the pilotless V1 rocket bombs was straining the population unbearably during the day, and depressing them by forcing them to return to sleeping underground at night. The London Blitz had long been ended, but once again these new weapons were filling the mortuaries and casualty wards with civilians.

Although she was apprehensive at going into an unknown field – nursing men who had experienced deprivation, brutality and torture – Eve was glad to be going from London; except that she worried over Connie.

'Darling, I am indestructible, and I am more away than actually in London.' Even so, Eve had seen the blast destruction and the terrible injuries that could be caused by the missiles.

Before going into weeks of virtual isolation from the outside world at the Oaklands Centre, Eve arranged to spend the weekend split between Georgia and Mont Iremonger. Her foster-sister and foster-grandfather, as she jokingly referred to them. She and Georgia had not seen one another since the Christmas after Eve's home had broken up and she had lodged for a while in Station Avenue.

'I often think of it, wasn't it super, Georgia?' Eve said when they were comfortably settled with tea and cigarettes in armchairs in the front-room at Georgia's, which was now a comfortable clutter of books and pictures, unpolished furniture and fluffy debris.

'Talk about self-indulgent, we ate our entire month's sweet ration in bed on Boxing Day morning.'

Instead of a nurse and an administrator, twenty-five years old and serious about their work, they became for a few minutes the sort of excitable, giggling girls that neither of them had ever been.

'And you made that great soufflé instead of Christmas pudding.'

'Oh, and what about Christmas Eve afternoon down at the kitchens, didn't you just love it?'

'I never thought to see Mrs Farr wearing a tinsel crown . . . and what about Marie's party with all those Americans?'

Since the upheaval of Eve's mother leaving and the installation of a WAC from Texas into The Cedars, the already friendly relationship between Georgia and Eve became more confident. They talked openly with one another, each of them discovering the unexpected joy of having an intimate woman friend who neither made judgements nor expected faultlessness.

That Christmas had been the first either of them had spent entirely free of any commitments, and they had enjoyed it.

'How is Nick?'

'Still in Liverpool. Hoyes staa'ted speekingk with a foony accent.'

Eve laughed and tossed a cigarette which Georgia caught in mid-air and lit thankfully.

'Craven A – you life-saver, I swear there hasn't been a decent gasper in Markham for two years.'

'They're about again. Supplies will reach the backwaters eventually.'

'Why is it other places seem to get stuff we haven't seen since the outbreak?'

'Perhaps Whitehall thinks it is enough that our houses are still standing.'

It passed through Georgia's mind that Eve might not know that her old home was in a neglected state. She had seen the garden herself whilst door-to-door collecting for the Spitfire Fund – a fallen tree left where it fell across the lily pond, the beautiful little palm-house sagging, dustbins scavenged by cats and foxes, tipped over and rolling around, verdigris on the door-brasses and grimed-in dirt on the windows. Nobody had answered her call, the place had the appearance of being abandoned. Now was not the time to mention it.

'It's a shame Nick can't get a transfer back to the South.'

'Maybe.'

'Georgia?' Astonished, Eve dropped her bantering tone. 'I thought you loved the guy.'

'Aah . . . don't read anything into that "maybe" one way or the other. I thought there was a time when I'd die if he didn't come, but . . . I don't know . . . I think it's like Mrs W. next door, she used to cry a lot when Dick became a POW, but she seems to be content enough now. I think she's discovered that she's Mary Wiltshire, not just Dick Wiltshire's wife. It will be interesting to see how they get on when he's back again and discovers that Mary can mend plumbing, do bits of wiring and use a hammer and saw. Dick's nose will be out of joint. I just hope that she doesn't let him push her down again. He'd never have let her bleach her hair, or get a little job. I can just hear him – "A woman's place is in the home, Mary" . . . "I've been home ten minutes, Mary, what's happened to the dinner?" . . . "I'll have no Littlewoods Club in my house – what we can't pay cash for, we'll go without."

'Now look at her, the front of her hair bleached and put up in a Victory roll *and* she's running a profitable little line in Mail Order stuff, to say nothing of a bit of black market. But I can't talk, I was nearly as bad with Hugh. Girls, like me and Mary especially, are brought up to be married women.'

'You've proved you can do a manager's job really well: there's bound to be a place for you somewhere.'

'I can't think where. The men will come back and women will get shooed into dolly's houses and play-kitchens. Everyone will forget that women drove tractors and lorries, worked lathes, did welding . . . yes, and organized workers. They will pretend that we are helpless outside the home.'

'And a lot of women will collude in the pretence. As Connie did. Do you realize that never once in the twenty-five years before she left did she say that she had learned to fly an airplane.'

'Imagine, being able to do something like that, and everybody else thinking that you were only good at arranging dinner parties and dressing well.'

'Seeing her as she is now has made a difference to me. I thought that I would continue nursing as a career. It's a pity if we can't hold on to the progress women have made as a consequence of this war.'

'Equality for Women isn't the favourite horse to back.'

'I suppose you are right: men have been going off fighting since the year dot, and whilst they were gone, women did everything they weren't supposed to be capable of doing when the men were at home, such as fending off wild animals and farming crops.'

'And when the men had had enough, they came back and filled the women full of babies. It happened after 1918 as it must have after the Crusades. "Oh no, Lancelot, *please* not all that again," my Lady said, "I'd much prefer a new breast-plough to a new baby."

' "Dear Lady," said the knight, "hast lost thy senses? Breast-ploughs are for men. A lady's place is in the home with a nice little baby and a nice little roasting spit. Keep," ' Georgia said, giggling, ' "within the keep." '

'Oh yes, "A lady's place is within the keep." "But, my Lord," said she, "I have been running the castle and the farm and the dairy, as well as bringing up the kids for ten years. I've made a very good job of it, no labour trouble at all, and it's all been so much more interesting and worthwhile than embroidering samplers."' Eve knelt with exaggerated humility. ' "And my Lord, this be not fair." '

' "Blame your mother, honey. When you came out female and no rod of authority – you drew the short straw." '

Caught up in their silly mood, they fell about laughing.

'Oh, Eve, you don't know how good it is to have somebody to talk to and let down my hair with. I have to be so formal and capable in my job, and all the voluntary things I get involved with. I've gained the reputation for being good with ideas and organizing, so I get roped in to do absolutely every voluntary thing.'

'Seriously – what will you do? The training I am to undergo is to do with the situation when the war ends – it will be over now within a year at the most I should think – but this is just the beginning of a career for me.'

'I'm not going back into the dolly's house. I must earn my living. Women have had a little taste of freedom and found it addictive. I seem to have got used to living for myself. I don't know that I want to share.'

'One does get used to the idea of being on one's own. Then one begins to resent intrusion. I have to admit that I wasn't entirely delighted when I heard that I was being shipped back to Markham. I've grown to like not being answerable to anyone but myself.'

'I think that is what Nick can't understand. He thinks it is to do with him – but it is to do with me.'

'D'you know, at first, when Davey went missing, I had such terribly vivid dreams of him, erotic and terrifying at the same time – awfully mixed up. Then I went through a phase – it was when I first started work at the hospital – a phase of thinking I heard his voice everywhere, and believing that every time I turned back the blanket on a stretcher, it would be David lying there. Pretty soon after that phase, I knew that he wasn't coming back.' She stubbed out her cigarette and immediately lit another. 'Oh Georgia, I have to tell somebody or I'll burst. It has to be you, I could never talk to Connie . . . in any case, she lives in her own world. I have been going nuts since I left Markham. Connie said something . . . it seemed to bring me to my senses – "as dissolute as your father," she said. I just let fly at her. Since I've been in London I've been with dozens of different men – the hospital bike, give anybody a ride.'

'Eve! Don't!'

'It's true. I did it with great purpose.' She shook her head in apparent amazement at herself. 'Honestly, I didn't care much what they looked like, they only had to be the right shape and size.'

Georgia's brows puckered as she observed the changes in Eve Hardy. She had lost the plumpness that had made her look so girlish when they had first met five years ago. Now, as she sucked deeply on her cigarette, drawing in her cheeks, the fine bones of her face showed clearly. Her skirt, utilitarian to the point of extreme skimpiness, had wriggled up to her thighs, but she made no attempt, as she once would have done, at modestly covering her liquid-stockinged legs. And whereas at one time she would have sat with still hands and followed the conversational trends of others, she now frequently gestured and moved her body as she talked. She had picked up some of Connie Hardy's mannerisms.

'God, if anyone else should hear this, but I've got to get it off my chest, Georgia, there's nobody I'd tell except you. Talk about a Denise Robins romance! But just hear me out. There has always been this great moment of utter passion with David that I wanted to relive, it became a kind of obsession. The first time we went to bed was more wonderful than I had imagined it could be. Our affair was enchanting – our families were the Montagues and Capulets – Davey was an heroic Romeo with his medal on the dressing-table and he made my transition from virgin to woman total ecstasy.' She smiled. 'In Probationer language . . . the first time we did it, we hit the high spot and I've been hot for it ever since.' She inhaled tobacco deep into her lungs. 'But he fucking well went away and didn't fucking come back.'

'Not Denise Robins, honey – unexpurgated Lawrence.'

'You can mock, but he was wonderful – it's only now that I've had all these other men that I realize just how wonderful. I have come to the conclusion that a man who thinks of the sex thing as involving two people is very rare, and a good many of them don't really know what a woman is *for*. And it is not only the English – believe me . . . I've had League of Nations experience.'

'And so you took to your bed with all these men, looking for another bout of total ecstasy?'

Eve shook her head, smiling to herself. 'No – it sounds quite awful really, and I don't expect you to understand.'

'Try me.'

'It was that for a few seconds . . . each time I . . . you know . . . reached the top, it *was* Davey with me. Not raising his ghost or anything as potty as that, but it was the only way that I could bring him back and I wanted him so desperately. You see, I could not remember what he looked like the rest of the time, but each time I made love . . . for those few moments I have him back . . . remember him clearly.'

Georgia did not try to meet Eve Hardy's eyes but said quietly, 'You aren't the only one who fantasizes or forgets faces. Strange thing, I can remember every detail of Hugh, but Nick is a blur.'

'So, each time you see Nick afresh, you can fall for him all over again.'

'I suppose that it is a bit like that. The trouble is there are so many other real faces in between – and they're fun to be with and they don't expect commitment, aren't looking for much more than a free meal and a roll in the hay – not that they get that. If I really loved Nick, wouldn't his face blot out the rest?'

'If that's true, then I don't love David. I have only one photograph, taken when he joined the navy, and now . . . he looks such a boy in it. Strange isn't it, but wherever he is, he's on the sunny side of thirty and is probably totally different from the boy who deflowered me so beautifully.'

Georgia smiled and blew a long, slow stream of thoughtful smoke at the ceiling. 'Aren't you seeing anybody at all that you like?'

'Only you, honey, and blondes aren't really my type – I like ward sisters with large starched pygidiums.'

'Eve Hardy, you're terrible! I don't know what a pie . . . whatever is, but it sounds vulgar.'

'Turtle's arse. We're a pretty coarse bunch – Probationers and Improvers and nurses generally.'

'You've changed.'

'Or my true nature is surfacing – as decadent as my father.'

'Rubbish! You'll calm down again once you're back in Markham. So many people are flying off in all directions, it's no wonder we're all becoming strange.'

'Are we?'

'Well aren't we?'

'My family has gone to pot, that is true.'

'Hugh and Hugh's Floozie have a son.'

'Oh Georgia . . .'

'He wants a divorce. I've started it going. I'm refusing to apply for maintenance.'

'It's the sensible thing to do. Connie should do the same. Clean break.'

'No roof over our heads though.'

'Is that right?'

'It's a man's world.'

'God! Connie's flying sorties over the Channel or somewhere, whilst my disgusting daddy is holed up in the country with his Floozie. Bloody hell, Georgia, it's not fair is it?'

'If you're after fairness, be sure you get born with the necessary appendages.'

'What news of Nick?'

Georgia shrugged her shoulders. 'He hasn't been here for weeks, and what can you say on the phone in three minutes? Every time he rings he says, "Marry me", but it's grown into a bit of a joke. I sometimes wonder what he'd say if I said yes.'

'He'd jump on the next train of course.'

'Then why doesn't he jump on now?'

'Because you go hot and cold on him and he can't stand keep having his heart broken?'

'What did I say . . . the strain of five years of war is sending us all round the bend.' She jumped up from the armchair and changed her expression and tone. 'That's enough of all that. Let's eat! Listen, have you got a bike?'

'Round at Mr Iremonger's.'

'Then let us picnic tomorrow and have an old-fashioned day of normality and self-indulgence. I promised I'd take Leonora up to Farley Mount on the new bike her mother got from her Littlewoods Club. Mary won't let her go on her own.'

'You can't blame her, with all the army camps around here. I'd love a picnic. I'll be going to Mr Iremonger's this afternoon: do you mind if he comes too? I did say I'd spend a day with him before I disappear into Oaklands. He's super about the countryside.'

'Oh do, and bring the dog. Bring anybody.'

Leonora was thrilled to bits to be going out with Mrs Kennedy and her friend.

Because she had been in a gym display at the Grammar School to which she had won a scholarship, her mother had unpicked a pair of her Dad's navy-blue trousers and out of them had got a pair of pleated shorts and a bolero.

'You're so clever, Mum, nobody'd ever know.'

'Well I should like them to know, Lena,' Mary Wiltshire had said primly. 'Nothing to be ashamed of in Make-do and Mend; you should be proud.'

To Leonora, the Make-do and Mend campaign was epitomized by such freaky things as the grey trilby hat of her Dad's that her Mum had steamed and bent and wore decorated with lampshade braid, and by brooches made from clusters of silver-painted beech-mast or painted shells or everlasting flowers, and by hair bows made of hoarded toffee-papers and by belts woven from hundreds of bits of folded cellophane. She felt no pride in the substitutes, only embarrassment for the wearers, and a hunger for the real pre-war things that she could still remember.

She longed for prettiness, almost pined to know how it must feel to have a second pair of shoes; to own some item of clothes that did not have a 'Utility' label; that would show the dirt and was not hard-wearing or sensible; to twirl, in a wide skirt with petticoats, as Judy Garland or Ann Blythe did in the pictures.

'I don't know what I'd do if I didn't have a Mum who could magic up things like this.' Leonora had to admit that the outfit was really pretty smart and gave her Mum a hug.

'Oh, go on with you, cupboard love. I still think I should have made the legs longer. They're hardly decent, and you're growing so quickly . . .'

Before she went to call for Mrs Kennedy, scooping up her hair like Betty Grable in the photo she had in her film scrap-book, Leonora inspected herself this way and that in the landing mirror. I could pass for eighteen easily. Which was true. Her deep eyes, straight nose and well-modelled face gave her a serious, un-girlish look. Dropping her thick, cascading hair, she ran her hands over her stomach and hips, arching her back to maximize her bosom and then felt the contours of her thighs and neat behind. If I had high heels my legs would be as good as Betty Grable's. Which was true also.

'If there'd been a bit more material, I shouldn't have had to cut them so short.'

Leonora jumped and blushed, not knowing whether her mother had just arrived at the bottom of the stairs or whether she had been watching.

'No, Mum, they're just right; if they were any longer the girls would call me Baggy-britches – everybody wears them like this.'

'Well just watch what you're doing when you sit down . . . and when you get off your bike. You shouldn't cock your leg over like a boy.'

Oh, Mum, she longed to say, Don't keep nagging all the time. But that would have led to a long lecture about having to be both mother and father at once and bearing the responsibility of bringing up two children, and the town full of soldiers, and women alone and nobody caring. Leonora had heard it so often that not a word of it adhered any more. Instead she said, 'It's the only way to stop getting oil on your socks and shoes, Mum.'

'You know what I mean: economy is one thing, but that last lot of panties have got hardly any gusset to speak of and I don't know what knicker elastic is made of these days, when you can get it at all. Now get off, Georgia will be waiting.'

Leonora, thinking how obsessed with knicker elastic her mother had become, went next door to Georgia who wore red slacks and french knickers, and gave Leonora an occasional cigarette and treated her like a woman.

Today Georgia had bunched her hair on top with a georgette scarf and wore white linen tennis shorts coupled with a white gypsy-neck top tucked into a yellow belt. Leonora had to wait until they were out of sight of Station

Avenue before she scooped up her own hair, removed her neat bolero, opened the top three buttons of her blouse and tied its tail in a knot above her midriff.

She understood precisely the meaning of the phrase, Feeling like a million dollars.

It was a fine weekend at the start of the growing and harvest season, when those who were not sticky and stinking with the sweat of hard farm labour, might believe that Eden must have been like Hampshire on that day. Clear, fresh skies, warm, soft air that carried sound for miles. Slow-moving brick-red cows arranged themselves in buttercup pastures to please the eye of a painter such as Mont Iremonger. Fidgety downland ewes nibbled white and red clover whilst their Sunday-dinner offspring, unconscious of their succulent reputation, gambolled prettily enough to illustrate the month of April on a calendar.

Eve, cycling ahead beside Mont with Yap, called back, 'Isn't this absolutely wizard!'

'Super,' Georgia shouted. 'I haven't been out of town for months.'

1989

Mrs Giacopazzi sorted through a file of photographs making last minute decisions about the illustrations for *Giacopazzi Territory*, the book of beautiful illustrations of Hampshire locations that were connected with Giacopazzi and her novels. There was something about the sketch Monty Iremonger had done on Farley Mount that revealed more of her youthful self than the photographs.

What a good painter he was.

Long after his death, a dozen or so of his Markham water-colours, hanging in the local Trust House that had once been Monty's local, had been 'discovered' by a London art critic who had written about them and so made Iremongers desirable and rare. Monty had left most of his paintings to Eve, who had never sold any or even exhibited them. Occasionally, usually on Georgia's birthday, a little water-colour would come by special delivery with just the message, 'For Georgia from Eve'.

All these years putting off and putting off doing anything about meeting. It wouldn't have been so difficult: Eve and I both had the money and the means to arrange it. Always tomorrow, next month, next year. How has it all gone so quickly? One day we are young and the next the party's over. But there's always been so much, so much to get done. To write the books, to get the money to be secure.

She went to the window of her suite.

Park Lane, the roads around Marble Arch and the Cumberland Hotel, as far as the eye could see, were solid with unmoving traffic moving in the shimmering haze of exhaust fumes and reflected heat.

Room Service delivered a tray of Malvern water and ice.

'How do you manage to keep going in London?' she asked the young man as he set the tray beside her. 'Look, do you see that woman down there? I've been watching her. She obviously got fed up with sitting in the traffic jam so she paid off her taxi. She's been trying to get off that little grassy island for five minutes, but she daren't step off in case the traffic moves.'

The waiter held back the voile curtain and took a polite interest in Madam's observation.

'Is a bad place to get out of a taxi-cab. No crossings, no traffic-lights. She can be there till tomorrow.'

'No, see . . . she's getting back in the same taxi she paid off just now. She's laughing . . . How can she laugh . . . how can she even breathe?'

'Is better than Barcelona, madam.' He was smiling cheekily at her.

'Is that where you are from?'

'Not exactly . . . but everyone knows that waiters are called Manuel and they come from Barcelona.' He poured the chilly Malvern. 'Will that be all, madam?'

'Thank you.' She handed him a pound coin which he accepted with a polite nod.

'Madam, London is the most exciting place in the world. I love it even if I die from the traffic gasses. Is not always like this . . . not always full of flocks of chattering starlings with cameras and backpacks. This week is Chelsea Show. Today railway strike, it makes much more cars but everybody wants to come to London, madam. Is the most exciting city in the world.'

'Perhaps it is not true that youth is wasted on the young.'

Not understanding, he nodded and left, and she returned to the window, smiling at the thought that she would soon be far from the most exciting city in the world, she would be standing high on the Downs where she lived and have neither sight nor sound of any combustion engine other than perhaps their own tractor.

Chelsea Week. That meant that it was almost round to D-Day again. Forty-five years since Overlord, and nearly fifty since war was declared. It must have been about this time of year that Eve and I met for the first time. Quite an anniversary. I suppose there will be fiftieth anniversary celebrations of singing the old songs, letting off fireworks, taking the children for a nice evening out to watch mock battles.

We're a warlike nation . . . too many Hughs, not enough Nicks. In Markham Park, nothing had ever been erected to celebrate one single peaceful human achievement, only a cenotaph and a grey cannon on a pedestal, no work of art or bandstand or lily-pond – just the weapon and the names of the young flesh and blood and bones of Markham's young men.

She turned again to the small water-colour sketch that was to be the cover illustration of *Giacopazzi Territory*. A gifted man, Monty, and nobody had realized. They should erect a statue of him. She smiled to herself – Montague I, the painter/postman. Six foot of solid postman's uniform with cycle clips. A lot better in the Market Square than Mr Palmerston.

Fifty years since he had done the little portrait. Was this young Georgia Kennedy, painted standing at the top of the hill with the outline of the Farley Monument in the background, already beginning to slide down the slope of time? Or had she been at the bottom of a new career preparing to climb up? Who cares. There can't be a lot more slope left. For a while she had thought that *Eye of the Storm* had left her written out. When there's nothing to say, shut up. But not yet. There's always something else to say.

Meeting Eve again, meeting Leonora, Dorothy and Mrs Farr – not Farr, Mrs O'Neill now – they would make her mind fizz. She knew that the need to write would begin to well up, building pressure until she would shut herself away for six months. Shut the door on the beautiful bowl of a valley she practically owned outright now, on the Downs and the fields; shut her ears to the muffled thud of cloven hooves and the pattering of dung as the cattle went down the lane, to the clop of hooves as the others rode out on to the Downs, to the hiss of rain as it drove across the valley, and to the human sounds of village life.

Even now, before *Eye of the Storm* was in true book form, it had started again. Even as she had been standing watching the great snarl-up around Marble Arch, she had begun to think about this woman who had been marooned on the grassy island in the midst of all that aggressive traffic fighting for each inch of territory.

Plump and white-haired in her silk trousers and loose jacket, the woman had calmly looked at the pond and wandered around on the grass, apparently oblivious to her predicament at the hub of the welded mass of traffic, before she became aware of the craziness of her situation. She had laughed with the taxi driver, shrugging her shoulders and throwing up her hands, then got in and sat in the back, still expressing with her hands and laughing. What was she doing? Something positive, exciting probably. Where was she going? Somewhere enjoyable without any stress or hassle. But what had brought her to this point in her life?

I suppose writers have a kind of Fallopian tube in which the first cell of ideas form, which then become fertilized by something like this incident, and which are eventually born as full-blown books. I hope that I die with my tube still unemptied.

This woman in the midst of all that revving and roaring was calm and unruffled, amused even, at finding herself on a tiny grassy island with water and flowers and trees . . .

A spot of safety . . .

Markham was thus in the midst of war . . .

The Town Restaurant kitchens at its calm centre . . .

1944

After they had left the bounds of Markham, it was obvious that something big was about to happen.

Among the trees that bounded pasture and meadows, along the hedged margins of potato and cornfields, in stands of timber, in orchards, spinneys, forests and woodlands and every piece of land large enough to take a cookhouse or tent, soldiers were encamped.

The British nation had been waiting for D-Day for months. The Americans – who had received a warm reception when they had eventually come into the war, now took second place in British affections to the Russians. Uncle Joe Stalin and his suffering people had revived the War Effort which had become tedious in its endlessness. But it was GI Joe who was encamped in southern England. Thousands of young Americans, many of them black, were a curiosity to children – and their source of undreamt-of sweetness in the form of Hershey bars. Newly arrived, these soldiers had had no time to meet the locals in the way that the first-comers had met the Partridges. The closest to the local population these encamped Americans got was to offer gum or Lucky Strikes to passers-by. Few had much idea of where they had been dumped. Hamp-shier? As in Noo Hampshire, well, wadda ya know!

They had a better idea of why they were there. The Big Push, the Second Front, D-Day.

As the two women, the girl and the old man rode out into the countryside, they passed long lines of trucks, jeeps and tanks tended by girl-hungry GIs who whistled with appreciation at the display of legs. Say, will ya just get that neat ass! Hey, Doll. Over here, Honey.

'Just wave, Leonora,' Georgia said. 'But for God's sake don't fall off or there's no knowing what might happen to you in those shorts.'

Leonora flushed with pleasure at being included in the intimacy of such adult suggestiveness.

She and Mrs Kennedy had laughingly raced on past the other two and were now leaning against a gate waiting for them.

'Mrs Kennedy?'

'Georgia.'

'Oh, I keep forgetting. Georgia, your friend looks different.'

'That's what living in London does for you.'

'I like her better than before. She looks more . . . sort of grown-up.'

Georgia laughed. 'That's what she said about you.'

Leonora flushed again. 'Did she really . . . that I look grown-up? Really? I didn't think she took much notice of me.'

'Bloody hell, Lena, with a face and figure like yours at fifteen, there's never going to be many people who don't notice you when you're a woman.'

Leonora turned and leaned on the gate, knowing that the tingling in her breasts she was feeling at Georgia's compliment would show through her thin white blouse and she still didn't know how to deal with those signals except to fold her arms across them. She was fascinated with what was happening to her body and she and her small group of friends spent a lot of time comparing the phenomena of their womanliness.

From the top of the hill they watched Eve, Mont and the dog making their way at the pace of Yap and the old man. As they passed a small encampment, soldiers came out and played with the dog. Eve accepted a cigarette and then a whole pack. Even from this distance, it was easy to see that Eve was being charming and vivacious. Leonora observed how it was done. Georgia sat on the step of the stile and Leonora on the grass beside her.

'I wish that this day would last for ever, Georgia.'

'Goodness. There'll be better days than this.'

'Not when I'll feel happier than I do now.'

'There will be. The occasional day that's going to have some bit of ecstasy.'

'You mean falling in love?'

'Not necessarily, it can be . . .'

Leonora waited, watching her idol, her ideal, as her mind drifted to thoughts that made her eyes soften and her mouth lift, almost talking to herself as though Leonora was not there.

'. . . it can be fulfilment. Discovering something about yourself that you never suspected.'

'Like what?'

'Lena Wiltshire, your mother would have fits if she knew the sort of conversations you lead me into.'

'That's why it's so super being with you. Mum thinks that if she keeps my hair in a pigtail and my legs in lisle stockings and my chest under a gymslip, she can keep me as a child and I'll not get into "trouble". But she can never bring herself to say what the trouble is. I know – she means losing my virginity.'

'You can't blame her. Because she knows that it would be more than only losing your virginity . . . I mean, do you even know what a Durex is? A girl of fifteen who looks like you do . . . I dare say all she sees is trouble. I imagine when she sees your legs growing long enough to reach your bottom and a profile that's about perfect, she imagines your Dad coming home and finding a pram in the hallway.'

'Fat lot she knows about me then.'

'Your Mum's an attractive woman – she knows what it's all about. She knows how it feels to think about love and sex. She knows how easy it is to go overboard if the opportunity presents itself at the right time – or rather the wrong time.'

Leonora opened her mouth to exclaim, but Eve and the old man came cycling up. Her *mother*? Mam, in her funny jumpers made from two or three unravelled old ones, in her 'turned' coat and mended stockings, attractive? Thinking about love and sex? And Dad . . . even when he had joined up he had been old. Could a man like Dad be attractive to a woman other than Mam?

He had been gone for years. A prisoner-of-war in Germany. It was as though he had disappeared from her and Roy's life. Until recently, when for the first time German POWs had come to Markham and changed her ideas, if she thought of her Dad at all it was as an anonymous man in thick, dark-brown battledress with a huge yellow circle in the middle of the back, an uninteresting, featureless man like any one of the hundreds of Italian POWs who had lived for years in a camp behind a barbed-wire fence on the Winchester road. Scruffy Eyeties who Leonora did not associate with the idea of love and sex. But the German POWs were different from the Eyeties who slouched on the roadsides and smiled. The Germans looked sullen and angry and attractive. Dad would be like them, angry at being imprisoned in Germany.

Perhaps her Mam and Dad were attractive. That was the thing about being with Georgia, she often made one see things in a different light.

As Eve had said, Mont Iremonger proved to be the perfect companion to appreciate the countryside on such a day. He and Georgia had met a few times since she and Eve had become close friends, but he could never feel at ease with her in the way he did with Eve. It no longer seemed strange to him that Eve would let herself into his kitchen and drop into an armchair as easily and familiar as you like.

He sat in flannel shirt, serge trousers with braces and belt, and a well-worn cap, as large and solid as an outcrop of rock on the soft downland. 'There! Only water-colour sketches, but I reckon I've caught the likenesses.'

His subjects exclaimed their delight at the little portraits which were as simple and moving as a Manet sketch. The two women he had done in profile, heads arranged so that seen as a pair they either faced or turned from one another, whilst Leonora he had painted full-length, propped up on her elbows watching skylarks ascending. It was months before she realized that the answer to her thoughts about her 'old' father was contained in what the old postman had seen – a girl in the pose of a voluptuous woman. A picture that would have disturbed Mary Wiltshire had she ever seen it.

Georgia and Leonora saw to the food and the boiling of the picnic kettle. Eve, who was edgy at the prospect of starting at the Oaklands Centre, went off with Mont to get firewood. They were easy in one another's company.

He knew that she never saw her father these days, or went to The Cedars, even though she still had a lot of her things at the old house: her white car on its bricks, her gramophone and jazz records, books and clothes. Mont never talked about all that unless she asked. And coming up the hill she had asked.

'Is the Councillor still coining it in?' She no longer called Freddy Hardy, Pa or, my father.

'So they say, but there, you know Markham for gossiping on about what they don't know about.'

'It's probably true, they don't miss much in Markham.'

'They say since he got the contract for supplying all the bread and cakes for the NAAFIs, he's rich as Croesus.'

'And the women?'

'Well . . . I wouldn't know about that. The house looks a mess though. He does a lot of partying. He and Vern Greenaway had an up and a downer at a Council meeting apparently.'

'What about?'

Ever since he had heard the rumour about the affair, Mont had known that it would come to her ears. Best if it came from him. It wasn't easy.

'Vern accused him of malpractice or something in front of the whole Finance Committee.'

'Connie said he fiddled everything, and did not have a straight bone in his body. But she says a lot of bitter things about him.'

'From all accounts, it's a bit more than fiddling extra petrol coupons.' He stopped to throw a stick for Yap. 'You don't want to hear all this. It's probably all a tale . . . a nine-day-wonder . . . you know how it is in this place.'

'Even if it is, I shall feel less of a fool knowing what is being said.' Ever since she knew that she was to come back to Markham, Eve had made up her mind to clear up the clutter of her life and do some of the things that she should have done ages ago. 'I intend going up to The Cedars to sort out my stuff, so it's better if I know.'

'Well, there's apparently some sort of investigation going on. He's supposed to have set up a lot of little companies without declaring his connection with them and giving himself a whole load of valuable contracts. There's some plans for new housing estates after the war and he's bought up the land.'

'And Mr Greenaway found out?'

'I suppose so . . . I don't know that the rest of the Council was bothered – Councillor Hardy always kept them sweet, they knew they'd be sure to get their cut without putting their heads on the block. But you know Vern Greenaway, straight as a die and not afraid to open his mouth. I don't know if it's true, but people are saying that there won't be no hushing it up, it's being taken to the County and they reckon the Ministry is asking questions.'

'Thanks for telling me, Monty.'

'It's a shame to spoil such a lovely day.'

'I'm a big grown-up girl now, Monty.'

'I can still see the little gel in a pink dress and white socks running down the drive for the letters.'

'I was always so impressed with your uniform – the only

uniforms I'd ever seen then was yours and the doorman at the Picture House. Oh dear, Monty, what a family you got yourself mixed up with. I'm surprised that you want to associate with any of us. There'll be a scandal about this affair . . . mud sticks and I'm a Hardy.'

'Don't put yourself down, my dear. You are the best thing that has happened to Mont Iremonger in forty years or more. Lord love you, what other pensioner gets to take out the three beauties of Markham.' Fondling and playing with the little dog to cover his embarrassment. 'An't that right, little Yap? You and me has a good time together.'

1989

Leonora drove her hire-car towards Hursley, trying to recall what it had been like that day in 1944 when she had gone to Farley Mount. In this country, the media was building up towards what looked like being a great climax of old film and tattoos and fireworks on the fiftieth anniversary of VE day in September. It had already had one bite of the cherry with a D-Day anniversary last month, when Leonora had heard on the car radio, as she toured the UK like the American tourist she now was, wartime songs she had not heard for fifty years, yet whose words she could still remember without falter.

As she watched for a break in the Clearway lines, she hummed to herself. That day in 1944 when they had come along here on their cycles, this road had been narrow and pale grey and bendy, and it had been ribbed with silvery tracks of all the tanks that had gone along it assembling for D-Day. It was now a wide, black orderly highway with road junctions where there had then been dusty unsurfaced lanes slipping off to unsignposted villages. In spite of there having then been such a concentration of men and vehicles, today's constant stream of cars seemed to be so much more stressful and obtrusive.

Or does it only seem like that because I was fifteen and more aware of me than of what was going on?

More aware of Waldemar.

Waldemar, blond and startlingly blue-eyed, who was so attractive in his POW clothes with the diamond target between his shoulders. Waldemar, still wearing his Luftwaffe cap against regulations. Waldemar Altzheiber, who had been one of the gang of hired labour cutting the hedges round the field at the back of Station Avenue.

On the day of the picnic, Waldemar was too new a phenomenon to understand. He was the enemy her Dad had been fighting, he was a Luftwaffe pilot who had probably dropped bombs all over England . . . and yet he would not keep out of her thoughts or her dreams – such dreams . . . dreams that made her afraid in case she should talk in her sleep and Mam should hear.

That day, as today, had been burning hot. That entire summer of '44, as this one of '89, had been long and hot and dry. But the air then had been light and easy to breathe, because the roads then were empty of most traffic except military. Today there was a constant stream of cars, some doing ninety, and vast container lorries with continental registrations doing speeds that caused a slip-stream.

She came to the Farley Mount turn-off. Everything had changed. It looked as though the place had become part of the tourist and leisure industry. She parked and walked to where they had all posed for the old man to draw them. Mam had never known about that sketch: Waldemar had taken it back when he was repatriated and had returned it to her on the day they married. Twenty years difference in their ages, yet the marriage had been good whilst it lasted. Greater difference in age than there had been between Little-Lena and Mrs Kennedy when they had gripped hands so tightly the day before the war had broken out.

She sat beside the odd monument to a horse and lit a cigarette as she had done fifty years ago, but now without the kind of ceremony of Georgia's cigarette case and flint-sparking lighter, without the excitement of being invited to accept a symbol of modern womanhood. 'Have one, but don't tell your mother.'

Leonora Altzheiber was both excited and apprehensive at the prospect of meeting Georgia Kennedy again. For fifty years she had kept another secret which Mrs Kennedy had confided in her. At the time, no one else knew why she had disappeared from Markham, where she had gone, and why she had left so suddenly – not even Eve Hardy had known. Georgia Kennedy had told only young Leonora Wiltshire – and it had been painful to know.

1944

Summer

In the small world of the Dinner Kitchens, girls and women came and went. Perhaps to bigger money-making munitions; or because of a pregnancy caused by an over-glamorous romance with a Yank leading to expectations of a ranch in Texas; or – in the case of evacuated families – to return home to Bomb Alleys that had gone quiet. Almost an institution now, but certainly not establishment, were four of the women who had been there from the early days – Dorothy and Marie Partridge, Mrs Farr and Georgia.

At some time or other during those years, there were shortages of almost every kind of food and ingredient. Fortunately not everything ever disappeared at the same time. If the hated yellow dried-egg was in short supply, then the even more hated vivid yellow custard powder substitute came in. If the dried household milk which wasn't very popular disappeared, lovely sweet tinned condensed milk came in. Fifty per cent of all sausages disappeared when they were cooked, as the high proportion of water-soaked cereal they contained exploded through the skins – nobody ever saw a sausage unless it was laid open as though dissected. Mrs Farr and Dorothy devised potato toppings and gave them a catchy name – but they were still Bangers. Somebody always came up with something, so that The Markham Town Restaurant came to have a much better reputation than the usual run of British Restaurants which were the pay-dirt of comedians.

There was a shortage of jam-jars, but throughout the year Dorothy would offer local children threepence a dozen for clean jars or a slice of bread pudding – the spicy smell of which almost always weakened their resolve to take the money. In summer Georgia organized, through the schools, hedgerow hunts for berries, and paid spot cash to the young scavengers who thought they were on to a good thing because blackberries and rosehips were free and plentiful around Markham. Ursula and her helpers used every pound of sugar allocation and every bottle of pectin for jam-making, bottled plums by the stone and dried apples by the hundredweight.

Marie had become Queen of the Till. Pretty and always looking fresh and nicely made-up, she was popular and had her regulars who brought her a few duck-eggs or a string of onions and a bunch of sweet-williams and, on occasions, perhaps a banana or orange or some similar rare delicacy from a crate 'dropped' whilst off-loading at Southampton Docks.

She and Paula often went out together, sometimes to the Air Force administration offices, or to a dance at the Yankee base, and once or twice to a social at Oaklands but, although Marie felt sorry for the boys there, she couldn't stand what she saw in their frightened eyes and the way they went quiet and withdrawn, even when they were supposed to be on the mend. 'I don't know how nurses like Eve Hardy can stand it.'

But Paula would carefully coat her Cyd Charisse legs with leg make-up and dance with any of the Oaklands boys, however close to breaking point they were. 'Poor little things. They're only kids who have been frightened out of their wits at the terrible things they've seen.' And she would hold them close and kiss them goodnight and try to make them feel like men again.

The Partridge family was not what it had been. It seemed a lifetime since Charlie joined up. Bonnie, ten years old now, mentioned him only because people talked of him to her: he was no more real to her than Jesus or God, but if people said there was Dad and Jesus, then there probably were.

Harry came and went in his well-pressed sergeant's uniform, red beret and glossy boots, never there for more than twenty-four hours, going back to wherever another batch of men needed training into the techniques of leaping into mid-air suspended from a canopy of silk that they hoped would unfold, and if it did unfold would not carry them behind the enemy lines.

As the war dragged on and every able-bodied labouring man not essential to the war effort was being called up, Sam Partridge had only a boy of fourteen to help keep the park going. No model of the abbey fashioned from growing sempervivums had been made for years, nor any patterned carpets of miniature plants; even the herbaceous borders had been left so long to their own devices that all lupins were blue, all hollyhocks pink and single, and marigolds grew from every crevice of the retaining wall.

This summer it all seemed too much. The weather was depressing: as he went about trying to keep some control over the acres of grass and trees, he seemed to hear the turf cracking open it was so dry. On some days he hadn't the heart even to go near to the old bowling green with its display of ox-eye daisies and bents and had consciously to put out of his mind the vision of its old velvet lushness, when a good player could bowl a wood along the rink and know that there was not one to touch it for miles.

At the time when the Germans were driving their way towards England or into Russia, Sam had plotted their advances and retreats with pins and flags on maps, but once the fighting was taken into countries like Greece, Africa and the Philippines, he felt no personal involvement. He would have preferred a simple confrontation with the Germans in the place where he had left his legs.

'I shan't put up with much more of him, he's making everybody's life a misery,' Dolly declared frequently to Paula and Marie.

'What can anybody do, though?'

'I don't know. But I reckon it's only my job and you and Bonnie stops me sticking the bread-knife in him at times.'

'Oh Mum, that's not like you.'

'Isn't it? You'd be surprised, Marie. Since Mr O'Neill's been trying to make this documentary film, life hasn't hardly been worth living.'

'You'd think he'd be proud they chose you.'

'Proud! He's jealous.'

'Of Mr O'Neill?'

'You'd think it was a film about a scarlet woman dancing the can-can instead of how ordinary women are managing homes and jobs.'

Dolly didn't miss the look that Paula and Marie exchanged.

'I think he believes that every woman in Markham is scarlet,' Paula said.

It came to a head one hot evening when Dolly had stayed behind at the Dinner Kitchens for Niall O'Neill to do some filming there. Bonnie was having a last evening at the swimming pool which was about to be closed down because the filtration plant had packed up and it had been commandeered anyway. Marie and Paula were waiting in Dolly's kitchen for Bonnie to come in.

Sam made the same sort of remark that he had made frequently about Dolly and married women generally always gadding about when Paula turned on him furiously.

'Ever since I was little we've all made excuses because of your legs,' Paula said harshly. 'You've been sarcastic to me, bitter to Mum, who God knows has had enough to put up with your moods. Is it her fault you haven't got a decent pension? She's made something of herself, but have you ever given her one word of praise or encouragement? Never!'

Marie's pent-up feelings about years of not wanting to say anything because she was only the daughter-in-law were now unleashed by Paula's righteous attack and she could not hold back. 'And the same goes for Charlie,' she said. 'Till he joined up, he done everything he could for you, never a morning went by without he didn't come in and see you was all right, and you never had it in you to say anything but what it was to interfere in our lives. Don't have a tanner on the horses, Charlie, go to your Union meeting, Charlie, time you hoed up your potatoes, Charlie. He was nearly thirty when he went in the RAF and you was still treating him like you was the head of *our* family instead of Charlie. And now I hear you starting on Bonnie. She's *my* daughter. I don't want her brought up in your ways. All right, she has to fend for herself sometimes when I'm at work, but there's nothing wrong with that. Can't you see that you're turning everybody away from you. Everybody loves you, but you make it bloody hard for us.' She flushed at the first swearword she had ever said outside her own four walls.

The old man's eyes narrowed, but Paula wouldn't let him fill the pause.

'Especially Harry. He's been trying since he was two to get you to give him a hap'orth of praise, but you've been as stingy with your praise as you've been with your love.'

He did not reply, but sat there and said nothing, letting it all pour over him until Bonnie's bicycle bell sounded and she and Dolly were heard chattering happily in the kitchen.

Dolly had put her head round the door and seen their faces all turned from one another and felt the tension and had known better than to throw a match into that particular box of dry matchwood.

Brightly, she said, 'What do you think? The chip-shop was open, and it's only Monday. They had some real cod extra to their allocation, so they opened an extra evening. She was only going to let me have two pieces, but Bonnie come along so she let her have two and she checked him for another one.'

Sam Partridge's heart ached to see Charlie: there were

times when he felt sick at the thought of him being God-knew-where and in God-knew-what danger. Now they had all turned on him, except Charlie. Two and a half years and he hadn't hardly clapped eyes on his son.

'Would you like me to come with you, Eve?'

'Would you, Monty? I don't know why I should, but I feel quite edgy about it. Isn't that silly, it was my home for twenty-five years.'

'It's only natural after a bust-up like that.'

They cycled through the silent, early-morning Sunday town. Along the wide main Winchester Road with its respectable large bay-fronted semis with front gardens, past small terraces, mean-windowed narrow cottages, Edwardian villas with uncontrolled wistaria and unpruned forsythia, past Victorian residences with monkey-puzzle trees, all temporarily in free neighbourly association now that they shared the same absence of railings and gates, the same emergency water supply, street wardens and stirrup-pumps. Beyond the railway arch a pub and, where the ground began to rise so that Mont and Eve had to dismount, potato fields and a clapped-out old mansion, and at the crest the cottage hospital in its flowery grounds where they stopped to take breath as the heat of the late spring began to shimmer off the roofs of Markham.

'It's not such a bad old place,' Mont said, mopping his red face.

'I think it's lovely from here. Looks as though it hasn't changed in hundreds of years.'

'Well it has, you know. Only the bricks and mortar are the same. Everything else has been changed out of all recognition by the war, and it won't ever go back.'

'What about Oaklands when it's finished being a hospital, and the Chapel Hall when they close down the Town Restaurant, and the munitions factory and the little engineering works – Georgia and I were talking about it. All those women having their small freedoms for the duration of the war. How can they cope with going back to their old domestic life, playing second fiddle?'

' "How they goin' to keep 'em down on the farm, now that they've seen Paree"? D'you know that song?'

'Sort of.'

'It's all happened before. Not only just to women. Ordinary blokes go in the Forces, get to see foreign parts, camels, pyramids, icebergs. Some of them get two or three stripes and find they're as capable of organizing the setting up of a camp as their old bosses were of setting up a factory.' Slowly they resumed the last half-mile along the road towards Eve's old home, making no attempt to cycle, Eve content to listen to the old man who had carried their mail along this route twice a day all her growing years.

He sweated and puffed a little, but did not stop his flow. 'There'll be them who fly in aeroplanes or sit in holds of the big liners, sub-mariners and others who've been behind barbed-wire for months. It only needs one man to say out loud what he's been thinking – "There's something wrong somewhere" and they'll all see that there is.'

'My Ma says there are Reds everywhere.'

'And Lady Connie might just be right.'

They had arrived at the entrance to The Cedars drive, along which a hundred years ago a white tourer tied with satin ribbons had been driven by a plump blonde girl who used to be the daughter of the house.

They halted briefly. She said, 'Oh,' and they walked on towards the house where they propped their bicycles against a sagging, overgrown pergola. She rang the door-bell but there was no response. 'There's no car about, so he probably isn't here.' She tried her key, but it would not turn in the lock.

Mont tried. 'There's one already in . . . oh, it's open. Do you want me to go and have a look round. We should have brought Yap.'

Eve laughed, 'Oh yes, he'd soon sink his gums into an intruder. Come on, let's go and find some boxes and get my stuff packed.' As she walked through the hallway, she called out, but there was no response.

'The place looks deserted, don't it?'

'Look in here, Monty, everything's packed up.'

Of all the furnishings that had once made The Cedars unique, the only items remaining were the great velvet curtains and voile drapes, the rest was in packing-cases or furniture crates. Swiftly she ran upstairs, where she found her own room tidy and neat, as she had left it. Her clothes were as she had left them, except that each hanger had a Mothak ring and all the drawers contained bags of crystals.

In her parents' room she found a few shoes and some odd items of women's clothing that were certainly not Connie's. A blouse label read 'Greenleaf and Gale – New York'.

Mont found plenty of empty cartons left by the packers, to which Eve quickly transferred her few possessions and stacked them in the corner of her old room. 'He's leaving, Monty.'

'Looks like it.'

'Then there's probably some truth in what Mr Greenaway found out.'

'You don't want to jump to conclusions. It might be that he just finds the place too big.'

'That needn't stop him telling me and Connie.'

Mont Iremonger kept his thoughts to himself. What sort of a man is it runs out on his own daughter without saying anything?

'Perhaps he was going to tell you.'

'Perhaps he still thinks David Greenaway wasn't good enough for me. Perhaps he thinks I'd go running to Mr Greenaway and give the game away.'

Picking up a raffia bag of trinkets that she wanted to take with her, she quickly left the room. 'Come on, Monty, let's go and have a look at her.'

The white tourer had been jacked up in an outbuilding at the back of the house. As they crunched their way along the gravel drive, a two-tone horn sounded.

'That's my car horn.'

The double doors were wide open and a wide ray of sun like a spotlight picked out an apparently naked woman sitting at the wheel of Eve's car.

'Say, Fred, can I have this? It sure is neat.' She turned and saw the two silhouettes against the sun. 'What the hell do you think you're doing creeping in here like this?'

Eve did not move, but stood looking at the girl. She was probably a year or so younger than Eve, suntanned, groomed and very pretty.

'More to the point – what are *you* doing. Now get *out* of my car.'

The young woman was obviously used to doing as she was told. As she jumped down from Eve's car she revealed that her only garment was a skimpy sunsuit of such colourful good quality that Eve knew it could not have been bought in England.

Eve turned on her heel and went towards the house with Mont.

By now, Eve and Mont were ahead and inside the kitchen door, which Eve bolted against the young woman.

In the echoing breakfast-room, Eve said, 'I suppose that's his latest. I needn't have behaved like that. The drawing-room windows are open if she wants to get back in.'

'I thought you behaved very ladylike. She's a common bit of goods if you ask me.'

'What am I going to do now?'

'What we were going to do anyhow, pile your boxes in the hall ready for the van to collect.'

'I don't want to see him.'

The sound of a motor car crunching gravel, voices and the rattle of keys.

Eve went into the hall where her father and the girl had just come in.

'Evie! Sweetheart.' Effusively, he came towards her, but she moved so that his kiss only brushed the air beside her ear. Eve smiled at the girl over his shoulder.

'You obviously didn't tell her you had a big grown-up daughter.'

'Hell, Fred, you didn't. Nor about that little automobile being hers.'

'Go and get dressed, Suzi.'

She went. Mont backed into the kitchen, leaving Eve and her father standing in the echoing entrance hall.

'It looks as though you're leaving.'

'I would have been in touch.'

'After you had gone?'

'I was going to arrange for your things . . .'

'And Connie's?'

He shrugged.

'You needn't have done it without telling me, Pa.'

'I have to go quietly, Evie . . . you understand?'

'No.'

'I'm leaving Markham.'

'I can see that.'

She wanted him to tell her. The rumours about a conspiracy investigation had become the talk of Markham. Gossip had it that there were a group of businessmen involved in everything from fraud to embezzlement.

'I would have got in touch.'

'I'm your daughter. A father doesn't just pack up house, go away and then just get in touch with his daughter . . . not a normal father. He says goodbye, exchanges addresses.'

'I've had a lot on my mind.'

Eve looked towards the ceiling from where sounds of Suzi came. 'I can see.'

'Don't judge, Eve.'

'Who's judging? Is she going with you?'

'Well, actually, I am going with her.' He smiled wryly. 'Of all places, Las Vegas: it's where she's from. Her family's pretty well-heeled. Casinos. It's all fixed.'

'And the house?'

'When the dust has died down, I shall arrange for it to be sold.'

'And the factory?'

He avoided her eyes, 'I've been bought out. Part of a deal with Carnutzi Brothers – Suzi's family.'

'Suzi Carnutzi.' She raised her eyebrows slightly. 'Sorry, that was cheap.'

'At least Suzi doesn't think that I'm cheap, as your mother did.'

'I really don't want to know.'

'I'm sorry about the house.'

'And Connie?'

His voice hardened. 'Look, Eve, no matter how it might have appeared to you, it wasn't all that bad.'

'It never looked at all bad to me. To be honest, it came as a shock to me when Connie went.'

'Once the physical thing had finally gone out, there wasn't anything left. Now maybe that's a difficult thing to swallow about your parents. But I can't let you go off thinking Connie was a saint and I was the sinner. I like women, always have, and I never thought a bit of extra-marital fun was too serious. When the house is sold, I shall make a settlement on her.'

'I don't think she'll divorce you.'

'I'm not short of money, Eve. And there's a will in case . . .'

'I don't want to know any of it.'

'Listen.' His voice was low and insistent. 'For a goddam minute stop putting on airs and listen.'

Eve heard the word 'goddam' and knew that her father no

longer existed. Goddam. Her mind hung on to the word . . . a strange and embarrassing Americanism that Freddy Hardy would have ridiculed. He would become as brown and hard as Suzi Carnutzi. She would buy him jackets with large checks and he would wear strange, un-English shoes.

She scarcely heard the rest of his attempt at reconciliation. 'When I get to America and the deal is settled, you will find your bank account quite full. Suzi will never want for a brass farthing, the Carnutzis are rolling in it. When I gave you a present, I always did the wrong thing in Connie's eyes. Tasteless, no style – like the diamond clips and the car . . . Con would have bought a dark green car, wouldn't she? But I am me, and I never did have the advantage of an upper-class upbringing like hers. But then she never had the advantage of knowing how to get rich like me. She might have despised me, but she never looked down on my cheque book. So don't you, Evie.'

'I've always loved the car. You wouldn't have given it to her?'

'Give Suzi your car? Evie baby! I have already arranged for old Thornton at the garage to keep it until you want it again.'

'Thanks. I have to go, Monty's waiting, and I'm due at a wedding later this morning.'

'Are you still at the same Nurses' Home in London?'

She shook her head. 'I've been in Markham since June – at the hospital at Oaklands.'

'You might have told me.'

'I . . . You can always get hold of me through Georgia Kennedy. You know . . ?'

'Yes, I know Georgia Kennedy.' He smiled too enigmatically for Eve.

Not Georgia . . .

'I shall see you again, shan't I?'

'Oh yes. Once the dust has settled . . . the war's nearly over. You must come to Vegas.'

Ursula Farr and Niall O'Neill were married at Markham's Civic Offices in July and held a lunch-time reception at the Town Restaurant.

The Press, who would have loved to get wind of such a gathering, were not told that O'Neill who was now one of the foremost makers of Government documentary films, was to marry the woman who, as a militant girl, had caused such uproar in the House of Commons gallery.

There were no name-cards at the long tables: people sat with whoever they happened to find themselves at the time. Two men with very cut-glass accents, who had been boys at the 'experimental' school where Ursula as a very young woman was cook, sat either side of Georgia. One of them was Sir Henry somebody who said, Hello, my name's Henry, Ursula tells me you're the brains behind all this. The other one, whose name was Perry, told scurrilous and hilarious behind-the-scenes stories about Clark Gable's false teeth and Jean Harlow's lack of underwear.

Marie found herself sitting beside a friend of Ursula's, a woman called Dora who talked sense about peace and throwing away life and about the way to stop the war.

Dorothy discovered that the friend of Niall's by whom she was seated was quite a famous poet – though you'd never guess. He wrote the words for some of Niall's films.

Eve, who immediately recognized George Lansbury, charmed and was charmed by him.

Poor old Sam, said Dolly when she knew: he would have given anything to see George Lansbury.

Most of Niall's friends were male and getting on in years, whilst most of Ursula's were female and young: Eve, Georgia, Marie, Pammy, who was now a pregnant GI bride, Trix in WAAF uniform, Cynth. And Hildegard, a stumpy young woman – where she had come from no one knew, except the bride and groom, and possibly Mont Iremonger for whom she had been keeping house since he had developed leg ulcers. It was to have been a temporary arrangement, but she had stayed on after his leg healed. They rubbed along very well because neither interfered with the other.

It was quite late in the evening when Ursula and Niall walked with some of their guests to the railway station. Now, instead of black-out restrictions, there was a 'dim-out', so that windows need be covered only by normal curtains; pubs had taken down door shutters so that here and there orange pools of light shone out; and in streets where lamps could be shut off in an emergency there were, here and there, glimmering lights after five years of complete blackness at night.

'Markham looks alive again,' Ursula said, as they stood waiting on the gas-lit platform.

Henry, who had been seated next to Georgia, said, 'The Germans can't hold out much longer.'

Perry, the other one, said, 'They're still not entirely out of the game. Those bloody V2s scare the hell out of me.'

'It seems to me,' said Niall, 'that everybody's jittery in London. With good reason. I've heard that they are coming over at the rate of six or eight a day.'

Silently, until the huge blast, one fell two streets away from where Connie Hardy was walking, blowing down a garden wall which fell across her back.

After the wedding reception, Eve went back to Oaklands and Georgia to her home. As Georgia rounded the corner she saw Harry Partridge outside her house just propping up the great Vincent motor bike on which she had ridden pillion to the coast. Her pulse-rate rose. Harry Partridge's company was just what she needed. Nothing heavy, nothing serious.

Her relationship with Nick had become a bit of a mess.

Earlier in the year, they had decided to take a few days holiday together, perhaps each thinking that something might happen to clear the air between them. Although it would be the first time they had slept together, Georgia had not intended that either of them take the step too seriously. They went to the Isle of Wight, staying as a couple at a down-at-heel Ventnor hotel which had been splendid before the war. From the time they met on the quayside at Southampton and went aboard the paddle-steamer, each of them was over-aware that they were heading for bed together at last.

Georgia's awareness made her nervous. She had known for ages – for ever perhaps – that there would come a time when she and Nick would be lovers. But there was something unspontaneous and calculated about the way they were doing it. Bookings, coupons, time-tables – preparations that took the romance out of it. Yet, since she and Harry had rolled together on the beach, she had felt released enough from her marriage to make love with Nick – almost duty-bound to make love with him having done so with Harry.

It was early in the season, so that there were not enough other guests for them to go unnoticed. The proprietor was an army officer on leave and he was about everywhere, enjoying his old role as mine host. His wife, who had run the place for six years, was trying to come up to her usual scratch now that she was back under his eye. So that what with those two hovering to make their guests welcome, and the curiosity of the few elderly guests and long-term residents, Georgia felt awkward and very aware of the double room booked in Nick's name and Liverpool address.

The proprietor's, 'Let me take that bag, Mrs Crockford,' had made Georgia cringe with embarrassment at the ridiculous deception. It was the stereotypic film situation for illicit love. The woman always forgets her name and blushes confusedly at some blunder. In their room, Georgia found the sight of the double bed even worse. Two white pillows propped against its varnished headboard, two precisely flanking night tables and lamps, two bath towels, two hand towels, two upturned glasses. The only shared things were a mirror and the high bed itself. This Georgia tried to ignore, it seemed so . . . so *arranged.*

She wondered whatever it was that had made her believe that she could make love with Nick for the first time in such a commercial set-up?

Blessedly, the dinner gong sounded, obviously pleasing the proprietor. 'You arrived just in time. Time to wash your hands. We have only one serving . . . shortage of staff, of course.'

After a very good dinner of unexpected guinea-fowl with purple sprouting and baked potatoes, and rarely seen home-made ice-cream, they went out. As yet, the Island had not adopted the 'dim-out', so that the town was lit only by the rising full moon. They strolled down the steep road from the hotel, hand in hand like young sweethearts, then up again to the cliff-top where there were neglected anti-invasion obstacles and barbed-wire protecting the high mast on the grassy downlands that overlooked the sea. There Nick spread his greatcoat, and they sat down and looked out to sea.

'Nick?'

'Ah . . . peace, and the sea, and the woman I love.'

'Nick. I've got to be honest with you – I felt very awkward and stupid at the hotel.'

'You don't need to tell me, I'm not surprised. It all seemed such a set piece. I saw the ludicrousness of it. Two adults wanting only to sleep together and make love, yet they have to flaff around like we did at dinner.'

'It's not only that. I think from that time you came to the house with the dahlias I knew that there would come a day when we would do something like this, and then when it comes to it . . . oh, that hotel . . . that bedroom. I just suddenly went off it, I don't know why. I'm sorry.'

He squeezed her hand and fingered her wedding ring until he had removed it. 'Perhaps it is to do with this.' This was the first time that she had been without the ring since Hugh had put it there.

He sucked her empty finger. 'There, now he's gone. You must have known that I wanted you then . . . badly, you don't know how badly. But then I'd wanted you for ages before that.'

'And I've wanted you. Time and time again I've imagined how it would be, and it was always in one of the places where we used to mess about when we were kids. That's probably why that awful bedroom seems such an anti-climax.'

He combed back her hair with his fingers and grinned, 'No such inhibitions, I'm afraid: I'd have had you any-where, anytime. I came that night aching for you . . . you kept me waiting nearly five years – and I'm still waiting.'

'Don't tell me you haven't had girls in Liverpool.'

'Celibacy for me is not having Georgia Honeycombe, which means that I've lived in life-long celibacy. Georgia, Georgia, how did we get like this?'

'Like. . . ?'

'Talking about it, afraid of it. That's not *us*. What happened to us between those old days in Emberley and now?' He kissed her and she relaxed into the warmth of him.

'We got older . . . grew up . . . became adults.'

'Something else happened, you stopped being Georgia Honeycombe . . . at least you tried to.'

'You still call me that.'

'So that you won't forget who you are.'

'The country girl . . . the innkeeper's daughter? And what about Nicky Crockford who used to quote poetry at the drop of a hat?'

He laughed warmly.

> *'All through that summer at ease we lay,*
> *And daily from the turret wall*
> *We watched the mowers in the hay*
> *And the enemy half a mile away,*
> *They seemed no threat to us at all.*

'There. Crockford still showing off his ability to memorize.'

'I remember thinking of that bit the day when we saw the bombers and the dog-fight and the farm caught fire . . . then suddenly they were a threat.' She gently fingered the puckered area of his brow that was a burn-scar caused that day.

'I feel that I'm still pretty much Crockford, the country lad. I remember when you were still Georgia Honeycombe, and we were all so physical and full of ourselves, and I was oh so hungry for you and too shy and proud to tell you because of what you might say.'

'Physical . . . yes, we were, weren't we? You used to lift my plait and kiss the back of my neck and I was too gauche to tell you how much I loved it.'

He lifted her heavy, golden hair, pale as his own white head in the moonlight and moved his lips in the hollow of her neck.

'Yes . . . like that. Now that I'm all grown up, I can tell you I love that . . . ask you not to stop.'

'How easily we used to throw off our clothes and jump into the lake without a second thought, and yet this evening we both tiptoed around that bedroom as though the bed was enemy territory.'

Inevitably she thought of Harry and the isolated cove, of lying uninhibited and naked with Harry Partridge. Now the spring tide was coming in roughly, hitting the shore far below, moving a bar of shingle that shushed-shushed as each wave came and receded.

Why was there this barrier between her and Nick, the man she had wanted since before she knew why she wanted him?

When Nick had first suggested they go to Ventnor, she had fantasized them in the scene that one never actually saw in films – the scene that is behind the door when it shuts upon the camera. Rhett Butler sees Scarlett undoing her own dress, Scarlett O'Hara sees that the bed is a low divan spread with coloured shawls and cushions; only Rhett sees her expression when they make love once quickly and then more slowly. With Nick in her fantasy it would be perfect.

More perfect than with Harry?

For her, that thought had come between them. She could not trust herself to enjoy Nick in the way she had enjoyed Harry. Harry had been casual, no consequences, no strings attached. But Nick . . . ? I love Nick. It's that . . . the love . . . the commitment.

'It wasn't "*we*", it was me. It's my fault, I'm stupid with apprehension.'

'Apprehension? Oh Georgia.' He put his arms more tightly about her and drew her close.

'I think that I'm afraid that it won't be good enough, and that I shall be so anxious that it will turn out to be the same half-cocked thing that it has always been with Hugh. I'm afraid that perhaps it won't work out because when we were little we were like brother and sister. I'm afraid it would not turn out to be the best thing that ever happened to us – I couldn't bear that.'

'Tears, Georgia Honeycombe?' He had touched them with his tongue. 'It will be good. Good, good. I promise you. With you and me, it can't be anything else. It will be like this.' He caressed her intimately for the first time. He groaned gently as though it was he who had been caressed by her. 'We were never brother and sister, and so what if we were? So what if we are? I should still touch you like this, caress you like this.'

As he lay close to her she could feel his stomach gradually contract with contained laughter. She undid a button of his shirt and slid her hand inside, catching the hair on his chest with her scarlet nails.

'Oh Georgia Honeycombe, wonderful, desirable Georgia Honeycombe, with skin like silk and hair like honey . . . kiss me and tell me that you never did believe that anything to do with me could be half-cocked.'

Then she laughed with him, and he heard the voice of the girl who used to be wild and joyful. The fresh wind was chill through his open shirt, but her lips warm and moist in the dished hollow of his chest. With the sea surging and the red light of the tall mast above them and the moon whitening the Downs, they made love. Their first, long-delayed consummation had been urgently and quickly good, their second soon afterwards in the hotel room was good . . . good.

She sat back panting.

'Lovely!' he said. 'That was more wonderful than I dreamed of it. Nick Crockford's dream come true – to be pinned down and forced by Georgia Honeycombe. I love you, Georgia. I always have and always shall.'

She, satiated and alive, looked down and kissed him. A long kiss that occupied her mouth so that she should not commit her feelings to reckless words which, although they might be true, if said aloud would be too binding. *And I love you, Nick Crockford.*

That was weeks ago. He had gone back to Liverpool, and the joy of their love-making weekend was dulled by a return to the misconnections, crossed lines, lines engaged and the, 'Three minutes – your time is up', interjections of a wartime liaison conducted by telephone.

They had seen one another only once since, when he had come unexpectedly into her office holding Pete by the hand. Pete at six years old was a most attractive child, with his father's physique and Nancy's large thickly-fringed eyes and full mouth. Until then, Georgia had never much thought of Nick in the role of father. The sight of him, huge and gentle, holding the hand of the child he had fathered upon Nancy, had plunged her into a strangely erotic mood.

She felt embarrassed and confused in front of the child, by a sudden upsurge of desire which, although he addressed the boy in a neutral voice, was evident in Nick also. He did not flirt or call her Georgia Honeycombe, but he did not appear able to take his eyes from her. Not only desire for each other, but love. If Georgia and Nick had not been in love before, then they were now. The child seemed to be the catalyst.

He was obviously proud of Pete, sitting with him held encircled in his long arms and legs. He had wanted to show him off to her.

'He's a super kid, Nick.'

'Pete's going to live with his Grandpa now, aren't you, Pete?'

The boy had looked up at Nick and nodded. 'Just till Daddy comes back home . . . you said, didn't you, Daddy?'

'That's right, as soon as the war's over. Then you will live with both me and Grandpa.'

'And Mrs Dancer.'

'Well, Mrs Dancer's going to help Grandpa out.'

'With the washing.'

Nick had smiled and nodded, obviously touched by the boy, loving him more than he had ever let on, more than Georgia ever guessed. 'And nobody's going to hurt you in Grandpa's house, are they, son?'

The boy had looked at his boots and shaken his head. Georgia frowned questioningly, and Nick nodded.

'Been having a bad time of it lately has our Pete. Nancy's signalman has been heavy-handing him. I went there on the off-chance to see Pete and when I saw the state of him, I just brought him away, didn't I, Pete?' He ruffled the boy's hair.

'But you've no legal claim. Won't they . . . ?'

'Let them try! But they won't. He knows I'd go through every court in the land, and he won't have any stomach for that. In any case, he just don't want Pete there now they've got kids of their own – that's the trouble. Six-year-olds want a lot of time and attention.' He pulled the boy to him. 'But Daddy and Grandpa want you all right, Pete, don't we?'

'And what about Nancy?' Georgia asked.

'She's got her hands full with the other ones, and she's relieved that Pete's out of reach of the signalman. Nancy won't make any trouble for me.'

Georgia had wanted to ask, Did you have Pete at home when you asked me to marry you? But she thought that she knew him better than that. He would have told her about Pete straight off and been honest about it. Even so, she had not been one hundred per cent sure – he obviously loved Pete and it would be only natural to think of his welfare first, of somebody more permanent than old Mrs Dancer.

Since then they had spoken a few times by telephone, having only the standard three minutes. Nick was still in Liverpool, but had applied for a transfer back to the south. Within weeks of their wonderful days together on the Isle of Wight, their honeymoon love seemed to have soured.

So that was why her pulse raced when she saw the Vincent parked outside her house. The one thing that Harry Partridge was not was serious.

Inside the house, he gave her a long hard kiss and an appreciative caress. 'Ah, Georgia, lovely, scrumptious Georgia, I could eat you. I've only got a couple of days. Are you free to be eaten?'

'As air,' she said gaily.

'Come on then, get those glad-rags off and put on your hot red pants and we'll be away. Do you fancy Brighton and a little bit of 'ows your father?'

She laughed, loving the uncomplicated feelings that his

spontaneity bubbled up in her. 'September's a bit late in the year for any seaside larks, isn't it?'

'I wasn't thinking of the beach . . . more of The Metropole, say?' He raised his eyebrows questioningly.

'The Metropole! Goodness, how grand.'

'Why not?' Lighting two cigarettes and handing one to her, he was challenging her with directness.

'Absolutely, Harry – why not?'

As she was putting a dress and toiletries into an overnight bag, she caught sight of herself in the dressing-table mirror. Her cheeks were flushed, her eyes bright and a smile raised the corners of her mouth, and she recognized the features of happiness. Harry Partridge. His intentions were as unambiguous as her own. An occasional lover with no ties, no complications, no guilt. No one but herself to consider.

She smiled at the happy woman.

Georgia Honeycombe, you are a free woman.

Fifty Years On

1989

17th September

Georgia Giacopazzi, whose now famous name had come to her in 1945 by way of a pencil stabbed at a newspaper, descended the narrow stairs of Markham's foremost hotel. Compared to the unstarred, luxurious and exclusive places she was booked into by her publishers, The Coach House was far down market: here the rooms were inconvenient and small, and the smells of tobacco, beer and cooking seeped and wafted and grew stale in the low-beamed narrow passageways. Today, dull and humid after the long, hot summer, the place seemed smaller and darker than she remembered it. But then it was a long time ago.

It was to The Coach House that Hugh had brought her on her first date with him. It was in those days the only licensed premises where middle-class Markhambrians might gather without brushing shoulders with hoi polloi darts players. Its original use had still been discernible then in its yard and stables, which were now all conversions with white clap-board, white-painted tables.

The receptionist, aware of the kudos of so famous a guest as the novelist Giacopazzi, leaned eagerly across the desk-flap. 'Good morning, ma'am, is everything satisfactory?'

Georgia smiled and nodded. 'Is there a member of staff on duty to show my guests where to go when they arrive?'

'All arranged, ma'am.'

Georgia went to the small reception room she had reserved and looked out across Markham's town square. On the face of it, the square was very little different from fifty years ago. None of the buildings she used to pass on her way to work all through the war was much changed, though many of them had changed use. The old Post Office depot was a new estate agents', the old estate agents were still there, the air-raid shelters-cum-toilets under the Town Hall were entirely gone, the greengrocer-fishmonger's had become yet another estate agents' and a pet supplies shop. The Congregational Church, the banks and chemists were there, but what had been the bus waiting-room was now an olde shoppe with olde windows. Where do sweethearts go these days?

Lord Palmerston was back in his place of dominance. Beyond the statue, Georgia could see the beautifully restored Georgian cottage that used to be her office, and the archway leading to Mrs Farr's old house and the Town Restaurant.

Forty-five years to the day since Harry Partridge, with hundreds of other parachuted men, had jumped to defeat in battle from an aeroplane above Arnhem. Of all the men in her life, Harry had been the most fun. Good-time Harry. She had often wondered whether, that weekend at the Metropole in Brighton, he had known that his regiment was preparing for that impossible battle. He had been the perfect carefree partner for a day and the perfect lover for a night.

1944

September

Harry Partridge breathed softly close to Georgia's ear. 'Georgia, are you awake?'

She turned lazily towards him and linked her arms around his neck, her eyes still closed, smiling. 'No. But don't let that stop you.'

Smoothing back her tousled hair, he looked at her in the clear coastal light. 'It's been great, Georgia. The dinner, the dancing, wandering down The Lanes like there was no tomorrow; but the greatest thing has been you. Not just last night, not only the way you give yourself up to love-making, but it's great knowing you.'

She raised herself on one elbow and looked at him. His weathered, handsome face with its uncontrollable cowlick lock of hair that fell forward, his clever eyes and small nose that was like Dolly's, and teeth so fine that when her tongue had moved over them she had imagined shining bone china. 'You talk as though we won't do this again.'

'Oh we will. Of course we will. But I wanted you to know that you are important to me.' He tilted back her head so that she had to open her eyes and see that he was sincere. 'Remember the day on the beach when we talked about what it would be like for people like us after the war, there being a social upheaval and there being a class-less society?'

Georgia nodded. 'Shall I ever forget!'

'That's when I started to think about coming here with you . . . not just for a twenty-four-hour pass quickie fling, but about *us* coming here together. I imagined after the war things being different so that we would sometimes come to places like this . . . you know . . . spontaneously, any old time, as the fancy took us.'

'Mm – that would be nice.'

'I was doing a jump, and for a second or two I thought my 'chute wasn't going to open, and it flashed through my mind, Bugger all, Harry Partridge, you missed your chance . . . you shouldn't have waited. Then the harness buckle unjammed and she opened and I landed like thistle-down.' He chuckled. 'That taught me a lesson better than all my Dad's lectures ever did . . . Don't put off till tomorrow what you can do today.'

'Harry! Don't joke about it. How awful, that's the most petrifying thing I can imagine.'

'Not half as petrifying as being a thousand feet above Salisbury Plain, dropping like a stone, and knowing that there was a beautiful woman you had put off till tomorrow that you could have done today.'

'Harry!'

'So, Prude, I made up my mind that I would not wait until after the war for things to change, but I would make some changes of my own. And I'd always imagined coming here with somebody elegant and intelligent and beautiful.'

'Sergeant Partridge, you are a man who knows how to make a woman feel wonderful.'

He trailed an appreciative hand down the curves of her body. 'Not difficult with material like this to work on.'

'I remember, that day on the beach, you said that we were two of a kind. Somebody else once said the same thing to me. I really didn't know what to think about that . . . to be of a kind with Harry Partridge with his reputation – Harry Partridge, the free spirit, Good-time Harry?'

She linked her arms tightly about him, inviting him closer, enjoying the luxury of the surroundings and a voluptuous feeling of liberty. 'I think you knew me better than I knew myself. But now – I know myself very well. I know that my basic nature is joyful. I think *that's* what makes you and me two of a kind. Joyfulness. It's a word that loses its meaning as soon as we are old enough to know its definition.'

'And what about the other one? Does he – it's got to be a he? – does he make three of a kind?'

'I suppose, yes. The two of you have a lot of ideas in common – free love, free hospitals, free lawyers and all those other freedoms.'

'And have you done this with him?'

She didn't respond.

'It's all right. I'm not the jealous type. When I say free love, I mean equality.'

'Except that women aren't quite as free as men. The woman always takes the rap if there is one.'

'I'd never do that to a woman. I always, always take precautions.'

'So do I, but there are accidents. I've often thought that I am one.'

'I don't believe in them, it's either carelessness or intention. Your parents had you because they intended to give life to a beautiful creature called Georgia.'

He hugged her.

She laughed and tousled him.

'I'll tell you what you are, Georgia, you are a natural-born nonconformist. However briefly, I'm glad that we're inhabiting the same world at the same time . . . imagine, supposing one of us had been born fifty years before the other, or I was a Martian . . .'

Drawing back the covers, she flirted her hand down the length of his body. 'Too terrible to contemplate, to be on a world where there's no Harry Partridge.'

As though they feared to think it, they made their final hours of love-making last a long time.

1989

17th September

Yesterday, when it had been gusting and showery, Georgia Giacopazzi had put on mackintosh, walking shoes and tied a scarf round her head and, unrecognizable as the Giacopazzi of a million dust-jackets, had gone to search the town to see if her memory had played her any tricks.

What she had not expected was the way Markham had become 'Yaah'd' as the young ones at home would have called it – meaning, that instead of Yes or the rural Oh-ah, Yaah was the affirmative 'in' word of the moment, and of the dominating class of present-day Markham. By the end of the war, there had not been more than a handful of cars about the place, now they were everywhere, side-lighted Volvos, BMWs, Mercedes, G-registration Sierras, and 'limited edition' shopping cars by the score. The traffic of an affluent community which parked on double yellow lines and took the ticket rather than carry a box of vegetables.

Station Avenue was now pedestrianized and heavily draped with restless frizia trees. What had been the boys' school, facing the terrace which had included the Kennedys' and the Wiltshires' houses, was now the core of an IBM and media-person enclave which, having discovered the simple unspoiled country town, changed its simple nature by living in it.

Monty's house was the local office of a computer software manufacturer. She had glimpsed the Capability Brown park and outwardly unchanged Oaklands estate from a bridge over the river. Its days as a hospital long over, the mansion was now part of the brown, signposted tourist trail. Also unchanged was Markham's other estate, where Dolly, Marie, Pammy and Trix had lived.

She did not go to see what had happened to the site of The Cedars.

One of the terrible consequences of wars was what happened to families like the Partridges and the Hardys . . . not that the two families had ever had much in common – except that in 1939 they had been intact.

Mrs Giacopazzi's mind drifted as it often did when she was engaged in writing. By that last Christmas of the war, there wasn't one of the women who had not had their heart broken. Only Ursula was not touched directly – her anguish was in seeing what had become of the women who had come and gone through the Town Restaurant kitchens.

1944

Markham, at the still centre of the storm of war, was not blitzed or fire-bombed, or shelled or rocketed, but the very stillness of the place seemed, after five years of ills being done to them at a distance, to create the ideal environment for moths and wood-beetles to chew away at the old self-satisfied society.

After the Normandy landing in the spring, the whole country thought that by the autumn the war would be over, but as the summer ground on, there were times when it looked as though there would never be a conclusion to it.

That year, after five years combating the dreary and austere with ingenuity and nous; the fear and anxiety with wit and sympathy, there gradually came about a change in the atmosphere in the back rooms and kitchens of the Town Restaurant.

Dolly had put her finger on it. 'One thing after the other, it's like we're being punished for five years of being happy together.'

The 'one thing after another' was Paula telling her mother about being pregnant, and then Georgia coming over to tell them that Connie Hardy had suffered damage to her pelvis and back.

'Look at it like this, Dorothy, Paula's predicament might appear to be trouble just now, but there'll come a time when it will be water under the bridge.'

'I never thought I'd be the one to say it, but it's never been the same since Mrs Hardy and Eve went away, and I keep thinking about what happened up there at The Cedars. I know that's nothing to do with Paula and Robbo, but we used to be such a happy group.'

Ursula looked hard at her good friend. 'Dorothy, this isn't like you.'

'And I think our Harry's carrying on with Georgia, but she's never said anything and I can't ask a thing like that.'

'And what about Harry?'

'I couldn't never ask him about his women friends. But it's hurtful, you'd think they'd say.'

'There's probably nothing in it, I don't think Georgia's particularly interested in men at all at present. What we all need is another day out, Dorothy, a day at the sea. You will get it more in perspective. Water under the bridge, dear, you see if I'm not right about that.'

But Ursula was not right, except where Paula's trouble was concerned. Harry's death never did flow away, but stayed dammed up in Dolly to flood and threaten to drown her for the rest of her life.

The beginning of the end seemed to have started with Paula. Throughout the years when Robbo was in Africa she had never missed a week without writing to him, but as the months and months passed she found less and less to say to him. Her job was mundane and unchanging, and she could scarcely say very much to him about her voluntary work in canteens or her popularity at camp dances – he was a docker, with a man's eye view of a wife's place in the home, and Paula knew that mention of anything that might spark off jealousy must be censored from her letters.

But then Paula fell in love.

When she began to be morning sick, only Marie knew of it and only Marie too knew who it was that Paula had been going out with so often, and so who was likely to be the father. Nothing would have dragged that out of her, or that he was part of Operation Overlord and was unlikely to return to this country, but would go back to America from where he came.

'What are you going to do, Paula?'

'*Do*? What do you think I'm going to do – I'm going to have the baby I've wanted for years.'

'But Paula, it will be . . .'

'Don't say it, Marie! It will be my baby, the one everybody thought I couldn't have because there was something wrong with me.'

'What about Robbo?'

'Look, Marie, because I thought I couldn't get pregnant I went all the way with Louis . . .'

'Louis! I thought it must be. Paula! How *could* you? With Louis . . . I know he's nice and good looking and has plenty of money but . . .'

'Don't, Marie. Don't say something you'll regret when my baby is your niece or nephew. I love Louis and want his baby more than anything.'

'I don't know what your Dad's going to say. He thinks you're Greer Garson and Phyllis Calvert rolled into one.'

'It will give him a chance to put his philosophies into practice.'

Marie didn't even like to think about Robbo.

Born on Christmas Day 1944, Paula Carter named her daughter Louisa, after her father. For a few days, the only way of detecting that she was of mixed race was in her faintly purple nails and the black cap of black crimpy hair.

'Oh, Paula,' Dolly said. 'She makes me want to cry because she is so beautiful.'

And so little Louisa was. Lusty, healthy and beautiful in that way of children who inherit only the choicest of genes of the Anglo-Saxon and the Negro races.

Robbo took the news badly – worse than anybody had imagined. He was not so much disturbed that Paula was pregnant by another man, but that her pregnancy was an advertisement of his own inadequacy.

A great, strong stevedore whose wife couldn't get pregnant until she got there with some Yank who was swanning around England whilst decent Englishmen were fighting in some hole full of foreigners and flies.

It was as well that he did not get to know that Louis was a Negro or that he was a popular jazz musician, or that he and Paula had fallen in love. It was bad enough as it was, for Robbo had gone berserk in camp, driving wildly off in a stolen vehicle which he had crashed and wrecked. He had written Paula a vile and threatening letter that could only have passed a censor who thought that women like this one deserved it.

As soon as he could do so, Robbo went to his commanding officer for advice on divorce and made plans to emigrate to the Rhodesian copper-belt where strong men were needed and pay was fantastic. His Chaplain had talked to him about the woman taken in adultery and advised Robbo to think charitably. 'Such mistakes happen in time of war.'

'Not to me they don't.'

Sam Partridge, like everyone else except Marie, had never for a moment dreamed that Louisa would be anything but fair-haired and white-skinned, but Paula placed the perfect baby in Sam's arms and he was won over before he knew that she would grow coffee-skinned. Paula never told him that Louis was an officer until she heard that he was safe and wanted her to go to France and live with him there.

In any case, the shadow of Harry hung so darkly over the family that the colour of Louisa's skin was entirely irrelevant.

The news of the failure of the airborne landing at Arnhem had filtered through almost at once, at first in rumours. Sam Partridge heard of it from an airman in the King William whilst he was having a quiet sit in the Four Ale Bar mulling over what to do about Paula who was getting so big that she could no longer disguise it. Markham did *talk* so.

'It was on the news. Airborne landing.' Sam's attention

was caught. 'Some place called Nijmegen . . . a lot of dead. And for nothing as far as you could read between the lines.'

The airman could not possibly have known that the old man who limped and stumbled from the bar was not swaying because he was the worse for ale, but that he had a Paratrooper son – one who had risen to sergeant and who was his secret pride and wonder. Sam and Harry had been getting on a bit better lately, especially since Harry had said he would soon be going on an officer training course. Sam visualized the peaked cap, the polished shoes and the Sam Browne belt when Armistice Day parade came, but it didn't do to let kids know you were proud of them in case they started to get above themselves, and Harry was bad enough already.

When Dolly went dark-eyed and gaunt into work the following day, all the women knew why. 'I couldn't bear to be at home. I don't know what I should have done if I didn't have this place to come to. As soon as I heard, I thought, I wish it was tomorrow so that I could be with the girls. I can't bear the waiting. I'd rather be at work. Sam's different, he's sitting at home. Won't say a word hardly. I said to him, You know Harry, always lands on his feet, he's probably safe and sound. You sitting here waiting for a telegram is like tempting fate; but he said, if the worst has happened then I want to know straightaway, I don't want no telegram boy going all over the place looking for me. Neighbours knowing before I do.'

Sam had sat at home for days tempting fate, but no telegram or news of his safety came. Then, because of an administrative blunder, they received first a letter through the regular post.

Dear Mr and Mrs Partridge,

Your son, Harry, was known to me more as a friend than my NCO. I cannot tell you how grieved I am for your loss and for his loss to the regiment. He was an exceptional soldier and an exceptional friend.

Sadly I have many letters of condolence to write, but this to you I have written first – I suppose because of those who died in the terrible battle in which we have been engaged, Harry Partridge is most directly in my thoughts. His loss is personal, we have been close friends ever since we started out together in '39. He, like myself, was a motor bike enthusiast, and we spent many days together tootling around the countryside. It was on these jaunts that he told me of the Partridge family. He loved, and was enormously proud of you, his mother and father who against the odds have brought up children of whom any parent would be rightly proud. You will, of course, know these things, but I am sure that you will like to know how much he loved and admired you, Mrs Partridge, and what understanding and compassion he felt for his father. I believe it was from you, Mr Partridge, that he gained his great sense of justice.

The loss of a son – and for me of a personal friend – is one of the terrible consequences of going to war, but when one of the consequences is the waste of such soldiers as Harry – men of intelligence, ideals, and depth of vision of the future – one wonders whether without them there will be a future for England worthy of their death. I know that Harry's great ambition was to become a Member of Parliament – his death is England's loss too.

I have officially recommended that Harry receive the highest military award for bravery.

Sincerely
John Clark (Capt.)

The telegram arrived days later.

Charlie was still posted overseas. He was hit very hard when he was notified of Harry's death. In his letters home he scarcely mentioned it. 'Our Charlie's grieving inward. I know him,' Dolly said.

Marie, who knew him equally, agreed. 'I only hope he don't do something silly.'

But he did.

Charlie Partridge, when refused compassionate leave, went absent without leave and on the run. As he went AWOL when the wing he was attached to was preparing for an attack upon the enemy, he had committed the offence for which a good many serving men had faced the firing squad.

It was 1945, and within sight of peace by the time the Military Police caught up with Charlie. The long months in the glasshouse finished him: when he returned to Markham he was rigid-faced and moved jerkily. There were nights when Marie could hardly bear it when she was awakened by him sobbing silently in his sleep.

Perhaps it was fortunate that Sam Partridge never did hear about Charlie, although many said the outcome would have been the same.

As Sam had always said, Markham people would *talk*. Suicide over his son in the Paras, they said.

That he was found floating in the park river he had been clearing of water-weed, and that the inquest found that he had drowned by Misadventure, meant nothing to the Markham gossips. They declared their own verdict: Suicide whilst the balance of his mind was disturbed, they said. This death-watch beetle talk that could eat into the structure of any family was partly scotched by Vern Greenaway, who wrote an obituary for the *Markham Clarion*, praising Sam, the well-known Markhambrian, old soldier and long-term fighter for justice and a fair society. Suicide, they said. And who can be surprised?

Later, there appeared another column reporting the posthumous presentation to Sam and Dorothy Partridge of their son Sergeant Henry Partridge's award for bravery.

A pity he committed suicide before he collected the medal, they said.

Only days after hearing of Harry's death, Georgia answered a request by her solicitor to visit his offices. Dark, aching days.

'Not the news you would have wished, Mrs Kennedy, but your husband wants to sell the house. Very generous terms – he offers you half, which should be quite enough for you to buy a little cottage somewhere in the town.'

So what! Harry was dead and Hugh offered her the proceeds of half a house. Not much of a deal.

'All I want, Mr Fox, is a decree nisi. It is my husband's house, but I would be pleased to have the car and some of the furniture if that can be arranged.'

'Mrs Kennedy, in your own interests . . .'

'No, Mr Fox, he had two years of my time without pay for which I was well-fed and clothed and had free accommodation. Please get it settled as soon as possible.'

After five years in her job, with few goods in the shops, travel either limited or forbidden, and only The Picture House open for entertainment, Georgia estimated that she had accumulated enough money, from savings out of her salary and the legacy from her parents, to keep her going until 1947.

Because of the stressful atmosphere that seemed to pervade both her office and the kitchens these days, it was not the best of times to make positive plans. But plan she must for a future in which she would not be pleasantly and conveniently employed by the Government. A future in which she avowed that she would be Georgia – be herself.

At work, the pleasant cocoa and tea breaks were no longer the intimate and happy affairs of the previous four years. New women had come in, replacing Connie and Eve and Pammy and Trix; the Red Cross and WVS women seemed to change weekly and keep themselves aloof from the kitchen workers.

Only Ursula seemed to be unscathed. In fact Ursula – the radical suffragist, the revolutionary, the one-time scourge of Parliamentarians – plumped out a little and throve on marriage with Niall O'Neill.

The warmth of the sorority that had first tasted its freedom in the kitchens of the Town Restaurant escaped through holes blown out by the hurt that had been done to several of their number. There was no topic that was not a minefield. They went for their breaks and often only talked work or smoked hungrily, silently and fiercely, drawing smoke low into their lungs and returning it like flame-throwers. Ursula, ashamed of her ineffectualness and inability to help 'her' girls, no longer seemed even to notice cigarette smoke in previous forbidden areas.

Georgia missed the atmosphere badly. She desperately needed their support, but most of them were all far, far worse off than she was. Eve had not been to the house or called in at the office for months now. When Georgia wondered if Eve was avoiding her, she told herself that she was being paranoic about people avoiding her. First Dolly, now Eve.

Eve had phoned once or twice, sounding bright . . . 'Terribly sorry not to have seen you, Georgia. This place is a mad-house. God, that's the sort of thing we have to watch in here . . . but you know what I mean. Anyway, darling, we absolutely *must* get together soon.' But something always turned up to prevent Eve from coming. Georgia understood: Connie was now out of hospital, but the V2 had left her with irreparable hips and so ended the career which had filled her life.

Marie was worried sick over Charlie, grieving over Harry and helping Paula with the baby.

Dolly became thin. Georgia was convinced that Dolly was avoiding her. The returns and lists which Dolly used to bring into the office after work, and which they both used as an excuse to talk for five minutes about what the latest film was like, or exchange a magazine, or to laugh at the latest half-baked directive from the Ministry of Food, were left on her desk when she was out.

If it was grief, then Georgia understood, but she would have liked her to have talked about Harry, to have talked about him herself, told Dolly what a gift of a man he was. Perhaps then Georgia might have been able to tell her about that last weekend in Brighton, when instead of visiting his mother and father he had spent his last two-day pass to make love with Georgia in a classy hotel in Brighton. But perhaps Dolly knew. Perhaps she could not bring herself to talk to the woman he had preferred to his mother to spend his last free hours with.

Georgia knew that it was time that she made the decision about what she must do. The house would be sold and she must decide where she would live. If she was to break with Markham, then it must be now. A clean break. A new start.

Ever since her mother's and father's funeral, she had kept in touch with her aunts and uncles. She wrote to them often, and occasionally visited on a snatched weekend or even a week's holiday – once a few days at Christmas, sleeping soundly under the uneven roof, awakening to the sound of clucking and lowing, and the smell of woodsmoke and two centuries of stored apples and hams.

In this place, she soon saw how much of a joke it was that the Honeycombes had said that she was a real country girl. Until she came to pay visits to the small farm in this neglected corner of Hampshire, she realized that she had scarcely known the meaning of the word.

What went on at Croud Cantle Farm was magic to Georgia. Magic from the pouring of rennet into the zinc basins filled with milk, the separation and eventual pressing into cheese moulds, to the smoking and charming of the bees housed in old-fashioned skeps against a sunny wall, and the taking of their honey.

Whilst she was there, she felt alive.

She walked the Downs. Her favourite place was at the top of Tradden Raike which rose from behind the farmhouse, from where she could look down upon the quiet valley whilst, behind her, ancient, restless beeches moved constantly in the up-current from the valley. Sometimes she rode John Honeycombe's horse, going cross-country through the village along the old bridle-path beside the river, or out over the wider metalled road towards Old Winchester Hill.

When looking down upon the farmhouse from the Downs, she scarcely dared allow herself to believe that the place did actually belong to her. Not morally, for Hyacinth and Uncle John had farmed the place both before and after Georgia's father had brushed from his heels the dust of his home village.

Uncle John was as quiet a man as Hyacinth was extrovert. What came into her head, she usually said aloud. 'Now you're shut of that man you was married to, I reckon 'tis time you thought serious about what you're going to do.'

'I'm going to do my job. I love it. It's a good position and when it comes to an end, then I shall probably apply for the Civil Service exam. There are some good opportunities for women attached to the Navy at Portsmouth.'

'Oh Georgia! Don't kid yourself. You wasn't cut out to be no Civil Servant. You should get a hold of that young Crockford fellow and the two of you should get wed and start raising a fambly.'

Georgia often wondered why it was that she could smile amiably at Hyacinth when she expressed such opinions, yet had it been her mother who had behaved similarly, then Georgia would have bridled and said it was none of her business and stop interfering.

The decision that Georgia had to make involved a laboriously written letter from Uncle John.

We don't get no younger and the place is getting a bit much for me and her. We put the whole of our lives into making something of the place and it would break Hyacinth's heart if it was all for nothing. We don't rightly know what to do because as you know the place wasn't never ours but was Thomas's your father's and so by rights is yourn. I know Hyacinth has been on to you to come here, but as I told her a thousand times, that's not practical even if you was married to somebody and in any case you set your heart on being somebody, not a farmer. Anyhow, Hyacinth has kept on to me to write and ask you and I see the rightness of her argument because it wouldn't be right for her and me to keep going and spiling the place because our rumaticks don't get no better with the years. What this place needs is a good strong pair of hands, and it's what we haven't got. And I can't seen young men wanting to come back here once they get their demob. Anyhow, one way or the other we wants to hand over your rightful inheritance to you. There won't be no trouble us getting out, because there's been a couple of alms-houses empty here for more than a year because there be few true Cantle folk left to qualify to get one. Hoping we shall hear some good news from you. Hyacinth sends her love but that's all of her messages I am going to write else I should want another sheet of paper, you know what she's like.

Your affectionate Uncle John Honeycombe

Georgia, in answering John Honeycombe's letter, promised that she would soon visit him and Hyacinth. She was tempted to go to them now, she felt unwell from unreliable periods and aching rib muscles which depressed her because she could not get relief from the nagging. She longed to go over to the farm at Cantle to be fussed over for a few days by Hyacinth. Although she was pleased to be leaving Hugh's house, the little one in Newton Lane had looked cramped and felt cold. The memory of the rosy warmth of the spacious kitchen in the farmhouse at Cantle was tempting: living there where life, ruled by seasons and weather, went on much as it had a century ago, and where one would not be affected so much by the dragging on of the war.

She was not interested in food and made herself very hasty and indifferent meals, or brought home bits and pieces of left-overs from work. Harry, Eve and Nick intruded on her thoughts constantly. It did not seem possible that Harry had become one of hundreds of bodies in a war-grave: it often seemed to her that it was as though he had been buried alive.

She had not seen Eve for weeks and was hurt by her

avoidance, so that when she recognized Eve's voice on the telephone a few weeks before Christmas, Georgia held back her usual enthusiasm.

'Hello, stranger . . . I thought you had emigrated.'

'Georgia, I am sorry, but you know how it is, the weeks go by.'

'For God's sake, Eve, you're only a mile away, not in Timbuctoo.'

'We've had a lot of new patients.'

'I've really missed you. It's been so awful lately.'

'Hasn't it just! Absolutely bloody.' She stopped.

'Eve? Are you all right?'

'Of course, right as ninepence.' Another moment's pause, then her voice came over tight and high. 'Only thing wrong is this morning bloody sickness . . . it's a difficult fact to hide in a place like this.'

'Oh, Eve.' Now it was Georgia who was silent, then she said, 'Eve, just come. Don't say anything else . . . we can't talk over the 'phone, just come as soon as you can.'

'Oh, I don't know . . . you don't want to hear my troubles.'

Eve arrived the next evening amidst Georgia's packing-cases and general mess of house-clearing, looking a lot like the old, plump Eve. Except that now it was more a thickening and swelling that gave her this appearance than youth and a soft line.

'I'm sorry about this mess, I'm packing up.'

'So I see. Going far?'

Georgia hunched her shoulders.

'Not somebody else who was going to go away without saying?'

'Of course not. I've only just made up my mind . . . anyway, that's not the burning issue here.' They stood facing one another for a moment: Eve's weeks of avoidance, and Georgia's apparent secrecy stood between them; but

Georgia stepped over those obstacles and they stood, arms tightly around one another.

'Thank God for friends, Georgia.'

'A friend you could have come to before now and said that you were . . .'

'Up the spout, in the club?'

'. . . pregnant. You don't have to put a face on here. Let's have a drink. Come on, it's marginally better in the front room and the cigs are in there.' They went through into the other room, touching one another with relief at being in each other's presence again.

Eve shook her head. 'Can't smoke these days . . . makes me sick as a dog. Anyway, the nicotine probably gets into the baby's blood or something. But Tottie and I could do with a Scotch.' She placed both hands over her belly.

'You're sure then? It *is* a baby, and not just a miss or two because of the worry about your mother or vitamin starvation? My Curse has been all over the place lately; the Welfare ladies reckon it's lack of vitamin B – I'm eating Marmite . . . well, when I can get it.'

'Perhaps you've got my trouble – for sure Marmite won't cure that.'

'Not on your life. I'm making plans, and they don't include cots and prams.'

'Well . . . my plans have to. I'm well over four months. One of the docs at Oaklands had a feel.'

'You aren't going to get . . .'

'Married to the father? No father. He was just a quick trick for both of us – and in any case . . . he bought it!'

'Oh Eve. Did he know about the baby?'

'No – it's as I said, one of those quickies that seem such a good idea at the time. It was my day off . . . Oh God . . . so sordid . . . you know how it goes.'

'That wasn't what I was going to ask you. I meant, you're not going to have an abortion? You always said that you knew the right doctors in Harley Street.'

'Have it fixed? Not on your life. I don't much care now who the father is, little Tottie is in there and starting to move. Here, give me your hand . . . put it there. I've nursed abortions that have gone wrong. Not for me! In any case, why not have little Tottie? I've only got Connie in her wheelchair and my randy old man who's cleared off. Why are you looking so straight-faced, Georgia darling? Don't tell me you're shocked.'

'Of course I'm not shocked, I was only wondering what you are going to do. You can't go back to your mother's flat again, not with a baby and the V2s.'

'Lord, no. Connie couldn't do with babies about the place – she's writing some sort of book about her exploits; I doubt if she'll get permission to publish until the war's over. She's got a super little ground-floor flat now, right in the heart of London with an amenity garden and trees, quite sweet. She's not all that badly off, plenty of people around her. Taken to wearing long skirts and she sits there or gets wheeled about by her admirers, quite the queen bee. Being a grandmother won't be her style. Certainly not having Tottie about the place.'

'If you had said . . .' Georgia waved at the packing cases, 'I might have held on to the house a bit longer.'

'Georgia my love, that's really sweet of you, but I have got myself some very suitable accommodation right in the heart of Markham.' She laughed, a little stridently. 'Give the old Markham gossips something to sup with their beer. Freddy Hardy's girl's up the spout and gone to live with the postman. That's right – I'm going to live with Monty. He's so *nice*, he's like a child waiting for Christmas. Did you know he's got this Jewess there? She's quite decent, too – doesn't look it, but she'll be smashing with Tottie – I'm sure of it.'

'You're going to live with Monty and Hildegard?'

'It's a perfect arrangement. Monty's like an old hen at the prospect of a baby, he's doing up a cot and painting ducks on it, and Hildegard was a nanny before she escaped from wherever she's come from.'

Georgia went very quiet.

'I'm really, really sorry, Georgia. I haven't meant to keep you out of things. I kept telling myself I should come and see you.'

'Then why didn't you? That foreign woman who hasn't been in the town five minutes knows all about it, but not me. I thought we were supposed to be friends.'

'For God's sake, Georgia!' She downed her neat whisky and held out her glass. 'Why do you think I didn't come to my best friend . . . my only real bloody friend. I was ashamed! I was a-shamed! I couldn't bring myself to tell you I'd got myself a bun in the oven. You would be the same with me, you know you would: you are as much of a smart arse as I was about not getting caught. I couldn't bear it at first, so I just ignored all the signs and put them down to the stress-factor that they keep telling us about at Oaklands. When I think of all the men I've slept with . . . and I let myself get in the club on a one-night stand. A casual roll in the hay. I wasn't even all that keen . . . and he was never at all my type. I don't even know how it happened – I never go out on a date unless I'm wearing my diaphragm, but I wasn't on a date, so I hadn't got it . . . but he said he was OK . . . maybe it's not just a story, maybe they do put a hole in every tenth one to keep the birth-rate up. Hell, Georgia, I don't know how it happened. It happened!'

'Hey, wind down, Eve, this is me – Georgia. Am I so intimating that *my* only real friend can't tell me she's pregnant . . . made a mistake?'

'Darling, no, of course you are not. It's me, it's me. Now I'm here I can't understand why it was that I didn't come to you at once. Oh, but I did feel such a fool just when I was boasting about the wonderful prospects of my specialist nursing career.'

'Here, have another drink and don't be so damned dramatic.'

'I wish I had come earlier, but now that I have, do let's try and get back on to our old footing. Tell me about these plans you are making. What's all this moving business then?'

'I've got a chance of a little place in Newton Lane – one up, one down and a sort of kitchen-scullery. The decree nisi will soon be granted – it's only a matter of time and I shall no longer be Mrs Kennedy.'

'Sounds cosy.'

'It will do until I make my fortune. I'll make us some Welsh rarebit. Here, read this whilst I'm in the kitchen. It's from my Uncle John. Tell me what you think.'

After a few minutes, Eve followed Georgia into the kitchen and perched on the table. 'This,' she flicked the letter, 'this is what you really want, isn't it? We've all got a fantasy of our particular place in the sun – this one's yours, it sticks out a mile, Georgia. I don't know why you are even *thinking* about Newton Lane.'

'I'm taking the cottage precisely because the farm *is* a dream. If I'm anything at all, I am practical.'

'You and Nick? Tilling the good earth. It could be idyllic, couldn't it?'

Georgia smiled wanly and shrugged her shoulders. 'Farming is many things, but it's not an idyll if you're the one doing it.'

'Nick's the right type. He always seems to thrive on exposure to the elements.'

'He's got big responsibilities now. He has taken Pete away from Nancy. The child's living with Nick's father until Nick gets released, but Mr Crockford is not a well man to have charge of a seven-year-old. I know what Nick would like, he'd like me to give up my work and go and live at Roke Acre. No strings except love, he said. Romantic, isn't it? But I couldn't! Back out at Emberley again . . . with

Nancy's child and old Robert – I should shrivel and wither away. For God's sake . . . I'd be a housewife again!'

'So why not go to your Uncle John's? Be a farmgirl.'

'I'm an administrator. Not just anybody can take over a farm. I hardly know how to milk a cow.'

'Well, you asked, and I've told you what I think. You should go for the dream, Georgia.'

Georgia dished up the supper. 'Oh, let's eat and not try to sort out my problems as well as yours.'

'Hey, come on. My problem is sorted and yours are not problems, they're choices.'

It was quite late when Georgia watched Eve pulling on her knitted cap. 'Come and see me again soon.'

'I won't stay away again – promise. I finish at Oaklands in a month, we'll see a lot of one another, and I'll need someone to pace the waiting room when I go into labour.' She kissed Georgia affectionately. 'Thanks, Georgia. I'm not really as flip as I sound you know. I don't want anybody knowing about how I got Tottie. I'll let her grow up before I tell her. Having a bastard baby isn't the thing a girl chooses; but I should never have married . . . It was Harry Partridge.'

For a moment it didn't sink in. 'What was?'

'Tottie, Pudding Club, bun in oven, the quick trick, idiot. It was dear fun-time Harry with his "Honestly, I'll be careful," his "Trust me, I wouldn't let it happen for both our sakes." '

'I can't believe it, I thought you hardly knew him.'

'I didn't really, but he was good fun – you knew he would never get too heavy. You know what he's like, you went out with him, didn't you?'

Georgia forced herself to be flip. 'Only for a ride on the old Vincent and the odd quick trick, like you say.'

By Christmas, Georgia had moved some of the furniture into the Newton Lane cottage and arranged the sale of the rest. It was a cosy enough place downstairs, but the bedrooms when no fires were lit in them were icy. On Christmas Eve, Georgia put on a little stand-up supper for her friends.

Georgia's relationship with Nick tottered on. Since their days together back in the spring, they had been together on only a few occasions, and not at all since Harry and the Metropole. Now he had gone home on seven days Christmas leave, and said he would put Pete to bed and then come.

He had stayed overnight in the Station Road house once or twice, but since he had taken Pete away from Nancy, he had never done so. 'I'm sorry, Georgia, but he's my kid, I have to be there whenever I can. He's still getting used to the change. My responsibility. It's one of the things a man doesn't think about when he's rolling in the hay.' She knew that tonight being Christmas Eve, he would be sure to want to get back to see to Pete's presents. She really did not mind: since the shock of Harry's death so soon after their scatty and delightful weekend in Brighton, her appetite for sex had diminished.

Ursula and Niall O'Neill, who lived only yards away from Georgia, came with Dolly who, for the first time in her married life, was staying away from home at Christmas and spending two days with the O'Neills. In one of Paula's dresses, she looked strangely unmotherly and less than her fifty-five years.

Eve came, looking plump and pretty, and talked with cheerful animation about her expectations of Tottie but, Georgia noticed, not to Dolly Partridge. Was it right not to tell Dolly that Harry was the father? They had talked about it briefly, but Eve's opinion was that the whole thing was too complex.

'Can you imagine, Georgia! Dolly Partridge discovering that her precious Harry left the Partridge family a legacy? She would smother me. I don't want Tottie to be a

Partridge, or a Hardy either. I shall register her as "Father Unknown" and tell her who her father is when she understands how easy it is to cop it. Young girls before they get the urge can be devastatingly judgemental. Dear Monty says she can have his name. Tottie Iremonger? Sounds quite pleasant.'

Nick was helping Georgia in the tiny back room. 'You're quiet.'

'It's a patch I'm going through.'

'Do you want to talk about it? I could stop on for an hour.'

'Talking won't do much good . . . it's just *everything*! My life has got itself in tatters, fragmented – this house, the divorce, my job. And Uncle John wants to get out of the Cantle farm. I've got to pull it together again.'

'Would you come to Emberley for lunch? Tomorrow if you like. You could talk about it. It helps. Pete wants a party and Mrs Dancer has made a cake. I know it's not this swish buffet kind of thing that you like, but Pete and my Dad will love it if you came.'

He stood there, big and slightly abashed, as he used to when he was a youth and came into the Honeycombes' kitchen to ask if she was coming out. Suddenly she would have loved to have taken his large, knuckly hands and led him up to the icy bedroom and burrowed with him under the eiderdown till morning and awoken with a clear mind in a carefree world.

'I'd love to come.'

'Thanks, Georgia.' He bent to her level and they kissed with the same longing and passion as they had back in the Spring, before Georgia's emotions had become confused.

'Oh dear, I forgot my bike tyre's gone. The car's back on the road, but I haven't any petrol allocation.'

Lighthearted at the prospect of her spending the day at Emberley, he laughingly swept her up in his arms. 'I'll carry you.'

At that moment, Eve came in. 'Don't tell me that at long last the hero's going to carry off the fair lady. I thought you never would.'

'Chance would be a fine thing. Do you know anybody who does black market petrol?'

Eve, now well into her pregnancy, looking blooming and prettier than ever, laughed and put on a funny voice. 'You want nice petrol? I get.'

The last Christmas Day of the war was a terrible day for Georgia. Eve had told Nick where to find her father's stash of petrol, and he was going to cycle over from Emberley to get one of the cans. It was a long time, if she ever did, before Georgia stopped blaming herself for mentioning using the car to go to Emberley. *If I had been content to borrow Eve's cycle, none of it would have happened.* It was a long time too, before she could once more shake off the notion of divine retribution.

She was already edgy when, after waiting about, ready to leave for two hours after Nick had arranged to call, he had not arrived. Then a police sergeant and a constable arrived.

'Sorry to disturb you on Christmas Day and all that . . . but there's been this accident, ma'am. Bottom of Longmile Hill by the T-junction.'

Georgia's expression became fixed.

'The only clue we could find as to who the victim was is this letter with your address inside. Do you know a Mister Nicholas Crockford?'

Her blood withdrew from her veins and seemed to be pumping only through the valves of her heart and going no further, the thud echoing and banging in her ears. Her insides became shrivelled and chill and her mouth dry.

'You look a bit dicky, you'd better sit down, ma'am. Are you family?'

'No, close friends, we grew up together. He was on his way to call on me.'

'We haven't been able to get in touch with the next-of-kin yet . . .'

'He's not *dead*?'

'No, no, ma'am – not dead . . . injured bad.'

'How did it happen?'

'It appears he was carrying a can of petrol. We've only got the driver of the jeep's word. He says the bike swerved and a can of petrol went over and caught light. One of them must have been smoking or just lighting up, or it could have been a spark from the metal dragging on the road.'

'He didn't smoke.'

'Well, we shall be asking them sort of questions later.'

She looked blankly at them. 'He can't talk, ma'am. The hospital says his trackier, that's his throat, and his lungs got burnt from breathing in the burning petrol. They got him under sedation.'

'For a moment I thought you meant that he'd been killed.'

'He's got some burns, and his breathing is bad.'

Having established who the casualty was, the two policemen tramped back to the station to secure the use of a vehicle so that his lady friend could be taken to see to the victim's child and the next-of-kin who was apparently pretty ill. The policemen then relaxed their respective ranks – it being Christmas morning.

'I reckon she's a bit more than a friend to our man, Constable.'

'Ah, and I'll tell you something else, Sarge – she's got a bun in the oven or I'm a Dutchman.'

'Can't say that I noticed that.'

'Five times my missis has been that way – it don't necessarily have to show much for me to be able to tell. She was too thick on the waist for such a slim bit. And, apart from that, there was a box of raspberry-leaf, which an't much use for anything except a woman in the family way. I'd say she was three or four months. You get a nose for it.'

The grizzled sergeant pursed his lips as he did when he was being jovial with his men. 'Five kids? I reckon you must have a bit more than a nose for it, lad.'

1945

When, on 7 May, the Board of Trade announced that red, white and blue bunting not costing more than one and three a square yard was to be sold without coupons, Georgia had no interest in anything other than that her waters had broken and Hyacinth Jepp was awaiting the first birthing she had attended at Croud Cantle for decades.

And on 8 May, when it was announced that there were to be two days national holiday to celebrate victory, Georgia had already given birth prematurely by about three weeks. The baby was a girl named Dixie who, Hyacinth declared, was so beautiful that she hurt your eyes enough to fair make them water.

Nick, who had for a while been in and out of hospital, nursed Dixie for hours in his slowly healing arms and said that she was balm for the soul. He still had many puckered scars, his lungs were clearing, but his throat was still quite gravelly. He and John Honeycombe had taken to one another at once, and since Nick's discharge from the Fire Service, John had taken Nick under his wing and vowed to have him back on his feet in six months.

The old farmer had taken up residence in one of the Cantle village alms-houses, but Hyacinth had stayed on, 'Just till you'm over the birthing, Georgia', revelling in 'putting a bit of flesh on Pete's little bones' and cadging baby wool and clothing coupons for Georgia's baby. For those months of waiting, except that Nick's father's health was deteriorating, life in the cottage was placid. John Honeycombe would sit on in the evening, telling Pete true and untrue tales about the old days when he was a sparky lad the same age as Pete, until Hyacinth would shoo him off home until next day when he would return to tend the animals and teach Nick the basics of running the small mixed farm.

It seemed as though as soon as Georgia had made her decision to retreat to Cantle, her condition began to be obvious. Hitherto, that state of mind in which she tried to ignore her condition had kept her flat and slim. Before she left, she had written a short note to Ursula apologizing for her sudden departure, but explaining nothing except that Nick had had an accident and that she was going to look after Pete. She felt disloyal to the women with whom she had discovered love and friendship, but she felt so desperate about her situation that she wished only to cut herself off and to start again.

She took Pete away from the Markham school, leaving his head teacher with the impression that the boy was returning to his mother in Bristol.

She arranged for the now ailing Robert Crockford to go into a residential home where he would be properly cared for. As well as making the journey back and forth to visit Nick in hospital.

And, as soon as he was released, she brought Nick to Croud Cantle Farm.

Then, having settled Pete in the village school, Nick to recuperate before the great ingle fireplace and later in the open air of the farm, Georgia began to put into action the plan about which she had told Eve. Because of all the unexpected responsibilities that had gnawed away at the substance of her plan, it was in tatters.

Her plan had been to live at the farm, employ a foreman to run it, whilst she gave herself two years in which to see whether she could write a successful book. But having admitted to herself that her aching ribs and missing Curse were not caused by lack of vitamin B but due to being pregnant, and having taken on the care of Pete and Nick, the only bit of her dream that she salvaged was to try to write the book that had been gathering like a boil on her mind. Something good came out of it though, for now that Hyacinth and Uncle John saw that the farm was safe in Honeycombe hands, they continued to tend the place as they had always done.

Within days of coming to Cantle, Georgia bought what appeared must be the only available typewriter in Hampshire, and set about writing as though time was terribly short. During odd moments of idleness in her office she had made a map of a fictional town and worked out a plot and a resolution. During her five months of waiting, that map and plan gradually became a mystery story with some love interest. A publisher's reader reported that 'some of the love scenes in which the detective, Miss Fern Goodlands, was involved, are perhaps somewhat "spicy" for the readership' and that 'an attractive woman sleuth is a somewhat avant-garde idea for such a thriller'.

The publisher, however, saw the chance of publicity in a curvaceous sleuth named Fern, and offered a contract.

The success of Georgia Kennedy's first book led to a contract for others. By the time Dixie was ten years old, her mother was becoming famous for the sexual adventure of her female characters, her winding plots, violated corpses and dramatic endings. Dixie was not the only one to ask, 'Why do you always write about death, Ma?' Indeed, it is something that Georgia Kennedy herself would have liked explained to her.

Nick had to accept the fact that she would never marry him, but was content that they live together as lovers. When Georgia became pregnant with Tessa, she was not carelessly gotten as was Pete, or accidentally as was Dixie.

When her divorce became absolute, Georgia legally took back her old name – Honeycombe.

Once having settled on the farm in that Hampshire valley, she and her family never left. As Georgia's books brought in ever-increasing royalties, she was able to buy land that had once belonged to her family and acres that had been neglected and bring it all back to the extraordinary fertility that had once made the valley part of the foodbowl of England. She bought derelict cottages and abandoned farmhouses, and restored and extended Croud Cantle where her forebears had lived for two hundred years.

From time to time, she thought about the Town Restaurant Women, she always read the *Markham Clarion*, saving any bits about the families she had known. When Leonora had her first success in the theatre, Georgia subscribed to a clippings service.

In 1989, fifty years after the incident that had brought the women together, Georgia Honeycombe had returned to Markham for the first time since she had left it.

1989

17th September

Driving towards Markham on seemingly the first dull day for months, Leonora Altzheiber's companion asked, 'Would you ever want to go back to live in your old home town, Leonora?'

Leonora Altzheiber, as she always did, considered the question before giving a glib answer. 'Only if I could go back to Markham some time in the summer of 1944, before Georgia became all complicated and cleared off, and if I could stop time going beyond the summer. I was still innocent, virginal and happy.'

Her companion, the artist Fenella Standing, turned to look at her. 'If you ask me you've still got the hots for your precious Georgia.'

'Jealousy doesn't suit you, Fenny. And in any case . . .'

'In any case . . .?'

Leonora Altzheiber yanked the lighter from the dashboard of the car and pressed it hard on the tip of her cigarette. 'In any case . . . she let me down.'

'Because she went off with her lover and had a baby? And not necessarily in that order.'

Leonora went silent for several minutes. 'It wasn't like that. She let me down by leaving me to find my own way out of Markham. It is true that she was pregnant when she left . . .'

'And poor little Lena had her nose put out of joint.'

'Oh Fenny! You do like to bitch it up sometimes. Her nose was not put out of joint. Quite the opposite . . . she was the only one in whom Georgia confided. Georgia told me she was pregnant ages before that Christmas when Nick had an accident and they went away. Nobody knew except

Little-Lena, not Nick, not even Eve Hardy. I was the only one to know. And I still know the quite vital bits Georgia has chosen to leave out of her book. She has copped out. But I know.'

' ". . . And everyone will know, because you told those blabbering trees . . ." ' Irritatingly to Leonora Altzheiber, her friend sang and hummed the old Ink Spots song.

'Well, they won't, Fenny dear, not from me.'

'Frau Altzheiber! You do still have a yen for your heroine.'

'You might not know a single one, Fenny, but there are nice people dotted around the world, and Georgia Kennedy was one of them.'

Experienced novelist though she was, Georgia Giacopazzi knew that she would be hard pressed to describe the emotion she felt when Mrs Partridge and Mrs O'Neill arrived at The Coach House. In herself, emotion manifested itself in an aching throat from trying to smile and not to cry. Dumbly shaking her head, she embraced the two old women.

'Mrs Partridge! And Mrs Farr,' was all that she could manage as she clung to them.

Ursula chewed her mouth and Dolly wiped her eyes. 'Come on now, ease off or you'll knock me off my stick.'

A round-faced woman in a smart suit and an expensive hair-do was with them.

'You didn't mind me bringing Bonnie? She's a fan of yours. Read all Georgia's books, Bonnie, haven't you?'

'Bonnie? All these years and I've still had you fixed in my mind as a rather better edition of Shirley Temple.'

'She's got two shops as well as the one Marie started,' Mrs Partridge said proudly.

The waiters hovered and Georgia Giacopazzi turned to Ursula who was standing easily, legs apart and evenly balanced as she had always done.

'Mrs Farr,' Georgia clasped her hands again. 'I can't get over you, you are just the same.'

'You must need your contact lenses then, Georgia. I'm a stringy old lady who intends to hang on as long as she can.

'It's a strange occasion, this one. Not one that either Dorothy or I could have expected to have lived to see when we first met. I was curious to see what you and Eve would be like.'

Mrs Partridge said, 'Is it all true?'

Late that night, when the reunion was all over, Georgia Honeycombe sat in the ingle seat of her own room and recalled most vividly that moment facing Mrs Partridge when she had asked, Is it all true?

Other images. Leonora and her partner – whatever that term might imply. Georgia Honeycombe remembered how Leonora had made an entrance. The hotel manager had flourished open the door and ushered in Leonora Altzheiber. Sifting through the jumble of impressions Giacopazzi recalled moving forward to greet her and seeing at once that Leonora Altzheiber was the kind of woman who always made an entrance, a woman for whom doors were always opened with a flourish by some senior member of staff. It was not only her long-legged height and handsomeness, but a self-assurance that she was *Somebody*. Elegant and stylish, she turned the heads of both men and women.

Georgia Honeycombe sipped the smooth brandy and listened to the comfortable sounds of Pete clattering chains and calling to animals, and passed on in her thought to her reunion with Little-Lena.

'Leonora!'

'Mrs Kennedy, we meet at long last.' Her voice had been throaty and sexy, a voice used to command and public speaking. She had shaken hands strongly and kissed the air at both sides of Georgia's cheeks. 'Strange meeting. Goodness, it is a long time since I cried, but I believe I shall not help it. I doubt if Fenella is aware that I'm even capable of it. You have no idea what influence this lady had on me, Fenny. Georgia, let me introduce my partner, Fenella Standing.'

Georgia, in shaking hands with the well-known young sculptress whose flame-red shaggy hair she wore as a kind of trade-mark, had detected signs of challenge in the young woman's tight bottom lip, chin-up expression, but the girl had been polite. 'I'm glad to meet Leonora's famous friend. I've certainly heard *so* much about you from her. You really are as your book jackets show you – I had assumed they were re-touched portraits.'

At home, she recalled acknowledging the compliment with a smile. With her youth and looks, she can be generous with the odd crumb of compliment, but Desmond Morris would tag that challenge as sexual. She can't think I'm interested in Leonora! Leonora's use of the term 'partner' was intentionally ambiguous and androgynous. Leonora Altzheiber had a gossip-column reputation for taking lovers of all persuasions. Georgia Honeycombe knew well enough about gossip-column reputations – they sold whatever it was one had to sell. Leonora Altzheiber belongs to my Giacopazzi world, the one that says, Never mind what they write so long as they spell your name right.

Leonora had seemed determined to set the tone of their meeting on a light, sociable level with cocktail conversation. 'You know Fenny's work?'

'Of course, and admire it.'

'Really?' said Leonora Altzheiber. 'All those horses and stags in a state of rut – I can't stand them. But Fenny's all right.'

Now, with only a table-lamp and the flickering fire, Georgia allowed herself to consider the phenomenon of Frau Altzheiber. It's all put on. Somewhere inside the beautiful, hard amber is the trapped fossil of Little-Lena Wiltshire. She's beautiful, successful, no doubt fawned upon – what a problem she would have if she still had the Wiltshires in her life. Mary and Dick would always be on to her about grandchildren. Roy! I forgot to ask her about Roy. The amber theatre director had asked about Eve Hardy.

'Eve is coming.'

'She's a titled lady, isn't she?'

'If you count foreign titles.'

'With a name like Altzheiber, I have to.'

'She married a Marquis she met in London during the war – one of her "League of Nations" lovers, I believe.'

'And she got the Hardy fortune?'

'No, the Marquis had one. Freddy Hardy had another family in America. I was sorry when I read of Waldemar's death.'

'Right! One of the good guys, you know.' For a moment the defensive shutters had opened and vulnerable Little-Lena Wiltshire had peeped out. But only for a moment.

The sculptress had wandered off into the adjoining orangery with her drink, obviously only here at The Coach House because she was, for the present, smitten by Leonora.

'What's this *for*, Georgia?' Leonora had asked, waving her hand at the luxurious buffet and bar. 'Is it curiosity? Or do you expect reaction to what you've written about us all. It's what novelists do, isn't it?'

'Not I. Sentiment . . . curiosity too, I imagine. Once I had resurrected the past, I simply did not want to die without trying to gather together those of us who are left.'

'You are not dying?' Without very much concern.

Georgia, the chameleon, watched herself slipping into the language of the glitterati.

'Not as far as I know. At least, no more than anybody – but I'm getting on.'

'I know, we all are. You are seventy-two, Georgia. And I am sixty. And we both look damn good and know it. Are those Markham's famous centenarians? I can see they are. I must speak to the O'Neill widow. I have cornered the market in Niall O'Neill's films – they are pure gold, irreplaceable, part of film history. Ha . . . and they're all *mine*.'

Georgia Honeycombe gave herself some more brandy and stood it to warm on the ingle shelf. Leonora did it beautifully, the glitterati bit. She was taller than most women, long-legged and sexual, as she had been at sixteen.

Then the reception room door had opened and Nick's great body had stood filling the space. As always when he entered a room, all faces had turned, and as always she had felt an erotic flicker at seeing him. He had stood there carrying Belle as he had carried Pete and Dixie and Tessa and in turn all of their children. This morning, under his weight, their bathroom scales had registered two hundred and thirty pounds and, when he remembered not to stoop, he was well over six foot tall. What did Leonora see? A weathered and white-maned man getting on in years, but still handsome, wearing his lion hair to his collar to cover the old burn scars? Or was she able still to see something of the younger Nick she had fantasized over in her developing years? He was still there for Georgia: intelligent, sensitive, caring eyes looking out from a weather-beaten face. As a gesture to the occasion he had dressed in his Harris tweed, and looked as though it and he were designed for each other. From the way he carried Belle, anyone could see that he was a family man who was at ease with children.

'Leonora, you remember . . ?'

'I know who it is . . . Nicholas.' Her gaze had run appreciatively up and down. 'Hello, Nick – long ages no see. I was going to marry you and you ran away.' She laughed, and Giacopazzi – as she had become once Leonora appeared – remembered thinking that Leonora's bridgework and porcelain capping were as beautiful and as expensive as her own. 'Just look at you – you're still one hell of a man, Nick. Perhaps it's still not too late for us to elope.' She had linked his arm and at once drew him towards the orangery. 'Come where it's quiet, I want to ask you *everything*.'

Georgia Honeycombe had guessed that Leonora wanted to take him to where the sculptress was. When she had been writing *Eye of the Storm* she had wondered whether she had gone too far with Little-Lena's burgeoning sexuality, when at sixteen she was unbuttoning her blouse so as to tie it at the midriff to show off her breasts to the soldiers billeted in Markham, and rolling up shorts till there was no leg left to them. Is she still putting her goods in the window, but not selling? But perhaps she had sold: after all she was only a teenager when she had married Waldemar Altzheiber and put her foot on the first rung of her particular ladder of success. At sixty, she's got off the art of seduction in public better than anyone I ever saw do it.

Now, the fumes of the warm brandy were relaxing. She did not try to order her impressions but let them take her over as she did when brain-storming ideas for a new novel. It was as well that she was not at present involved in writing anything, for when she was working on a novel she relied on being up and at her computer by five o'clock – drinking brandy always made her sleep on.

She recalled how Eve had come in with much the same kind of flourish as Leonora, but with much less awareness of the interest she created.

For Giacopazzi the novelist, the coming together of Tottie and Dixie was drama of a high order. For Georgia Honeycombe, mother to Dixie and great-grandmother to Belle, that event was fraught with danger, as was the meeting of Eve and Dorothy Partridge.

The door of the reception room had opened and a sturdy little boy of Belle's age with fair curls had raced into the room and stood staring. For a moment she had thought that it was Belle. When he had seen that he was the centre of attention, he had turned and run back to Eve and the group of people with her to whom he obviously belonged.

'Eve! I was beginning to think you might not come after all.'

'You said bring family – so I did.'

'All of them?' Georgia Giacopazzi quickly took in the family entourage who followed. Entourage is the apt word, she thought.

'Do you mind?'

'Absolutely not. At last I may satisfy my curiosity.'

Eve's family fussed her and Hildegard into armchairs. A family used to money and having things their way and oblivious to the attention their entrance had created.

'This then is great-grandson Joshua.' Still holding Belle, Georgia picked up the little boy, who was obviously quite used to attention. 'You are beautiful.'

She heard Eve draw in a short breath 'Oh! It's . . .' and was about to add something but changed her mind. 'Don't tell him, Georgia, he knows it. It's true of course.' She went to take the baby, but was beaten to it by Hildegard. 'And this is his Papa, Fergus.' Eve's hand stretched towards the young man she obviously adored, '. . . and my daughter, Melanie – whom you once met as a small bump.'

'I remember you well,' Georgia said. 'But you were called Tottie in those days.' Melanie was exactly as Georgia had always imagined she would look, a lot like Dixie – very like Harry. Would Dolly see it?

Melanie's English was Americanized. 'I am still called Tottie quite often, but Hildegard doesn't like it, do you, Hildy? Thinks it rather common.' She was swish and urbane, but there was something about her that Georgia Honeycombe liked. That she carried the likeness of Harry Partridge perhaps?

Suddenly, Nick was beside her, carrying a tray of drinks, having apparently escaped from Leonora Altzheiber.

'Nick doesn't recognize me, Georgia,' Eve said.

Nick Crockford looked blankly at the regal old woman, but quickly recovered his composure. 'Of course I recognize you – Eve.'

She had held out her hand to be helped to her arthritic feet by Nick Crockford, who kissed her offered cheek. 'Nick, come, you must be the one to take me over to meet Mrs Partridge again. How I love to have a large man to lean on (arthritic ankles, Nick – for my sins, I dare say. How on earth does Georgia move so easily?) I say! Can you imagine . . . one hundred years old. I hope that I can make it.'

Still deep in thought, Georgia Honeycombe automatically turned the last glowing log and added another, pleased to find that it was aromatic applewood. She recalled that there had come a moment at lunch-time when, as Eve had been sitting with Dorothy Partridge and Ursula O'Neill, she had looked around the reception room and thought, 'Thank God the young people came; it would have been too ghastly without their chatter.' As she had looked on at the incongruous coming together of the two old Markham families of Partridge and Hardy, Georgia Honeycombe had observed something of the same hardness still in Eve as there had been during the time when she was nursing. Imperious and elegant as she had become as a titled lady she probably still enjoyed shocking people.

The five women sat together, demonstrating by their grouping and manner that they were for the moment excluding the other people in the room. Leonora Altzheiber joined them.

Eve said, 'So, Mrs Partridge, now you know that Freddy Hardy's daughter was Harry Partridge's whore, what have you got to say to her?' She smiled, showing that she still had her own teeth.

The old lady did not return the smile. 'He'd have probably ended up living on Longmile Hill if he hadn't been killed, perhaps even somewhere better – Longmile isn't much cop these days. What I've got to say is, I never did think over-much of the lot that lived up there. If he wanted to have a posh whore . . . well that was up to him. And seeing you got family that's got Partridge blood, then I say it won't do them any harm.' Mrs Partridge was a match for Eve, who flicked a look at Georgia and said nothing.

Dorothy Partridge continued, 'Only thing I want to know is, did you love my Harry?'

At once Eve said, 'Good Lord, no. He liked women, but I don't think he was mature enough for *a* woman, not to marry – certainly not for *me* to marry, if that's what you were wondering. But he was pretty good fun, and he looked good in uniform.'

Mrs Partridge turned to Georgia Honeycombe. 'Did *you*?'

'I . . . don't know. When I began writing, I did wonder whether I might find out . . . and if so, I wondered how I would feel about him. I guess that if I did love him, it's all gone. I do know that I love Nick. I did then and I still do – seventy though we are. I loved being with Harry, he was very physical and full of dreams about what life would be like in the future – I loved that.'

Recalling it now in the familiarity of her own study, she saw that it had been a tricky moment. What would she have said if either herself or Eve had said that they did love him. In deference to the old lady, Giacopazzi had left out of *Eye of the Storm* the great anger she had felt when she discovered that she was pregnant. And that Harry Partridge – the great expert on love-making, the lover who was always prepared and wouldn't ever get a woman pregnant – had, from what he had once confessed, probably impregnated one girl before he joined the forces, and had certainly managed to do so to two more. Thank the pill for small mercies; a pity it hadn't been discovered before.

The situation had been changed by Belle hurling herself on to Georgia's lap.

'Have you met this bit of nonsense?' she had said to no one in particular. 'She is my great-grandchild, known as Belle.' Georgia tickled her belly, which she loved; Belle wriggled her sturdy legs. 'She belongs to my granddaughter, Tess, and her man, but I claim her on the grounds that I'm addicted to her and that Dixie's too young at forty-four to be a grandmother.' Having had her petting, Belle had wriggled down to be with her new-found playmate, Joshua.

The atmosphere eased. A waiter topped up their glasses. Then Ursula O'Neill had asked, 'Why did you write the book?'

'Why?' She considered for a few moments, as she did when being interviewed on camera. 'I don't know really; perhaps because what happened during those six years was so important to the rest of my life . . . probably all of our lives. What happened then has had consequences for me for the rest of my life.'

Eve, gazing into space, rather tipsy and flushed, nodded. 'David was killed. Our house burnt down. My Pa ran off with a girlie. My Ma got a wheelchair. I got Tottie. Harry was killed . . . and I made friends with a famous writer of detective books.'

Leonora did not take her eyes off Georgia, who continued, 'I had wanted to write something about the war years, for once to get away from what I always do. I wanted to tell a story about a group of people who met during the war, but not one full of battle-scenes and Spitfires and blitzes. I wanted to write a love story, and when I began to think about it, I realized that I had lived one.'

'You mean about my Harry?'

'No. It was about *love*. Not romance . . . about the discovery of all sorts of love.'

'You said it wasn't a romance, Ursula, didn't you?'

'For nearly six years didn't we women love one another? You can't call it anything else, can you? I loved Eve for defying the Markham gossip-mongers and turning out to be so strong after so many awful things had happened to her. I loved you, Mrs Partridge, and Marie and Bonnie and all your family for what you were . . . nice, decent Markham people. And Ursula for always being so supportive and unshakeable: she was the centre of our lives, we poured our troubles over her and she never drowned in them. In a way I even loved Eve's mother for having the guts to get out and do what she did. None of that was romance . . . but it was love.'

Ursula prodded, 'But why did you write it using real names and events? You could have made it more fictional.'

'I did try doing that, but I couldn't manage it. I needed to call you Mrs Farr, and to call Mrs Partridge Dolly – because she actually thought of herself as Dolly. No way could I have written about how I felt about *the* Dolly Partridge, or how she looked or how she spoke – not if I had called her Beryl Chapman or Edith Mitchell.'

Leonora Altzheiber blew out a long stream of smoke. 'You use a word-processor, don't you? It would have been easy enough to change the names when you had finished. No one would have been any the wiser . . . except us.'

'I tried that too but . . . it was like . . . killing you all off. So I decided to do it in the way that I have. There is nothing in the book that I didn't see, hear, or wasn't told by the people concerned. It will be called a good many things – but nobody can say that it isn't the truth.'

Leonora dragged on her cigarette. 'The truth, the whole truth, and nothing but the truth. So help you God?'

The women looked at the two children who had become part of the circle. Seated on the floor, sharing a plate, head to head, they were totally absorbed in picking out bits that took their fancy and stuffing them, flat handed, into their mouths.

'Proper little pigeon pair,' Dorothy Partridge said, and immediately looked across the room to where Dixie and

Melanie were standing side by side, absorbed in watching the group of old women seated together.

And Giacopazzi the novelist saw dawning in Dorothy Partridge's eye that which she had expected to see earlier when Dixie and Melanie had met for the first time, but had not. It had been the babies who had revealed the truth.

'I remember my Harry as though it was yesterday, all fat and blond, just like that.'

Georgia Honeycombe rose from her ingle seat and stretched her shoulders as Leonora had done that lunch-time.

'*That's* why you wrote the book, Georgia.' She laughed and downed the last of her wine. 'And it's why you've gathered us all together here . . . it's exactly like the ending of a classic Giacopazzi mystery, except that there is no detective as you usually have. No corpse. Just two cute children who are standing in for a skeleton in your cupboard. Did you chicken out when you wrote the book? Or did you want to see what happened here today so that you could write your last chapter?'

Georgia Honeycombe said, 'The fifty years since we met have flashed by. I simply wanted to be with you all once more, Lena . . . in the little time that's left before we are gone.'

Giacopazzi wanted to be back in her study, facing the blue screen of her VDU.

1989

Towards the end of the writing of the novel which she thought of as her war book, Georgia Kennedy had still not decided whether or not it would be wise to include the revelation that Harry Partridge had been careless enough to father not only Tottie, but Dixie also.

Her editor had wanted it left out on the grounds that although such coincidences may *be* quite common in real life, nevertheless *Eye of the Storm* would appear in the fiction list. The hassock and cassock schooling of Georgia Honeycombe was, at times, apt to be a bit strong for the laid-back Giacopazzi. The Honeycombe part of her wanted to be honest, and fair to Eve. Now, again in a doubtful mood, she imagined the reviewers' criticism: *Giacopazzi's propensity for drama and surprise is now so necessary to the seasoning of her books that she cannot write without that extra shake and pinch, even in a book that purports to be based upon fact . . .*

She recalled Eve's words when they had met in London, back in the summer. 'It was not much of a surprise to me, Georgia,' she had said. 'When you left Markham without so much as a word, I guessed that you were probably pregnant, and I worked out that it couldn't have been Nick's little bun.'

It was September of the long hot summer of 1989, the day of a reunion with some of the women. Georgia carried the last of her drink to the window. The sky was clear again, this summer seemed to be going on and on. For years to come, English people would remember it as they remembered the summer of '76, and people as old as herself remembered the summers of '39, '40 and '41.

The floodlights that were left on all night to deter any possible rustlers of their valuable breeding stock lit up the yards that were close to Pete's house.

She thought of Pete, reliable and intelligent, as good and caring a farmer as one would find anywhere. She saw the bathroom light go on in Pete's house. At last, probably reluctantly, Pete would leave the farm alone for five or six hours. Pete had gradually become her son. In the early days, when he was bewildered and lost, Georgia had given him some affection, and he had returned it with a lifetime of love. She had grown to love Pete a great deal – 'This is our son, Pete. He's the best farmer in Hampshire.' She knew that he sometimes found her sudden demonstrations of affection embarrassing, but she knew equally that he would not want her to alter.

Pete had been eight years old when she had brought him here, and now he was a man who had reached the age when he needed to put on glasses to read. How angry Georgia Kennedy had been at the time, and with what difficulty did she hide her frustration.

She had worked out what she must do so that, once the war ended, she need never again return to the domestic role she had filled at the beginning.

Hugh's love affair with Floozie had freed her of a bad marriage, her parents' legacy had freed her of the necessity of going out to work for a year or two, the women at the Town Restaurant had freed her of her own stereotyped ideas of a woman's place, and Harry Partridge had freed her of her inhibitions about sex. She was ready to travel the world and write novels. Footloose and fancy free described precisely what she expected for herself in the future.

But, as she felt the bonds which had restrained her ever since she had become a woman loosen, so, during the last months of the war, did others tighten. A four months pregnancy from an accident with a man who died a hero. A feeling of responsibility towards Pete who had nowhere to go except back to his mother's violent marriage. A feeling of duty to Nick who loved and needed her.

When she had arrived here at the farm, she had been so angry. Her bright and footloose future she now saw as a long and reluctant Lenten denial. It was a wonder that Dixie hadn't come into the world red and screaming.

'Why did you write the book?' Ursula O'Neill asked.

'Because I wanted to write something about the war. Something but not about Spitfires and Blitz and men machine-gunning and going into battle. I wanted to tell a love story. When I came to do it, I found that I had lived one.'

Dorothy Partridge's shrewd eyes in the puffy old face searched Georgia.

'And was this here love story about my Harry?'

'No, it is about more than that kind of love. It's about several different kinds of love and what it did to us, about men going away, and women getting a bit of freedom and about what the war did to love.'

'So you wouldn't say it was romance then?'

'No. It's a love story. Didn't we women love one another? You can't call it anything else can you? It occurred to me whilst I was writing it, that it was a bit like having a love affair . . . Romance is too shallow a word. *Eye of the Storm* is a love story.'

Lying back on a soft sofa, she stretched above her head the arm with the hand holding the brandy glass, and watched the flickering flames of the fire glittering the cut glass.

Tomorrow, I shall go out on the Downs. Perhaps I'll ride a bit . . . work off this brandy. Or maybe I'll go to London and see what they think about the idea for the new book. Or get Nick to go over the plan for the trout tanks with me. Perhaps I'll take Belle to the pond.